U0004170

騎鵝歷險記

The Wonderful Adventures of Nils

中英雙語典藏版

賽爾瑪·拉格洛芙——著

李毓昭、Velma Swanston Howard——譯

鐘文君、Bertil Lybeck——繪

晨星出版

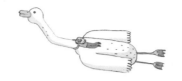

第 1 章
男孩

精靈　三月二十日，星期日

　　從前，有個身材高瘦、動作敏捷的十四歲男孩，他沒什麼本事，成天喜歡做的事就是吃和睡，除此之外最愛調皮搗蛋。

　　星期日早晨，男孩的父母親正準備去教堂。男孩穿著襯衫，坐在桌邊，心想這下可好，爸媽都要出門，他有好幾個小時可以自由玩樂。「真棒！我可以把爸爸的槍拿下來把玩射擊，沒人管我。」

　　可是父親似乎猜中了男孩的心思，人都走到門口了，卻又停下來，轉身對他說：「你不和我們去教堂，至少要在家裡唸唸講道集。你願意嗎？」「願意，我一定會唸的。」男孩雖然嘴巴這麼說，心裡卻想著，如果他不想唸，當然就不會唸了。

　　男孩媽媽迅速地從壁爐邊的書架取下《路德講道集》，放在窗前的桌上，翻開當天要讀的那一篇。她還翻開《新約聖經》，放在講道集旁邊，最後把大扶手椅拖拉到桌前。

　　父親走到男孩身旁，嚴厲地說：「好好唸！我們回來時，我會一頁一頁地考你，要是你漏掉一頁沒唸，就有苦頭吃了。」

　　「這篇講道總共有十四頁半，」母親叮嚀。「你要馬上坐下來唸，不然會唸不完。」

　　他們說完就出門了。男孩在門口目送他們時，感覺好像中計了。「他們一定正在慶幸想了個好辦法，讓我在他們上教堂禮拜時不得不坐下來看書。」

可是他的父母親並沒有在慶幸什麼，反而相當苦惱。父親抱怨著兒子又笨又懶，上了學校也無心唸書，一點用處也沒有，連叫他看鵝都不放心。母親不否認這些批評，可是她最擔心的是兒子的頑劣。他會虐待動物，對人也不懷好意。母親說：「但願上帝讓他冷酷的心變得溫和！不然他會給他自己和我們招來不幸。」

男孩站了許久，考慮要不要去唸講道集。他終於得到結論：這次最好聽話。他坐進扶手椅，開始讀書。可是他低聲唸了一會兒，那咕咕噥噥的聲音似乎有催眠作用，讓他打起瞌睡。

外頭的天氣十分晴朗，木門半掩，在屋裡聽得見雲雀的啼唱。母雞和鵝群在院子裡漫步，牛隻也感覺到春天的氣息，不時哞哞叫著，表示嘉許。

男孩一邊讀書一邊打盹，與睡意搏鬥。「不行！我不可以睡。」他心想：「不然整個早上我都唸不完。」可他還是睡著了。

他不知道自己睡了多久，有一道輕微的響聲把他吵醒。

窗臺上的小鏡子正對著男孩，幾乎能從裡面看到整個屋內。男孩抬起頭來，正好看到鏡子，瞥見母親的衣箱蓋開著。

他的母親有一個束著鐵條的橡木箱，向來不准別人碰。裡面收藏著祖母留給她的物品，她非常愛惜那些東西。其中有幾件過時的農婦裝、漿好的白麻頭巾，以及沉甸甸的銀飾品。他母親也曾想要丟棄這些舊東西，卻又捨不得。

這時，男孩從鏡中清楚地看到箱蓋掀開著。他不明白怎麼會打開，因為他單獨在家時，母親絕不會讓那只珍貴的箱子開著。

他擔心是小偷溜進屋裡，他不敢動，只是靜靜坐著盯著鏡子。

　　他等著小偷現身時，看到箱子的邊緣有黑影。他一看再看，不敢相信自己的眼睛。那個起初像影子的東西變得越來越清晰，很快就看出那是個真的，是活生生的精靈——跨坐在箱子的邊緣上！

　　男孩確實聽說過精靈的故事，但是從沒想到他們竟然這麼小巧，坐在箱子邊的那個精靈不會比一隻手掌高。精靈有一張年老的臉，布滿皺紋，但沒有鬍鬚，身穿黑長袍、齊膝褲，戴著寬邊黑帽，他的衣著整齊美觀。他從箱子拿出一塊繡花布，坐在那裡端詳著上頭的舊式手工，沒有注意到男孩醒了。

　　男孩雖然感到驚訝，但一點也不害怕，那麼小的東西有什麼好怕的。何況精靈的神情專注，完全沒有察覺到四周的動靜。男孩心想，戲弄他應該很好玩，例如把他推進箱子，再闔上蓋子。

　　他一看見捕蝶網就伸手去拿，然後跳起來朝箱子邊緣揮過去。男孩根本不知道自己是怎麼辦到的，可是真的網住精靈了。可憐的小傢伙栽倒在網子深處，沒辦法掙脫。

　　起初男孩只是小心地搖晃網子，讓精靈無法站穩，也無法攀爬上來。

　　精靈可憐兮兮地求饒男孩釋放他。他說多年來一直在賜給男孩一家好運，男孩應該善待他。如果男孩肯放他走，他願意給他一枚舊硬幣、一把銀湯匙和一個像他父親的銀錶一樣大的金幣。

　　男孩覺得精靈承諾的東西不算多，可是捉到精靈之後，他開始害怕了，覺得自己正跟不屬於這個世界的怪異東西打交道，他很樂意擺脫精靈，馬上答應這筆交易。他停止搖晃網子，讓精靈爬出來。可是當精靈幾乎要爬出網子時，男孩又想到應該要求更多財富和好東西，至少應該要求精靈把講道集的內容塞進他的腦子裡。「我真笨，怎麼能讓他跑掉！」這麼想著，他開始粗魯地搖晃網子，所以精靈又跌了下來。

瞬間，男孩挨了個結實的巴掌，覺得整顆頭都要碎掉了。他被甩出去，從一面牆撞到另一面牆，最後倒地不起，失去意識。

醒來時，屋裡只有他一個人。箱蓋是闔上的，捕蝶網好端端地掛在窗邊。要不是頭和臉頰因為挨了耳光而感到熱辣，他會相信是一場夢。「無論如何，爸媽都會認為我是在做夢。」他心想：「他們絕不會因為精靈而饒過我沒唸講道集，我最好趕快開始唸。」

可是當他起身要走到桌邊時，發覺事情不太對勁。屋子不可能變大，但為什麼桌子變得比平常還要遠呢？那把椅子又是怎麼一回事？它看起來不會比之前大，可是他卻得踩著底下的橫桿，才能爬上座位。桌子也是一樣，他必須爬上椅子扶手，才看得到桌面。

「發生什麼事了？」男孩說。「一定是精靈對桌子和椅子，還有整個屋子都施了魔法。」

講道集仍放在桌上，看似無異，可是一定有哪裡有問題，因為他如果不站在書上，就一個字也看不到。

他唸了幾行字後不經意地抬起頭，視線落到鏡子，馬上大叫：「哎！那還有一個！」鏡中有個戴著帽兜，穿著皮褲的小傢伙。

「啊，他的穿著和我一模一樣。」男孩說，他吃驚得拍著雙手。這時他看到鏡子裡的人也做出同樣的動作。他拉拉頭髮，捏捏手臂，扭動身體，鏡子裡的人都馬上照做。

男孩繞著鏡子跑了幾圈，看看有沒有小人藏在後面，可是什麼也沒發現。他開始嚇得全身發抖，現在他明白了，那個精靈對他施了魔法，鏡子裡的影像就是他自己。

野鵝

男孩無法相信自己變成精靈了。他想著：「這一定是一場夢，等一下我就會變回人類了。」

他站在鏡子前，閉上眼睛，希望幾分鐘後睜開眼睛時，一切都已過去。但事與願違，他的個子還是那麼小。就某方面來說，他和之前沒有兩樣。淡黃色的頭髮、遍布鼻子的雀斑、皮褲和襪子上的補丁都和之前相同，唯一的差別是全部都縮小了。

他可以確定，站在這裡等再久也沒用，必須想想辦法，而他想到的最聰明的辦法是去找那個精靈，和他講和。

男孩一邊哭一邊祈禱，答應做到所有他想得到的事。再也不說話不算話、惡作劇，或是在聽講道時睡著。只要他能夠變回人類，他願意成為樂於助人的乖孩子。可是無論他怎麼許願，都沒有用。

突然之間，他記起來曾經聽母親說過，精靈都住在牛棚裡，就決定去那邊看看。幸好屋子的門半開著，不然他根本搆不到門拴。他輕易地從門口溜出去。

他來到門廊，尋找他的木鞋，因為他在屋裡只穿著襪子，正想著要如何穿上那雙笨重的大鞋時，看到門階上有一雙小鞋。精靈竟然設想周到，對木鞋也施了魔法。這下子他更不安了，因為精靈顯然要折磨他很久。

　　有隻灰色的麻雀在屋子前面的木頭地板上跳躍。他一看到男孩就大叫：「啾啾！啾啾！看這個呆頭男孩尼爾斯！看這個拇指大的尼爾斯‧霍爾加松！」

　　院子裡的鵝和雞都轉過頭來看，然後發出嚇人的咯咯聲。公雞喊道：「活該！咕咕咕！他扯過我的雞冠！」母雞也一起叫著：「活該！」鵝聚在一起，抬頭問道：「是誰讓他變成這樣的？」

　　奇怪的是，男孩聽得懂他們的話。他吃驚地站在門階上聽，同時自言自語：「一定是因為我變成精靈了，所以聽得懂鳥語。」

　　他受不了母雞一直說他活該，就朝他們扔出一顆石頭，大吼：「閉嘴，你們這群畜生！」

　　可是母雞不再怕他了，整群母雞衝過去，圍著他，出聲叫罵：「你活該！你活該！」

　　男孩想要逃跑，雞群卻在後面追著，直到他覺得耳朵快要聾了。要是他們家的貓沒有走過來，也許他永遠也擺脫不了。雞群一看到貓就安靜下來，假裝只是在啄地上的蚯蚓。

　　男孩迅速跑到貓那裡說：「親愛的貓咪！你一定知道這一帶所有躲藏的地方吧？乖小貓，告訴我哪裡可以找到精靈？」

　　貓咪沒有立即回答。他悠閒地坐下來，尾巴優雅地在腳掌上圍成圈，兩眼瞪著男孩。那是隻大黑貓，胸前有一塊白斑，毛皮光滑、柔軟，在日光下顯出光澤。他的爪子內縮，暗灰色的瞳孔瞇成

細縫，看起來很溫馴。

「我知道精靈在哪裡，」貓咪柔聲說，「但我不會告訴你。」

「親愛的貓咪，你一定要告訴我！」男孩哀求。「你看不出他對我施了魔法嗎？」

貓的眼睛微睜，透出一道寒光。他轉了一圈，發出滿足的呼嚕聲，然後回答：「就因為你經常拉我的尾巴，所以我要幫你嗎？」

男孩生起氣來，忘記自己已經變小了。「哦！那我要再去拉你的尾巴。」他說著，跑向那隻貓。

那隻貓一轉眼豎起每一根毛髮，拱著背，伸長四肢，爪子在地上刮搔，尾巴變得又粗又短，耳朵往後縮，口吐唾沫，睜大的眼睛閃現火花似的光芒。

男孩不想對貓示弱，就又向前一步。貓跳起來撲向男孩，把男孩推倒，前腳按著他的胸部，張大的嘴巴對著他的喉嚨。

男孩感覺到銳利的爪子穿透他的衣服，刺進皮膚，犬齒碰到他的喉嚨。他盡可能大喊救命，卻沒有人過來。以為自己一定沒命了，卻發覺貓縮回爪子，把他放開。

「看在女主人的份上，放你一馬。我只是讓你知道，現在我們兩個之間誰比較佔上風。」貓說完就走開了，變回和之前一樣溫和。男孩羞愧得說不出話來，只好趕緊去牛棚找精靈。

那裡有三頭牛，年紀都很大了。可是男孩一進來，就引起一陣怒吼和騷動，足以讓人以為裡面至少養了三十頭牛。

「哞，哞，哞，」三頭牛一起叫喊。男孩聽不清楚他們說什麼，因為一隻比一隻吼得更大聲。

男孩想問精靈的事，可是聲音進不去他們的耳裡。就像之前他把陌生的狗放進去時一樣，他們猛踢後腿，搖晃側腹，頭伸直，牛角對準了男孩。

「過來！」五月玫瑰說。「我要踢你一腳，讓你難以忘記！」

「過來，」金百合說。「我要你在我的角上跳舞！」

「過來，去年夏天你用木鞋扔我，我要讓你嚐嚐那是什麼滋味！」星星說。

五月玫瑰是年紀最大、最聰明，也是最生氣的。「你過來，我要讓你吃點苦頭，因為你曾經多次害你媽媽打翻牛奶桶，也因為你，她常常站在這裡為你掉眼淚。」

男孩很想跟他們說，他很後悔做了那些壞事，以後一定會乖乖的，只要告訴他精靈在哪裡。可是那三頭牛不肯聽他說話，不斷叫罵，男孩害怕他們會掙脫繩子，覺得現在最好安靜地離開牛棚。

男孩沮喪地走出來，他知道這裡不會有人願意幫他找到精靈。他爬到農場圍牆上，想著如果不能變回人類會怎樣。爸媽從教堂回來時一定會很吃驚。消息會傳到全國，人們會從四面八方跑來看他。也許爸媽會帶他到城市的市場供人觀賞。候鳥乘風飛行，穿越波羅的海飛向北方。野鵝排成人字形飛著。

野鵝看到在農場漫步的家鵝時，就會飛近地面大叫：「一起來吧！一起飛向高山！」家鵝都不禁抬頭傾聽，可是都理智地回答：「我們在這裡過得很好。」

這天的天氣特別晴朗怡人，隨著一群群野鵝飛過，家鵝變得越來越興奮。有時他們會拍動翅膀，但總是有一隻母鵝跟他們說：「別傻了，跟著那些傢伙會挨餓受凍的！」

有隻年輕的鵝名叫莫爾登，對旅行產生憧憬。他說：「要是再有一群飛過來，我就要跟他們走。」

真的又來了一群野鵝，和之前的鵝群一樣大聲叫喊，年輕的公鵝莫爾登回答：「等一等，等一等，我來了。」

他張開翅膀，升到空中，可是他不習慣飛行，很快就掉下來。

儘管如此，野鵝們聽見了公鵝莫爾登的叫聲，就折回來慢慢飛，看他有沒有跟來。

「等一等！」莫爾登再度嘗試飛起來。男孩坐在圍牆上，每句話都聽見了。他心想：「如果這隻大公鵝飛走了，對爸媽來說是很大的損失。」光想到這一點，他便忘了自己有多弱小，跳起來用雙臂抱住公鵝的脖子。「不行，你這次先別走。」他大叫。

公鵝正想著如何騰空飛起，來不及甩掉男孩，就帶著他飛到空中了。

他們一下子就飛到高空，男孩倒抽一口氣，才剛覺得可以把手放開時，已經離地面很高，掉到地上一定會沒命。

唯一能做的就是讓自己舒服一點，所以他騎到公鵝的背上，把手插進羽毛中抓緊，才不會摔下來。

大方格布

男孩覺得頭暈眼花，過了很久才恢復神智。風呼嘯而過，羽毛的沙沙聲和拍動翅膀的聲音聽起來彷彿暴風。十三隻鵝飛在他旁邊，一邊振翅一邊呱呱叫著。

過了一會兒他才清醒過來，覺得應該問問鵝群要帶他去哪裡。可是並不容易，因為他不敢往下看，他確信自己一看就會頭暈。

野鵝飛得並不高，因為新夥伴無法在稀薄的空氣中呼吸。也因

為這樣，他們飛得比平常緩慢。

　　男孩朝底下瞥了一眼，感覺好像鋪著一大塊布，由許多大小不同的格子拼湊而成。「我到底是在哪裡？」他很想知道。

　　他只看到一塊塊格子。有的是菱形，有的是長方形，沒有一個是圓的或彎的。「下面這塊大方格布到底是什麼呢？」他自言自語，並不指望聽到回答。

　　可是圍在他旁邊的野鵝隨即喊道：「田地和草地。」

　　他這才認出鮮綠色的格子是裸麥田，灰黃色的格子是去年夏天收割完的田地，褐色的是老苜蓿地，黑色的是廢棄的放牧地或犁過的休耕地。

男孩看到一切都變成格子時，不禁哈哈大笑。可是野鵝聽到他的笑聲，就以斥責的口氣大喊：「肥美的土地！」

　　男孩正經起來，心想：「你居然還笑得出來，想想是誰遇到了一個人類所能遇到最悲慘的事！」他嚴肅了一會兒，但不久又笑了出來。他習慣了騎鵝和飛行速度，可以一邊抓著鵝背一邊想事情。

　　他們經過一些裝著高大煙囪的笨拙建築，四周有許多小房子。「這裡是糖廠。」公雞群嚷著。男孩在鵝背上吃了一驚。他認得這裡，因為離他家不遠。

　　去年曾來這裡打工，不過從上面看起來，全部都變了樣。

　　當時他認識了看鵝女孩歐莎和小麥茲，很想知道他們是否還在這裡。要是他們知道他正在飛過他們的頭頂，不知道會怎麼說！

　　野鵝從家鵝頭上飛過去時是最快樂的！他們會飛得很慢，同時往下叫喊：「我們要飛到山上。你們要一起來嗎？」但家鵝回答：「這國家還是冬天，你們太早出國了。飛回來！飛回來！」

　　野鵝們飛得更低了，好讓底下的鵝聽得更清楚。「一起來！我們會教你們飛行和游泳。」家鵝生氣了，不肯再回答。

　　野鵝們飛得越來越低，幾乎要碰到地面，然後快如閃電地升空，彷彿受到驚嚇。「哎唷，哎唷！」他們大叫。「這些傢伙不是鵝，他們只是羊，只是羊。」地上的鵝聽了都氣壞了，紛紛叫罵。

　　男孩聽見這番嘲諷時笑了，但想起身上的惡運，又哭了起來。但過沒多久又笑了。

第 2 章
來自凱布訥山的阿卡

傍晚

　　大公鵝莫爾登很得意，因為能夠與野鵝在南方的鄉野上方盤旋，逗弄家鵝。但到了傍晚時分，他就覺得疲倦了。他盡量深呼吸，加速拍翅，但還是落後了幾隻鵝身的距離。

　　野鵝注意到家鵝跟不上，就呼叫領頭鵝：「阿卡！阿卡！」「什麼事？」領頭鵝阿卡問道。「白鵝落後了。」「告訴他，快飛比慢飛省力。」領頭鵝大喊，依然保持著同樣的速度前進。

　　公鵝盡可能聽從建議加快速度，但是很快就精疲力竭，而朝著底下區分耕地和草地的垂柳墜落。

　　「凱布訥山來的阿卡，阿卡！」飛在後面的野鵝再度喊叫。

　　「你們就不能讓我安靜地飛嗎？」領頭鵝不耐煩地喊道。

　　「白鵝要摔到地上去了。」

　　「告訴他，要是沒有體力跟上來，就回家去！」領頭鵝大叫，無意減速。

　　「啊，原來是這樣！」公鵝心想。他明白了，野鵝根本不想帶上他，引誘他離家只是為了好玩。

　　他在隊伍後面慢慢地飛，心想著該掉頭還是繼續前進。背上的小傢伙跟他說：「親愛的公鵝，你很清楚你從來沒有飛行過，跟著野鵝飛到拉普蘭是不可能的。要不要在毀掉自己之前掉頭回去？」

小毛頭這麼不相信公鵝的能力，更讓他決定要繼續飛。「你再多嘴，我就把你扔到我們經過的第一條水溝。」憤怒使他力氣大增，開始飛得和其他鵝一樣好。

當然他是撐不久的，但也不需要苦撐太久，因為太陽快下山了。鵝群在日落時，降落在維木布湖邊。「看來我們要在這裡過夜了。」男孩心想，從公鵝背上跳下。

太陽已經落下，寒氣從湖上逼來，黑暗籠罩大地，森林開始傳來啪嗒聲響。

飛行時的愉快心情已經消失，男孩滿懷不安地尋找旅伴。現在他只有公鵝可以依靠了。公鵝倒在降落的地方，看起來好像快要死了，脖子癱在地上，眼睛閉著，氣息微弱。

「親愛的公鵝，試著喝口水吧。走兩步就到湖邊了。」

可是公鵝一動也不動。男孩以前會虐待動物，對公鵝也不例外，但現在公鵝是他僅有的依靠，開始擔心會失去公鵝。

男孩想要把公鵝拖到水邊，就開始推他，可是公鵝又大又重，費了很大的力氣才辦到。

公鵝把頭伸進水裡。起初他在軟泥中動也不動，但不久又抬起頭來，甩掉眼睛上的水，用力吸氣，在蘆葦與海藻間得意地游著。

白公鵝憑運氣捉起一隻河鱸游到岸邊，放在男孩前面。「這是要感謝你把我弄到湖邊。」

這是男孩那天第一次受到親切的對待，高興得想擁抱公鵝，但他沒有這麼做。

他摸摸身上是否帶著小刀。沒錯，還掛在褲子後面的鈕扣上。

當然刀子
也縮小了，比火
柴棒還短，但還是可以用
來刮去魚鱗。他很快就把魚吃掉了。

　　男孩吃魚時，公鵝靜靜地站在一旁。在他吃完後，
公鵝低聲說：「我們碰上了高傲的野鵝，不把家禽放在眼裡。」

　　「我注意到了。」男孩說。

　　「要是我能和他們一起飛去拉普蘭，讓他們知道家鵝也有這
個能力，那會是一大勝利。」

　　「是啊。」男孩拉長聲音說，因為他不相信公鵝辦得到，卻
又不想潑他冷水。「可是我不認為我能單獨完成這段旅程，我想
問你能不能和我同行？」公鵝說。男孩只想回家，但公鵝的話讓
他很驚訝，不知道該怎麼回答。

　　「我真的應該回到父母身邊。」男孩說。「我會在秋天時送
你回家。」公鵝保證。「我會帶你到家門口才離開。」

　　男孩心想，也許暫時不讓父母親看見也好。公鵝的提議令他
有點心動，他正要答應時，聽到後面傳來轟隆聲。野鵝一起從湖

上飛了起來，然後站著抖掉背上的水。接著呈一縱列，由領頭鵝率領，往公鵝和男孩這裡走來。

野鵝過來之前，公鵝只來得及對男孩低語：「簡單介紹自己就好，不要跟他們說你是誰。」

野鵝停在他們面前，禮貌地點頭致意，公鵝也跟著做了許多次。行完禮後，領頭鵝說：「現在我們想要知道你們是誰。」

「我沒什麼好介紹的。我是在去年春天生於斯堪諾爾，後來被賣到霍爾加松家，就一直住在那裡。」公鵝說。「你沒有可誇耀的家世，怎麼敢加入野鵝的行列？」領頭鵝說。「可能是因為我想要讓你們野鵝看看我們家鵝的能耐。」

「那就看你的表現囉！」領頭鵝激他。「我們已經知道你對飛行有多了解。但也許你其他方面的技巧不錯，譬如說游泳？」「不，那方面我不在行。」公鵝說。他覺得領頭鵝好像打定主意要他回家了，就隨便敷衍。「我從來沒有游過一個水坑。」「那麼我猜你是個短跑選手了？」領頭鵝說。「我沒看過家鵝跑步，我自己更沒有跑過。」公鵝回答，使場面更僵。

公鵝現在可以確定，領頭鵝說什麼也不會帶他走了。不過出乎他的意料之外，領頭鵝說的是：「你很敢講話，即使剛開始什麼都不懂，只要有膽量就能當個好旅伴。要不你跟我們一起待幾天，讓我們看看你有什麼本事？」「我很願意！」公鵝高興得不得了。

領頭鵝接著用嘴巴一指，說：「你身邊這個是誰？」「我的夥伴。他一直都是看鵝的，對我們的旅程很有用。」公鵝說。「對家鵝來說或許有用。他叫什麼名字？」公鵝遲疑了一下，不知道該怎麼稱呼男孩，因為不想讓野鵝知道他的名字。「他叫小拇指。」公

鵝回答。「他是精靈嗎？」領頭鵝問。「你們野鵝什麼時候睡覺呢？」公鵝想要引開話題。「我的眼睛差不多要閉上了。」

看得出和公鵝說話的野鵝很老了。她全身灰白，沒有黑斑紋。頭部比其他的鵝大，腿比較粗，腳掌也更破爛。羽毛僵硬，肩膀瘦削，頸子細長。這些都是年老的徵兆。只是她的眼睛更明亮，顯得比其他鵝年輕——那是時光無法改變的。

她高傲地對公鵝說：「你要知道，我是阿卡，飛行時在右邊離我最近的是伊克西，左邊是卡克西。再來，右邊第二隻是科米，左邊第二隻是奈加。再後面是維西和庫西。他們和飛在最後面的那一隻都是名門子弟！別把我們當成和誰都處得來的傻蛋，也別以為我們會讓任何報不出祖先名字的人和我們一起睡。」

領頭鵝說話時，男孩突然站出來。公鵝那麼坦率地介紹自己，卻迴避有關他的問題，令他很不是滋味。「我不想隱瞞我的身分。我名叫尼爾斯‧霍爾加松，是農夫的兒子，在今天之前我是人類，只是今天早上……」他一說出自己是人，領頭鵝就倒退三步，其他鵝退得更遠。他們都伸長頸子，對他氣憤地咆哮。

「打從在湖邊看到你，我就在懷疑了。」阿卡說。「現在你可以馬上離開。我們無法忍受隊伍中有人。」

「你們野鵝該不會害怕這麼小的人吧！他明天就會回家了，你們讓他和我們一起過夜吧。讓這麼可憐的小不點在夜裡單獨面對鼬鼠和狐狸，我們誰都擔不起這個責任。」

領頭鵝靠近了些，但看得出來她還是充滿恐懼。「我從經驗學會怕人，不論個子大小。但如果你能擔保他不會傷害我們，他就可以和我們一起過夜。不過我們的住處可能不適合你和他，因為我們要在那裡的浮冰上睡覺。」

　　她以為公鵝聽到這些話就會改變主意，公鵝卻滿不在乎地說：「你們好聰明，知道要選擇那種安全的地方睡覺。」

　　「你負責叫他明天自己回家。」

　　「那我就得離開你們，我已經發誓絕對不離開他。」公鵝說。

　　「隨便你。」領頭鵝說。

　　她說完就鼓翅飛到冰上，其他的野鵝也隨後跟去。

　　男孩覺得很難過，因為不能去拉普蘭了，而且在寒冷的戶外過夜也讓他感到害怕。「我們會在冰上凍死的。」

　　可是公鵝心情很好。「這裡並不危險，只是拜託你快點去撿乾草，能拿多少就拿多少。」

　　男孩抱來一堆乾草後，公鵝咬著他的衣領，把他舉起來，然後飛到冰上。野鵝已經在那裡熟睡，嘴巴都塞在翅膀下面。

　　「現在把乾草鋪在冰上，讓我們有地方可以站，我也不會凍僵。你幫我，我也幫你。」公鵝說。

　　男孩照做之後，公鵝把他塞進翅膀裡。「這裡會很溫暖。」男孩舒服地埋在絨毛中，因為疲累，他一下子就睡著了。

夜晚

　　半夜浮冰漂移，直到一角觸及岸邊。湖的東邊有一座公園，狐狸斯密爾住在那裡。夜裡出來覓食時瞥見那塊浮冰，走了過去。

　　斯密爾快要靠近鵝群時，他的爪子在冰上刮搔，鵝群醒了，拍動翅膀，準備飛離。可是斯密爾的動作很快，他飛撲過去，一口咬住一隻鵝的翅膀便跑回陸地。

公鵝展翅時，男孩已經醒了。他趺在冰上，坐在那裡發呆，看到一隻小長腿狗叼著鵝在冰上跑著，他才明白發生了什麼事。

男孩馬上去追那隻狗。他聽到公鵝在喊：「小心啊，小拇指！」可是他覺得那麼小的狗沒什麼好怕的，就繼續往前衝。

被狐狸叼住的野鵝聽見男孩的木鞋在冰上啪啪響著，幾乎不敢相信自己的耳朵。「那小不點居然以為他能把我從狐狸口中救出來？他會掉到冰縫裡面去的。」

但雖然是黑夜，男孩還是可以看清楚所有裂縫和窟窿，而一一跳過去，因為他現在有精靈的夜視力。

男孩對狐狸大叫：「放開那隻鵝，你這土匪。」斯密爾不知道誰在叫他，只是加快步伐，沒有浪費時間回頭看。

狐狸直接進入森林，男孩一次又一次地對那隻狗大叫，要他放下獵物。「你是哪一種狗呀？偷一整隻鵝，怎麼不覺得羞恥呢？馬上放下她，不然就要讓你的主人知道你幹的好事！」男孩跑得很

快，終於趕上狐狸，並且抓住他的尾巴。「現在我要把鵝搶走。」他叫著，但用盡全力也無法阻止狐狸。狐狸拖著他繼續跑，地上的枯葉在他四周飛舞。

這時狐狸知道追趕他的東西傷不了他，就突然停下來，把鵝放在地上，用前腳壓住，以免鵝飛走。他本來想要去咬斷鵝的脖子，卻又不禁想要戲弄一下男孩。「快點去跟我主人告狀，因為我要把這隻鵝咬死了。」

男孩看到這隻狗有個尖鼻子，再聽到他粗啞的聲音，不免吃了一驚。現在又聽到狐狸在取笑他，就生起氣來，把尾巴抓得更緊，身體靠在山毛櫸樹幹上。在狐狸張口要咬鵝的喉嚨時，男孩猛力一拉，狐狸嚇得退後好幾步，野鵝吃力地搧翅飛走了。由於有一個翅膀受了重傷，幾乎不能用，而且森林暗得看不見，她無力去幫男孩，就穿過枝枒飛回湖上了。

斯密爾撲向男孩。「得不到那一隻，我就去抓另一隻。」男孩因為救了野鵝而興高采烈，起初他哈哈大笑捉弄狐狸。但斯密爾耐力十足，男孩開始擔心自己最後會被捉住。他看到一棵跟竿子一樣細的小山毛櫸樹，就放開狐狸尾巴，爬了上去。斯密爾氣急敗壞地在那裡轉了好多圈。

「不用繼續跳你的舞了！」男孩說。

斯密爾受不了敗給這個小不點的恥辱，就趴在樹下緊盯著他。

男孩跨坐在細枝上很不舒服。小樹長得不高，男孩無法跳到別棵樹上，也不敢爬下來。他快要凍僵了，而且睏得不得了，卻擔心一打瞌睡就會摔下去。

太陽終於露臉，灑下日光，驅走夜間的恐懼，萬物開始活動。

男孩知道太陽是在告訴所有小生物:「醒來吧,走出你們的巢穴!我在這裡!現在你們不用再害怕了。」

湖上傳來野鵝的叫聲,他們準備要飛行了。很快的,十四隻鵝都飛越了森林。男孩出聲叫喚,但是他們飛得那麼高,聽不見男孩的聲音。鵝群可能以為狐狸已經吃掉他了,也不想花心思去找他。

男孩懊惱得幾乎哭出來,幸好有太陽掛在那裡,金光閃閃,笑容滿面,為整個世界增添勇氣。「尼爾斯,只要我在這裡,你就沒什麼好擔心的。」

鵝戰　三月二十一日　星期一

要中午時,一隻鵝單獨從濃密的樹冠下飛起,然後在樹幹和樹枝之中遲疑地穿梭,飛得很慢。斯密爾一看到她,就離開山毛櫸樹,偷偷地跟蹤。野鵝沒有躲避狐狸,反而緊靠著他飛。斯密爾跳起來捉她,但沒有捉到,野鵝繼續飛向湖邊。

不久又飛來一隻鵝,沿著同樣的路線,飛得更低、更慢,同樣離斯密爾很近。斯密爾又高高跳起來,耳朵擦過她的腳。那隻鵝毫髮無傷地飛向湖面。

過了一會兒,又來了一隻鵝,仍然緩慢地低飛,在枝枒之間穿梭的能力好像比較差。斯密爾使勁一跳,幾乎要碰到了,但那隻鵝還是全身而退。

接著來了第四隻。她飛得那麼緩慢,又那麼笨拙,斯密爾以為要捉住她是輕而易舉的,可是擔心再度失手,就沒理會。她沿著同樣的路線飛,飛得那麼低,讓狐狸不禁蹤身一躍,尾巴都掃到她了,但是她迅速閃開,保住性命。

斯密爾還在喘氣時，有三隻鵝排成一列飛了過來。斯密爾又試了一次，還是沒有得逞。

　　不久又來了五隻鵝，飛得比之前的鵝好。儘管她們似乎有意引誘斯密爾跳起來，但斯密爾沒有上鉤。過了很久，一隻鵝單獨飛過來。這是第十三隻了。她年紀很大，全身灰白，而且只有一邊翅膀可以用，飛得歪歪斜斜的，幾乎碰到地面。斯密爾不僅撲了過去，還追著她，一路跑向湖邊。可是這回還是徒勞無功。

第十四隻鵝過來了，這隻很漂亮，全身雪白。搧動巨大的翅膀時，彷彿為黑森林射入一道亮光。斯密爾一看到他，使勁全力跳得有半棵樹那麼高。可是這隻白鵝仍然安全飛走了。

突然之間，斯密爾想起看守的囚犯，抬頭去看那棵小山毛櫸樹，果然如他所料，男孩不見了。

但斯密爾沒有時間懊惱，因為第一隻鵝從湖邊飛回來，在樹冠下低飛。儘管運氣欠佳，斯密爾還是蹤身跳起。不過他太性急了，沒有考慮距離，撲了個空。接著的第二隻、第三隻和整群鵝，都飛得又低又慢。她們在斯密爾頭上盤旋，然後猛然下降，好像在引誘斯密爾出手。斯密爾一路追隨，儘管跳得很高，還是屢試屢敗。

這是斯密爾最倒霉的一天。他已經不年輕了，曾多次被狗追趕，聽過子彈在耳邊呼嘯，但這一切都比不上這次捕鵝的挫折。

到了下午，斯密爾不僅累垮了，也氣瘋了。他開始把什麼東西都看成鵝，連光影也去追，連一隻小蝴蝶也不放過。

終於，斯密爾癱倒在一堆枯葉上時，野鵝才停止捉弄他。「狐狸先生，現在你應該知道敢惹阿卡的下場了吧！」他們在他耳邊喊完這句話才飛走，還他清靜。

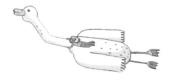

第 3 章

尼爾斯美妙的旅程

農莊 三月二十四日 星期四

　　有人在維木布湖邊的榛樹林裡捉到一隻母松鼠，帶回附近的農莊。看到她蓬鬆的尾巴、聰明好奇的眼睛和靈巧的小腳，所有人都很高興，拿出有小綠屋和鐵絲輪的舊松鼠籠。小綠屋設有門窗，讓母松鼠在裡面吃飯、睡覺。他們在裡面用葉子鋪了張床，再擺上一碗牛奶和幾個堅果。鐵絲輪可以讓她在裡面跑上跑下、兜圈子。

　　大家覺得一切都安排得很妥當，可是母松鼠似乎不太滿意，一直垂頭喪氣地坐在房間角落，偶爾還會苦惱地尖叫，既不吃東西，也不碰轉輪。

　　人們在廚房忙得不可開交，沒有人注意母松鼠，或是去看她進食了沒有。只有一個老婦人因為不能幫忙而覺得不是滋味，就坐在起居室的窗邊往外看。

　　為了排出熱氣，廚房的門開著，亮光洩入院子，老婦人看到對面牆上的裂縫和小洞，松鼠籠就掛在最明亮的地方。她注意到松鼠從房間跑到轉輪，再從轉輪跑到房間，整晚跑個不停。她覺得那小動物坐立不安的情況有點奇怪，但她以為是強光使松鼠睡不著。

　　牛棚和馬廄之間有一扇寬大的門，同樣被照得通亮。夜深時，老婦人看到一個小傢伙偷偷溜進來。他不比一個掌寬高，穿著皮褲

和木鞋，和工人一樣。老婦人一點也不害怕。因為她早就聽說這一帶有精靈，而且精靈會帶來好運。

　　小男孩一進入鋪石板的院子，就直接跑向松鼠籠。由於它掛得很高，精靈得去倉庫拿一根棍子，頂在籠子上，然後像水手爬纜繩一樣爬上去。到達時，他搖搖小綠屋的門，好像要把它打開。老婦人沒有起身，因為她知道小孩在門上加了掛鎖，以免鄰居小孩來偷松鼠。由於小男孩無法把門打開，母松鼠就走到轉輪那裡，和小男孩談了很久。後來男孩順著棍子滑下來，從院子的門跑出去。

　　老婦人以為當晚不會再看到精靈了，但還是留在窗邊。過了幾分鐘，他回來了，腳步匆忙地跑向松鼠籠。老婦人看到他手上拿著東西，不知道那是什麼。他把左手上的東西放在地上，把右手拿的東西帶到籠子裡。他用木鞋猛踢窗戶，打破玻璃，然後把東西拿給母松鼠，再溜下來，拿著地上的東西爬上去，接著飛快地跑開。

　　老婦人不能再坐著不動了，她慢慢走向院子，站在抽水筒的影子裡等精靈回來。這一幕還有一個好奇的觀眾，那就是屋裡的貓。他悄悄走過來，在旁邊站住，離那道光只有兩步遠。在三月寒冷的夜晚，他們倆等了好久好久，老婦人正想進屋，就聽見地板上的腳步聲，看到那小精靈再度跑來，和之前一樣兩手都拿著東西，那東西一邊蠕動一邊嘰嘰叫著。老婦人恍然大悟，原來精靈是跑回榛樹林，幫母松鼠把幼鼠帶來，以免他們餓死。

　　老婦人站在那裡不動，深怕驚擾到他們，而精靈似乎沒有察覺到她。他正要把其中一隻幼鼠放在地上時，看到家貓在旁邊閃著一雙綠眼睛。他兩手各拿著一隻幼鼠，不知如何是好。

　　他轉身張望，看到了老婦人，沒有遲疑很久就走向前，把手舉

高。老婦人不想辜負他的信任，就彎身撿起幼鼠，等男孩把另一隻
帶上去，再下來拿這一隻。

第二天早上，農莊的人聚在一起吃早餐時，老婦人一五一十地
說出前晚看到的事。他們當然都笑她只是在做夢，幼鼠怎麼會在那
麼早的季節出生。

可是她很肯定，要求他們去看看松鼠籠。他們去了，看到葉子
床上有四隻半光著身子、半盲的小松鼠，至少有兩天大。

農莊主人看到幼鼠，就說：「不論事情是怎麼發生的，可以確
定的是我們這個農莊做了一件對動物和人都很可恥的事。」他把母
松鼠和所有幼鼠拿出籠子，放在老婦人的圍裙裡。「把他們送回榛
樹林吧。」他說：「讓他們重獲自由！」

威特朔沃爾　三月二十六日　星期六

兩天後，又發生了件怪事。一早有一群野鵝飛到威特朔沃爾大
莊園附近的田裡。

野鵝覓食時，幾個小孩走了過來。警戒心強的鵝拍起翅膀，提
醒同伴有危險。整群野鵝都飛起來了，唯獨一隻白鵝無動於衷，還
抬頭對他們喊：「不必飛走啦！只是一群孩子。」

男孩正在樹林邊的小丘撿松果，剝裡面的松子吃。小孩離他很
近，他不敢越過農田去找白鵝，而是躲在一片乾燥的薊菜葉下，大
聲警告白鵝。白鵝卻堅持留在地上，一次也沒抬頭去看那些孩子的
動向。等白鵝終於抬起頭來，他們已經近在眼前。他嚇呆了，忘了
自己會飛，想要逃跑。但是小孩把他逼進水溝，在那裡抓到他。兩
個較大的孩子把他夾在腋下，帶著他離開。

男孩看到時，想要馬上把公鵝搶回來，但想起自己弱小的身軀，而跌坐在小丘上，用拳頭捶地。

公鵝拚命求救：「小拇指，快來救我！」男孩在焦急中開始大笑：「哦，對，我是最適合解救你的人選！」不過他還是站起來，跟著公鵝。他想：「我無法救他，但至少要知道他被帶到哪裡。」

他在一條小徑上看到他們通向樹林的腳印，就繼續跟隨。

不久來到一個十字路口。那群小孩一定是在那裡分散開來，因為兩個方向都有腳印。男孩正感到絕望時，在一片石南小丘上看到一片白鵝毛，明白那是公鵝在為他指路。他穿過整片樹林，每次快要迷路時，都有白鵝毛指引他。

男孩忠實地跟著鵝毛離開森林，走過幾片田地，再沿著一條

路，轉進通往一座莊園的林蔭大道。男孩看到那座壯觀的莊園，就知道公鵝的命運了。他心想：「那群小孩一定是把公鵝賣到這裡來，他可能已經被宰了。」但是非得確定不可。

男孩毫不考慮地跑向東邊通往院子的高大拱門，不知該往哪裡去的時候，聽見後面傳來腳步聲，他急忙躲到拱門邊的水桶後面。

那是出來遠足的高中生，約有二十人，有一人走到水桶邊彎身喝水。他脖子上掛著一個用來採集植物的金屬盒子，他顯然覺得它礙事，而把它甩到地上。盒蓋開了，裡面有幾朵春天開的花。

盒子掉在男孩面前。他知道這是進入城堡的機會，就走了進去，藏在銀蓮花和款冬花下面。他才剛藏好，年輕人就撿起盒子，掛在脖子上，啪的把蓋子闔上。

高中生終於進入城堡，男孩卻沒有機會爬出盒子，不得不跟著他們參觀所有房間。因為老師不斷地停下來解說，他們走得很慢。

男孩以往容易急躁、不耐煩，但他在這一天學會耐心。他已經動也不動地在盒子裡待了一個小時。

最後老師帶領高中生回到院子，講起人類為了製造工具、武器、衣服、房屋和飾物所耗費的心力。不過這些話男孩都沒有聽到，因為那學生又渴了，他偷偷溜進廚房找水喝。既然被帶進了廚房，男孩不小心用力壓到盒蓋，使盒子彈開，但那個學生並沒有特別留意，只是再把它蓋上。廚子看到就問他，盒子裡是不是有蛇。

「沒有，只有幾棵植物。」學生回答。

「裡面有東西在動。」廚子堅持說。

學生只好打開蓋子，讓她知道她看錯了。「妳自己看……」

話還沒說完，男孩從盒子裡頭一跳就跳到地上，跑向門外。女

僕還來不及看清楚，就急忙追了過去。

老師還在講課，被叫聲打斷。「捉住他，捉住他！」所有學生都跟在男孩後面追捕。男孩跑得比老鼠還快，他們想在門口攔住他，他卻幸運地跑出屋外。

男孩不敢跑上大道，而轉往另一個方向。他穿過花園進入院子。一大群人在後面跟著，又笑又叫的。可憐的小傢伙拚命跑，好像逃不掉了。

他匆匆經過一個工人的屋子，聽見鵝的叫聲，瞄見門口有一撮鵝毛。終於找到公鵝的下落了！他快速爬上臺階走上門廊。大門關著，他進不去。追捕他的人們越來越靠近他了，而屋裡的公鵝也叫得越來越淒厲。在這緊要關頭，男孩終於鼓起勇氣，用力敲門。

一個小孩來開門。男孩看到屋子正中央坐著一個女人，緊緊抱著公鵝，正要剪斷他的羽毛。她並不想傷害鵝，只是要讓公鵝加入自己的鵝群，而修剪他的翅膀，以免他飛走。

幸好男孩早了一步，門打開時，只有兩根羽毛隨著剪刀落下。看到一個小傢伙站在門檻上，女人以為他是妖精，而嚇得把剪刀掉在地上，兩手握緊，忘了抓緊公鵝。

鵝一得到解放，就跑向門口，邊跑邊唧起男孩的領子，在臺階上張開翅膀，飛到空中，同時優雅地揮動脖子，讓男孩滑到平滑而鬆軟的背上。

他們就這樣飛走了，所有威特朔沃爾的人都在下面凝望。

鄂威德修道院領地

野鵝戲弄狐狸的那一整天，男孩都躺在廢棄的松鼠窩裡睡覺。

他在傍晚時醒過來，覺得很煩惱，心想：「我很快就要被送回家，父母會看到我這個樣子！」他抬頭看到野鵝在維木布湖上沐浴，沒有一隻提到他回家的事。男孩心想：「也許他們以為白鵝太累了，沒辦法在今晚送我回家。」

第二天早上，鵝群在黎明時醒來。男孩確定他非回家不可了，可是很奇怪，野鵝准許他和白鵝加入他們清晨的翱翔。男孩猜想那是因為野鵝認為要吃飽才能展開那麼長的旅程。

野鵝飛越湖泊東邊的鄂威德修道院領地，那裡有一棟高大的城堡、設計優美的庭園，以及矮牆和涼亭。樹木蒼翠，修剪整齊，草坪上開著美麗的花。

野鵝確定那裡空無一人時，就朝著一個狗舍低飛，大叫：「這是什麼小棚子啊？」

那隻狗立刻從裡面跑出來，氣得對空中吠叫。

「你們這群流氓！竟然說這是小棚子？難道看不出來這是石砌的大城堡嗎？你們看過小棚子外面有那麼多建築嗎？你們想必知道有許多小棚子有自己的教堂、佃農房舍吧？你們在空中看到的土地沒有一片不屬於這個小棚子的，汪、汪、汪！」

那隻狗一口氣說了這麼多話，野鵝則在空中盤旋，聽他講到喘不過氣來，才大喊：「你何必這麼生氣啊？我們說的不是那座城堡，我們只是想了解你的狗舍，笨蛋！」

男孩聽到這個玩笑時哈哈大笑，心裡想著：「跟著野鵝穿過整片鄉野，一路飛到拉普蘭，可以聽到多少好玩的事啊！在災禍上身時，能參與這樣的旅程是再好也不過的。」

鵝群飛到領地東邊吃草根，一待就是好幾個小時。男孩則是去

找榛樹，看看有沒有去年秋天留下來的堅果。他在路上不斷地想著
這段旅程。如果能一路跟著野鵝，不知道會有多快活。儘管會挨餓
受凍，但可以不用工作和唸書。他心想，如果媽媽知道他靠生魚和
冬天的乾果過日子，不知道會說什麼。

　　鵝群填飽肚子後飛回湖上，在那裡玩到將近晚餐時間。

　　野鵝們向白公鵝挑戰，要他參加各種活動。他們比賽游泳、跑
步、飛行。雖然白公鵝竭盡全力，還是每次都輸給野鵝。男孩始終
坐在公鵝背上幫他加油，同樣玩得很盡興。

　　「這種生活正合我味。」男孩爬到公鵝的翅膀底下時想著。
「可是到了明天，我大概就會被送回家了。」

　　除了要被送回家之外，他什麼都不怕。可是星期三，野鵝還是
沒說什麼，就和星期二一樣，男孩對這種野外生活越來越滿意。

　　星期三他堅信野鵝會讓他待下來，但是又失去了希望。

　　星期四和其他日子一樣展開，男孩在庭園覓食時，阿卡走過
來，問他有沒有找到東西吃。他說沒有。阿卡就幫他找到一顆乾燥
的葛縷子，所有小種籽都在裡面。

　　男孩吃完後，阿卡說他在庭園亂跑太魯莽了，問他曉不曉得有
多少敵人要提防，畢竟他那麼弱小。但是男孩一點也沒想到，於是
阿卡開始說給他聽。

　　在庭園一定要提防狐狸和貂，而在湖邊時，就要想到水獺。坐
在石牆上時，不能忘了會從小洞鑽出來的鼬鼠。如果想要在樹葉堆
上睡覺，就要先看看有沒有冬眠的小青蛇。一旦去到空曠的草原，
就要注意在空中盤旋的老鷹和鴛。在灌木叢中，他可能會被雀鷹抓
走。到處都有喜鵲和烏鴉，千萬不能大意。天黑後就要注意有沒有

騎鵝歷險記

大貓頭鷹的聲音，因為他們能神不知鬼不覺地捕獵。

男孩並不怕死，但不想被吃掉，就問阿卡要怎樣保護自己。

阿卡開口教導男孩，必須與所有小動物和樂相處，例如松鼠、兔子、燕雀、啄木鳥和雲雀。只要和他們交上朋友，他們就會在有危險時警告他，為他找地方躲藏，盡力保護他。

但後來男孩照著阿卡的建議去找松鼠幫忙時，他卻說：「你休想從我這裡或其他小動物身上得到什麼。難道你以為我們不知道你是那個看鵝的尼爾斯，你去年搗毀燕子窩，打破椋鳥蛋，把小烏鴉扔到泥坑裡，還用陷阱捉鴿子，把松鼠關到籠子裡？你最好自己想辦法，你該慶幸我們沒有聯合起來對付你。回去找你的同類吧！」

以前聽到這些話，他是不會善罷干休的，但現在他只擔心野鵝知道他曾經那麼頑劣。儘管個子小，他還是有能力去破壞鳥巢，可是他變乖了。星期四他都在想，野鵝會不會因為他從前的頑劣而不肯帶他去拉普蘭。那天晚上，聽到松鼠的太太被偷走，小孩開始挨餓時，他就打定主意要幫忙。

男孩星期五來到庭園，聽到紅腹灰雀在每個灌木叢中唱歌，描述松鼠太太的經歷，以及尼爾斯冒著生命危險，把幼鼠送去給她。

男孩確定阿卡和那群野鵝都聽說了整件事，然而他們卻一整天都沒有開口叫他待下來。

星期六早上，他們來到草原時，狐狸斯密爾已經在等著把他們趕來趕去，讓他們不得安寧。阿卡馬上飛到空中，帶著鵝群飛越平原和山丘，來到威特朔沃爾地區。公鵝就是在威特朔沃爾被偷走的，要不是男孩設法營救他，可能再也找不到他了。

星期六晚上，男孩帶著公鵝回到維木布湖，以為會得到讚許，

卻沒從阿卡和野鵝那裡聽到他渴望聽見的話。

　　星期日又來了。自從男孩中了魔法，已經過了一個星期，他還是只有一丁點大。可是他不想再為這件事煩心了。

　　他坐在湖邊茂密的柳樹下吹蘆葦笛時，看到阿卡和其他野鵝排成長龍往他這邊走來。他們的速度出奇地慢，舉止莊嚴，男孩知道，他們現在要跟他說明白了。

　　阿卡終於停下腳步時說：「你也許覺得奇怪，你把我從狐狸那裡救出來，我卻沒跟你道謝。可是我向來是用行動表示感謝，我曾派使者聯絡對你施法術的精靈。起初他根本不想理睬，可是我不斷傳話給他，告訴他你和我們在一起表現得很好。他接受了，而且表示你一回到家，就可以恢復原樣。」

　　一開始聽到野鵝的感謝時，男孩非常高興，但當她說完時，男孩卻感到非常悲傷！他一句話也沒說，轉身哭了起來。

　　男孩喜歡的是現在愉快的日子，和在空中自由飛行的旅程。他難過地大叫：「我不要當人類，我想和你們去拉普蘭。」「那個精靈不好惹。這次不領情，以後再求他就難了。」阿卡說。

　　男孩這輩子不曾關心過父母親、老師、同學。不論是工作還是遊玩，都讓他覺得厭煩，所以他誰也不想念。

　　男孩大叫：「我要跟你們去拉普蘭，這就是為什麼我整個星期都很規矩。」阿卡說：「如果你想去，我不會拒絕你，可是你要先考慮好，是否真的不想回家。你可能有一天會後悔。」

　　「不會！沒什麼好後悔的。我從來沒有這麼快樂過。」男孩說。「那就依你吧。」阿卡說。

　　「謝謝！」男孩說完後，高興得想要大哭。

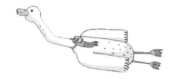

第 4 章
格里敏城堡

黑鼠和灰鼠

　　格里敏城堡位於離大海不遠的斯堪尼東南部，那是座高大而堅固的石造建築，從好幾公里之外就看得到。

　　尼爾斯與鵝群雲遊四方時，格里敏城堡並沒有人居住，但不是沒有房客。每年夏天都有一對鸛鳥住在屋頂的大巢裡，閣樓也有一對灰色貓頭鷹居住，暗廊垂掛著蝙蝠，廚房爐子裡住著一隻老貓，地窖則有幾百隻老黑鼠。

　　老鼠在動物之間的評價不高，但是格里敏城堡的黑鼠例外，因為他們與敵人作戰時格外勇猛，在族群遭受不幸時堅忍不拔，其他動物提起他們時總帶著幾分敬意。黑鼠曾經統御斯堪尼，在每一間房舍出現，但現在已幾近滅絕，只在老舊而偏僻的地方出沒。沒有一個地方像格里敏城堡一樣有這麼多黑鼠。人類當然也曾努力去消滅黑鼠，但成果有限。將黑鼠逼入絕境的是是灰鼠。

　　起先灰鼠並不敢進入黑鼠統領的城市，但隨著數量增加，膽子越來越大，就開始搬進黑鼠遺棄的廢屋，揀食黑鼠不屑一顧的垃圾。不到幾年，他們就壯大起來，占據黑鼠的閣樓、地窖。

　　很難了解為什麼黑鼠無法團結起來殲滅灰鼠，也許是因為相信自己不會衰敗。後來在斯堪尼找不到地方棲身，只剩格里敏城堡。

這座古堡日夜都有攻防戰發生。由於黑鼠守衛嚴密，打起仗來視死如歸，也幸虧古堡安全可靠，他們始終能擊退來敵。

鄰近地區的灰鼠仍不斷地找機會攻進城堡。人類把古堡當成糧倉，除非攻占這個地方，不然灰鼠不會停戰。

鶴鳥　三月二十八日　星期一

站在維木布湖上睡覺的鵝群，一早就被空中的叫聲吵醒。「特立勞，特立勞！名叫特立勞的鶴要跟野鵝阿卡和她的同伴問好。明天我們要在克拉山表演大鶴舞。邀請阿卡與她的同伴一同參加。」

阿卡抬起頭回答：「謝謝，也向他問好！」

鶴群聽了就飛走了，但野鵝仍聽得見他們的叫聲迴盪在山林中：「特立勞問候大家，明天我們要在克拉山表演大鶴舞。」

野鵝很高興接到這個邀請。「你很幸運能夠看到克拉山的大鶴舞。」他們對白公鵝說。

「看鶴舞有這麼稀罕嗎？」公鵝問。

「那是你做夢也想不到的事！」野鵝回答。

「現在我們得想想，明天去克拉山時，要怎麼安排小拇指，免得他受到傷害。」阿卡說。「我們不能丟下小拇指一個人！」公鵝說。「如果那群鶴不准他看表演，那我就待在這裡陪他。」

「沒有人類可以參加克拉山的動物集會。」阿卡說。「我可不敢帶小拇指去。不過待會兒再談這件事，先找東西吃比較要緊。」

這一天她照常去遠離狐狸斯密爾的地方覓食，一直飛到格里敏古堡南方的濕地才降落。

濕地另一邊有一道很寬的石牆。傍晚男孩抬頭想要請求阿卡帶他一起去克拉山看大鶴舞時，他的視線正好落在那面牆上。他嚇得輕叫一聲，所有野鵝都抬起頭，往那裡看。起初野鵝和男孩以為牆上的圓灰石都長了腳在跑，但很快就看清楚，那是一群老鼠。他們彼此靠得很近，一排排地跑著，數量多到有一陣子遮住了整堵牆。

男孩向來很怕老鼠，從他還是人類時就怕了，何況他現在這麼弱小，兩、三隻老鼠就能制服他。他站在那裡看著，不斷地發抖。

但是很奇怪，野鵝似乎同樣討厭老鼠。等老鼠走了，還抖一抖身體，好像羽毛沾到了泥巴。

「這麼多灰鼠跑出來，不是好兆頭。」伊克西說。

突然來了一隻大鳥，在他們之間降落。他有一對又大又黑的翅膀、紅色的長腿和粗大的嘴，使他的外表顯得憂鬱。

阿卡馬上整理翅膀，一邊靠近那隻鸛鳥，一邊不斷行禮。雖然是初春，阿卡看到他並不驚訝，因為她知道母鸛鳥飛越波羅的海之前，公鸛鳥會先來檢查鳥巢有沒有在冬天受損。令阿卡覺得奇怪的是，鸛鳥竟然會來找她，因為鸛鳥通常只跟同族來往。

「我想你家沒有受損吧，艾爾曼里奇先生。」阿卡說。

鸛鳥一開口就要訴苦，可是他欲言又止，起初只是發出嘎嘎聲，後來才用微弱的沙啞聲說話。格里敏城堡屋頂瓦上的巢被暴風吹壞了，在斯堪尼找不到食物，斯堪尼的人偷走了他所有的東西，他們為了種田而排掉沼澤的水，他想要離開再也不要回來。

鸛鳥忽然問鵝群，有沒有看到前往格里敏城堡的灰鼠。阿卡回答說有，他就開始說，勇敢的黑鼠多年來如何保衛城堡。「但今天晚上，格里敏城堡將會落入灰鼠的手中。」鸛鳥嘆著氣說。

「為什麼是今晚呢？」阿卡問。

「因為黑鼠相信所有動物都會趕到克拉山，所以昨晚幾乎全部都去了那裡。」鸛鳥說。「可是你們看到了，灰鼠都留下來了，而且正在集合，打算在今晚突襲城堡。那裡只有一些無法去克拉山的老弱黑鼠在看守，所以灰鼠應該會得逞。多年來我和黑鼠相處得很愉快，真不想和他們的敵人住在一起。」

阿卡明白了，原來鸛鳥是在生灰鼠的氣，才會來找她訴苦。「你有送信給黑鼠嗎？」她問。

「沒有，那沒用。他們還沒有趕回來，城堡就會被攻陷。」鸛鳥回答。「不要這麼武斷。」阿卡說：「有一隻老鵝很願意去阻止這種野蠻的行為。」

鸛鳥一直盯著阿卡，因為阿卡並沒有適合作戰的爪子和嘴巴，再說她在白天活動，天一黑就要睡覺，而老鼠是夜間開戰的。

但阿卡顯然決定幫黑鼠。她命令伊克西把鵝群帶到維木布湖。但鵝群不同意，於是她說：「我相信你們聽話對我們比較好。我要飛到那座大古堡，如果你們要跟，人類看到我們，就會把我們射下來。我唯一想要帶的人是小拇指，他可以幫我，因為他視力很好，而且能在夜間保持清醒。」

男孩那天正在鬧彆扭，他挺胸站出來，正想說他不想插手灰鼠的戰事，請阿卡另請高明時，鸛鳥一看到他就咕嚕叫著，好像在大笑，然後快如閃電地用嘴巴夾起男孩，把他拋到幾公尺高的空中。這個動作他重複了七次。男孩一直在尖叫，鵝群也在喊：「艾爾曼里奇先生，你在幹什麼？他不是青蛙，他是人啊！」

鸛鳥終於把男孩放下來，男孩毫髮無傷。他對阿卡說：「現在我要飛回格里敏城堡了。我離開時，住在那裡的動物都很擔心。當我告訴他們野鵝阿卡和小拇指會過來救援時，他們肯定會很高興。」鸛鳥說完，就好像箭矢離開拉緊的弓，沖天而去。阿卡知道他在開玩笑，沒放在心上。她等男孩找到被鸛鳥甩掉的木鞋，就把他放在背上，跟著鸛鳥走了。男孩生著悶氣，那紅長腿的傢伙竟然以為他長得小就沒用處。他要讓鸛鳥看看，西威門荷格的尼爾斯有什麼本事。

　　過了一會兒，阿卡就站在格里敏城堡的鸛鳥巢上。鸛鳥巢邊坐著兩隻灰色貓頭鷹、一隻灰條紋老貓，以及十二隻眼睛水亮、有暴牙的年邁老鼠。這群動物在平常是不會和睦相處的。

　　所有黑鼠都不說話，顯然非常絕望。或許很清楚，無法保衛城堡和自己的性命。兩隻貓頭鷹以空洞如鬼魅的聲音說起灰鼠的殘暴，因為他們不會放過任何一顆蛋和鶵鳥。老貓相信那麼多灰鼠進來城堡，一定會把他咬死。他不斷責怪黑鼠：「你們怎麼這麼笨，讓最厲害的戰士離開？你們怎麼能相信灰鼠？真是不可原諒！」

　　十二隻黑鼠都沒有吭聲。儘管心裡也不好過，鸛鳥還是忍不住要逗逗老貓。「別擔心，家貓湯米！你沒看到阿卡媽媽和小拇指過來拯救城堡了？你大可放心，他們會成功的。我要站在這裡睡覺，等明天醒來時，絕不會有一隻灰鼠還留在格里敏城堡。」

　　男孩對阿卡使眼色，示意要把站在巢邊縮起一腳的鸛鳥推下屋頂，但是阿卡阻止男孩。阿卡一點也不生氣，反而自信滿滿地說：「我這個老人家如果連這點事都沒辦法解決，那就太差勁了。只要能熬夜的貓頭鷹先生和太太肯為我送信就夠了。」

　　兩隻貓頭鷹都很願意。阿卡請貓頭鷹先生去找離開的黑鼠，要他們快點回來。貓頭鷹太太的任務是去找住在隆德大教堂尖頂的貓頭鷹弗拉瑪，但內容是祕密，阿卡是以耳語告訴貓頭鷹太太的。

捕鼠人

　　一群灰鼠終於找到通往地窖的洞口時，已經是接近半夜。這個洞是在牆上的高處，但灰鼠以疊羅漢的方式，讓他們最勇敢的那隻很快地來到洞口。她在那裡坐了一會兒，等來自內部的攻擊。她傾耳聆聽，但一切都很安靜，於是鼓起勇氣，跳進漆黑的地窖。

　　一隻隻灰鼠跟著領隊進到裡面。他們都以為會受到黑鼠伏擊，直到地窖地板擠不進更多老鼠時，他們才敢前進。

　　灰鼠一進去就聞到堆在地上的穀物氣味，但現在不是享受戰利品的時候。他們沒有遺漏任何一個小洞，都沒有發現黑鼠。

　　灰鼠進入堡主的大宴客廳，那裡和其他房間一樣空洞、冰冷。他們還爬上最高的四樓，那只是一個空曠的大房間。他們唯一沒去查探的地方是屋頂上的鸛鳥巢。就在這時，貓頭鷹太太叫醒阿卡，通知她弗拉瑪同意她的要求，把她要的東西借給她。

　　由於灰鼠已經仔細搜查過整個城堡，認為黑鼠已經逃走不再抵抗，因而興沖沖地奔向穀物堆。

　　可是灰鼠們還沒有吞下第一顆穀粒，就聽見庭院傳來尖細的笛聲。灰鼠抬起頭來，不安地聽著，放下穀物往前跑了幾步，但又忍不住轉過身來繼續享用。

　　尖銳的笛聲再度響起，這時奇妙的事情發生了。一隻、兩隻……整群老鼠都離開穀物堆，循著捷徑跑下地窖，離開屋子。仍有許多灰鼠留在城堡裡面，捨不得離開花了那麼多心力征服的格里敏城堡。但同樣受到笛聲的牽引，激動地穿過牆上的洞，爭先恐後地離開城堡。

院子正中央站著一個正在吹笛的小傢伙，旁邊圍繞著心醉神迷的老鼠，而且越圍越多。有一度停止吹笛，將拇指放在鼻子上，對老鼠擺動指頭。那群老鼠準備要撲過去咬死他了，他才又開始吹笛，老鼠也就再度臣服。

小傢伙讓所有灰鼠都離開格里敏城堡以後，慢慢從院子走到馬路上。所有老鼠都跟在後面，因為笛聲在他們耳中是那麼地悅耳，完全無法抗拒。

小傢伙走過許多彎道，繼續吹著笛子。那支笛子非常小，是用動物角做的，沒有人知道它的來歷。教堂尖頂的貓頭鷹是在隆德大教堂的壁龕裡面發現它的。她曾經拿給渡鴉巴塔奇看，猜想那是人類以前用來制服老鼠的東西。那隻渡鴉是阿卡的朋友，阿卡因此知道這個寶物。

老鼠果然無法抗拒笛聲。男孩在星光下不斷地吹奏，整群老鼠跟隨在後。他一直吹到日出，讓老鼠跟著他一路遠離格里敏城堡。

第 5 章

克拉山的大鶴舞

三月二十七日 星期二

　　雖然斯堪尼有許多雄偉的建築，但沒有一座像古老的克拉山一樣有那麼美麗的峭壁。壯觀的景色加上碧藍大海，晴朗的天空，使遊客在夏天紛湧而至。每年所有動物都會來到這裡集會，這是自古以來的傳統。

　　這一天的天氣總是很好。鸛鳥是優秀的天氣預報師，如果會下雨，他絕不會叫動物來集會。天空清澈，視線毫無阻礙。

　　動物們看到一片片小灰雲慢慢越過平原，然後有一片飄向克拉山，在遊戲場上空停住。整團雲開始呱噪，彷彿是由聲音組成的。它時起時落，終於降落停在小丘上，小丘一下子就布滿了灰色雲雀、各種顏色的美麗燕雀、有斑點的歐掠鳥和黃綠色山雀。

　　阿卡和鵝群最後才抵達，這在所難免，因為要飛越整個斯堪尼省，而且她醒來時必須先去找小拇指，那時他已經對灰鼠吹了好幾個小時的笛子，離格里敏城堡很遠了。找到男孩的並不是阿卡，而是鸛鳥艾爾曼里奇先生。鸛鳥特別出去找他，把他帶回巢，請他原諒昨晚的無禮。男孩非常高興，也和鸛鳥成了朋友。阿卡對他也很親切，頭在他手臂上磨蹭了很多次，稱讚他救了患難中的動物。

　　但男孩不想平白受到嘉許。他說：「不，阿卡媽媽，我這麼做並不是要幫黑鼠。我只是要讓艾爾曼里奇先生知道我有點用處。」

男孩說完，阿卡就轉頭問鸛鳥，是否適合帶小拇指去克拉山。鸛鳥馬上回答：「當然要帶他去。他昨晚為我們受苦，能夠回報他是我們的榮幸。昨天對他那麼無禮，讓我很難過，所以應該由我來背他去集會地點。」

依照克拉山的慣例，當天的節目由烏鴉的飛行舞開始。烏鴉一結束，兔子就上場了。他們排成一列往前跑，有的是單隻一列，有的是三、五隻，全部立起身體，耳朵朝各個方向搖晃。他們轉圈、跳高、用前掌拍打後掌。有些不斷地翻筋斗，有些則像輪子一樣翻滾。有一隻用單腳旋轉，另一隻則倒立行走。整個場面凌亂無序，但是古怪有趣，讓動物看得呼吸加快。

緊接著上百隻深褐色羽毛的松雞跳到遊戲場中央的大橡樹上。樹梢那隻鼓起羽毛，垂下翅膀，翹起尾巴，露出雪白的底毛。然後他伸長脖子，發出深沉的喉音：「喀、喀、喀。」接著閉上眼睛，輕聲說：「嘻、嘻、嘻。多好聽啊！嘻、嘻、嘻。」三隻最靠近的松雞就開始唱歌，然後再下面的十隻也加進來，直到上百隻松雞同時出聲，同樣唱得渾然忘我，使其他動物跟著陶醉，心想：「對，春天真的來了，寒冬已經過去。春天的火焰正在大地上燃燒。」

看到褐色松雞表演得如此成功，黑色松雞就忍不住了。由於沒有樹可以跳，他們跑進遊戲場。灌木長得很高，觀眾只看得到美麗的尾羽和粗嘴巴。他們開始唱：「咕、咕、咕。」

黑松雞與褐松雞比賽時，有隻狐狸趁著大家專心看松雞表演時，偷偷溜進野鵝的小丘。等到被發現時，他已經來到小丘上。一隻鵝看到他，立刻大叫：「野鵝，小心啊！」狐狸一口咬住她的喉

克拉山的大鶴舞

嘍，但是野鵝聽見了她的叫聲，全部飛上空中。他們一飛起來，其他動物就看到狐狸站在野鵝的小丘上，嘴裡叼著一隻死鵝。

狐狸斯密爾破壞了遊戲場的和平，一定要給予懲罰。沒有一隻狐狸為他說情，因為他們都知道，一旦這麼做，就會被趕出遊戲場，再也不能進入。斯密爾失去了狩獵場和住處，不得不去異地討生活。最年長的狐狸一咬掉斯密爾的右外耳，所有的年輕狐狸同時撲向斯密爾，斯密爾只能趕緊逃跑。

這一切都在黑松雞與褐松雞的表演賽發生的。但是松雞們唱得很投入，沒有受到野鵝小丘上的混亂干擾。松雞的表演賽一結束，公鹿就出來表演摔角。有幾對公鹿同時較勁，鹿角一撞就纏在一起，迫使雙方後退。

所有動物都感染到激戰的情緒，儘管紛紛鼓起翅膀、脹起頸羽和尖爪，他們對彼此沒有敵意。如果那些公鹿再角力一會兒，每個小丘上可能都會發生爭戰，因為他們都渴望表現出生命力。

這時有一陣低語傳遍每一個小丘：「鶴鳥來了。」

那些披蓋著灰暗羽毛的鳥兒，以一種神秘的狂放舉動，滑落在小丘上。他們往前滑行，轉著圈，一會兒飛一會兒舞。翅膀優雅地舞動，前進。他們的舞蹈既奇特又美妙，彷彿一團幻影在表演，令人目不暇給。現在第一次來克拉山的動物都明白了，為什麼這個集會要以鶴鳥之舞命名。因為舞蹈具有野性，又能喚起甜美的渴望。所有動物都不再想著打鬥，鳥兒與四腳動物們都想從此飛向雲端，一窺雲朵另一頭的祕密，留下沉重身軀，翱翔到無邊無際的地方。

一年之中，動物們只有這麼一次會渴求那無法獲得的生命奧祕，也就是舉行大鶴舞的這一天。

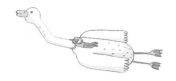

第 6 章

雨天

三月三十日 星期三

　　這是旅程中的第一場雨。野鵝們在維木布湖一帶時，天氣還很好，但是他們動身前往北方的那一天，就開始下雨了，而且連下好幾個小時。男孩坐在鵝背上全身濕透，冷得發抖。

　　出發時，天氣還很晴朗。鵝群在高空穩定地飛行，不急不躁。阿卡帶頭，其他的鵝呈人字形排在後面。他們沒有停下來逗弄地上的動物，但也無法一直保持沉默，而隨著拍翅的節奏，不斷發出平常撫慰的叫聲：「你在哪裡？我在這裡。你在哪裡？我在這裡。」

　　第一道春雨落下時，草原和樹林上的鳥兒都興奮地大叫，聲音迴盪在空中。「現在我們有雨了，雨帶給我們春天，春天帶給我們花朵和綠葉，綠葉帶給我們蚯蚓和昆蟲，蚯蚓和昆蟲帶給我們食物。豐盛美味的食物勝過一切。」鳥兒們唱道。野鵝也很高興雨喚醒了多眠的植物，在結冰的湖面上穿孔。他們再也正經不起來，開始對鄰里愉快地呼叫。

　　這都是剛下雨的情形，等到雨連續下了整個下午，野鵝就不耐煩了，對著伊維湖四周的森林大喊：「你們還沒喝夠嗎？」

　　到了下午，他們在一大片沼澤中的矮小松樹那降落。有些小丘蓋滿了雪，有些則光禿禿地從半融的冰水坑中冒出。男孩躺在公鵝的翅膀下，因為濕冷而無法入睡。他不斷聽到嘎吱的聲音、窸窣的腳步聲和脅迫的話語，心中充滿恐懼。如果不想被嚇死，最好找個有燈光的暖和地方待著。

「也許我該去人類的地方過夜。」男孩心想：「在火爐邊待一會兒，再找點東西吃。我可以在天亮之前回去和野鵝會合。」

他從公鵝的翅膀底下爬出來，溜到地上，沒有吵醒公鵝和別隻野鵝，躡手躡腳地穿過沼澤。他不知道自己在哪裡，但是他記得降落前有看到一個大村莊，決定走向那裡。他找到一條路，不久就走上一條長長的街道，兩邊都種著樹，還有一個接著一個的花園。

房屋是木造的，蓋得很漂亮，大多數都有山牆和前院，鑲著雕刻的飾邊和玻璃門。男孩經過時，聽見人們坐在溫暖的木屋裡談天說笑。「我如果敲門要求進去，不知道他們會怎麼說。」

他沿路都有這個念頭，但現在只要他靠近人類，內心就膽怯了起來。「我多看看這個村子以後，再要求進屋好了。」

他來到一間有陽臺的屋子，大門在男孩經過時打開了，黃色燈光穿透漂亮的薄簾灑出來。從裡面走出一名少女，她靠在陽臺欄杆上說：「下雨了，春天就要來了。」男孩看到她時，心中有股翻騰，與想哭的感覺很像。這是他第一次對與世人隔絕感到難過。

不久之後，他走到一間商店，外面有一台紅色的播種機。他停下來看，然後爬上座位，假裝在駕駛。他心想，在田裡開著這麼漂亮的機器不知有多好玩。這一刻他忘了自己的模樣，接著馬上從機器上跳下來，油然升起更大的不安。當人類其實滿不錯的！

他走過郵局時，想到有那麼多報紙帶來世界各地的消息。看到藥店和醫生的房子，覺得人類真厲害，能夠對抗疾病和死亡。他來到教堂，想到人建造它是為了知道人世以外的世界，了解上帝和永生。他越走就越喜歡人類。

尼爾斯選擇繼續當精靈時，沒有考慮到會失去什麼，可是現在他非常擔心，也許再也不能恢復了。到底要怎樣才能變回人類呢？

他爬上臺階，在大雨中坐下來思考。「這事對只有一丁點大的我來說太困難了，」他這麼想著。「看來我還是要回到人類的世界，問問牧師、醫生、老師和其他有學問的人是否有辦法解決。」

他決定馬上起身行動，這時他看到一隻大貓頭鷹飛過來，停在路邊的樹上。接著又飛來一隻母貓頭鷹坐在屋簷下，開始大叫：「你回來啦，灰鴞先生？你在海外過得好嗎？」

「謝謝妳，褐鴞女士，我過得非常好。」灰鴞說。「我不在時，這裡有沒有發生不尋常的事？」

「這裡沒有，但是斯堪尼有。一個男孩被精靈用法術變得像松鼠那麼小，他後來和一隻家鵝去了拉普蘭。」

「這真是個天大的消息。他再也不能變回人了嗎？」

「這是祕密，灰鴞先生，但是我可以告訴你。精靈說，只要那個男孩好好照顧公鵝，讓他平安回家……」

「還有呢？」

「跟我一起飛到教堂的鐘樓，我就會全部告訴你。我怕這裡有人偷聽。」兩隻貓頭鷹飛走後，男孩把帽子扔到空中大叫：「只要我照顧公鵝，讓他平安回家，我就可以變回人類了！太好了！」

他一直叫著，直到屋裡的人聽到他的聲音為止。他趕緊以最快的速度走向沼澤，回到野鵝那裡。

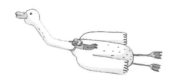

第 7 章
羅耐畢河畔

四月一日 星期五

　　野鵝和狐狸斯密爾都沒想到會在離開斯堪尼之後再碰上。斯密爾之前都一直都待在斯堪尼北部，卻沒碰到任何莊園，或是有許多獵物和美味小鹿的獵場，日子過得淒苦。

　　一天下午，斯密爾走在離羅耐畢河不遠的荒林中，看到一群野鵝飛在空中，其中一隻是白的，他馬上就知道來者是誰。

　　斯密爾馬上奔去獵鵝。一方面想要獲得美食，一方面也想趁機報復。他看著他們往東飛到羅耐畢河，然後改變航向，循著河流往南飛。他知道他們想要在河邊過夜，但是野鵝選了個安全的地方降落，讓他無法靠近。

　　這時仍是嚴寒的早春時期，樹木都光禿禿。野鵝很慶幸找到一片位於山崖邊的沙地，寬闊得足以棲身。前面是因融雪而奔湧不停的河水，後面是無法攀爬的岩壁，還有樹枝在上面遮護。

　　鵝群很快就睡著了，但男孩無法闔眼。他什麼都看不見，而且只聽到一點點聲音。萬一公鵝發生危險，他會無力搭救。

　　斯密爾站在山頂俯視那群野鵝。自言自語著：「你不能爬這麼陡的山，不能在那麼湍急的河裡游泳，而且山下沒有一寸土地能通到他們的休息處。」可是斯密爾躺在懸崖邊想著，即使不能把他們全部吃掉，也希望他們都死翹翹。

　　他聽到旁邊的大松樹有一陣腳步聲，接著就看到一隻松鼠被貂趕下樹。他們都沒有看到狐狸，斯密爾只是靜靜看著他們在樹木中追逐。松鼠在樹枝中輕盈地移動，而貂的爬樹技巧雖然不如松鼠，還是能在樹枝上攀爬，跟腳踏林中小徑一樣穩當。

　　松鼠一被抓到，追逐就結束了。斯密爾走到貂那裡，友善地打了聲招呼，恭喜貂捕到松鼠。貂雖然身材苗條，臉蛋漂亮，披著淡褐色圍巾，儼然是個小尤物，實際上卻是個森林流氓，所以沒理會狐狸。斯密爾說：「我很驚訝，像你這種狩獵高手竟然只想去追松鼠，而不去吃近在眼前的美味。」他停了一下，看到貂只是無禮地冷笑，就繼續說：「難道你沒看到底下那群野鵝？還是你爬山的本領不夠好，沒辦法下去抓他們？」

　　這次那隻貂拱著背，豎起每一根毛，對斯密爾撲過去。「你看到野鵝了？」他兇巴巴地問。「在哪裡？馬上告訴我，不然就咬斷你的脖子。」

　　斯密爾回答：「客氣一點，別忘了我比你大一倍。我只是想告訴你野鵝在哪裡，沒別的意思。」

　　貂立刻爬下懸崖，斯密爾則坐在那裡看著他像蛇的身軀在樹枝間跳動，心想：「那美麗的獵手是森林中最狠毒的。我相信那群野鵝拜我之賜會在血腥中醒來。」

　　斯密爾等著聽見鵝群臨死的慘叫聲，看到的卻是貂從樹上跌入河裡，水花濺得很高。沒多久就傳來用力拍翅的聲響，所有野鵝都匆匆飛了起來。

　　斯密爾原本想隨後跟去，但又好奇他們是如何保住性命的，於是坐在那裡等貂爬上來。那可憐的野獸全身都是泥水，不時地停下來用前掌擦臉。「我之前就料到了，你是個大笨蛋，一定會跌到河裡面去。」斯密爾輕蔑地說。

「我不是笨蛋，你也不必責怪我。」貂說。「我坐在最下面的樹枝上想著要怎麼把整群鵝扯爛時，就有個沒比松鼠大多少的小不點跳起來，把一顆石頭扔到我的頭上，力道很大，害得我掉進河裡。我還沒有站起來，他們就……」

貂不必把話說完，因為斯密爾已經跑得老遠，趕著追野鵝去了。這時，阿卡順著河流往南飛，來到榆巴瀑布。河在這裡鑽進地底，然後像透明玻璃一樣從一個狹縫墜落，在底下噴出閃亮的水珠和飛沫。瀑布下方有一些石頭，水在這裡沖激形成洪流。阿卡媽媽就在這裡降落。這裡是個好住處，尤其是在沒有人類走動的夜晚。

野鵝早已睡著了，男孩沒有睡意，坐在旁邊看顧公鵝。

過了一會兒，斯密爾沿著河岸跑過來。他馬上就看到野鵝站在冒泡的漩渦中，沒辦法過去。但他還是不死心，在岸邊坐下盯著他們，覺得很丟臉，自己獵手的名聲岌岌可危。

突然之間，他看到一隻水獺叼著一隻魚，從瀑布那邊爬上來。斯密爾就走過去。「你真了不起，那邊的石頭滿滿是鵝，你卻只抓一隻魚就滿足了！」

水獺卻連轉頭往河那邊瞥一眼都沒有。他和其他水獺一樣是個流浪漢，曾多次在維木布湖捕魚，也許認識這隻狐狸。他說：「斯密爾，我很清楚你會用什麼手段騙取一條鱒魚。」

「哦，原來是你啊，葛利普？」斯密爾高興地說著，因為他知道這隻水獺動作很機靈，而且是游泳高手。「你看不上那些野鵝，我不覺得奇怪，因為你根本到不了那裡。」但是水獺的腳趾有蹼，還有跟船槳一樣好用的硬尾巴，以及防水的皮毛，受不了有人說他無法游到瀑布那邊，立刻轉過身，看到河上的野鵝，就丟下嘴邊的魚，衝下陡峭的河岸跳進河裡。

如果夜鶯已回到榆巴瀑布，他們就會一天歌唱許多次，描述葛利普如何與急流搏鬥，因為水獺被波浪推開許多次，還被捲到河底，但是他奮力游上來，逐漸靠近野鵝。這段過程很驚險，值得夜鶯傳頌。

斯密爾盡可能看著水獺的行蹤，眼看他就要游到野鵝那邊了，卻在這時傳來尖銳的狂叫聲。水獺四腳朝天栽進水裡，像瞎眼的小貓一樣被水沖走。接著就是一陣拍翅聲響，鵝群又飛起來，去尋找另一個休息處了。

水獺很快就上岸，他一句話也沒說，只是開始舔舐前掌。斯密爾嘲笑他無功而返，他開口說：「那並不是因為我泳技不佳。我游到鵝那邊，正要爬上去時，一個小不點跑過來，用一種尖尖的東西刺我的腳。我痛得站不住，就被河水沖走了。」

他不用再說下去，因為斯密爾已經拔腿去跟蹤野鵝了。

阿卡不得不帶領同伴再度在夜裡飛行。幸好月亮還在上空，她可以靠著月光在附近找到另一個地方睡覺。離海不遠的南方有一處溫泉，四周蓋了許多旅館，吸引春天的遊客，在冬天倒沒有人造訪，所以許多鳥類會在嚴峻的暴風季節在建築物的陽臺上避難。

野鵝們在陽臺上降落，照例很快就睡著了。陽臺朝南，男孩就坐在那裡，欣賞大海和陸地連接的美景。

男孩注意到大自然是多麼的溫和可親，在夜裡的心情也變得比之前平靜。這時，他忽然聽到浴場花園那邊傳來刺耳的嚎叫聲。他站起來，在黯淡的月光下，看到陽臺下方的步道上有一隻狐狸。斯密爾又跟來了，但是看到野鵝們休息的地方，知道自己不可能靠近，就惱恨地狂叫。

狐狸這一叫，老阿卡就醒了過來。雖然她什麼都看不見，但認得那個聲音。她說：「是你半夜還在外面嗎，斯密爾？」

「對，是我。今晚安排的節目，覺得怎樣？」斯密爾回答。

「你是說，貂和水獺都是你派來對付我們的？」阿卡問。

「有好機會就要把握。」斯密爾回答。「妳曾經跟我玩鵝戰，所以我要跟妳玩狐戰。只要你們其中一隻還活著，我就絕對不放棄，即使要跟著你們到天涯海角，我也照跟不誤！」

「你至少應該想一想這麼做對不對。你有獠牙和爪子來跟蹤我們，我們卻沒有能力防衛。」阿卡說。

斯密爾以為阿卡在害怕，緊接著說：「那個小拇指和我作對很多次，只要妳把他交出來，我就和妳講和，再也不會去追捕你們任何一隻。」

阿卡回答：「我不會把小拇指交出來的。我們這群從年紀最小到最老的鵝，都願意為他犧牲生命！」

「既然你們這麼愛他，我就跟妳保證，我報復時一定先選他下手。」斯密爾說。

阿卡沒有吭聲，而斯密爾又嚎叫幾聲之後，四周就安靜下來。男孩躺在那裡，仍然醒著。現在是阿卡對狐狸說的話讓他睡不著。他作夢也沒想到會聽到這樣的話，居然有人寧可送命也要保護他。從現在開始，再也不能說尼爾斯‧霍爾加松不在乎任何人了。

第 8 章

卡爾斯克羅納

四月二日 星期六

　　卡爾斯克羅納市的夜晚籠罩著月光，平靜而美麗，但是在稍早之前的白天卻是風雨交加。或許是人們以為壞天氣會再持續，所以街上沒幾個人。

　　在城市如此沉寂的時刻，阿卡和鵝群正要飛向這裡。他們不想留在內陸，因為每次降落，狐狸斯密爾都會過來騷擾。

　　男孩在空中高飛，俯瞰底下的大海和島嶼時，覺得一切都好詭異。正想著今晚要勇敢一點，不要害怕時，看到某個非常嚇人的東西。那是座高聳的峭壁島，充滿尖尖的大石頭，黑色的石頭之間閃爍著金光。

　　可是鵝群降落後，男孩就驚訝地發現那些大石頭不過是一些房子，整座島是一座城市，閃亮的金光是街燈和明亮的窗框。岸邊停泊著許多船隻，陸地這邊的多半是划艇、帆船和近海輪船，靠海的那邊則是裝甲戰艦。

　　這是什麼城市呢？男孩猜得出來，因為他看過各種戰艦。他從小就喜歡船，儘管只在路邊的水溝玩過玩具船。他知道只有一座城市會有那麼多戰艦停泊，那就是卡爾斯克羅納。

　　這是個避開狐狸的安全處所。男孩開始考慮，是否要放下心來，爬進公鵝的翅膀過夜。對，睡一覺對他有好處。等天亮以後，就可以去看看碼頭和船隻。

但男孩知道，怎麼可能挨到早上才去看那些船。他睡不到五分鐘，就從翅膀底下溜出來，順著避雷針和水管爬到地上。

不一會兒就來到教堂前的大廣場。幸好這時廣場空無一人，只有一尊底座很高的雕像。那是一個高大的壯漢，戴著三角帽，身穿長大衣、齊膝短褲和笨重的鞋子，手上還拿著長拐杖，看起來好像很懂得利用它，因為他的表情很嚴肅，有一個大鷹鉤鼻和醜嘴巴。

「這個長嘴唇的人在這裡做什麼？」男孩叫道。他從來不曾覺得像今晚這麼渺小。他想說些大膽的話來振奮自己。後來他轉身走向那條通向海洋的大馬路。

沒走多遠，男孩就聽見有人在跟蹤他。那個人腳步沉重，而且用一根硬棍敲著地面，聽起來好像是廣場上的大銅人在走路。

男孩邊走邊聽身後的腳步聲，越來越確定他就是那個銅人。地面在抖動，房屋在搖晃。男孩想到之前說的話，開始恐慌。

「也許他只是下來散散步。他才不會因為我講了那句話就生氣。我又沒有惡意。」男孩心想。

男孩彎進一條朝東的巷子，想要擺脫後面那個人。可是銅人跟著拐進同一條巷子，使男孩害怕得不知如何是好。這時他看到右邊不遠的樹林中央有一間古老的木造教堂，就毫不考慮地跑過去。「只要我能進到裡面，就安全了。」他想。

他往前跑的時候，突然看到一個人站在砂石路上對他招手。「那個人會幫助我！」男孩安下了心，趕緊跑過去。那個人就站在路邊的矮凳上。他一靠近就嚇呆了，因為那個人是木頭做的。

男孩站在那裡瞪著他。那個人身粗腿短，有著紅潤的大臉、閃亮的黑髮和濃密的鬍鬚。他頭上戴著木頭帽，身上穿著褐色的木頭大衣，圍著一條木頭腰帶，腳上是寬大的木頭短褲和襪子，腳上套著黑木鞋。他的漆是剛上的，所以在月光下渾身發亮。他看起來很和善，男孩知道可以信任他。

他的左手拿著一塊木牌，上面寫著：雖然我是無聲的，但是我謙恭地懇求您，來丟個銅板吧，只要拉起我的帽子！

哦！所以這個人只是個捐款箱。男孩覺得完了，但是又想起祖父曾提到這個木頭人，他說卡爾斯克羅納的小孩子都很喜歡他。這個雕像相當老了，讓人覺得有好幾百歲的年紀，但同時又顯得那麼健壯、活力十足，就像人們想像中的古人。

男孩聽見那個人從巷道拐進教堂的墓園，所以也跟到這裡來了！男孩怎麼辦呢？

這時木頭人彎下身，伸出他褐色的大手。男孩直覺他是基於善意，就跳進木頭人手裡。木頭人把他舉高，放在帽子底下。

男孩才剛躲好，木頭人也才剛把手放回原位，銅人就在他面前站住，手杖往地上一敲，使木頭人在臺座上晃了一下，然後以宏亮的聲音說：「你是誰？」

木頭人舉起手，發出嘎吱嘎吱的聲音，回答時碰觸他的帽沿：「陛下，我是羅森博姆，以前在無畏軍艦上當水手長，服完役後在教堂當司事，最近被雕成木製捐款箱放在墓園裡。」

聽到木頭人說出「陛下」二字時，男孩嚇了一跳。現在他想起來了，廣場上的雕像就是建造這座城市的人。這個人一定就是卡爾十一世本人。

「今晚有沒有看到一個小傢伙在街上亂跑？他是個無禮的壞蛋，要是捉到他，我一定要給他一頓好看！」銅人說完，手杖又開始在地面上敲，顯得非常生氣。

「陛下，我確實看到他了。」木頭人說這話時，男孩透過帽子的縫隙看著銅人，害怕得發抖，但是聽到木頭人接下來的話語後鎮定下來。「陛下走錯路了。那小子當然會跑去躲在造船廠裡。」

「是嗎，羅森博姆？那就不要再站在臺座上，來幫我把他找出來。四個眼睛總比兩個眼睛好。」

但是木頭人感傷地說：「我謙恭地請求您讓我留在這裡。我因為剛漆過，所以看起來很健壯，但其實我又老又破，走不動了。」

銅人不能接受抗命。「這是什麼話？一起來，羅森博姆！」他舉起手杖，在木頭人的肩膀上敲了一下。「你不是挺結實的嗎？」

兩個人浩浩蕩蕩地一同走在卡爾斯克羅納的街上，來到造船廠外面的大門。門外有個看守的水兵，銅人趾高氣揚地走過去把門踢開，那水兵連假裝沒看見都不能。

他們一走進去，就看到以木橋隔開的大碼頭。銅人說：「你認為我們應該從哪裡找起？」

「那麼小的傢伙，很容易藏在模型間裡。」

門口右邊有一片狹長的陸地，蓋滿了古老建築。銅人走向一棟有低牆、小窗和大屋頂的建築物，用手杖把門打開，踩了幾級破爛的臺階，進入一個大廳，裡面裝滿配備齊全的小船。不用說也知道，那是以前為瑞典海軍所做的軍艦模型。

被帶進這麼一個房間，男孩覺得很驚奇。「想想這麼氣派的大船都是瑞典製造的！」

他有很多時間參觀裡面的陳設，因為銅人一看到那些模型，就把一切拋在腦後，從頭到尾都看得很仔細，而且問個不停。羅森博姆就為他介紹造船和指揮的人，以及那些人的命運。

因為他們對新戰艦並不了解，談最多的是那些精緻的老木船。「我看你並不懂得這些新東西，」銅人說。「我們去看看別的吧，我覺得看這些東西很有意思。」

這時他已經拋開找男孩的事。男孩在木頭帽子裡，覺得很安全，心情平靜。

兩個人就這樣在大廠房中閒逛，最後走到一個寬敞的院落，那裡陳列的是老戰艦的船長塑像。男孩從沒看過這麼奇妙的景象，因為那些塑像的臉是那麼的嚴肅，令人敬畏。他們是不同時代的人，男孩覺得在他們面前簡直是一無是處。

銅人在這時對木頭人說：「羅森博姆，為站在這裡的人脫下你的帽子！他們都曾經為祖國奮戰。」

羅森博姆和銅人一樣，已經忘了為什麼要出來走動。他想也不想就拿起頭上的帽子，大喊：「我向那些選擇這個港口，建立這個造船廠、重整海軍的人，以及讓一切重生的國王脫帽致敬！」

「謝謝你，羅森博姆，說得太好了。你是個好人，可是這是什麼東西啊？」

尼爾斯‧霍爾加松站在羅森博姆的禿頭頂上。他不再害怕，而是舉起他白色的尖頂帽大喊：「長嘴唇，萬歲！」

銅人將手杖往地上用力一敲，這時太陽升起，銅人和木頭人一起像雲霧般消失了。野鵝從教堂鐘樓起飛，在城市上方盤旋。大白鵝一發現尼爾斯，就俯衝下來把他接走。

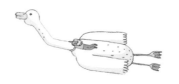

第 9 章

厄蘭南角

四月三日 星期日

野鵝飛到一座樹木繁茂的小島上覓食時，遇到了幾隻灰鵝。灰鵝很驚訝，因為野鵝通常是在內陸飛行的。

牠一隻看起來和阿卡一樣睿智的老灰鵝說：「斯密爾一定會跟著你們去拉普蘭。如果我是你們，我就不會直接往北飛，而是繞到厄蘭島，這樣才能澈底甩掉他。在厄蘭最南端的岬角至少停留三天，那裡有很多食物和同伴。我相信你們去了那裡絕不會後悔。」

這個建議確實高明，野鵝一吃飽，就啟程飛向厄蘭島。

四月三日至六日

厄蘭島最南端有一片王室領地，稱為「烏登比」。這塊土地相當遼闊，橫跨兩岸，也因為有大群鳥出沒而受到矚目。

那是一片布滿石頭和水灘的沙岸，以及一堆堆被沖上岸的海草。如果男孩可以選擇，他不會在這裡降落，但鳥群或許把這裡當成了天堂。鴨子和鵝走來走去，在草地上覓食，鷸鳥和其他岸鳥則在較靠近海邊的地方奔跑。潛鳥在海裡捕魚，而最熱鬧的地方是沿岸的水草堆。鳥兒們緊靠在一起，在那裡啄食小蟲。那數量一定很多，因為沒有一隻鳥兒抱怨不夠吃。

大多數的鳥都要飛到更遠的地方，只是休息片刻。一旦鳥群領袖覺得同伴恢復精神了，就會說：「準備上路。」

　　「不，等一等！我還沒有吃飽！」同伴說。「你們以為我會讓你們吃到飛不動嗎？」領袖說著，翅膀一拍就啓程了。

　　有一群天鵝沿著最外圍的海草堆蹲著。他們不想上岸，只想在水面上飄盪，偶爾把脖子伸進水裡，從海底撈取食物。每次拿到特別可口的東西就會大喊大叫，聽起來好像喇叭聲。

　　男孩聽見淺灘上有天鵝，連忙跑到海草堆那裡。他從來沒有近距離看野生天鵝，很幸運能夠跟他們靠得這麼近。

　　不只是男孩聽見天鵝的叫聲，野鵝、灰鵝和潛鳥也都從海草堆中游過去，圍成一圈凝望著天鵝。天鵝們揚帆般張起翅膀，頸子在空中優雅地伸展。有時候會有天鵝游到野鵝、大潛鳥或潛鴨跟前說些話，那些對象卻都不敢出聲回答。

　　一隻頑皮的小潛鳥受不了他們正經八百，他迅速潛進水裡，不久有一隻天鵝發出尖聲，猛然游開，快得產生泡沫。他停下時，繼續擺出高雅的姿態。接著又聽到同樣的尖聲，然後又是一聲。

　　潛鳥沒辦法一直潛在水裡，搗蛋的小黑點浮出來。天鵝紛紛撲向他，但看他可憐兮兮，又調頭不跟他計較。小潛鳥再度潛進水裡咬天鵝的腳。那一定很痛，最糟的是傷了天鵝的威嚴。他們一同拍翅發出轟然聲響往前衝刺，像在水面上奔跑，最後展翅飛上天空。

　　天鵝飛走後，大家都感到失落。有些鳥兒剛才還覺得小潛鳥的舉動很好玩，這會兒都開始責備他魯莽。

　　第二天早上，天空依然布滿雲霧。野鵝在草地上覓食，男孩則跑到岸邊採貽貝。那裡有很多貽貝，男孩想到明天可能會去到沒有

食物的地方，決定做個貽貝便當。他在草地上找到一棵強韌的老莎
草，用它編了個袋子。他做了好幾個小時，對成果很滿意。

　　午餐時間，所有野鵝都跑過來問他，有沒有看到白公鵝。「沒
有，他沒有和我在一起。」男孩回答。

　　「他剛才還和我們在一起，但現在找不到了。」阿卡說。

　　男孩跳起來，擔心得不得了。他問他們，有沒有看到狐狸、老
鷹，或是在附近看到人類。但都沒有，公鵝可能在霧中迷失了。

　　男孩尋找著失蹤的公鵝，有迷霧遮掩，不會有人看到男孩，但
他也很難看見東西。男孩沿著海岸往南走，一直來到最南端的燈塔
和霧砲那裡。到處都有困惑的鳥群，唯獨不見公鵝。他冒險走到鳥

登比領地，搜索樹林中每一棵中空的老橡樹，但都一無所獲。

一直找到天快黑時，男孩才轉頭回到東岸。他的步伐沉重，心情沮喪，萬一沒找到公鵝會怎樣，他不能沒有公鵝。

這時霧裡有個大大白白的東西正接近他。那是公鵝嗎？果然沒錯，他沒事！公鵝說，霧讓他頭暈，以至於整天都在遼闊的草地上轉來轉去。男孩欣喜得張手抱住白鵝的頸子，懇求他保重自己，不要再離開同伴了。公鵝答應他，絕對不會再這樣。再也不會了。

可是第二天早上，男孩沿著海邊撿貽貝時，鵝群又跑過來問他，有沒有看到公鵝。當然沒有。「那麼公鵝又失蹤了？他跟昨天一樣，又在霧中走失了。」

男孩趕緊去找。他發現烏登比牆有個地方坍塌了，可以讓他爬過去。他先在海邊遊走，然後登上小島中間的平坦高地。那裡除了風車，沒有其他建築物，而且草皮稀疏，底下的水泥都露出來了。

眼看快要黃昏了，還是沒有找到公鵝，非回到沙灘不可了。男孩好難過，他不敢相信他的旅伴已經失蹤，不知道該怎麼辦才好。

當他再度穿越圍牆，才聽到碰通一聲。他轉過身，看到有東西在牆邊的石頭堆上移動。他悄悄走過去，看到公鵝啣著幾根長草吃力地爬上石頭堆。公鵝沒有看到男孩，男孩也沒有叫他，因為他想要知道為什麼公鵝要這樣三番兩次地失蹤。

他一眼就明白了。石頭堆上躺著一隻小灰鵝，看到公鵝靠近就高興地大叫。男孩又走近一點，發現那隻灰鵝一邊翅膀受傷不能飛，她的同伴都撇下她走了。前天公鵝聽見她的叫聲而找到她時，她幾乎要餓死了。從那之後，他就一直為她送食物。他們倆都希望她能夠在他離開小島時復元，然而直到現在她還是不能飛，也不能走動。她很擔心,但是公鵝安慰她說,他這一陣子都不會離開。最後他道了晚安,答應明天再來。

公鵝一離開,男孩就偷偷爬上石堆。他很生氣,因為公鵝欺騙他,他想跟那隻灰鵝說,公鵝是屬於他的,必須帶他飛到拉普蘭,不能為了她留在這裡。但是一靠近小灰鵝,看到她小小的頭部極為美麗,全身羽毛彷彿柔軟的綢緞,目光楚楚可憐。

小灰鵝一看到男孩就想要逃走,但是左翼脫臼使她無法移動。

「妳不用害怕，」男孩說著，他沒那麼生氣了。「我是小拇指，公鵝莫爾登的同伴。」接著他站在那裡，不知道該說什麼好。

小拇指一說出他是誰，她就優雅地低下頭，以甜美得讓人不敢相信是鵝的聲音說：「我很高興你來這裡幫助我。白公鵝跟我說過，沒有人比你更聰明、更善良了。」男孩覺得很不好意思。他心想：「她一定不是什麼鳥，而是某個中了魔法的公主。」

男孩想幫助她，用手摸摸她的翅膀，找到翅骨。骨頭沒有斷裂，但是關節有點問題。他把手指按在凹槽上。「忍耐一下！」他說著，用力把管狀骨拉回原位。他的動作又快又準確，不像是第一次做這種事的人。但小灰鵝可能是太痛了，她尖聲一叫，就癱在石頭上，沒有生命跡象。男孩嚇壞了，他的本意是要幫助她，現在她居然死了。他覺得自己等於謀殺了一個人。

第二天早上，天氣晴朗，阿卡說該出發了。男孩跳到公鵝的背上，公鵝勉強緩慢地跟在鵝群後面。男孩很高興要離開這座島了，但是心裡也惦記著小灰鵝，並不想對公鵝說出昨天試圖治療她的事。突然之間，公鵝折回原路了。如果小灰鵝在那裡孤零零地生著病，他就不能跟著鵝群離開。但石頭堆上沒有小灰鵝的蹤影。「丹芬！丹芬！妳在哪裡？」公鵝大聲喊著。

「也許狐狸把她叼走了，」男孩心想。但在這時，他聽到有個甜美的聲音回答說：「我在這裡，莫爾登！我只是在晨浴。」小灰鵝從水面上飛過來，精神奕奕，而且光鮮亮麗。她說出小拇指幫她把翅膀拉回原位的事，還說她身體很好，可以跟著他們去旅行。

水珠灑在她絲綢般的羽毛上宛如珍珠。小拇指再一次感覺到，她其實是個小公主。

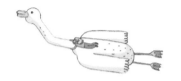

第 10 章

小卡爾斯島

風暴　四月八日　星期五

　　野鵝在厄蘭島的北端過了一夜，準備要飛向內陸。卡爾馬海峽上空刮著強勁的南風，把野鵝們掃到北邊，但他們還是努力地往前飛。接近第一個小島時，他們聽見巨大的轟隆聲，好像有一大群翅膀強健的鳥飛了過來，底下的水突然變成一片漆黑。阿卡急促收翅，幾乎在空中靜止不動，因而往海面落下。但是鵝群還沒有碰到水，暴風就捲起他們，最後將他們拋在海上。

　　野鵝不斷地嘗試飛回去，卻只是被吹得越來越遠。暴風已經把他們吹到厄蘭島外，眼前是一望無際的大海。

　　阿卡發現他們無法折返，心想不能讓暴風把他們趕到波羅的海的另一邊，於是在水上降落。浪濤洶湧，而且越來越大，浪頭越來越高。但野鵝並不害怕，反而樂在其中。他們不勉強自己游泳，而是蹲在上面，隨著海浪起伏，跟小孩子盪鞦韆一樣玩得很高興。他們唯一擔心的是會分散開來。幾隻陸鳥在暴風中經過，嫉妒地大喊：「你們會游泳，就安全了嗎？」

　　可是野鵝並不是毫無危險的。首先，在水裡飄盪使他們睏得要命。阿卡每隔一段時間就要大喊：「別睡著了，野鵝！萬一睡著了，就會被沖走。一離開就會走失。」

儘管極力抗拒睡意，他們還是一個個睡著，連阿卡自己也差點打起瞌睡。這時她忽然看到某種又圓又黑的東西升到浪頭。「海豹！海豹！」阿卡尖聲大叫，然後用力搧翅飛到空中。這一刻非常驚險，最後一隻野鵝飛離水面時，海豹已經近得可以咬住她的腳了。

　　他們鼓起勇氣，再度在水面上降落。但是隨波晃盪了一會兒，又開始睏了。海豹趁著他們熟睡時又游了過來。要不是阿卡那麼警覺，野鵝沒有一隻逃得掉。

　　暴風持續了一整天，最後阿卡開始懷疑他們能否倖存。野鵝已經精疲力竭，卻找不到地方休息。接近傍晚時，她不敢再躺在海上，因為那裡忽然塞滿了大浮冰，可能會被互相壓擠的冰塊撞死。有幾次試圖站在冰上，但不是被暴風掃進水裡，就是有殘酷的海豹爬上來。

　　日落時，野鵝飛到空中。天黑得特別快，真是糟糕，因為他們還是看不到陸地。天空烏雲密布，月亮躲了起來，無處不令人畏懼，連最勇敢的心也會膽寒。浮冰發出猛烈的碰撞聲，海豹唱出狂放的獵捕歌。天與地似乎即將崩毀。

羊群

　　男孩低頭望著大海一會兒，覺得它的怒吼比之前更大聲了。他抬頭看到前面聳立著凹凸不平的禿壁，距離不到幾公里。野鵝直接飛向懸崖，男孩覺得他們一定會在那裡撞成碎片。正疑惑阿卡怎麼沒有察覺到危險，他們已經來到了山前，野鵝飛進去一個拱形的洞口，暫時安全。

野鵝沒有因為脫險高興，而是先確認所有同伴都進來了。是的，唯獨隊伍左邊的第一隻鵝卡克西失蹤，沒有人知道她的下落。

　　但野鵝並沒有太擔心。因為卡克西很聰明，而且熟悉所有航道和習慣，當然知道要如何找到他們。

　　野鵝在洞穴裡環顧四周。透進來的光線讓他們知道這個洞又大又深。正慶幸有這麼好的地方過夜時，一隻鵝看到黑暗角落閃著一些綠圓點。「那是眼睛啊！」阿卡驚叫。

　　「有大型動物在這裡！」他們快速奔向洞口，但小拇指叫住他們：「不用逃！只是幾隻羊躺在牆邊。」

　　野鵝習慣了洞裡面的黯淡光線後，就能清楚看到那些羊。大羊的數量和他們野鵝差不多，但旁邊還有幾隻小羊。一隻有長彎角的老公羊似乎是他們的頭目。野鵝謙恭地走到他面前。「很高興在荒原碰見你們！」他們出聲致意，但是大公羊一動也不動，沒有表示歡迎。

　　野鵝以為這些羊不歡迎他們來這個洞避難。「你們不喜歡我們來這裡吧？」阿卡說。「但我們是逼不得已的，因為有暴風。我們在暴風中飄蕩了一整天，如果能在這裡過夜，那就太好了。」羊群沉默了好一陣子，只聽得到一、兩隻羊在嘆氣。一隻長臉老母羊終於以悲悽的聲音說：「我們所有人都不反對你們留下，但這裡是哀悼室，我們不能像以前一樣接待客人。」

　　「你們不用擔心，」阿卡說。「如果你們知道我們今天所受的苦，就會明白我們只要有個安全的地方過夜就很滿足了。」

　　阿卡說完，老母羊就站起來說：「我相信你們在惡劣的暴風中飛行會比留在這裡好。不過你們離開之前，我們至少可以提供這裡最好的招待。」

她帶領他們來到裝滿水的水坑。旁邊有一堆穀糠和草料。她請他們盡情享用。「今年冬天這個島特別冷，我們的主人給我們送來這些乾草和燕麥，以免我們餓死。我們只剩下這些了。」

鵝群馬上跑過去吃，覺得運氣不錯而心情愉快。他們注意到羊群憂心忡忡，以為羊本來就很容易緊張，不相信這裡會有危險。吃飽後，正想要和平常一樣站著睡覺，那隻大公羊站起來走向他們。

「如果要讓你們野鵝住在這裡，我就不能不盡義務告訴你們，這裡不安全。」他說。「我們不能留客人過夜。」

阿卡終於相信他是認真的，於是回答：「如果你們不允許，我們可以離開。但是能不能告訴我們原因？我們什麼都不知道，連這裡是哪裡也不曉得。」

「這裡是小卡爾斯島，位於果特蘭島的外海，只有羊和海鳥住在這裡。」公羊說。

「你們是野羊嗎？」阿卡說。

「差不多，」公羊回答。「我們和人類沒有關係，只是和果特蘭島的農人有個古老的協議，他們會在多雪的冬天提供飼料給我們，我們則讓他們帶走過多的羊。這個島很小，養不活太多羊。但通常我們整年都可以照顧自己。我們不住有門的房子，而是住在這種山洞裡。」

「你們冬天也住在外面嗎？」阿卡驚訝地問。

「是的，」公羊回答。「山上整年都有很好的糧草。」

「你們好像過得比其他羊好。」阿卡說。「到底是遇到了什麼不幸？」

「去年冬天很冷，海水結冰，有三隻狐狸從冰上跑上來，就一直待在這裡。要不是這樣，島上是不會有危險動物的。」

「哦！狐狸敢偷襲你們？」

「白天不會，我可以保護自己和同伴。」公羊說著，搖搖他的角。「但是狐狸會在夜裡，趁我們在洞裡睡覺時跑進來。我們盡量保持清醒，但是總有睡著的時候，他們就會偷襲。其他洞裡的羊都被他們殺光了，那些羊都和我們這群一樣大。」

「我們是這麼的無助，說起來挺難過的。」老母羊說。「我們保護自己的能力並不比家羊強。」

「他們今晚也會來嗎？」阿卡問。

「一定會的，」老母羊說。「昨晚他們偷走一隻小羊。只要這裡還有一隻羊活著，他們就會再來。別的地方也是這樣。」

「這樣下去，你們會全部完蛋的。」阿卡說。

「唉，過沒多久，小卡爾斯島上的羊就會死光光了！」母羊嘆著氣說。

阿卡站在那裡猶豫不決。她考慮了一會兒，轉頭對小拇指說：「你之前幫過我們很多忙，不知道這次能不能再幫我們？」他回答，「可以。」他很樂意。「真可惜，你不能睡覺。」野鵝說。「不知你是否能一直醒著，在狐狸來的時候叫醒我們，讓我們飛走。」

男孩聽了很樂意，因為再怎麼樣都比回到暴風中好，所以他答應不睡著。

他走到洞口，爬到一塊石頭後面避風，同時坐下來看守。

暴風減弱了，天空放晴，月光開始在海浪中玩耍。男孩走出洞口觀望。這個洞位於很高的山上，有一條陡峭的小徑通到山腳。他或許應該在這裡等狐狸。

這時他聽見爪子的刮搔聲，看到三隻狐狸爬上峭壁。男孩心想只叫醒鵝，讓羊群獨自面對惡運太說不過去了，決定另想辦法。

他快跑到洞口另一邊，搖晃大公羊的角，等他醒來，就騎到他的背上。「老爹，我們去嚇嚇狐狸！」男孩說。

他盡量保持安靜，但狐狸想必聽到聲音了，因為他們一到洞口就停下來商量。「裡面有動靜，」一隻說。「他們可能醒著。」

「你儘管走！」另一隻說。「反正他們不能拿我們怎麼樣！」

狐狸進入洞口時，停下來聞一聞氣味。「今晚要選哪一隻？」帶頭的那一隻悄聲說著。

「我們今晚拿那隻大公羊開刀吧，」最後那一隻說。「以後就輕鬆了。」

男孩坐在公羊背上，看著他們溜進來。「現在直接用頭去撞。」男孩輕聲說。公羊一撞，第一隻狐狸被推回洞口。「現在往左邊牴！」男孩說著，把公羊頭拉到那個方向。公羊使勁牴在第二隻狐狸的肚子。狐狸滾了好幾圈，才站起來跑掉。男孩本來還想給第三隻好看，但是他已經溜走了。

「我想今晚他們夠折騰了。」男孩說。

「我也是。」大公羊說。「現在你躺在我的背上，鑽進我的毛裡面吧！你之前一直被暴風吹刮，應該暖暖身，舒服一下。」

地獄洞

第二天，大公羊讓男孩騎在背上，帶他參觀這個島。公羊先爬上山頂，給男孩看看肥美的草地。男孩必須承認，這個島似乎是專為羊設計的，因為那裡除了羊愛吃的草之外，其他的植物並不多。

登上懸崖，就會發現值得欣賞的美景。首先是那一望無際的大海，只有岬角湧出白沫。東邊是果特蘭島，西南邊是大卡爾斯島，外表和這個小島相似。公羊走到山頂的每個角落，讓男孩俯瞰峭壁。他發現峭壁上布滿鳥巢，而下面的蔚藍海上有番鴨、三趾鷗、海雀和尖嘴鳥在忙著捕捉小鯡魚，那麼美麗，又那麼平靜。

「這真是個好地方，」男孩說。「你們羊住的地方很美。」

「沒錯！這裡確實很美。」大公羊說著，好像要多說些什麼，卻只是嘆了一口氣。他停了一會兒，就出聲提醒：「如果你自己來這裡，就要小心到處都有的裂縫。」這個警告來得正好，因為好幾個地方都有又深又大的裂縫。最大的那一個稱為「地獄洞」，深達數公尺，寬約兩公尺。「掉下去的話，大概就沒命了。」大公羊說。男孩覺得他這句話好像有別的含義。

接著大公羊把男孩帶到岸邊的狹地上。原來昨晚令他害怕的巨人只是高大的石柱。大公羊把它們叫做「巨石」。男孩覺得如果真有怪物變成石頭，應該就是那個樣子了。

岸邊的風景也很美，但是男孩比較喜歡山上，因為這裡陰森森的，到處都看得到死羊。他看到肉被吃光的骨骸，還有只啃了一半或連碰都沒碰的羊身，看了令人心痛。可見那些野獸獵羊純粹是出於好玩，只是為了獵殺。

大公羊並沒有在死屍前面逗留，而是靜靜地走開。男孩卻忍不住去看那恐怖的景象。

接著大公羊又開始爬山。到了山頂，他停下來說：「聰明能幹的人看到這裡的慘狀，一定會想要懲罰狐狸才甘心。」

「狐狸也要生存啊。」男孩說。

「對，」大公羊承認。「那些殺生量不比需求多的動物是為了生存，但是那幾隻狐狸是罪大惡極。」

「這個島的主人應該來幫助你們。」男孩說。

「他們划船來過幾次，」公羊回答。「但是狐狸都藏在山洞和裂縫裡，沒辦法槍殺他們。」

「你該不會是說，你和那些農人都無法對付他們，我這個小不點卻有辦法？」

「身體小但腦筋靈活的人就能擔負重任。」

他們的對話到這裡為止。野鵝正在高原上覓食，男孩在他們旁邊坐下。雖然沒有表現出來，但他確實為那些羊難過，也很想幫助他們。「我至少要跟阿卡和公鵝莫爾登商量這件事。」他心想。「也許他們能出個好主意。」

不久，白公鵝讓男孩騎在背上，越過山頂上的平原，飛向地獄洞。他在廣闊的山頂上悠哉地晃蕩，顯然不知道自己又大又白。沒有躲在樹叢或遮蔽物後面，就一直往前走。奇怪的是，昨天在風暴中吃盡苦頭，依然沒有比較謹慎。他的右腿跛了，左邊翅膀拖在地上，好像斷掉了。

看他一副四周都沒有危險的樣子，不時地啄食草葉，一點都不提防。男孩平躺在鵝背上，仰望著藍天。他已經很習慣待在鵝背上，可以站立，也可以躺下來。

公鵝和男孩如此悠遊自在，當然沒有注意到有三隻狐狸來到山上的平原。

狐狸知道要在空曠的平原掠取一隻鵝的性命幾乎是不可能，所以起初並沒有去追捕公鵝。但最後還是偷偷溜進一條長長的裂縫，試圖偷襲公鵝。

　　公鵝張開翅膀，但飛不起來。狐狸察覺他不能飛，高興地往前衝。他們不再躲在裂縫裡，而是爬上高原快速飛奔，以樹叢和凹洞為掩護，離公鵝越來越近，公鵝卻還不知道自己成了獵物。最後三隻狐狸同時跳起來，撲向公鵝。

　　公鵝終於發現了他們，他趕緊跑開，狐狸因而撲了個空。但公鵝只逃開幾公尺，而且還跛著腳，可憐的東西繼續拚命往前跑。

　　男孩坐在鵝背上面向後方，對狐狸尖聲喊道：「你們羊肉吃太多了，肥得連一隻鵝也追不到。」狐狸被他激怒，只顧往前衝。

　　公鵝直接奔向那條大裂縫，他拍拍翅膀飛過去。這時狐狸也緊追在後。

　　公鵝繼續跑著，男孩就拍拍他的背說：「你可以停下來了，莫爾登。」

　　這時後面傳來狂叫聲，接著是爪子的刮搔聲和沉重的落地聲。從此之後，再也不會看到狐狸的蹤影了。

　　第二天早上，大卡爾斯島上的守燈塔人看到前門底下有一小塊樹皮，上面刻著歪七扭八的字：「小島上的狐狸掉進地獄洞裡了。快去處理他們！」

　　守燈塔人依照指示做了。

第 11 章
斯莫蘭的傳說

四月十二日 星期二

　　野鵝愉快地飛越大海，降落在斯莫蘭島北部的許斯特縣。這個地方難以說是陸地還是海洋，因為處處都有海灣將陸地切成島嶼、半島和岬角。大海是那麼地蠻橫，只有丘陵和山巒能比它高，其他陸地都藏在水裡。

　　野鵝在高斯灣裡的光禿岩島上降落。他們看一眼岸邊就知道，春天在他們遊歷各島時已有一番表現。健壯的大樹還沒有長滿綠葉，但是底下的地面已被白色的銀蓮花、頂冰花和藍色的銀蓮花織成錦緞。

　　看到花毯時，野鵝擔心他們在南方耽擱太久。阿卡認為沒有時間在斯莫蘭尋找休息地了，第二天早上一定要往北飛越東耶特蘭。

　　這樣子男孩就不能去遊覽斯莫蘭了，他有點失望。他聽過的斯莫蘭傳說比其他地方多，很希望能親眼瞧瞧。

　　去年夏天幫人看鵝時，他幾乎每天都會遇見兩個也在看鵝的斯莫蘭小孩。那兩個孩子曾以斯莫蘭的來歷激怒他。

　　看鵝女孩歐莎太聰明了，不至於惹到他。讓男孩惱火的是她那愛講故事的小弟麥茲。

　　「尼爾斯，你聽說過上帝創造斯莫蘭和斯堪尼的事嗎？」他這麼問道，尼爾斯說沒有，他就開始講一則古老的傳說趣事。

「話說上帝在創造天地的時候，聖彼得走過來，停下來看看，然後問上帝說會不會很辛苦。『這事不太容易，』上帝說。聖彼得又看了一會兒，發現上帝創造一個又一個的陸地好像很容易，就很想試試看。『也許您需要休息一下，我可以在您休息時接手做。』聖彼得說。上帝回答：『我不知道你對這方面行不行，不放心讓你接手。』聖彼得很生氣，就說他相信他的創造會和上帝一樣好。

「上帝正好在創造斯莫蘭，一半都還沒完成，看起來好像是美麗的沃土。上帝無法拒絕聖彼得，他認為這件事已經起了個不錯的頭，應該任誰也無法搞砸，就說：『你要的話，就來證明一下我們之中誰比較擅長做這件事。你是新手，這件事已經起了頭，就由你來接手，我去創造新的土地。』聖彼得馬上答應，和上帝在不同的地方工作。

「上帝稍往南方走，著手創造斯堪尼。他沒多久就完成了，回頭問聖彼得是否也好了。『早就好了，』聖彼得說。從他的語氣可以聽出他對成品很滿意。

「聖彼得看到斯堪尼時，只能說那地方好極了。那裡的土地肥沃，易於耕種，不管從哪裡看過去都是廣闊的平原，連山丘都沒有。顯然上帝設想得很周到，讓人類可以舒適過活。『對，這是個好地方。』聖彼得說：『可是我覺得我做的比較好。』上帝就說：『那就去看看吧。』

「聖彼得接手時，那塊土地已經完成北部和東部了，所以他創造的是南部和西部，以及整塊內陸。上帝來到聖彼得完成的地方時，嚇得停住腳步，大聲說：『你是怎麼搞的啊，聖彼得？』

「聖彼得看看四周，同樣嚇呆了。他認為一個地方最好有很多熱氣，就收集了很多山石，堆成一片高原，這樣子就能靠近太陽，接收太陽的熱氣。他在石頭堆上鋪了一層薄薄的泥土之後，就覺得一切都妥當了。

「可是他去斯堪尼時，這裡下了幾場大雨，高原變成怎樣就不必多說了。上帝來檢查時，所有泥土都被雨水沖走，到處都是光禿禿的岩石，只有水多得積滿山上的裂口，到處都是湖泊和河川，更不用說淹沒大片土地的沼澤和池塘。最糟糕的是有些地方的水太多，有些地方又太少，形成乾旱的荒地，微風一吹，塵土飛揚。

「『你創造出這樣的土地有什麼目的？』上帝說。聖彼得 辯說，他原先是要造出一塊能從太陽那裡得到溫暖的地方。『但這樣會在晚上變得很冷，』上帝說。『因為寒冷也是來自天上。就算有少許植物能在這裡生長，我擔心它們也會凍死。』

「當然聖彼得沒有想到這一點。『這塊土地很貧瘠，而且會有霜害。沒辦法改善。』上帝說。」

小麥茲說完後，歐莎反駁說：「我無法忍受聽你一直在講斯莫蘭有多慘。你忘了那裡也有肥沃的土地，一片又一片的田野，跟斯堪尼這裡一樣，要種什麼都可以。」

「我沒辦法，」小麥茲堅持。「別人就是這麼說的。」

「我聽許多人說過，沒有比斯莫蘭更美麗的海岸了。想想那些海灣，那些莊園和樹林。」歐莎說。

「也別忘了，學校老師說，斯莫蘭南部的維特恩湖一帶是瑞典最富庶、最漂亮的地方。」

「對，沒錯」，小麥茲說，顯得很不安。

突然他抬起頭來說：「我們真笨！這些地帶都是上帝在聖彼得接手之前完成的，當然會很美好。可是聖彼得完成的部分就像傳說中說的，也難怪上帝看到時那麼難過。」小麥茲繼續講故事。「不過聖彼得並沒有氣餒，反而安撫上帝說：『別這麼難過。等我創造出能夠在山石和沼澤中開墾農地的人再說。』

　　「上帝已經忍耐到極限了，他說：『不！你可以去斯堪尼創造斯堪尼人，但是斯莫蘭人我要自己來。』上帝就創造了斯莫蘭人，讓他們腦筋靈活、知足愉快，勤儉能幹，能夠在貧地上生活。」

　　小麥茲閉上了嘴巴。如果尼爾斯也跟著閉嘴就沒事了，可是他忍不住要問，聖彼得有沒有創造出斯堪尼人？

　　「你自己覺得呢？」小麥茲那輕蔑的眼神讓尼爾斯一個箭步就衝上去揍他。可是麥茲只是個小孩，比他大一歲的歐莎馬上跑過去助陣。雖然她的性情溫和，但只要有人敢碰她弟弟，她就會像獅子一樣飛撲過去。

　　尼爾斯不想和女生打架，轉身就走。那天以後，他連看都不看那兩個斯莫蘭小孩一眼。

第 12 章

烏鴉

瓦罐

　　索耐爾布縣位於斯莫蘭島的西南角，地勢相當平坦。在雪開始溶化的四月初，可以清楚看出底下是乾燥的荒原、光禿的岩石和大片潮濕的沼澤。

　　尼爾斯和野鵝一同漫遊的時候，那裡有間木屋，四周有少許耕地圍繞著，但居住的人搬走，現在已是空屋，土地也荒廢了。

　　居民搬離小屋時掩上了擋板，插上窗鞘，門也關上了。但是玻璃窗破了，只塞著一塊破布。過了幾年落雨的夏天，那塊破布已經腐爛，最後讓一隻烏鴉順利地扯掉了。

　　其實荒原上的山脊並不像人們想像的那麼荒涼，因為那裡住著一大群烏鴉。當然他們並不是整年都住在那裡，他們會在在冬天遷到別處，秋天在約塔蘭的耕地上尋覓穀子，夏天就分散在索耐爾布縣，靠著鳥蛋、漿果和雛鳥過活。但是到了每年春天的築巢期，他們就會返回荒原。

　　扯掉窗戶破布的是一隻公烏鴉，名叫「白羽卡姆」，但總是被叫成「呆頭」或「呆腦」，因為他一向舉止笨拙，糊里糊塗，什麼都不會，只有被取笑的份。呆頭和其他烏鴉相比，體型較大也較壯，但是他仍然備受譏嘲。顯赫的家世也對他也沒有幫助。照理說，他應該是烏鴉群的首領，因為自古以來這項榮譽都屬於最年長的白羽，但是早在呆頭出生之前，他的家族就失去了這項權利，目前是由一隻殘暴的烏鴉掌權，名叫「旋風」。

權利轉手的原因是山脊上的烏鴉想要改變生活方式。也許有人以為烏鴉的生活方式都差不多，但其實不是。有一群烏鴉過著清高的生活，只吃穀粒、蚯蚓、毛蟲和死屍，有一群則專做流氓勾當，專吃幼兔、小鳥，洗劫每一個鳥巢。

古老的白羽家族作風嚴謹，在他們領導的時代，烏鴉們都不會做出讓其他鳥類批評的事。可是烏鴉的數量很多，生活又很貧困，無法忍受中規中矩的生活，所以開始反叛白羽家族，把權力交給最暴戾的鳥巢強盜，也就是旋風，而他的妻子「風氣」，惡劣的行徑僅次於他。在他們夫妻的領導下，烏鴉群開始過著比蒼鷹和鵰鴞更暴戾的生活。

當然呆頭在族群中沒什麼話語權。所有烏鴉都認為他一點都不適合當首領，和他的祖先不一樣。只要他不經常出糗，就不會有人注意他。有些較為明理的烏鴉說，也許呆頭這麼遲鈍是件好事，不然以他的出身，旋風和風氣不會讓他繼續待在這個族群裡。沒有烏鴉知道，是呆頭把破布扯掉的，因為他們不會相信他竟然敢靠近人類的居所，如果知道的話會很驚訝。這件事他自己也守口如瓶，這麼做是有原因的。在白天和有其他人在場時，旋風和風氣對他不錯，但是有天暗夜，夥伴都在樹枝上歇息時，他遭到幾隻烏鴉偷襲，差點沒命。從此以後每天太陽一下山，他都會飛進那間空屋。

一天下午，山脊上的烏鴉整齊地築好巢之後，旋風、呆頭和幾隻夥伴飛到荒原上的一個大坑裡。烏鴉覺得那絕不僅是一個砂石坑這麼簡單，他們飛下去翻動每一粒沙子，想要知道人類為何要挖這個坑。烏鴉翻攪時，有一邊塌下大量的沙石。他們急忙跑過去，看到落石中有一個加了木頭蓋的大瓦罐。出於好奇，他們開始在蓋子上啄洞，或是把它撬開，但都沒有成功。

他們困惑地看著蓋子時，聽到有個聲音說：「我可不可以下來幫你們？」他們抬起頭。有一隻狐狸蹲在沙坑邊緣瞧著他們。不論是顏色或身材，他都是他們看過的狐狸中最漂亮的一個，唯一的缺陷是只有一個耳朵。

「要是你肯幫忙，我們當然接受。」旋風說著，和其他夥伴飛上來。狐狸跳下去，咬一咬瓦罐，扯一扯蓋子，還是無法打開。

「你看得出裡面是什麼嗎？」旋風問道。狐狸把瓦罐滾一滾，傾聽裡面的聲音，然後說：「裡面一定是銀幣。」

烏鴉大吃一驚，倒抽一口氣，貪婪得眼珠子都要迸出來了。這麼說也許奇怪，但是在這世界上，烏鴉最喜歡的東西就是銀子了。

「聽聽裡面鏗鏗鏘鏘的聲音。」狐狸說，又滾了一次瓦罐。「我只是不知道要怎麼把它拿出來。」

「那就沒辦法了。」烏鴉說。

狐狸站在那裡，一邊用左前腳磨搓著頭，一邊想著：也許借用這些烏鴉的力量，可以把那個小鬼抓到手。「啊！我知道有個人可以為你們打開蓋子。」狐狸說。

「快告訴我們！」烏鴉紛紛叫道，興奮得跌進坑裡。

「只要你們答應我的條件，我就說出來。」

狐狸跟他們提起小拇指，只要把小拇指帶來荒原，小拇指就會幫他們打開蓋子。而他們回報狐狸的方式是，一旦拿到了銀幣，就馬上把小拇指交給他。烏鴉接受了這個條件。

遭烏鴉綁架 四月十三日 星期三

天一亮野鵝就醒過來找東西吃，動身前往東耶特蘭。他們過夜的那個小島又小又貧瘠，還好四周的水裡長著海草，足以填飽肚子。可是男孩就慘了，找不到一點東西吃。

他站在那裡又餓又睏地四處張望，看到一對松鼠在對面岬角的樹林中遊玩。也許那些松鼠有剩餘的存糧，就請白公鵝帶他去那裡要榛果吃。

白鵝載著男孩飛越海灣，可是運氣不好，那對松鼠在樹上追來追去，玩得太高興了，不肯停下來聽他說話，反而跑到樹林裡面去。他隨後跟著，一下子就讓等在岸邊的公鵝看不到他了。

男孩在白色的銀蓮花中費力地前進時，感覺有人在後面抓他。他回過頭，看到一隻烏鴉咬住他的衣領。他想要掙脫，卻又來了一隻烏鴉，咬住他的襪子，還把他撞倒。

如果尼爾斯立刻呼救，白公鵝一定會來救他，但男孩認為他能保護自己。他又打又踢的，烏鴉不肯放手，而且還成功帶著他飛起來。更糟糕的是，烏鴉飛得那麼魯莽，男孩的頭因此撞到樹枝，他眼前一黑，就昏過去了。

男孩再度睜開眼時，發覺自己已經高懸在空中。底下是一大片紅綠參半的絨毛地毯，有著不規則的圖案。烏鴉突然驟降，才知道原來那片大地毯長著翠綠的針葉樹和光禿的褐色闊葉樹。

這裡是什麼地方呢？他開始產生許多疑問。他為什麼不是騎在公鵝背上？為什麼被東拉西扯的，簡直要被撕成兩半了！他突然明白自己被一群烏鴉綁架了，公鵝還在岸邊等著，而野鵝們今天要飛到東耶特蘭。太陽在他身後，他知道自己被帶到西南方，所以底下的樹林地毯肯定是斯莫蘭。

過了一會兒，其中一隻烏鴉以拍翅的動作表達：「小心！危險！」他們在杉樹林中降落，把男孩藏在一棵濃密的松樹下，以免讓獵鷹看到。

五十隻烏鴉用嘴巴對準男孩，把他圍住。他開口說：「各位烏鴉，我想知道你們帶我來這裡的目的。」可是話還沒說完，就有一隻大烏鴉嚇他：「別動！不然就啄掉你的眼睛！」

那隻烏鴉顯然是說真的，男孩只得坐在那裡和烏鴉對看。

他看得越久就越不喜歡他們。他們的羽毛又髒又亂，腳爪上沾著乾泥，嘴角黏著食物渣。和野鵝很不一樣。

「我一定是落入匪徒的手裡了。」他心裡想著。

這時他聽見野鵝在空中叫他。「你在哪裡？我在這裡。你在哪裡？我在這裡。」

他知道野鵝都在找他，可是沒來得及求救，那隻應該是頭目的大烏鴉就在他耳邊說：「想想你的眼珠子！」他只好保持沉默。

過了一會兒，烏鴉發出起飛的訊號。男孩說：「難道你們沒有一隻夠強壯，可以讓我騎在背上？我覺得快被你們扯爛了。讓我騎在背上吧，我答應你，絕不會跳下來。」

「哎！別以為我們在乎你的感受。」頭目一口拒絕。裡面有一隻羽毛蓬鬆，翅膀上有一根白羽毛的大烏鴉走向前說：「旋風，讓小拇指保持完整對我們來說比較好。我來載他吧。」旋風說：「我沒有意見，但是別把他搞丟了！」

男孩這下滿意了，他想：「只是被烏鴉綁架就沮喪對我沒有好處，我當然能夠應付這批小壞蛋。」

烏鴉越過斯莫蘭，繼續飛向西南方。這是個美好的早晨，地上的鳥兒正在唱著最拿手的情歌。一隻歌 在幽暗的樹林裡不斷重覆唱著：「你好漂亮！沒有人像你這麼漂亮！」

男孩正好穿越樹林，聽了幾次同樣的旋律，就把手圈在嘴邊喊道：「這首歌我們早就聽過了！」

「你是誰？是誰在取笑我？」 鳥問道，想要知道對方是誰。

「這是被烏鴉綁架的人在取笑你的歌。」男孩回答。

這時烏鴉頭目轉過頭來說：「小拇指，小心眼睛！」

但是男孩心想：「我才不在乎呢，我可不怕你！」

他們一直飛向處處是樹林和湖泊的內陸。樺樹林中有一隻母森鴿坐在光禿禿的樹枝上，前面站著一隻公森鴿咕咕唱著：「你，你，你是整個森林中最美麗的，森林裡誰也比不上你，你，你。」

男孩飛越空中時，聽到公森鴿的歌，就不禁喊道：「別相信他！別相信他！」

「誰，誰，誰在亂說話？」公森鴿說，試圖看清楚喊叫的人。

「這是被烏鴉綁架的人在亂說話。」男孩回答。

旋風又轉頭命令他住嘴，但是背著尼爾斯的呆頭說：「讓他說吧，這樣子所有鳥兒都會覺得咱們烏鴉變得又機智又風趣了。」

「哎，他們才沒那麼笨呢。」旋風說著，但是他滿喜歡這個說法，就不再管男孩說什麼了。

他們看到一座古老的莊園，前面是湖泊，後面是樹林。一隻歐掠鳥站在風標的頂端大聲唱著：「我們有四個漂亮的小蛋！我們的巢裝滿了可愛蛋！」

歐掠鳥唱了一千次以後，男孩飛越那裡，對著他喊：「喜鵲會來偷走的！」

「是誰在恐嚇我？」歐掠鳥不安地拍翅問道。

「這是被烏鴉綁架的人在恐嚇你。」

這次頭目和其他烏鴉都覺得很好玩，滿意地呱呱叫著。

越飛向內陸，湖泊就越大，島嶼和岬角就越多。湖邊有一隻公鴨在母鴨跟前俯首說：「我一輩子都會對你忠實。」

男孩尖聲說道：「頂多撐到夏天結束。」

「你是誰？」公鴨說。

「被烏鴉綁架的人。」男孩喊回去。

晚餐時間，烏鴉在果園中降落。他們四處覓食，全都沒想要分一點給男孩吃。呆頭啣著帶有一些乾果的犬薔薇枝飛到頭目那裡說：「旋風，這給你吃。」

旋風不屑地聞一聞說：「這是適合你的美食。」

「我還以為你喜歡吃這個呢。」呆頭說著，隨手扔掉犬薔薇，好像很難過。那根樹枝就落在男孩跟面，他馬上撿起來吃個飽。

他們吃完就開始閒聊。他們興奮得七嘴八舌。「那沒什麼，我有一次去追快長大的小兔子……」還沒說完，就有另一隻插話。「招惹母雞或貓也許很好玩，可是去招惹人類就了不起了。我有一次偷了一根銀匙……」

這些話讓男孩聽不下去了，他說：「聽著，你們應該為那些壞事感到羞恥。我和野鵝們生活了三個星期，我只看過他們做好事。你們的頭目一定很差勁，才會縱容你們去偷去殺。你們應該改過自新，因為人類受夠了你們的勾當，會想辦法消滅你們的。」

旋風和其他烏鴉聽了都很生氣，想要撲過去把他扯爛。可是呆頭呱呱笑出聲，擋在他前面。「別這樣！」他說著，「你們把小拇指抓爛的話，風氣會怎麼說呢？我們還沒拿到銀幣呢。」

「你這怕女人的傢伙。」旋風雖然這麼說，終究放過了男孩。

太陽下山了，可是烏鴉們抵達那塊荒原時，天色還很亮。旋風派了一隻烏鴉去報訊，風氣就和幾百隻烏鴉從山脊飛過來會合。在震耳欲聾的呱呱聲中，呆頭對男孩說：「你在路上那麼有趣，那麼快活，我真的很喜歡你。所以我要給你一個忠告。我們降落後，他們會要求你做一件你可以輕易做到的事，你一定要當心！」

呆頭把男孩放在沙坑上之後，男孩就躺下來，好像累壞了。

「小拇指，」旋風說。「你給我起來！你要幫我們一個忙，那對你來說很容易的。」

男孩沒有動，假裝睡著了。旋風扯他的手，把他拖到那個古瓦罐那裡。「起來，小拇指，把蓋子打開！」

「怎麼不讓我睡個覺呢！」男孩打了個呵欠。「我今晚太累了，明天再說吧。」

「把蓋子打開！」旋風搖晃他。

「我這麼一個小不點要怎麼打開呢？它跟我一樣大啊！」

「打開！」旋風再次下令。「不然你可有苦頭吃了。」

男孩站起來，搖搖晃晃地走過去摸摸蓋子，手就垂下來了。「我平常不會這麼沒力的，」他說。「讓我睡到明天早上，我就可以想辦法打開。」

可是旋風失去耐心了，他飛過去扯他的腿。男孩用力掙脫，往後跑了幾步，從刀鞘抽出小刀，拿到身前威嚇。「你最好小心一點！」他對旋風大喊。

可是旋風氣得不顧危險，直接往前衝，刀子正中他的眼睛，插進頭部。男孩立刻把刀子抽回來，可是旋風撲撲翅膀，倒地死了。

「旋風死了！這個陌生人殺死了我們的頭目！」其中一隻烏鴉這麼一叫，立刻響起可怕的嘶吼聲，所有烏鴉都衝向男孩。呆頭在最前面，但是和平常一樣笨拙，張著翅膀在男孩四周飛，防止其他烏鴉靠過來啄他。

男孩心想情勢對他不利，不僅跑不掉，也沒地方躲藏。他忽然想到瓦罐，就用力打開蓋子，想要藏在裡面，可是裡面裝了滿到邊緣的薄銀幣。男孩彎下身，開始把銀幣扔出去。

旁邊圍得密密麻麻的烏鴉本來想要去啄他，看到銀幣，馬上忘了報仇這件事，急著去撿拾銀幣。男孩一把一把地往外扔，所有烏鴉，連風氣在內都忙著撿，撿到以後迅速地帶到巢裡面放。

銀幣都扔完了，男孩抬起頭來，看到只有一隻烏鴉還在沙坑裡，也就是有白羽毛的呆頭。「你幫了我一個你無法想像的大忙。」那隻烏鴉的語氣和之前不同。他說：「所以我要救你。坐在我背上，我帶你去躲起來，明天我會安排你回到野鵝那裡。」

小屋　四月十四日　星期四

第二天早上，男孩醒來，發現自己在一間屋子裡，一時還以為以為回到家了。

他又張望了一下，想要看看有沒有用得著的東西可以帶走。可是大部分東西都太大也太重，只有幾根火柴拿得動。

他先爬上桌子，用布簾盪到窗架上。他站在那裡，把火柴裝進袋子時，有白羽毛的烏鴉從窗子飛進來。「我終於來了，」呆頭停在桌上時說。「我沒有早點來是因為我們烏鴉要推選新頭目。」

「你們選了誰？」男孩問。

「我們選了不允許偷盜和不義行為的烏鴉，也就是之前還被叫做『呆頭』的白羽卡姆。」他說著，挺起胸膛，顯出威嚴。

「選得真好。」男孩說完，向他祝賀。

「你是該祝福我！」白羽卡姆談起過去由旋風和風氣統治的日子。

這時男孩聽見窗外傳來熟悉的聲音。「他在這裡？」狐狸問。

「對，他藏在這裡。」一隻烏鴉回答。

「小心啊，小拇指。風氣把想要吃你的狐狸帶來了。」白羽卡姆大叫。

還來不及多說什麼，狐狸斯密爾就衝進來了。腐朽的窗框被他一撞就破，斯密爾一轉眼就站在桌子上。男孩知道這小房子這麼低矮，狐狸要逮到他一點都不難。他立刻擦了根火柴，點燃一團棉絮，然後丟向斯密爾。火落在狐狸身上，他嚇得逃到屋外。

雖然男孩躲過了斯密爾的追殺，但現在他陷入更大的危險。那團棉絮的火蔓延到床上的帳子。他跳下來，想要把火撲滅，可是火燒得很猛。屋子很快就瀰漫著煙霧。逃到窗外的斯密爾看到裡面的情況，得意地大聲叫著：「小拇指，你要在那裡被活烤，還是出來找我？我當然想要吃掉你，但只要死亡找上你，我都可以接受。」

整張床都燒起來了，而且順著牆上的布條，爬向牆上的畫像。男孩跳到火爐上，想要打開爐門時，聽見有人把鑰匙插進鎖孔中轉動。「一定是有人來了。」他心想，覺得很高興。門打開時，他已經走到門檻上。眼前是兩個小孩。他沒時間去注意兩個小孩看到屋子起火時的表情，就從他們身邊跑出去。

他當然不敢跑遠，因為狐狸在等他。他也知道必須待在孩子旁邊。他轉身去看小孩是什麼人，但才看一眼，就跑過去大喊：「你好，歐莎！你好，小麥茲！」

男孩看到他們時，完全忘了自己的模樣。男孩感覺自己像在收割後的田地上放鵝，看到那兩個斯莫蘭小孩趕著鵝群走過來，就跑到石頭牆上跟他們打招呼。

可是那兩個小孩看到那麼一個小不點伸開雙臂跑過來，就互相抱著往後退，好像怕得要命。

　男孩看到他們那麼驚恐，才想起自己現在的模樣。沒有比讓人看到自己被施了魔法更糟糕的事情了。他滿懷著不再是人類的羞愧和悲傷，轉身就跑，不知道要跑到哪裡。

　來到荒原時，男孩看到灌木叢中有東西白白的，是白公鵝和丹芬飛了過來。白鵝看到男孩拚命跑著，以為有可怕的惡徒在追他，趕緊把他放在背上，帶著他逃離。

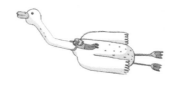

第 13 章

老農婦

四月十四日 星期四

夜深了，三個疲累的旅行者還在外面尋找住處。

天已經黑得沒有一絲光亮時，他們走到一個遠離其他人家，而且似乎沒人住的農莊。男孩心想：「無論如何，我們都得進去裡頭，不然找不到更好的地方了。」

三個旅行者進到院子裡。兩隻瞌睡蟲一停下腳步就睡著了，男孩則是仔細地張望四周。這個農莊並不小，除了住房之外，還有馬廄和燻製房、一排排糧倉和牛棚，全都顯得貧寒破舊。清醒的那個人弄清楚哪一間是牛棚之後，就叫醒睡著的旅伴，帶他們走到牛棚門口。幸好那道門只用一個鉤子扣住，他用棍子就能把它拔開。可是門一開，就有一隻母牛哞哞說：「女主人，妳終於來了？我以為妳不給我弄晚飯了。」

那旅行者發現牛棚不是空著，嚇著停在門口，但很快就看到裡面只有一隻母牛和三、四隻雞，於是鼓起勇氣說：「我們是三個窮旅行者，想要進來躲狐狸和人，不知道適不適合待在這裡。」

「這裡很適合，」母牛回答。「雖然牆壁很破，但狐狸進不來。只住著一個老農婦，她也不會去抓你們。但你們是誰啊？」

「我是從威門荷格來的尼爾斯，中了魔法變成了精靈。跟我來的是一隻灰鵝，和一隻讓我騎在身上的家鵝。」

「你們真是貴客啊。雖然我寧可是女主人來為我送晚飯，但還是歡迎你們。」

男孩讓兩隻鵝進入牛棚，讓他們躺在一個空槽裡，兩隻鵝很快就睡著了。男孩為自己用乾草鋪了個小床，以為也能很快入睡。可是那是不可能的，因為沒吃晚餐的牛一刻也靜不下來。她一直在棚子裡走來走去，抱怨說她很餓。男孩無法闔眼，只能躺在那裡想著這幾天發生的事。

他想到碰巧遇見的歐莎和小麥茲。那間小屋一定是他們在斯莫蘭的老家。現在他想起來了，他們曾經提過那間小屋和下面遼闊的荒原。他們剛好回去探望老家，現在那裡卻是一片火海。男孩很難過，自己給他們帶來巨大的傷痛。如果能重新當人，他會努力去彌補所有的損失和過錯。

思緒轉到那些烏鴉身上。想到救了他的呆頭才剛被選為頭目就被燒死，他難過得流下眼淚。

這幾天他真的很不好過，公鵝和丹芬能夠找到他純粹是運氣。

公鵝說，野鵝一發現小拇指不見了，就去問森林裡的所有小動物。很快就打探到他的消息，是被一群斯莫蘭烏鴉給帶走的。阿卡要野鵝兩隻一組去不同的方向找小拇指，然後不論有沒有找到，兩天後都要在斯莫蘭西北部的高山頂上集合。那座山很像被削掉的塔，因此稱為「塔山」。阿卡為大家說明去塔山的路線之後，野鵝就各自散開了。

白公鵝選了丹芬當旅伴，到處尋找時，聽到一隻 鳥在樹梢叫罵說，有個自稱被烏鴉綁架的人取笑他，他們跟 鳥談了一下， 鳥為他們指出那群烏鴉的去向。後來他們又分別遇到一隻公森鴿和歐掠鳥，才得以追蹤小拇指來到索耐爾布縣的荒原。

找到小拇指之後，公鵝和丹芬就開始往北飛向塔山。可是這段旅程很漫長，還沒有看到塔山，天就黑了。「只要明天到了那裡，我們就沒事了。」男孩想著，鑽進草堆，讓自己更溫暖。

母牛一直在發牢騷，而且突然對男孩說：「我的情況越來越糟。沒人來幫我擠奶或刷毛。我的槽裡沒有飼料，底下也沒有床可以睡。我的女主人傍晚時來過，但是她覺得很不舒服，必須回到屋裡，後來就沒有再來了。」

「可惜我太小了，沒有力氣，幫不上忙。」男孩說。

「我不相信你人小就不能幫忙。我聽說精靈的力氣很大，可以舉起一堆草，或是一拳打死一頭牛。」

「我和那些精靈不一樣。」他說。「不過我可以解開你的繩，把門打開，讓你去水坑喝水，然後爬到草棚上丟一些草給你吃。」

男孩真的這麼做了。可是他還沒有爬回草堆，母牛又開口了。

「要是再請你做一件事，你會生我的氣吧？」母牛說。

「不會，只要我做得到。」

「我想拜託你去對面的屋裡看看我的女主人怎麼了，我擔心她出事了。」

「不行！我不敢讓人看見。」

「你該不會怕一個生病的老婆婆吧？你不用進屋，從門縫窺看就可以了。」

「好吧，如果你的要求只是這樣。」男孩說。

他走了出去。外頭沒有星星和月亮，只有強風和暴雨。還沒走到那屋子，他就被吹倒兩次，第二次還被掃進水坑，差點淹死。

好不容易爬上臺階，上到門廊。門關著，但是底下鋸掉了一角，好讓貓出入，因此男孩要看到屋內的情況很容易。

他只看了一眼，就撇過頭往後退。一個灰髮女人仰躺在地板上，一動也不動，沒有呻吟，而且臉色白得出奇。

男孩記得他祖父死去時，臉色也是像那樣。死神一定是來得太突然，使得老婦人還沒有爬上床就死了。

他把屋裡的情況告訴母牛，母牛一聽就停止進食，嘆氣說：「我的女主人死了，那麼我也活不下去了。」

「會有人來照顧你的。」男孩安慰她說。

「啊，你不知道，我的年紀已經比一般上屠宰場的牛大一倍了，既然她不能照顧我，我也不想活了。」

她沉默了一會兒，但是男孩注意到，她既不睡覺也不吃草。不久之後，她又說話了。

「她躺在光禿禿的地板上嗎？」

「是的，」男孩說。

「她習慣來牛棚講心事。雖然我不能回答，但是我懂她說的話。她這幾天一直很擔心死時沒有人在旁邊，沒有人幫她闔上眼睛，把她的手搭在胸前。你能不能進去做這些事？」

男孩猶豫著。他記得祖父死的時候，母親很細心地處理每個細節。他知道這些事是必要的，卻不敢去接近死者。

母牛看他沒有回答，也沒有再要求，就開始談她的女主人。

話匣子一開就沒完沒了。首先是她養大的那些孩子，他們每天都會來牛棚，帶牲口到沼澤和樹林，每一個都又勤勞又快樂。至於農莊，也有很多可以說的。以前並不像現在這麼窮，雖然農地不多，但是長著豐盛的牧草。有一段時期每個牛棚都有一隻母牛，而現在空了的公牛棚也都養了很多公牛。女主人來開門時總是哼著曲子，所有母牛聽到她來都會高興地哞哞叫。孩子還小時，男主人就死了，女主人必須照料整個農莊，一手包辦所有事情。晚上她來擠奶時，常常累得哭出來。可是想到小孩，她就拭去淚水，愉快起來。「沒關係，只要孩子長大，就會有好日子了。」

可是孩子長大以後，就會有一種奇怪的念頭，想要出國。他們從來沒有幫過母親。有幾個小孩結婚生子之後才離開家，把小孩留在老家。那些小孩和她的子女一樣乖巧，會來照顧牛隻。晚上她還是會累得在擠奶時打瞌睡，但是想到那些孫子，她就會打起精神說：「好日子快來了，只要他們長大就好了。」

可是這些小孩長大以後，就去國外找父母親。沒有人回來，也沒有人留在家裡。農莊只剩下年老的女主人。

也許她從來沒有要求他們留下來陪她。她會對老母牛說：「你想想，瑞林娜，他們去外面可以過舒服日子，我能要他們留下來嗎？他們在斯莫蘭這裡，只有窮苦的未來。」

可是最後一個孩子離開時，女主人就垮下來了。她開始駝背，頭髮變白，走路也不穩當了。她無法工作，不能照顧農莊，所有地方都荒廢了，也把所有牛隻賣掉，只留下正在和小拇指說話的這頭老母牛。她讓老母牛活著是因為所有小孩都照顧過她。

她大可以請人來幫忙，但自從親人都拋棄她之後，她就受不了身邊有陌生人。也許她寧可看著農莊荒廢，反正沒有孩子會回來繼承。她不在乎窮困，只擔心孩子知道她過著苦日子。「只要孩子不知道就好了！」她蹣跚地走過牛棚時這麼嘆息。

孩子們一直寫信求她去他們那裡，但是她不答應。她不想到搶走她孩子的國家。她怨恨那個地方。「我也許很傻，那個國家對他們很好，我卻不喜歡，但是我就是不想看到。」

老農婦滿腦子只想著孩子和他們離家的原因。夏天來臨時，她會帶母牛去大沼澤吃草，自己在旁邊坐一整天。回家時，她會說：「你看，瑞林娜，如果這裡是肥沃的大片田地，而不是這種什麼都不長的沼澤，他們就不用離開家了。」

最後那晚，她比平常虛弱，也抖得更厲害，連擠奶都沒辦法。她靠在牛槽上說，有兩個陌生人去找她，要求跟她買那塊沼澤地。他們想要抽乾那裡的水，在上面種穀子。她覺得又高興又擔心。「妳聽到了嗎，瑞林娜，那裡可以長穀子呢。現在我要寫信叫那些小孩回來，他們不用離開了，因為可以在家裡吃到麵包。」她說完就進到屋裡面……

男孩沒有聽母牛說完。他推開門，穿過院子，走去探視原先害怕的死者。

小屋裡面並不像他以為的那麼貧寒。裡面有許多美國人家常見的東西。一個角落擺著美國搖椅，窗前的桌子鋪著華麗的長毛絨布，牆上掛著雕花相框，裡面是小孩和孫子的照片。櫥櫃上有一對燭檯，上面插著螺旋狀粗蠟燭。

男孩找到火柴，點亮那些蠟燭。並不是因為他需要亮光，而是因為他覺得這是哀悼死者的方式。然後他走過去，闔上老婦的眼睛，把她的雙手盤在胸前，再把她臉上稀薄的灰髮挪到後面。

他不再感到害怕，而是深沉的哀傷，因為她必須在孤單和期盼中度過晚年。他至少要在今晚為老婦人守靈。

男孩找到一本聖詩集，坐下來低聲唸了幾首。但是在唸誦時他停了下來，因為他開始思念父母親。

父母親竟然會思念小孩長達這麼久！他從沒想過這一點。想一想小孩離家之後，生活竟然會變得好像死了一樣！那他的家人會跟這個老農婦想念小孩一樣想念他囉！

這個想法令他欣喜，但是他不太敢相信。因為他向來不是那種會讓人想念的小孩。

但以前不是，以後也許會是。

四周有許多照片，都是那些離家的人。男人都長得高大強壯，女人則表情嚴肅。有些是戴著長面紗的新娘子，有些是盛裝的紳士，還有些頭髮捲曲的小孩，穿著漂亮的白衣服。他覺得這些人只是盲目地往前看，什麼都不想看到。

「可憐的你們，」男孩對照片說。「你們的母親死了。你們拋棄她，現在要補償也來不及了。可是我媽媽還活著！」

他閉上嘴巴，點點頭，露出笑容。「我媽媽還活著。」他說。「我爸媽都還活著。」

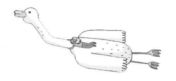

第 14 章

從塔山到大鳥湖

四月十五日 星期五

男孩幾乎整晚沒睡，但是天快亮時他睡著了，夢到父母親頭髮灰白，滿臉皺紋。他們說是因為太想念他了。他在晴朗的早晨醒來。他餵鵝和母牛吃早餐，開門讓母牛走去最近的農莊。等鄰居看到母牛自己過來，就會意識到不對勁而趕緊去她的女主人那查看。他們會發現她的屍體，然後埋葬她。

男孩和兩隻鵝離開，飛上天空，看到一座平頂的陡峭高山，那一定就是塔山。阿卡和其餘六隻野鵝在山頂上等待，一看到公鵝、丹芬和小拇指，他們發出一陣無法形容的拍翅聲與呱叫。

那天鵝群繼續上路，飛向青翠的山谷。他們心情愉快，又叫又鬧的，使有耳朵的動物都聽得見。

野鴨亞洛

陶庚湖是瑞典最大最有名的鳥湖，鳥類能有這樣的地方休息很幸運。可是不知道他們能擁有那裡的蘆葦和泥岸多久，因為人類不會忘記這座湖有相當大的一片沃土，經常提出把湖排乾的計畫。如果計畫通過，成千上萬的水鳥就要被迫遷移。

尼爾斯和野鵝旅行的時候，陶庚湖上有一隻名叫亞洛的野鴨，年紀很輕，在去年夏天出生，今年是他的第一個春天。他剛從北非回來，在湖還結著冰的時候就飛抵陶庚湖了。

　　有一晚，他和野鴨在湖上追跑玩樂時，有獵人對他們開槍，亞洛的胸部中彈。為了不落入獵人的手中，他拚命往前飛。等到力氣用盡時，已經往內陸飛了一陣子，掉落在湖邊的大農莊門口。

　　沒多久，一名年輕的長工走過來，看到亞洛，就把他撿起來。長工發現鳥兒還活著，小心地把他帶到屋裡，交給女主人。女主人撫摸亞洛的背部，幫他擦去滲濕頸羽的血，然後仔細觀察他。他明亮的深綠色頭部、白色頸環、紅褐色背部和藍色的翼鏡都太漂亮了，女主人迅速準備一個籃子，把亞洛放進去，把籃子拿到壁爐邊，還沒有放下籃子，亞洛就因為前面的折騰，累得睡著了。

　　過了一會兒，亞洛感覺有人在輕柔地推他。他睜開眼睛時，嚇得幾乎昏過去。眼前是個比人類還要危險傢伙——長毛狗凱薩，他正在好奇地嗅聞亞洛！

　　去年夏天亞洛還是隻小黃毛鴨時，每次聽到警告：「凱薩來了！」他就嚇得要命，希望不要碰到這隻有褐、白色斑點的狗。

　　可是很不幸，他掉在凱薩住的莊園裡，而他就站在眼前。「你是誰？」他叫道。「你怎麼進來的？你不是住在蘆葦岸嗎？」

　　亞洛好不容易才鼓起勇氣說：「別生氣，我會進來不是我的錯。我是因為中槍，而被女主人放在這個籃子裡。」

　　「原來是屋裡的人把你放在這裡的，他們一定是想要治好你。我倒覺得把你吃掉是比較聰明的做法。但不管怎樣，你在屋裡很安全，不必這麼害怕。」

　　亞洛第二次醒來時，看到前面有個碟子裝著穀粒和水。他還是

傷得很重，但覺得很餓。女主人看到他在吃東西，就過來撫摸他，好像很高興。就這樣一連幾天，亞洛不是吃就是睡。

一天早上，亞洛覺得好多了，就走出籃子，在地上走動，但沒走幾步就跌倒了。這時凱薩走過來張嘴叮起他。亞洛以為那隻狗要把他咬死，但是凱薩只是把他送回籃子。亞洛因此開始信任那隻狗，後來還會躺在狗的身邊。他們倆成了好朋友，亞洛每天都會在凱薩的前掌之間睡上幾個小時。

亞洛對女主人的感情更深，不僅不怕她，還會在她送食物來的時候，用頭去磨蹭她的手。每次她要出去，亞洛就難過得嘆氣，她一回來，亞洛就用自己的語言大聲歡迎她。

誘餌鴨　四月十七日，星期日

亞洛復原了，可以在屋裡飛來飛去。女主人經常撫摸他，她的小兒子也會去院子摘一些嫩葉給他吃。亞洛雖然已有力氣飛到陶庚湖，但是他不想離開他們，他不介意一輩子都待在這裡。

但是有天清晨，女主人在亞洛身上套上一條繩子，使他不能張翅，然後交給在院子發現他的長工。那個長工把他夾在腋下，帶著他走到陶庚湖。

長工踏上一隻小船，把亞洛放在船底，然後撐船到湖上。亞洛已經很習慣人類的善意，就對同行的凱薩說，他很感謝長工帶他到湖上，但不用把他綁得這麼緊，因為他根本不會飛走。凱薩沒有吭聲。這天早上他的嘴巴閉得很緊。

唯一讓亞洛覺得奇怪的是長工帶著獵槍。他不相信屋子裡的好人會想要去獵鳥。何況凱薩說過，人類不會在這時候獵鳥。

長工把船划到一個長滿蘆葦的小泥島，下船把一些蘆葦堆起來，然後藏在後面。亞洛可以在地上自由走動，只是翅膀上套著繫在小船上的繩索。

　　亞洛忽然看到以前和他在湖上玩的小鴨子。他們離得很遠，亞洛就大聲叫喚他們，一大群美麗的野鴨因此飛了過來。亞洛正在說自己得救的神奇經歷，以及人類有多麼友善時，後面就傳來兩聲槍響，三隻野鴨在蘆葦中斃命。凱薩跳出來，叼起他們。

　　亞洛這時明白了，人類只是為了要拿他當誘餌。三隻鴨子因而丟了性命。覺得自己應該羞憤而死，連朋友凱薩也以鄙視的眼光看他。回到屋裡時，他不敢再睡在狗的旁邊。

　　第二天早上，亞洛又被帶到淺灘。這次一發現有鴨子靠過來，就大叫：「走開！有獵人藏在蘆葦堆後面，我只是誘餌。」他們也確實離開了射程。

　　亞洛忙著出聲警告，連一枝草葉都沒有時間品嚐。他不希望又有鳥兒因為他遇害。多虧他，長工沒有發一槍就回家了。

　　凱薩的臉色沒有前一天那麼難看了，晚上他叼起亞洛，帶他到壁爐邊，讓他睡在他的前掌之間。然而，亞洛在屋子裡不再感到快樂，想到人類不曾愛過他，他就非常痛心。女主人和小兒子來撫摸他時，他都把嘴巴伸進翅膀裡，假裝睡著。

　　亞洛當了幾天悲苦的警戒員之後，湖上每隻鳥都認識他了。有天早上，他照常大喊：「大家小心！別靠近我！我只是個誘餌！」一個鷺鳧巢漂到他被繫住的地方。這並不稀奇，巢是去年做的，但亞洛還是盯著它看，因為它直接漂向小島，好像有人在駕駛。

　　鳥巢靠近時，亞洛看到一個小人坐在巢上，用兩根棍子往前

　　划。這個小傢伙對他喊道：「亞洛，盡量離湖水近一點，準備起飛。你很快就會恢復自由。」

　　幾秒鐘之後，鳥巢靠岸了，小傢伙藏在樹枝和草莖之間。亞洛站著不動，而且嚇呆了，深怕那個來搭救的人被發現。

　　接著有一群野鵝飛了過來。亞洛回過神去辦正事，尖聲警告他們，但他們還是在淺灘上方盤旋，只是飛在子彈射不到的高空。長工還是不斷地朝他們開槍，槍聲一響，小傢伙就跑上岸，抽出小刀迅速畫兩下，把亞洛身上的繩子割斷。「現在，飛吧，亞洛，趁那個人要重新裝彈！」他說完就跑回鷺鷥巢上，從岸邊划開。

　　獵人只顧著注意野鵝，沒發現亞洛被放走了，但是凱薩知道發生了什麼事，就在亞洛張開翅膀時，衝過去咬住他的脖子。

亞洛哀號，放走亞洛的男孩對凱薩說：「假如你像外表一樣值得敬重，就不會希望這麼一隻好鳥坐在這裡讓其他鳥兒受難。」

凱薩聽了這些話，他說：「飛吧，亞洛！你當誘餌鴨太可惜了。我並不是要你留在這裡，而是因為屋裡沒有你會很寂寞。」

排放湖水　四月二十日　星期三

屋裡沒有亞洛真的很寂寞。女主人懷念每次進屋時歡迎她的呱呱聲，但是最想念亞洛的是小男孩佩歐拉。他才三歲大，是個獨子，以前從來沒有過像亞洛這樣的玩伴。知道亞洛回到湖上的鴨群中時，他不斷想著要如何把他找回來。

亞洛躺在籃子裡時，佩歐拉跟他說了很多話，也相信鴨子聽得懂。他求母親帶他去湖上找亞洛，勸他回來，母親沒理會，這個小孩子卻從沒放棄這個念頭。

亞洛失蹤隔天，佩歐拉照常一個人在院子玩，凱薩則躺在臺階上。母親讓佩歐拉出去時，她說：「凱薩，要好好照顧佩歐拉！」

如果一切照常，凱薩就會聽話，男孩就不會出事。可是凱薩這幾天都心不在焉。他知道陶庚湖附近的農夫經常在商量排乾湖水的事，也差不多談好了。鴨子會離開，凱薩再也不能痛快地追逐獵物。他一直想著日後的不幸，而忘了看管佩歐拉。

佩歐拉難得單獨在院子裡，知道想去陶庚湖就要趁現在，於是打開門，沿著小徑走向湖邊，然後呼叫亞洛很多次。他等了很久，亞洛都沒有出現，於是到湖上找他。

岸邊繫著幾艘好船，只有一隻破舊的小船沒有繫住，因為它會

進水，沒有人要用。佩歐拉不在乎船底積著水就爬進去，也沒有力氣用槳，只是在裡面搖晃。佩歐拉很快就在湖上飄盪，叫喚亞洛。

小船在水上像這樣子晃動，自然會使裂縫越來越大，水灌了進來，佩歐拉卻不在乎。亞洛看到佩歐拉了，他高興得說不出話來，原來有人真的愛他。他箭矢似的飛到他的身邊，讓他撫摸。亞洛注意到小船已經浸入一半的水，幾乎要沉了。亞洛試圖告訴佩歐拉，但是他聽不懂。亞洛沒有耽擱，馬上飛去求救。

過了一會兒，亞洛回來，背上有一個比佩歐拉小很多的人。那個小傢伙立刻叫佩歐拉拿起小船底下的長竿子，用力划向一個蘆葦島。佩歐拉聽從了，和小傢伙合力划了幾下，然後走上小島。他們一離開，那隻小船已浸滿了水，沉到湖底去了。

這時農莊的人已經在找佩歐拉了，但到處都找不到。凱薩清楚農莊的人在找佩歐拉，不過他只是躺在那裡，好像事情和他無關。

後來有人在泊船的地方發現佩歐拉的腳印，那艘小船也不在原地。男主人和長工們立刻划船出去找男孩。他們在湖上搜索到深夜，連影子都沒看到。

佩歐拉的母親整晚都在岸邊的蘆葦和蒲草中尋找，顧不了腳深陷泥灘中，渾身濕透。每個人都以為男孩淹死了，但是她不願相信。她深感無力，心痛得不得了，絞著雙手，高聲呼叫孩子。

她聽到天鵝、野鴨和麻鷸在四周喧囂。很奇怪，他們並沒有在日落後安靜下來，而且有一些緊跟著她，另一些則是撲著翅膀飛掠而過。整個天空充滿了嗚咽和哀傷。

她覺得自己與這些生物的距離並沒有那麼遙遠，也比以前更了解鳥兒的生活。他們也要經常為家庭和小孩操心，和她一樣。要是排水的事定案了，這幾千隻鳥兒就要失去他們在陶庚湖的家了。她想把一個湖變成良田或牧場是不錯的點子，但應該是別的湖，應該是沒有幾千隻鳥在那裡生活的地方。

她懷疑這是否是兒子在今天失蹤的原因。上天是不是要藉由這份悲傷來打開她的心，以防止殘酷的事情發生？

她快步回到屋裡，和丈夫商量這件事。她提到湖上的鳥，說她相信上天在懲罰他們兩個。丈夫的想法和她一樣。

他站在那裡思索，這會不會是上天的旨意，在他打算簽約毀湖的前一天，讓陶庚湖奪走他的兒子。妻子不需多說，他就回答：「也許上天不希望我們擾亂祂建立的秩序。我明天會和其他人談一談，我想大家會同意，讓一切維持原狀。」

凱薩在爐邊聽得很仔細，等到可以確定他們的結論時，他走向女主人，咬著她的裙子，把她帶到門口。女主人想要掙脫。「你知道佩歐拉在哪裡？」她大喊。

凱薩高興地吠叫，用身體撞門。她把門打開，狗就領著他們跑到陶庚湖。才剛來到岸邊，他們就聽到湖上傳來小孩的哭聲。

佩歐拉在小拇指和鳥群的陪伴下，度過一生中最快樂的一天。但現在因為怕黑加上肚子餓，哭了起來。他很高興父母親和凱薩來找他了。

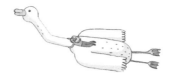

第 15 章
粗麻布與融冰

四月二十三日 星期六

　　東耶特蘭是一大片平原，南北兩邊各有一塊多山的森林地帶，在晨曦中閃亮，彷彿戴著金色面紗。而那片平原由一片片光禿的冬季休耕地拼湊起來，並不比灰色粗麻布好看。

　　但因為土地肥沃，人們想必對這片平原很滿意，而極力去妝扮它。男孩在高空看到四處散布的城市、農莊、教堂、工廠、城堡和火車站，如同大大小小的飾品，那些閃亮的屋頂和窗框就像珠寶，而村落的庭園就像胸針和鈕扣。這個景致散漫無序，但是非常壯觀，令人百看不厭。

　　野鵝沿著一條古老山路飛了一陣子，男孩突然出聲大叫。因為他坐在鵝背上，兩腳晃來晃去，把一隻木鞋踢掉了。

　　「公鵝，我的鞋掉了！」男孩喊著。公鵝回頭飛向地面。這時男孩看到兩個小孩子走在路上，其中一個把鞋子撿起來了。「公鵝，往上飛！我來不及把鞋子找回來了。」

　　看鵝的歐莎和弟弟小麥茲站在路上，研究著從天上掉下來的小木鞋。歐莎沉默了一會兒，最後她若有所思地慢慢說道：「麥茲，你記得嗎？我們回老家時，看到一個穿著木鞋的小傢伙騎在一隻鵝上面飛走。也許這就是他剛才經過時，從空中掉下來的。」

「對，一定是這樣。」小麥茲說。

他們把鞋子翻過來翻過去，看個仔細。

「你看，小麥茲，上面還寫著字呢！」歐莎說。

「眞的耶。可是字好小。」

「我看看！上面寫『西威門荷格的尼爾斯 · 霍爾加松』。」

「這眞是我聽過最神奇的事了！」小麥茲說。

四月二十八日 星期四

冰層在晨光中閃爍，看起來堅固而乾燥。雨水早已流進縫隙和洞孔，或是滲進冰層中，所以在孩子們的眼前是堅固的。

歐莎和小麥茲往北邊走，不禁思索如果直接穿過湖面，而不是繞過去，可以省下多少路。他們知道春天的冰層不可靠的，可是這裡好像相當安全。他們看到岸邊的冰層有差不多八公分厚，也看到一條可以走的小路，而且對岸看起來好近，一小時就可以走到。

「來吧，我們試試看。」小麥茲說。「只要注意看前方，不要掉到洞裡面就沒事。」

就這樣走到湖上。冰面並不滑，很容易走。上面的水比預料中的還多，到處都有滲水的窟窿。在這種地方要小心，幸好現在是大白天，可以看得很清楚。

他們快速往前走，來到維恩島時，一個老婦人從窗戶看到他們，就跑出小屋，揮手叫他們回頭，還拚命喊著什麼。他們知道她是在警告自己不要再往前走了，可是他們覺得前面並不危險，一切都這麼順利，離開冰層就太笨了！

他們經過維恩島，眼前是一塊有十公里長的冰塊。這裡有許多水坑，使他們不得不繞來繞去，但這對他們來說很好玩，可以比賽誰找到的冰面最堅固。他們不累也不餓，反正有一整天可以耗，每次遇到障礙就哈哈大笑。

他們不時抬頭去看對岸。雖然他們已經走了整整一個小時，但對岸還是離得很遠。這座湖是這麼的寬闊，出乎意外。

「對岸好像離我們越來越遠了。」小麥茲說。

風越來越強，兩個小孩沒有任何屏障，衣服被吹得緊貼在身上，走起路來很不方便，冷風是這段旅程中遇到的第一個阻礙。

吃驚的是，刮風的聲音竟然這麼大。他們來到瓦倫大島的西邊，離北岸很近，風聲突然越來越大，他們開始覺得不安。

他們忽然想到，這巨響是海浪在岸邊沖激的聲音。可是這座湖蓋滿冰層，這似乎不可能。

無論如何，他們停下來，看到一道白堤穿越冰面。他們起初以為那是雪堆，後來就發現那是披著白沫的波浪。他們二話不說，手牽著手快跑。那道白浪突然往東邊撲了過去。他們身處極大的危險之中，害怕整片冰層都會裂開。

「歐莎，冰層要溶化了！」小麥茲說。

「是啊，可是我們還可以跑上岸。快逃！」歐莎說。

其實大風和波浪要清除湖上的冰，還有很多工作要做。最棘手的部分是使冰層裂成碎片，但還要使這些碎片互相撞擊、消蝕、溶化。目前還剩下很多堅硬的冰塊。

對小孩來說，最大的危險是他們無法看到全貌，不曉得哪裡有跳不過去的缺口，或是能立腳的浮冰。沒有頭緒地跑來跑去，反而離陸地越來越遠。最後他們不知所措，嚇得站在冰上哭了起來。

這時一群野鵝迅速飛來，大聲喧囂。最神奇的是兩個小孩從呱呱的鵝聲中聽到一句話：「你們要往右邊走，右邊！」他們馬上依指示移動，但不久就遇到另一條大裂縫而停下腳步。

呱呱的鵝聲中再度傳來清楚的話語：「站著不要動！」

兩個小孩沒有交談，只是照做，站著不動。不久之後，浮冰漂近，可以跨越了，他們再度手牽著手往前跑。不僅是這場險境，得到的神祕救援也令他們畏懼。

他們很快就停下腳步，而且立刻聽到聲音：「直接往前走！」

這場引導持續了半個小時，他們終於涉水上岸，抵達岬角。雖然已經踩在堅實的陸地上，他們還是驚魂未定，沒有回頭去看波浪加快推擠浮冰的情況，只是拼命往前跑。在岬角上跑了一段路之後，歐莎突然停下來。

「等一下，小麥茲，我忘了一件事。」她說。

歐莎又回到湖岸，在袋子裡摸索，然後找出小木鞋。她把木鞋放在能清楚看到的石頭上，然後跑回小麥茲那裡，沒有再回頭。

但是她一轉過身，就有一隻白鵝從天上俯衝下來，像閃電一樣啣起木鞋，飛天而去。

第 16 章

水災

五月一日～四日

暴雨連日侵襲梅拉倫湖北部，天空昏暗，狂風吹嚎，大雨敲個不停。人類和動物都知道，這是春天來臨前，不可缺的徵兆，儘管難以忍受。

整個梅拉區中，耶斯塔灣是最安全的水鳥棲息地。這裡有低岸和淺灘，長滿蘆葦。許多天鵝住在這裡，完全不受侵擾，因為附近的城堡主人禁止所有人打獵。

新看門狗

野鵝安心地站在蘆葦堆上睡覺。尼爾斯卻餓得睡不著。「我得去找點吃的。」他說。他不假思索就跳上蘆葦叢中的木片，撿起一根小棍子，開始划向岸邊。

剛上岸，他就聽到撲通一聲。他停下腳步，看到一隻母天鵝在窩裡睡覺，隨即瞧見一隻狐狸走幾步跳進水中，偷偷走向天鵝窩。

「喂，喂，起來，起來！」男孩喊著，用棍子在水面上敲打。

母天鵝站起來，但是動作不快，狐狸想撲向她的話一定辦得到，狐狸卻是直接跑向男孩。

小拇指看到狐狸撲過來，立刻跑開。男孩跑得很快，可是再怎麼快也比不過狐狸。

離港灣不遠的地方有許多小屋的窗戶透出燭光。男孩往那跑去，可是他心裡明白，還沒有跑到最近的屋子，狐狸就會逮到他。

狐狸有一度幾乎可以捉到他了，可是他迅速閃到旁邊，回頭跑向港灣。狐狸錯過了機會，接近男孩時，男孩已經跑到兩個男人的旁邊，他們正要回家。

那兩人又累又睏，儘管男孩和狐狸一直在前面跑來跑去，卻沒有注意到。男孩也沒有跟他們求助，只要能跟著他們走，他就很滿意了。「狐狸一定不敢靠過來。」他想。

可是狐狸還是跑來了，或許是認爲那些人會把他當成狗。

「那隻偷偷跟著的狗是誰的？」其中一個人問道。

另一個人停下腳步往後看。「滾開！」他說著，把狐狸踢到路邊。「你在這裡做什麼？」

狐狸後來就保持一段距離，但還是跟在後面。

這時兩個人進屋了。男孩很想跟著進去，可是來到門階上時，他看到一隻毛茸茸的大看門狗從窩裡衝出來迎接主人。男孩改變主意，留在屋外。

「喂，看門狗！」男孩一等那兩人關上門就低聲說。「不知道你今晚願不願意幫我捉一隻狐狸？」

那隻狗的視力不好，也因爲被拴住而心浮氣躁。

「什麼，捉狐狸？」他生氣地吠叫。「是誰在尋我開心？你過來，我要給你好看。」

「不要以爲我不敢靠近你。」男孩說著，跑向那隻狗。

狗看到他的時候，吃驚得說不出話來。

「我就是和野鵝一同旅行的小拇指。」男孩自我介紹。「你聽說過我嗎？」

「麻雀有稍微提到你，」狗回答。「他們說你個子雖然小，卻做了許多奇妙的事。」

「我到目前為止都很幸運。」男孩說。「可是現在我快完蛋了，除非你幫我忙。有隻狐狸在跟蹤我，他在轉角那邊埋伏。」

「你以為我聞不出來？」狗回答。「我們很快就能解決他。」狗說著，跳到鍊子所能容許的最遠處，然後狂吠了好一陣子。「今晚他應該不敢露面了。」狗說。

「光是叫一叫是不會嚇跑他的。」男孩說。「他不久就會回來這裡，但也希望他回來，因為我指望你去抓住他。」

「你是在開我玩笑嗎？」狗問。

「帶我進去你的窩，我會告訴你該怎麼做。」

男孩和看門狗進到窩裡面，靠在一起小聲說話。

漸漸的，狐狸從藏身的地方伸出鼻子，隨著男孩的氣味來到狗窩，隔著一段距離坐下來，思索著要怎麼引他出來。

突然，看門狗探出頭來他吠叫：「走開，不然就過去抓你！」

「我要在這裡待多久就多久，你管不著！」狐狸回應他。

「滾開！」狗再次以威脅的口氣說。「不然，過了今天晚上你就沒機會打獵了。」

可是狐狸只是咧嘴笑著，待在原地沒動。

「我知道你的鍊子有多長。」他說。

「我警告你兩次了，」狗說著，走出他的窩。「要怪就怪你自己吧！」

狗說完就撲向狐狸，一點都不費力，因為他沒有被拴住。男孩已經解開他的頸圈。

　　他們激戰了一會兒，勝負很快就分了出來。狗贏了，狐狸躺在地上不敢亂動。

　　「別動，不然就咬死你！」狗說著，叼住他的頸背，把他拖進窩裡。男孩拿著鍊子，把項圈圍在狐狸的脖子上，牢牢拴住他。狐狸在整個過程中都乖乖地躺著，不敢亂動。

　　男孩綁好後，笑著對狐狸說：「斯密爾，希望你會當一個好看門狗。」

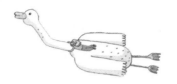

第 17 章

歐莎和小麥茲

　　尼爾斯和野鵝一同旅遊的那一年，大家都在談論兩個走遍全國的小孩。他們來自斯莫蘭省的索耐爾布縣，曾與父母親和四個兄弟姊妹住在荒漠上的小屋。

　　兩個小孩，也就是歐莎和麥茲還小的時候，有個流浪的女人來求宿。雖然屋子供一家人住已經很擠了，母親還是在地上為她鋪了個床。她在夜晚咳得很厲害，孩子們覺得連屋子都在搖晃。到了早上，她病得無法繼續流浪。孩子的父母親很好心，把自己的床鋪讓給她，父親還去找醫生買藥。

　　頭幾天那女人像個野蠻人，不斷地要人伺候，卻一聲謝謝也不說。後來她變得比較溫和，最後要求把她抬出去，讓她死在荒原。

　　主人不答應，她才說這幾年都和一群吉普賽人四處流浪。她沒有吉普賽血統，而是一名富農的女兒，卻跟著流浪漢離家。她相信是一個恨她的吉普賽女人害她染上這種病的。那個女人還詛咒所有收容她進屋或對她和善的人，都會面臨同樣的命運。她相信這一點，才會請求他們把她抬出去，不想給好心的人家帶來惡運。可是這家人沒有照做。他們雖然會擔心，但不是那種無情的人。

　　她不久就死了，惡運也連番而來。以前家裡充滿歡樂。雖然他們很窮，但日子沒有那麼苦。父親是做編織梳的，母親和小孩在一旁協助。他們從早到晚都在工作，但是過得很愉快。

女病人死後的幾個星期，對小孩來說簡直是一場惡夢。他們不知道這段時間是長還是短，但是記得家裡總是在辦喪事。他們接連失去兄弟姊妹，小屋到最後變得一片死寂。

母親還是能打起精神，父親就不太對勁了。他無法工作或說笑，從早到晚都坐著，抱頭苦思。

第三次喪事過後，父親發狂說了一段話，嚇壞了小孩。他不明白為什麼災禍會降臨。他們那麼好心幫助那個女人，難道世界上的邪惡比善良佔上風嗎？母親努力去勸他，還是無法安撫他。

幾天之後，父親最疼愛的大姊也病倒了。一知道連她也必須離開這個世界，父親就離家了。母親什麼話也沒說，但是她覺得他離開也好，以免精神失常，因為他沉浸在怨憤裡：上帝怎麼讓一個壞人製造這麼多罪惡？

父親離開後，他們變得窮苦無依。剛開始父親還會寄錢回來，但後來一定是境遇不佳，就再也沒有寄了。

大姊出殯後，母親就鎖上小屋，帶著僅剩的兩個小孩離開。她南下到斯堪尼，在尤芝伯亞糖廠找到工作。她是個好女工，又勤奮又開朗，每個人都喜歡她。她經歷過這些不幸，依然堅強地過日子，許多人都感到驚訝。有人提到她兩個健壯的小孩時，她只是說：「我也會失去他們兩個。」聲音沒有顫抖，眼裡也沒有淚水。她已經習慣不再盼望。

不過她擔心的事沒有發生，疾病反而降臨在她身上。她是初夏來到斯堪尼的，還沒秋天就離開人世，留下兩個無依無靠的小孩。

他們的母親生病時，經常要兩個小孩記住，她從來不後悔收留那個女病人。只要做對的事情，對得起良心，死亡一點都不痛苦。

母親去世之前，爲孩子安排了一些事。她請屋主讓孩子繼續住在她的房間。只要孩子們有地方居住，就不會對其他人造成負擔。她知道兩個孩子能照顧自己。

歐莎和麥茲只要肯幫忙看鵝，就能保留原來的房間，因爲很難找到小孩做這種工作。如同母親的預料：他們確實能養活自己。女孩會做糖果，男孩會刻木頭玩具，拿到農莊去賣。他們有做生意的天分，很快就開始跟農人批來蛋和黃油，賣給糖廠工人。歐莎是姊姊，才十三歲就跟成年女性一樣可靠。她不愛說話，個性嚴肅，麥茲則是活潑健談。姊姊經常說，他比鵝還聒噪。

兩個小孩在尤芝伯亞住兩年後，有天晚上學校辦了一場演講。雖然那是給成年人聽的，但兩個斯莫蘭小孩也在觀眾席中。演講人提到一種可怕的疾病，也就是每年在瑞典使多人死亡的結核病。

聽完演講，他們在教室外面等候，看到演講人走出來，就手牽著手，鄭重地走過去，要求跟他談談。

這個外地人覺得很奇怪，但還是親切地傾聽。他們說起家裡發生的事，問他是否那些家人就是死於他所說的那種病。

「很有可能，」他回答。「因爲不太像其他疾病。」

如果父母親知道兩個小孩那天晚上聽到的事情，就可以保護自己，燒掉女病人的衣服，把屋子擦洗乾淨，也不再使用舊床褥，兩個孩子所哀悼的家人就可能都還活著。演講人說，他不確定一定是這樣，但是他相信只要懂得預防，就不會染病。

歐莎和麥茲隔了一會兒才提出下一個問題，因爲那是最重要的。不，那吉普賽女人把病傳給他們並不是因爲他們接觸了她所痛恨的人，也不是某種特別的東西奪走他們的性命。演講人跟他們保證，沒有人能夠用這個方式把病傳給別人。

小孩向他道謝後就回家了。那晚，他們兩個談了很久。

第二天，他們辭掉看鵝的工作，要到別處去。去哪裡呢？去找父親。他們一定要告訴他，母親和其他小孩是死於一種普通的病，而不是因為一個懷恨的人。他們很高興知道這件事，現在他們有義務告訴父親，因為他可能還在設法解開這個謎。

歐莎和麥茲先是回荒原的老家，但抵達時意外發現小屋著火了。他們從牧師公館那，打聽到有個鐵路工人在瑞典最北邊的拉普蘭馬爾姆山看到他們的父親。他曾在礦坑工作，可能還在那裡。聽到孩子們要去找父親時，牧師拿出地圖，指給他們看馬爾姆山有多遠，勸他們不要去。可是孩子們說一定要找到父親，因為父親是抱著哀愁離家的，他們一定要告訴他，那些想法錯了。

為了省錢，他們不買火車票，決定步行前往。他們一點也不後悔這麼做，因為整趟旅程非常美好。

離開斯莫蘭之前，他們在一戶農莊停下來買食物。女主人很有愛心，詢問他們的身世，他們就把家裡的事都說出來。

「哎呀！哎呀！」孩子們敘述的時候，她不斷嘆氣。後來她殷勤地招待他們，還包給他們一大堆東西，一毛錢也不收。他們起身告辭時，農婦叫他們到了下一個教區就去她弟弟的農莊。孩子們當然很樂意。

「替我問候他，然後跟他說你們的遭遇。」農婦說。

他們倆到過的每個農莊都有個結核病患者。歐莎和麥茲就這樣無意中走遍全國，教導人民如何對抗那種可怕的疾病。

鵝群還在拉普蘭的某一天，阿卡帶男孩來到馬爾姆山，發現小麥茲不省人事地躺在礦坑口。歐莎和麥茲是在不久前抵達的。那天早上，他四處行走，希望能碰到父親。他太靠近礦井了，被爆破的飛石擊中。

小拇指立刻跑到礦井邊緣，對礦工大叫，有個小男孩受傷了。

馬上有工人跑出來，把他扛到他和歐莎留宿的小屋。他們想盡辦法救他，但還是晚了一步。

小拇指非常同情可憐的歐莎，很想安慰她，可是他知道，他現在這個樣子，去探望只會嚇到她而已。

小麥茲的葬禮結束後，歐莎獨自待在小屋，坐在那裡，一件件地回想弟弟說過的話和做過的事。豐富的回憶勾起她的思念，沒有他，日子會很難過。最後她伏在桌上哭了起來。

「小麥茲不在了，我該怎麼辦呢？」她嗚咽著。

到了深夜，歐莎勞累了一整天，終於睡著了。她夢到小麥茲輕輕地打開門，走進房間。

「歐莎，妳要去找父親。」他說。

「我不知道他在哪裡，要怎麼找呢？」她在夢中回答。

「妳別擔心，」小麥茲以他平常快活的語調回應。「我會派人去幫妳。」

就在這時，她聽到了敲門聲。真的有人在敲門，而不是在夢裡。可是她沉浸在夢中，無法分辨真假。走去開門時，她心想：「這一定是小麥茲派來的人。」

她想的沒錯，小拇指來告訴她父親的下落了。他看到歐莎不怕他時，就簡單說明她父親的位置和找到他的方法。

男孩說話的當下，歐莎逐漸回過神來，等他說完時，她已經完全清醒。想到自己正在和精靈交談,她嚇得顧不得道謝或說其他的話,立刻把門關上。

　　她這麼做的時候,似乎看見精靈的臉上浮現痛苦的神情,可是無法不那麼做,因為太害怕了。她爬上床,用被子蒙住頭。

　　雖然她害怕精靈,卻感覺得到他對自己的善意。第二天,她聽從他的話,出發去尋找父親。

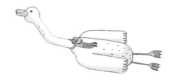

第 18 章

與拉普人共處

　　七月的一天下午，魯沙亞呂湖一帶下起可怕的大雨。拉普人通常夏天都待在戶外，這天只好鑽進帳篷，正當他們圍著火堆喝咖啡時，有一艘船從基律那瓦拉划過來，停靠在拉普人居所的岸邊。船上走出一名工人和一名十三、四歲的女孩。拉普人養的狗蜂擁而上，大聲吠叫，一個當地人從帳篷探出頭，看看出了什麼事。

　　「你來得正好，索德保！」他說。「我們正在煮咖啡。下這麼大的雨，誰都不能工作，進來跟我們講新聞吧！」

　　工人鑽進去，裡面的人正歡笑談天，他們從擁擠的空間挪出一個位置給歐莎和索德保。歐莎完全聽不懂他們的話，她呆呆坐著，好奇地看著，一切在她眼裡都很新鮮。

　　她突然低下頭，感覺所有帳篷裡的人都在看她。一定是索德保說出她的事了，因為現在拉普男人和拉普女人都把短菸斗從嘴邊拿下來，以敬佩的眼神望著她。她旁邊的拉普人拍拍她的肩膀，點點頭，用瑞典話說：「好，好！」一名拉普女人倒了一大杯咖啡，透過許多人傳給她。還有一個男孩，年紀與她差不多，從圍坐的人中擠出來，爬到她那裡。

　　歐莎覺得索德保是在告訴拉普人，她剛埋葬了小弟。她希望他能問問他們父親的下落。

　　精靈說他和拉普人住在一起，在魯沙亞呂湖的西邊紮營。由於沒有固定的載客火車到那麼遠的地方，她是搭沙石車來的。工人和領班都盡量幫忙，有個工程師請索德保陪她從湖上過來。她希望一到這裡，就能見到父親。她的目光焦急地看著他們的臉，可是都是當地人，父親不在這裡。

她發覺拉普人和索德保談得越多，表情就越嚴肅。拉普人搖搖頭，敲敲額頭，好像在談某個腦筋不正常的人。

她開始覺得不安，無法忍受被蒙在鼓裡的感覺，就出聲問索德保，他們是否知道父親的去處。

「他們說，他去釣魚了，」工人回答。「他們不確定今晚他會不會回營地。可是一等天氣放晴，就會有人去找他。」

他接著就回過頭，繼續和拉普人說話，不想讓歐莎有機會問更多榮・阿薩松的事。

次日早晨

烏拉・塞卡是地位最高的拉普人，他說要親自去找歐莎的父親，但是卻不急著出發，而是蹲在帳篷外面思考，該如何把他女兒到這的消息告訴榮・阿薩松。這需要一點手法，以免他受到驚嚇而逃跑。他是個怕小孩的怪人，經常說看到他們就會讓他悲傷得難以忍受。

烏拉・塞卡思考時，歐莎和拉普男孩阿斯拉克坐在帳篷前面的地上聊天。

阿斯拉克有上學過，會說瑞典話。他跟歐莎說明薩米人的生活方式，想告訴她，他們過得比其他人好。歐莎則認為他們的生活很可憐。

「妳不知道自己在說什麼！」阿斯拉克粗率地說。「只要跟我們過一個禮拜，你就會知道我們是這世上最幸福的人。」

老烏拉聽得懂瑞典話，只是不想讓別人知道。他在旁邊聽兒子說話時，忽然有了個想法，知道該怎麼把他女兒來找他的事告訴榮 · 阿薩松了。

烏拉 · 塞卡走到魯沙亞呂湖，沿著岸邊走一小段路，就碰到一個坐在岩石上釣魚的人。這個人頭髮灰白，背也駝了，眼神疲累，給人遲鈍、絕望的感覺。看起來好像背著過重的負荷，或是懷著解決不了的心事，因為挫敗而灰心喪志。

「榮，你在這裡待了一整晚，應該運氣不錯吧？」山地居民走過去，用拉普話說。

那人吃了一驚，隨即抬起頭。他的魚鉤上沒有餌，身邊連一條魚也沒有。他趕緊上魚餌，把釣線甩出去。

「有件事我想和你談談。」烏拉說。「你知道，去年冬天我有個小女孩死了，帳篷裡的人一直很想念她。」

「是，我知道。」釣魚人簡短地回答，臉上蒙著烏雲，好像不希望別人提起死去的孩子。

「傷心一輩子是不值得的。」拉普人說。

「我想是不值得。」

「我在考慮收養一個小孩。你覺得這個主意好不好？」

「那要看是什麼小孩，烏拉。」

「我跟你說說我知道的這個女孩。」烏拉就開始說，盛夏時節有兩個外地小孩，一男一女，去馬爾姆山礦區找他們的父親，可是父親不在，他們留下來等他，結果其中的男孩被石頭砸死了。

烏拉描述那個小女孩有多勇敢，得到每個人的讚賞和同情。

「她就是你想要帶進帳篷的女孩嗎？」釣魚人問道。

「是的。」拉普人說。「我們聽到她的故事都非常感動。有一個人說，這麼一個好姊姊一定能夠當一個好女兒，所以我們希望她來我們家。」

釣魚人沉默了一會兒。看得出來，他開口只是爲了應付朋友。

「這個女孩是你們的族人吧？」

「不是，」烏拉說。「她不是薩米人。」

「她是新移民的女兒，過慣了這裡的生活？」

「沒有，她從南部來的。」烏拉回答，好像這一點都不重要。

釣魚人開始有興趣了。

「既然這樣，我覺得你不能收養她。」他說。「我想她會受不了在帳篷裡過冬，她不是這麼長大的。」

「她可以和帳篷裡的好心父母和兄弟姊妹在一起。」烏拉堅持。「寒冷總比孤零零一個人來得好。」

釣魚人越來越想要說服烏拉放棄收養，他好像不能忍受瑞典小孩到拉普人家生活。

「你剛剛說她父親在礦場。」

「他死了。」拉普人直截了當地說。

「整件事你都打聽清楚了，烏拉？」

「何必這麼麻煩？」拉普人不屑地說。「我很清楚，如果他們的父親活著，他們何必走遍全國？要是有父親，他們需要自己照顧自己嗎？那女孩說父親還活著，可是我敢說，他已經死了。」

那個人把疲累的目光轉向烏拉。

「那女孩叫什麼名字？」他問。

那山地居民想了一下，回答說：「我不記得了，得問問她。」

「問她？她已經在這裡了？」

「就在營區裡。」

「什麼，烏拉！你還不知道他父親的想法就把她帶進去了？」

「管她父親怎麼想的！要是他還沒死，應該是那種不管孩子死活的人。有人要收養，他應該覺得高興。」

釣魚人丟下魚竿，好像變了一個人，迅速站起來。

「我想她的父親和別人不一樣。」山地居民繼續說。「我敢說，他可能是個傷心絕望，無法正常工作的人。這種父親對女孩有什麼用？」

烏拉還沒說完，釣魚人就沿著岸邊走上去。

「你要去哪裡？」拉普人問。

「我要去看看你的養女。」

「很好！」拉普人說。「來看看她吧。我想你會覺得她能成為我的好女兒。」

瑞典人走得很快，拉普人差一點就跟不上。過了一會兒，烏拉對同伴說：「現在我想起來了，要收養的女孩名叫歐莎。」

對方只是急著趕路，讓老烏拉高興得想要大笑。

他們看到帳篷時，烏拉又說了幾句話。

「她是來我們薩米人這裡找父親，不是來當我的養女。但如果她沒有找到父親，我會很樂意把她留在帳篷裡。」

釣魚人走得更快了。

「威脅說要收養他女兒時，一定嚇壞了。」烏拉在心裡暗笑。

帶歐莎來的基律那瓦拉人索德保當天要回去時，船上載著兩個人。他們手牽著手坐在一起，靠得很近，好像再也不會分離了。

這兩人是榮‧阿薩松和他的女兒。兩人都變得和前幾個小時不一樣了。父親的背沒那麼駝，外表也沒那麼疲倦了，他的眼睛變得清亮有神，煩惱許久的問題解開了。

而看鵝的女孩歐莎不再需要四處張望，因為她找到了父親，現在她又可以當個孩子了。

第 19 章
啓程回家

旅途的第一天　十月一日 星期六

　　男孩騎在鵝背上，在雲層中飛行。大約三十隻鵝整齊快速地往南飛。噗噗的羽毛聲和許多翅膀拍打空氣的聲響，讓他們幾乎聽不見自己的聲音。凱布訥山來的阿卡領頭，後面跟著伊克西和卡克西、科美和納葉、維西和庫西，公鵝莫爾登和丹芬。去年秋天加入團隊的六隻小鵝都已離開，自行生活。六隻老鵝所帶的二十二隻小鵝是今年夏天在峽谷中長大的，十一隻飛在右邊，十一隻飛在左邊，都努力和大鵝一樣保持一定距離。

　　可憐的小鵝不曾飛過這麼長的旅程，起初很難跟上速度。

　　「凱布訥山來的阿卡！」他們哀怨地叫著。

　　「什麼事？」領頭鵝嚴厲地問。

　　「我們的翅膀飛得很累了！」小鵝們訴苦道。

　　「飛高一點，就會輕鬆起來。」領頭鵝說，並沒有放慢速度。她說的沒錯，因為小鵝們飛了兩個小時後，再也沒有喊累。

　　可是在山谷中，他們習慣整天吃東西，所以很快就餓了。

　　「阿卡，凱布訥山來的阿卡！」小鵝可憐兮兮地叫著。

　　「又怎麼了？」領頭鵝說。

　　「我們餓得飛不動了！」小鵝哀聲說著。

「野鵝要學會吃空氣喝風。」領頭鵝說，繼續往前飛。

這些小鵝似乎真的在學習靠空氣和風維生，因爲他們又飛了一會兒，不再抱怨肚子餓了。

鵝群還在山區的高空，老鵝邊飛邊一路叫出所有山峰的名字，讓小鵝們記住。「這是波少陶考，這是沙耶陶考，這是梭里台馬。」他們叫了一會兒，小鵝們又不耐煩了。

「阿卡，阿卡！」他們煩躁地尖叫。

「怎麼了？」領頭鵝說。

「我們的腦子塞不進那些討厭的名字了！」小鵝叫道。

「你們的腦子塞越多東西，就越好用。」領頭鵝這麼回應後，繼續叫出奇怪的名字。

現在小鵝的翅膀終於長好，鵝群可以出發到南方了。男孩非常高興，騎在鵝背上又唱又笑的。除了想要離開拉普蘭的陰暗和寒冷之外，他還有別的原因。

剛到拉普蘭的那個星期，男孩一點也不想家。他覺得從來沒見過這麼美麗的地方。他唯一要煩惱的是，如何不被蚊子吃掉。

男孩很少看到公鵝，因爲這隻大白鵝一心只想著丹芬，一刻也不想離開她。小拇指一直和阿卡在一起，度過許多快樂的時光。

阿卡帶他飛到很遠的地方。男孩曾站在白雪覆蓋的凱布訥山，俯瞰冰河，參觀深山中的峽谷，窺看母狼養育小狼的洞穴。

自從他遇到歐莎，他就期盼有一天和公鵝莫爾登一起回家，再度當個普通人。他想要恢復人形，以免歐莎害怕跟他說話，再次當著他的面把門關上。

沒錯，他確實很高興他們終於要往南飛了。

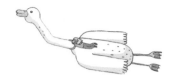

第 20 章
海爾葉達倫的傳說

十月四日 星期二

男孩在雨和霧中飛了三天，渴望找個隱密的地方睡個覺。鵝群終於飛下來覓食，讓翅膀歇一會兒。男孩看到附近的山丘上有個瞭望塔時大鬆一口氣，他拖著身子爬上去。爬到塔頂上時，他看到一群觀光客，立刻鑽進黑暗的角落，沉沉睡去。

後來那群遊客終於離開了，男孩從藏身的地方鑽出來。他沒看到野鵝，公鵝莫爾登也沒有來接他。他盡可能地大喊：「我在這裡，你在哪裡？」旅伴卻都沒有出現。他一點都沒想到他們會遺棄他，可是他擔心他們遇到不幸，正在想著該怎麼找到他們時，渡鴉巴塔基在他身邊降落。

男孩做夢也沒想到自己會那麼興奮地迎接巴塔基。「親愛的巴塔基，」他脫口說：「你在這裡真是太好了！你大概知道莫爾登和野鵝怎麼了吧？」

「我來是要轉達他們的話。」渡鴉回答。「阿卡看到有個獵人在山上走動，所以先走了，不敢留下來等你。騎到我的背上，你很快就會找到朋友。」

男孩騎上渡鴉的背，要不是有霧遮擋，巴塔基很快就能趕上鵝群。巴塔基飛到濃霧上方晴朗的高空，但還是沒看到野鵝。也許他

126

們是在下面的濕雲中盤旋。男孩和渡鴉大喊著，但沒有得到回應。

「運氣真不好！」巴塔基最後說。「但我知道他們是往南飛，等到霧散了，一定能找到他們。」

想到和公鵝莫爾登分離，鵝群也可能遭遇種種不幸，男孩就焦急不已。煩惱了兩個多小時之後，他對自己說，到目前為止還沒有發生不幸，不必因此消沉。

這時他聽到有公雞在鳴啼，立刻從渡鴉的背上傾身叫喊：「我們飛越的這個地方叫什麼名字？」

「這裡叫做海爾耶達倫。」公雞叫道。

「你那裡是什麼情形？」男孩問道。

「西邊是懸崖，東邊是森林，廣闊的山谷橫跨整片地方。」公雞回答。

「謝謝你。你描述得很清楚。」男孩喊。

男孩飛得更遠時，聽見底下的霧中有隻烏鴉在叫。

「這個地方住著什麼樣的人？」男孩大喊。

「善良而儉樸的人。」烏鴉回答。

「他們從事什麼行業？」男孩又問。

「他們養牛、伐木。」烏鴉回答。

「謝謝你，你答得很好。」

不久，霧散了，一樣很突然。男孩看到美麗的景觀，跟耶木特蘭一樣有高崖，但山坡上沒有大片肥田。村子離得很遠，農莊也很小。巴塔基沿著一條河往南飛，直到看到一個村莊。他在已收成的田地上降落，讓男孩下來。

「這塊地在夏天種穀子，你找找看有沒有東西可以吃。」巴塔基說。

男孩聽從建議，很快就找到一束穀穗。他撿起來吃的時候，巴塔基跟他聊了起來。

「你有沒有看到那座南邊的大山？」他問。

「當然有。」男孩回答。

「那是松山，以前那裡有很多狼。」

「也許你知道什麼有趣的狼故事，說來聽聽吧？」男孩說。

「我聽說，很久很久以前，松山的狼有次在追趕一個出來賣桶子的海德人。」巴塔基開始說。「他來自底下的海德村，離這個山谷有幾十公里。那時是冬天，他駕著一匹馬在育斯納河上滑行，大約有九或十隻狼在後面追他。那隻馬年老力衰，逃生的機會渺茫。

「那人聽到狼叫聲，看到有那麼多狼對著他狂奔時，亂了方寸，沒有想到應該把貨物扔出雪橇，以減少重量。他只是抽鞭趕路，但那些狼很快就離得越來越近。河岸沒有人煙，而最近的農莊也有二十多公里遠。他心想死期到了，嚇得全身僵硬。

「正當他癱坐在雪橇上時，看到冰上的松樹枝間有東西在動，發現那是人在走動時，他更加害怕了。

「那些野獸的對象不是他，而是一個名叫芬瑪林的窮苦老婦，她習慣在大小路上漫步，有點跛腳，背也駝了，所以從遠處就可以認出來。這個老婦人正在走向狼群。雪橇擋住了她的視線，所以那個人要是不警告她，繼續往前跑，她就會直接走向野獸口中，讓狼群把她撕碎，這段時間足以讓他逃開。老婦人拄著一根拐杖，走得很慢。要是不幫助她，她一定會沒命。但如果他停下來扶她上雪橇，她也不見得能夠逃生。那群狼很可能趕上他們，到時候他們兩

人和馬都活不了。他想，犧牲一條命來讓另外兩條得救是否比較好？但如果他因為沒有救老婦人而後悔，或是其他人知道他曾遇見她，卻沒有設法幫助她，他將會怎樣？多艱難的處境啊。『要是沒看到她就好了。』他自言自語。

「就在這時，狼群兇猛地嘶吼，馬縱身一躍，掠過那名行乞的老婦。她也聽見了狼嚎，而在那海德人經過的時候，老婦已經知道自己的命運。她站著不動，張著嘴巴，張開雙手想要呼救。但是她既沒有叫出來，也沒有跳上雪橇。好像有東西使她僵住了。『是我害的，』那人心想。『我經過時一定很像魔鬼。』他想要安慰自己，現在他肯定逃得掉了，可是在那一刻，他受到良心的譴責。他從來都不是懦夫，現在卻覺得一生都毀了。『無論怎樣，我都不能讓她單獨面對野狼！』」他說著，勒住馬。要讓馬掉頭非常困難，但他做到了，立刻回去找她。

「『快點上雪橇。』他粗暴地說著，氣自己無法拋下老婦人不管。」「『妳這個老太婆，偶爾也該在家裡待著！』他大吼。『現在我和我的馬都被妳拖累了。』那老婦人沒有吭聲，可是海德人沒心情體諒她。『這匹馬今天已經跑了五十多公里，而妳上來又不會使雪橇減輕重量。妳要知道，他很快就會累垮。』他說。雪橇的滑板在冰上發出嘎吱聲，可是他耳邊只聽得見野狼地喘氣聲，知道他們幾乎要追上他了。『我們都要完蛋了！』他說。『芬瑪琳，不論對你或對我，搭救妳都是件好事！』

「老婦人一直忍氣吞聲，但這時開口了。『我不明白為什麼你不把貨物丟掉，減輕重量。你可以明天再回來撿。』那個人很意外自己居然沒想到這個好方法。他把韁繩交給老婦，鬆開綁桶子的繩子，把桶子扔出去。狼群已經趕上他們了，但在這時停下來察看扔在冰上的東西，讓雪橇又領先了一些距離。『要是這樣還不行，你知道，我會主動給狼吃，你就可以得救。』老婦人說。

「她說話時，那人正想把一個大酒桶推下雪橇，卻突然停下來，好像拿不定主意是否要把它推下去，其實他是在思考別的事。『人和馬都身強體壯，怎麼能讓一個衰弱的老婦人為他們喪生狼口！』他心想。『一定有別的逃生方式。鐵定有的！都是我太蠢了，才想不出來。』他又開始推酒桶，然後又停下來，放聲大笑。

「老婦人很害怕，懷疑他精神失常了。可是海德人是在嘲笑自己的愚笨。有個辦法可以解救他們三個，而且簡單極了。他為什麼沒有早一點想到。

「『瑪琳，聽著，』他說。『妳願意給狼吃很了不起。可是妳不必這麼做，因為我知道怎麼解救我們，不必讓任何一個受害。不論我怎樣，妳都要在雪橇上坐好，一直去到林塞爾村。妳要在那裡叫醒村人，跟他們說我一個人在冰上被狼包圍，請他們來救我。』那人等到狼群幾乎趕上雪橇時，才把桶子滾出去，然後跳下來，鑽進桶子。那桶子很大，裝得下整個耶誕節日要喝的酒。狼群撲上去咬桶箍，可是桶子太重了，他們動不了，也碰不到裡面的人。他知道自己安全了，在裡面哈哈大笑。過了一會兒，他又正經起來。

「『以後面臨艱難的情況時，我會想起這個桶子，也會記住絕對不能對不起自己或別人，因為只要用心去想，總是會有第三個方法可以脫困。』」

巴塔基的故事到此結束。男孩發現渡鴉每次開口都有特別的含義，他聽得越久，想得就越多。「你為什麼要跟我講這個故事？」

男孩說。「我只是站在這裡望著松山時，碰巧想到這個故事。」渡鴉回答。

他們沿著俞斯納河繼續往南飛，過了一個小時，來到靠近海辛蘭邊界的考塞特村。渡鴉在一間小屋旁邊降落。這小屋沒有窗戶，只有一個活動遮板。煙囪冒著火星和濃煙，裡面傳來沉重的錘擊聲。

「每次看到這個鐵匠，」渡鴉說。「我就想起以前海爾葉達倫有一個鐵匠，曾邀請兩個厲害的鐵匠，來跟他比賽做釘子。其中一個來自達拉納省，另一個是韋姆蘭省。那兩個鐵匠接受挑戰，三個人就在考塞特這裡會合。達拉納省的鐵匠先開始。他打造了十二個釘子，每一個都平滑、銳利，好得不能再好了。接著輪到韋姆蘭的鐵匠，他也打造了十二個釘子，也都非常完美，而且只用了前一個人的一半時間。裁判看到他的表現，就對海爾葉達倫的鐵匠說，他不用試了，因為他不可能打造得比達拉納人好，也不會比韋姆蘭人快。

「『我絕不認輸！一定還有其他表現技巧的方法。』」海爾葉達倫的鐵匠說。他把還沒用爐子加熱的鐵放在砧子上，只是用鐵錘打熱，就製造出一個又一個釘子，沒有用到煤和風箱。從沒有一個裁判看過比他更會用鐵錘的人，因而判定海爾葉達倫的鐵匠是全國最好的鐵匠。」

巴塔基說完就沉默下來，讓男孩思考。

「你跟我講這個故事有什麼目的嗎？」他問。

「我只是看到老鐵匠時想起這個故事。」渡鴉隨口說。

這一人一鳥再度飛到空中，渡鴉帶著男孩往南來到小海達爾教區，降落在山脊長滿樹木的土墩上。

「你知道你站在什麼土墩上嗎？」巴塔基問。

男孩不得不坦白說他不知道。

「這是一個墳堆，」巴塔基說。「底下躺著第一個來海爾葉達倫開墾的人。」

「也許你又有故事要告訴我了？」男孩說。

「關於他的事情，我聽到的不多，但我想他是挪威人。曾經為挪威國王效力，卻捲入國王的不名譽事件，而必須離開那個國家。

「他後來去找住在烏曾塞拉的瑞典國王，得到一個職位。但是過了一段時間，他要求娶國王的妹妹，國王不肯把出身高貴的女子嫁給他，他就帶著她出走。不管住在挪威還是瑞典都不安全，但他不想搬到國外。但是他想，還是有路可以走，於是帶著僕人和財寶，穿過達拉納省，來到北邊荒涼的大森林。他就在那裡墾荒，建造房屋，開闢田園，成為第一個在這裡定居的人。」

男孩聽了最後一個故事，表情更加凝重了。

「你跟我講這些故事有什麼目的？」他又問道。

巴塔基晃一晃腦袋瓜，眼睛溜溜地轉動，一時沒有吭聲。

「這裡只有我們兩個，」他終於說。「我要趁機問你一件事。你有沒有問過，那個對你施魔法的精靈讓你變回人的條件是什麼？」

「我唯一聽到的是，平平安安地把白公鵝帶到拉普蘭，再把他帶回斯堪尼。」

「我猜也是，」巴塔基。「因為我們上次見面的時候，你那麼有自信地說，沒有比背叛信任自己的朋友更卑鄙的了。你最好問問

阿卡那是什麼條件，我敢說，她曾經去你家和那個精靈談過話。」

「阿卡沒有告訴我這件事。」男孩驚訝地說。

「她一定是覺得，你最好不要知道精靈說出來的每一個字。她當然比較想幫你，而不是公鵝莫爾登。」「巴塔基，你好奇怪，總是有辦法讓我煩惱，讓我困惑。」男孩說。

「這大概是真的，」渡鴉繼續說。「可是這次我相信你會感謝我。告訴你精靈實際上是怎麼說的：要是你能夠把公鵝莫爾登帶回家，讓你母親把他放在砧板上剁下他的頭，你就可以變回人類。」

男孩跳起來。「那只是你惡毒的捏造。」他氣憤地說。

「你可以自己去問阿卡，」巴塔基說。「我看到她和鵝群飛過來了。別忘了我今天跟你說過的話。總是有辦法解決困境，只要你肯去找。我很想知道你如何成功解決。」

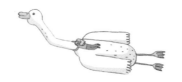

第 21 章

海島寶藏

十月五日 星期三

　　男孩趁著阿卡和其他野鵝分開覓食時，走過去問她，巴塔基說的話是真的嗎？阿卡並不否認。男孩要領頭鵝答應他保守祕密，不讓公鵝莫爾登知道。大白公鵝那麼勇敢，心胸那麼寬大，萬一他知道精靈的條件，可能會做出莽撞的事。

　　男孩悶悶不樂地騎在鵝背上，低頭不說話。他聽見野鵝對小鵝喊著，他們來到達拉納，可以在北邊看到定錢峰，現在正要飛越東達爾河，前往胡孟德湖，而底下是西達爾河。但是這些景色，男孩看都不看一眼。「我大概要和野鵝漫遊一輩子了，」他自言自語。「這些風景我可能會看得很膩。」

野鵝對他喊著，他們來到韋姆蘭，正沿著克拉河往南飛時，他根本漠不關心。「我看的河流夠多了，」男孩心想。「何必再去看另一條？」即使他有心觀賞風景，也沒有太多東西可以看，因為韋姆蘭北部只不過是一片單調的大森林地。不時可以看到燒炭磚窯，林中空地，或是幾間芬蘭人住的無煙囪矮屋。但大致來說，那麼遼闊的森林，會讓人誤以為遠在拉普蘭北部。

出海途中　十月七日　星期五

　　野鵝直接飛向南方。可是離開費里克倫之後，他們轉向飛越西邊的韋姆蘭和達爾斯蘭，前往布胡斯省。這是段愉快的旅程！小鵝已經習慣飛行，不再抱怨疲累，男孩也恢復了心情。

　　「莫爾登，你知道嗎？經過這趟旅行，我想如果整個多天都留在家裡會很無聊。」男孩說。「我們應該和鵝群一起出國。」

　　「這絕不是你的真心話！」公鵝說。既然已經跟野鵝證明了他的能力，他很甘願回到尼爾斯家的鵝窩。

　　「我想我從沒有看過底下的地面像今天這麼可愛！」他終於又開口。「那些湖好像藍絲帶。在西威門荷格定下來，不去見識更多東西，你不覺得很可惜嗎？」「我以為你想回家讓父母知道，你這個男孩變得有多好。」公鵝說。

　　他整個夏天都夢想著在霍爾加松家前的庭院降落，讓鵝、雞、牛和貓，以及母親看到丹芬和六隻小鵝時，會有多驕傲，所以聽到男孩的提議並不高興。「莫爾登，再也看不到這麼美麗的景色，你不覺得遺憾嗎？」男孩說。

　　「我寧願去看南部平原上的肥田，也不要看這些貧瘠的山丘。」公鵝回答。「可是你很清楚，如果你想要繼續旅行，我是不會和你分開的。」「這正是我想要的回答。」男孩說。他的語氣透露出他鬆了一大口氣。

　　「以後我可能每天都會想念不須冒險犯難的生活。」他想。「不管怎樣，還是要安於目前的生活。」

　　他沒有跟大白鵝透露這個想法，因為鵝群正以全速飛越布胡斯省，而公鵝飛得那麼喘，沒有力氣回答他。

太陽沉到地平線上，隨時都有可能在山丘後面消失。但鵝群還是繼續往前飛。男孩望著廣闊無邊的大海，以及光線柔和的橘紅色落日，感受內心的平靜。

野鵝的禮物

快到半夜，月亮高懸在空中，鵝群在費耶巴卡再過去的小石島上睡覺，阿卡卻搖著頭，甩掉睡意。她走去叫醒伊克西和卡克西、科美和納葉、卡西和庫西，然後用嘴巴搖了一下小拇指，讓他驚醒過來。「什麼事，阿卡媽媽？」他問著，急忙跳起來。

「不是什麼大不了的事，」領頭鵝安撫他。「只是今晚我們七個在一起很久的同伴要飛一小段路到海上，你要不要一起來？」

男孩知道，要不是有重要事情，阿卡不會叫醒他，因此立刻爬到她的背上。野鵝們飛越海邊的一長串大小島嶼，來到空曠的海面上，抵達維德大群島。這些島低矮多石，在月光下顯得相當大。

阿卡在其中最小的一個小島降落。上面有一個圓形的灰色石山，中間有一道寬大的裂縫，讓海朝裡面丟進白沙和少許貝殼。男孩從鵝背上滑下來，正欣賞著兩個漂亮貝殼時，聽到阿卡叫他。

「你一定很困惑為什麼要離開航線，飛到西海來。」阿卡問。

「老實說，我確實很納悶，」男孩回答。「可是我知道，你不會無緣無故這麼做的。」

「你很看得起我，」阿卡說。「可是我擔心你現在會失望，因為我們這一趟可能白費工夫。」

「很多年前，我和兩隻老鵝在春季飛行時遇到可怕的暴風，被

吹到這個島上，發現四周只有茫茫的大海。我們擔心來到太遠的地方，沒辦法回到陸地，就在這些光禿山崖間的波浪中降落，被逼得連待了好幾天。」

「我們餓得要命，有一次冒險飛到島上的裂縫中找食物，但一片草葉也沒找到，只看到許多綁得很緊的袋子半埋在沙子裡。我們希望袋子裡裝著穀子，就把布袋啄破，結果掉出來的不是穀粒，而是閃亮的金子。那種東西對我們野鵝沒有用，我們就沒動它。沒想到經過這麼多年，今年秋天我們會想要找到那些金子。」

「我們不知道那些財寶是不是還在，但還是飛到這裡，想請你幫忙找一找。」

男孩雙手各拿著一個貝殼，跳進裂縫中，開始鏟起沙子。他沒有發現袋子，但是挖了一個深坑之後，就聽到金屬的鏘鏗聲，然後找到一塊金子。他接著用手指挖，摸到沙子裡有很多錢幣，就趕緊回到阿卡那裡。

「袋子都爛掉分解了，」他大喊。「錢都分散在沙子裡。」

「太好了，」阿卡說。「現在把沙坑填回去，蓋好沙子，不要讓人看出這裡有人動過。」

男孩照做，從裂縫爬出來時，野鵝排列整齊，由阿卡帶頭，莊嚴地走向他。男孩感到非常驚訝。

這群鵝在他面前停下，對他低頭行了很多次禮，慎重得讓他不得不脫帽還禮。「事情是這樣的。」阿卡說。「我們野鵝在想，要是小拇指為人群做事，就像幫了我們野鵝很多忙一樣，他們一定會在他離開時給他豐厚的報酬。」

「我並沒有幫忙你們，是你們把我照顧得很好。」

　　「我們也覺得，」阿卡繼續說。「有個人陪我們經歷這段旅程，他離開我們的時候，不應該還和來的時候一樣窮。」

　　「我覺得我今年和你們在一起學到的事情，比金子和土地還寶貴。」男孩說。

　　「既然這些年來金幣一直在石縫中沒人領，我想應該由你拿走。」野鵝說。

　　「妳不是說需要這些錢嗎？」男孩提醒她。

　　「我們確實需要它，作為你的報酬，讓你的父母親以為你一直在替富貴人家看鵝。」

　　男孩轉頭瞥了一眼大海，才直視阿卡明亮的眼睛。

　　「我覺得很奇怪，阿卡媽媽，我還沒有告辭，妳就給我報酬，叫我離開。」他說。「只要我們野鵝還在瑞典，你就可以和我們在一起。」阿卡說。「我只是要趁著來不必離開航線太遠時，告訴你財寶的所在。」

　「可是感覺還是很像我還沒要走，你就打算甩掉我了。」小拇指抗議道。「我們在一起度過那麼多美好的時光，我想妳應該讓我跟著你們出國。」男孩這麼說的時候，阿卡和其他野鵝都伸長脖子，身子挺直，嘴巴半開，倒抽一口氣。

　「我從沒想到這一點。」阿卡回過神來說。「在你決定要跟我們走之前，你最好聽聽我派人去你家跟精靈談判時，從精靈那裡聽到的消息。他說無法改變讓你變回人的條件，還說農場的情況很糟，你最好儘快和鵝回家。你父親為弟弟借錢做保人，但弟弟倒債跑了。你父親還借錢買了一匹馬，才騎一次馬就跛了腳。除非能得到援助，不然你父親要賣掉兩隻牛，農場也非放棄不可。」

　男孩聽完，就皺起眉頭，拳頭握得緊緊的，指甲深陷進肉裡。

　「這精靈真殘酷，訂了這種條件，使我不能不回家幫助父母親。可是他不能叫我因此背叛朋友！我的父母親是正直的人，我知道他們寧可沒有我幫忙，也不要我昧著良心回家。」

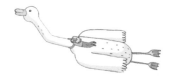

第 22 章
飛向威門荷格

十一月三日 星期四

　　十一月初，野鵝越過哈蘭山，飛向斯堪尼。在前幾個星期，他們都在法耶平市一帶的平原上休息。尼爾斯盡量提起精神，但很難與命運妥協。「只要離開斯堪尼，去到外國，」他心想。「我一定不會再有所期待，心裡就會好過些。」

　　一天早晨，野鵝終於出發，前往哈蘭省。

　　鵝群繼續往南順著狹長的沿海地帶飛行時，男孩倚在鵝背上，對底下的陸地目不轉睛。

　　他看到山丘逐漸消失，平原在底下伸展，遼闊的大海直接與陸地相連。這裡沒有森林了，由平原統治，一直延續到地平線。這裡的土地由一片又一片的田地組成，令男孩想起斯堪尼。他看著看著，一會兒快樂一會兒難過。「我離家不遠了。」他想。

　　旅程中，小鵝們多次問起老鵝：「外國是什麼樣子？」

　　「等一等！你們就快看到了。」老鵝回答。

　　鵝群經過哈蘭山，在斯堪尼飛了一陣子之後，阿卡喊道：

　　「快往下看！外國就像這樣。」

　　這時他們飛越索德爾山，綿延的山巒覆蓋著山毛櫸樹，到處聳立著華麗的城堡。

「外國就像這樣嗎？」小鵝們問。

「有樹林的山就像這樣。」阿卡說。「只是並不常見！等一等！你們就快看到大致的情況了！」

阿卡率領鵝群飛向斯堪尼平原。小山毛櫸樹環繞著草原上的湖泊，每一個湖泊都有宏偉的莊園妝點，閃著粼粼波光。

「快往下看！」領頭鵝說。「在外國，從波羅的海岸邊到阿爾卑斯山脈都是這個樣子。再過去我就沒去過了。」

小鵝們看過平原之後，領頭鵝往下飛到厄勒海峽岸邊。潮濕的草地緩緩伸向大海，有些地方是高堤，有些是流沙，沙子在那些地方形成沙洲和沙丘。

「快往下看！外國的海岸就像這樣。」

阿卡飛了很長一段時間之後，突然在威門荷格的沼澤上降落。男孩不禁想到，她飛越斯堪尼只是為了讓他看到，他的家鄉比得上世界上任何一個地方。

從看到第一棵柳樹林開始，他就想家想得心痛。

第 23 章

回家

十一月八日 星期二

　　天氣陰沉有霧，鵝群在教堂四周的大草原上覓食午休。阿卡走到男孩身邊說：「看來最近的天氣都會很平穩，我們明天就能飛越波羅的海了。」

　　「真的嗎？」男孩簡短地回答，因為他的喉嚨緊縮，幾乎無法說話。他還是抱著希望：在斯堪尼解除所受的魔法。

　　「我們現在離西威門荷格很近，」阿卡說。「我想你或許想要回家看看。下次要再見到你的家人，可能要隔很久。」

　　「不要比較好，」男孩遲疑著，但是從他的語氣聽得出，阿卡的提議令他很心動。

　　「只要公鵝和我們在一起，就不會發生意外。」阿卡說。「我想你最好去看看家人。雖然你不是正常男孩，或許還幫得上忙。」

　　「妳說的沒錯，阿卡媽媽。我應該早點想到。」男孩衝動地說。他和領頭鵝立刻飛向他家，沒多久阿卡就在包圍小農莊的石牆後面降落。

　　「感覺遇見你們好像只是昨天的事而已。」

　　「不知道你父親有沒有槍。」阿卡突然說。

　　「他確實有，」男孩回答。「就是為了那把槍，我才會在那個

星期天早上待在家裡，而不去教堂。」

「那我就不敢在這裡等你了，」阿卡說。「你最好明天早上到史密格胡克角跟我們會合，這樣子就能在家裡過夜了。」

「啊，先別走，阿卡媽媽！」男孩求她，從牆上跳下來。

他無法解釋為什麼，但總覺得有事情會發生在他或野鵝身上，使他們無法碰面。

「妳一定看得出來，我很痛苦，因為不能恢復原形。可是我想對妳說，我不後悔去年春天跟你們離開。」他接著說。「我寧願喪失變回人的機會，也不要錯過那趟旅程。」

阿卡回話之前喘了一下。

「有件小事我應該之前就告訴你，但因為你並沒有要回家，我就覺得不必急著說。但現在我還是說出來好了。」

「妳知道我向來都會聽妳的話。」男孩說。

「小拇指，要是你曾經從我們身上學到什麼，就不會以爲人類可以獨佔整個地球。」野鵝嚴肅地說。「要記住，你有很大的國家，可以輕易留幾塊光禿的石島、幾片淺水湖和沼澤、幾個荒僻的懸崖和偏遠的森林給一無所有的動物，讓我們在那裡安靜地過活。我這一生受盡了追逐和捕獵，要是有個地方能庇護我這種鳥兒，不知道會有多快慰。」

「是的，要是我有能力，一定很樂意幫忙。」男孩說。「可是我再也不可能有力量影響世人。」

「我們站在這裡講話，好像永遠見不到面了。」阿卡說。「不過當然，我們明天就會再碰面。現在我要回同伴那裡了。」

她張翅飛起後又折回來，用嘴巴撫觸小拇指，然後才飛走。

雖然是大白天，卻沒有人在農場走動，男孩要去哪裡都可以。他先跑到牛棚，因爲他知道可以從牛隻那裡得到最詳細的消息。

牛棚看起來相當淒涼。春天時這裡還有三頭漂亮的母牛，但現在只剩下一頭，也就是五月玫瑰。看得出來，她很想念同伴。她悲傷地垂著頭，幾乎沒有碰秣槽裡的草。

「你好，五月玫瑰！」男孩說，毫不害怕地跑進她的欄裡。

「我爸媽好嗎？貓和雞好嗎？星星和金百合怎麼了？」

五月玫瑰聽到男孩的聲音覺得很驚訝，好像想要去牴他，可是她現在不像以前那麼暴躁，只是先仔細瞧瞧尼爾斯。

他的個子跟離開時一樣小，穿著同樣的衣服，卻完全變了個人。在春天離開時，尼爾斯的腳步沉重而緩慢，說話會拖長音調，眼神呆滯。回來的這一個卻精神抖擻，說話俐落，目光炯亮。雖然長得小小的，舉手投足之間卻充滿自信，令人敬重。儘管他本身看起來不太快樂，卻能讓別人感到快活。

「哞！」五月玫瑰叫道。「他們說你變了，我一直都不相信。歡迎回來，尼爾斯！我很久沒有這麼高興了！」

「謝謝你，五月玫瑰。」男孩說，很高興受到她的歡迎。

「現在跟我說說爸媽的事。」

「自從你離開以後，他們遇到的都是苦難。」五月玫瑰說。「整個夏天，照料那匹馬很花錢，他卻只能待在馬廄，不能幹活。你父親心腸太軟，不能射殺他，卻又賣不出去。因為那匹馬，他不得不賣掉星星和金百合。」

有件事男孩非常想要知道，卻無法直接問，因此說：「我媽發現公鵝莫爾登飛走時，一定很難過吧？」

「要是她知道莫爾登是怎麼離開的，她就不會太擔心莫爾登。最令她傷心的是，兒子帶著一隻公鵝逃家。」

「她真的以為我把公鵝偷走了嗎？」男孩說。

「她還能怎麼想？」

「爸媽一定以為，我跟流浪漢一樣到處流浪吧？」

「他們覺得你一定過得很糟，」五月玫瑰說。「他們就像失去最親愛的人一樣為你感到悲傷。」

男孩聽到這句話，就跑出牛棚，來到馬廄。

馬廄很小，但是乾淨整齊。各方面都顯示出，父親盡力為新馬安排舒適的環境。那匹馬身強體壯，看起來被照顧得很好。

「你好！」男孩說。「聽說這裡有匹馬生病，應該不是你吧，你看起來那麼健壯？」馬轉過頭來，直盯著男孩。「你是那個兒子？」他問。「我聽了很多他的壞話。可是你面相和善，要是不知道你被變成精靈，我不會相信你就是他。」

「我知道我離開農莊時，名聲不是很好。」尼爾斯承認。「我媽以為我是小偷。可是不管怎樣，我都不會在這裡待很久。現在我想知道，你哪裡痛？」

「可惜你不能久待。」馬說。「因為我感覺我們會當好朋友。我的腳裡面有東西，像刀尖之類的刺，讓我覺得痛。那東西刺得很深，醫生找不到，我也無法走路。要是你能把我的問題告訴你父親，他就能夠幫我。」

「幸好你不是生病。」尼爾斯說。「我要馬上處理這件事，好讓你復元。你不介意我用刀子在你的蹄子上刻字吧？」

尼爾斯才剛刻好，就聽到聲響。他打開馬廄的門，窺看外面。

他的父母親回來了，他們憂傷得面容憔悴。母親的臉上有很多皺紋，而父親的頭髮都白了。她正說著要去跟她的姊夫借點錢。

「不行，我不要再借錢了。」父親說著，走過馬廄。「沒有比欠債更難受的事。我寧願把房子賣掉。」

「要不是為了兒子，我不在乎賣房子。」母親反對。「要是他回來了，變成可憐的窮光蛋，而我們又不在這裡，他怎麼辦呢？」

「妳說的沒錯。」父親說。「可是我們可以請接收這裡的人好好對待他，跟他說我們很歡迎他來找我們。不管他變成怎樣，我們一句話都不會罵他，對吧，孩子的媽？」「對！只要他能回來，除了問他有沒有在路上挨餓受凍，我什麼都不問！」

父親和母親進屋了，男孩無法再聽見他們的談話。

雖然以為兒子走上歪路，他們卻還是這麼愛他。當他知道這一點時，好想投入他們的懷抱。

「可是看到我變成這樣，他們可能會更傷心。」

他站在那裡猶豫不決時，有一輛馬車開到門口。男孩吃驚得差點叫出聲，因為從馬車上走下的是看鵝女孩歐莎和她的父親！

他們手牽著手走向屋子。走到一半時，歐莎拉住父親說：「爸爸，你要記著，不要提到木鞋、鵝群，或是那個像尼爾斯的小傢伙。就算那個人不是尼爾斯，也和他有關係。」

「當然！」榮・阿薩爾松說。「我只會說，妳在找我的路程中，他們的兒子幫了妳很多次，所以我們來這裡，想要幫點忙回報一下，因為我在拉普蘭發現鐵礦，發了大財，有用不完的錢。」

他們進入屋裡了。男孩很想聽聽他們在裡面說什麼，卻不敢冒險靠近。沒多久他們就走了出來，他的父母親送他們到門口。

他的父母親顯得很高興，好像重獲新生。

訪客都離開了，父母親卻還在門口目送。

「聽到尼爾斯做了那麼多好事，我再也不傷心了。」母親說。

「也許他做的好事沒有他們讚賞的那麼多。」父親多心地說。

「他們特地來這裡表示尼爾斯幫了他們很多忙，所以很想幫助我們，這不是很好嗎？孩子的爸，你應該接受他們的好意。」

「不行，孩子的媽，我不想拿任何人的錢，不管是送我們還是借我們都一樣。我要先把債還掉，然後再繼續打拚。我們還沒有很老，對不對，孩子的媽？」父親邊說邊開心地笑著。

「把我們花了那麼多時間和勞力的地方賣掉，你竟然覺得很好玩。」母親說。

「妳知道我為什麼會笑。」父親說。「之前想到兒子走錯路，我就灰心喪志。現在知道他還活著，而且過得不錯，妳以後就會看到我還有一些能耐。」

母親獨自進屋，男孩趕緊在角落躲好，因為父親走到馬廄這裡來了。他過去照舊檢查他的蹄子，想知道他哪裡不對勁。

「這是什麼！」他大叫，看到刻在蹄子上的字。

「拔除腳上的鐵刺。」他念出字，察看四周，但還是用手指摸索蹄子底部，仔細察看。

「這裡真的有一塊尖東西！」他說。

男孩蜷縮在角落裡時，農場又有訪客了。事情是這樣的，公鵝莫爾登發現自己離老家不遠，就無法克制衝動，想要讓老朋友看看他的妻子和兒女，於是帶著丹芬和小鵝飛回家。

公鵝抵達時，院子裡都沒有人，他充滿自信地到處走動，給丹芬看他以前當家鵝時過得有多奢華。

看完整個農場之後，他發現牛棚的門開著。

「來這裡看一下，」他說。「妳就會知道我以前是怎麼過活的。這和我們現在的沼澤、濕地生活完全不一樣。」

公鵝站在門口，窺看裡面。

「這裡沒人，」他說。「過來，丹芬，妳可以看到鵝窩。別怕，沒有危險。」

丹芬和六隻小鵝跟著公鵝走進鵝窩，看看大白鵝還沒有加入野鵝的行列時過得有多雅緻，有多舒服。

「等等！這裡還有些飼料。」他快跑過去，開始大口吞食。

可是丹芬很緊張。「我們出去吧。」她說。

「我再吃幾粒。」公鵝堅持。不一會兒他尖叫著跑到門口。可是太晚了！門碰地一聲關上，女主人站在外面，還上了門拴。他們被關起來了！

　　母親跑進馬廄時，父親已經爲馬拔掉蹄子上的鐵刺，正滿意地撫摸他。

　　「孩子的爸，過來看我捉到什麼了！」

　　「等一下！先來看這個，我知道馬的毛病在哪裡了。」

　　「我相信我們要走運了，」母親說。「你想想看，去年春天失蹤的大白鵝應該是跟著野鵝飛走的。他帶了七隻野鵝回來了。他們直接走進鵝窩，我已經把他們都關在裡頭。」

　　「那眞是不尋常，」父親說。「可是最好的是，我們再也不必以爲兒子離開時偷走了那隻公鵝。」

　　「你說得對極了，孩子的爸，」她說。「可是我想今晚必須宰殺他。過兩天就是吃烤鵝的馬丁節。我們要趕快準備，才來得及拿到市場上去賣。」

　　「公鵝才剛帶著一大群家人回來，我覺得把他殺掉太殘忍了。」父親反對。

　　「要是情況好一點，我們可以留著他，可是我們要搬離這裡了，不能養鵝。現在來幫我把他們帶到廚房。」母親說。

　　他們一起走出去，過了一會兒，男孩就看到父親兩個胳膊下分別夾著公鵝莫爾登和丹芬，和母親一起進屋。

　　公鵝大叫：「小拇指，快來救我！」如同他之前危急時的反應，雖然他並不知道男孩就在旁邊。

　　尼爾斯聽見了，卻在牛棚門口遲疑不前。

　　沒有立即行動並不是因爲他知道公鵝被宰殺對他有好處，在那一刻他根本沒想到這一點，他只是不想被父母親看到。

「他們已經夠痛苦了，難道我要讓他們更難過嗎？」他想。

可是當他們把公鵝帶進去，關上門之後，男孩就克制不住了。

他跑過院子，跳到門前的木板路，跑進門廊，照舊脫掉木鞋，然後走到門口。他不想暴露在父母親面前，因此沒有舉手敲門。

「可是這關係到公鵝的性命啊，」他自言自語。「從我上次站在這裡以後，他就是我最好的朋友。」

他頓時想起他和公鵝在冰凍的湖上、在暴風雨中的海上，以及遭野獸捕獵的驚險。他的內心充滿感激，戰勝了擔憂，敲起門來。

「是誰？」父親開門問道。「母親，你不能碰那隻公鵝！」男孩大喊。躺在凳子上，雙腳被縛的公鵝和丹芬都歡喜地叫出聲，讓男孩確定他們還活著。另一個驚喜的叫聲，來自他的母親！

「哇，你長高了，也變帥了！」她喊道。

男孩沒有進去，只是站在門階上，因為不確定會得到什麼樣的回應。「感謝上帝，你回來了！」母親說，又哭又笑的。「進來，兒子！進來！」「歡迎你！」父親再也說不出別的話了。

但男孩還是在門檻上逗留，不明白為什麼看到他這副怪模樣，他們還這麼高興。這時母親走過來抱著他，把他拉進屋裡，他才知道發生什麼事了。

「爸，媽！」他喊道。「我是個大男孩，我又是個人類了。」

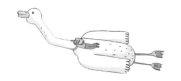

第 24 章

告別野鵝

十一月九日 星期三

　　男孩在黎明前起床，走向海邊。天還沒亮，他就單獨站在史密格漁村的東岸。他曾經去牛棚叫醒公鵝莫爾登，可是他不想離開家，一句話也沒說，只是把嘴巴塞進翅膀裡，繼續睡覺。

　　這天看起來會是個好天氣，跟去年春天野鵝來到斯堪尼那天一樣。沒有一點風，海面上也沒有任何漣漪，男孩想到野鵝將會有個美好的旅程。他有時候覺得自己是精靈，有時候是人。看到路邊的石牆時，他還會先確定後面沒有動物或禿鷹埋伏，才敢跨過去。他很快就覺得好笑，滿心歡喜，因為他身大體壯，什麼都不必害怕。

　　到了海岸，他站在岸邊，讓野鵝看到他高大的模樣。

　　這天有許多候鳥遷徙，鳥叫聲持續不絕。男孩想到只有他懂得鳥兒們的對話，不禁露出笑容。野鵝飛過來了，一群接著一群。

　　「那群鵝沒有來跟我告別，希望他們不是我的鵝群。」他心想。他好想告訴他們他不再是精靈，而是個人類了！

　　來了一群飛得更快，也更聒噪的鵝群，他憑直覺知道那一定是他的鵝群，卻無法那麼確定。那群野鵝放慢速度，在海岸上盤旋。

　　男孩知道是這群沒錯，他聽到阿卡的叫聲，卻不懂她說什麼。

　　「這是什麼意思？野鵝換了語言了嗎？」他覺得奇怪。

他對他們揮動帽子，沿著海岸奔跑、大叫。「我在這裡，你在哪裡？我在這裡，你在哪裡？」

　　可是這樣子似乎只是把他們嚇跑了。他們飛向海面。他終於明白了。他們不認得他了。他無法叫喚他們，因為人類不會說鳥語。他不會講他們的語言，也無法理解。

　　雖然很高興魔法解除了，但因此要跟老夥伴分開令他非常難過，他坐在沙灘上，用手蒙著臉。再望著他們有什麼用？

　　他聽到了搧翅聲。阿卡媽媽不忍離開小拇指，所以折了回來。看到男孩坐著不動，她才敢飛過來。突然之間，有什麼東西指出他的身分，她在他身邊降落。

　　尼爾斯發出驚喜的叫聲，把阿卡攬進懷裡。其他的野鵝也在周圍擠來擠去，用嘴巴撫觸他。他們呱呱叫著，祝他一切順利。男孩也對他們說話，感謝他們讓他加入，一同經歷美好的旅程。

　　野鵝頓時奇怪地安靜下來，從他身邊退開，好像在說：「哎呀！他是個人類，不了解我們，我們也不了解他！」

　　男孩站起來，走向阿卡。他撫摸她，輕輕拍她。他也對從一開始就在一起的伊克西、卡克西、科美和納葉、維西和庫西做了同樣的動作，然後走向內陸。他很清楚鳥類的悲傷不會持續很久，所以要趁他們還在為失去他感到難過時離開。

　　他跨過岸邊的草地，轉身望著許多群飛向大海的候鳥。所有鳥群都在發出引誘的叫聲，只有一群野鵝安靜地飛著，直到從男孩的視線中消失。他們的隊伍整齊，速度暢快，翅膀搧得安穩有力。

　　男孩非常眷念那群夥伴，幾乎希望能再變為小拇指，與野鵝一同飛越陸地和海洋。

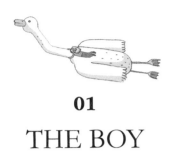

01

THE BOY

THE ELF *Sunday, March twentieth.*

Once there was a boy. He was—let us say—something like fourteen years old; long and loose-jointed. He wasn't good for much. His chief delight was to eat and sleep; and after that—he liked best to make mischief.

It was a Sunday morning and the boy's parents were getting ready to go to church. The boy sat on the edge of the table, in his shirt sleeves, and thought how lucky it was that both father and mother were going away, and the coast would be clear for a couple of hours. "Good! Now I can take down pop's gun and fire off a shot, without anybody's meddling interference," he said to himself.

But it was almost as if father should have guessed the boy's thoughts, for just as he was on the threshold—ready to start—he stopped short, and turned toward the boy. "Since you won't come to church with mother and me," he said, "the least you can do, is to read the service at home. Will you promise to do so?" "Yes," said the boy, "that I can do easy enough." And he thought, of course, that he wouldn't read any more than he felt like reading.

In a second his mother was over by the shelf near the fireplace, and took down Luther's Commentary and laid it on the table, in front of the window—opened at the service for the day. She also opened the New Testament, and placed it beside the Commentary. Finally, she drew up the big arm-chair.

His father walked up to the boy, and said in a severe tone: "Remember, that you are to read carefully! For when we come back, I shall question you thoroughly; and if you have skipped a single page, it will not go well with you."

"The service is fourteen and a half pages long," said his mother. "You'll have to sit down and begin the reading at once, if you expect to get through with it."

With that they departed. And as the boy stood in the doorway watching them, he thought that he had been caught in a trap. "There they go congratulating themselves, I suppose, in the belief that they've hit upon something so good that I'll be forced to sit and hang over the sermon the whole time that they are away," thought he.

But his father and mother were certainly not congratulating themselves upon anything of the sort; but, on the contrary, they were very much distressed. Father complained that he was dull and lazy; he had not cared to learn anything at school, and he was such an all-round good-for-nothing, that he could barely be made to tend geese. Mother did not deny that; but she was most distressed because he was wild and bad; cruel to animals, and ill-willed toward human beings. "May God soften his hard heart, and give him a better disposition!" said the mother, "or else he will be a misfortune, both to himself and to us."

The boy stood for a long time and pondered whether he should read the service or not. Finally, he came to the conclusion that, this time, it was best to be obedient. He seated himself in the easy chair, and began to read. But when he had been rattling away in an undertone for a little while, this mumbling seemed to have a soothing effect upon him—and he began to nod.

It was the most beautiful weather outside! The cottage door stood ajar, and the lark's trill could be heard in the room. The hens and geese

pattered about in the yard, and the cows, who felt the spring air away in their stalls, lowed their approval every now and then.

The boy read and nodded and fought against drowsiness. "No! I don't want to fall asleep," thought he, "for then I'll not get through with this thing the whole forenoon." But—somehow—he fell asleep.

He did not know whether he had slept a short while, or a long while; but he was awakened by hearing a slight noise back of him.

On the window-sill, facing the boy, stood a small looking-glass; and almost the entire cottage could be seen in this. As the boy raised his head, he happened to look in the glass; and then he saw that the cover to his mother's chest had been opened.

His mother owned a great, heavy, iron-bound oak chest, which she permitted no one but herself to open. Here she treasured all the things she had inherited from her mother, and of these she was especially careful. Here lay a couple of old-time peasant dresses, and starched white-linen head-dresses, and heavy silver ornaments and chains. Several times his mother had thought of getting rid of the old things; but somehow, she hadn't had the heart to do it.

Now the boy saw distinctly—in the glass—that the chest-lid was open. He could not understand how this had happened. She never would have left that precious chest open when he was at home, alone.

He was afraid that a thief had sneaked his way into the cottage. He didn't dare to move; but sat still and stared into the looking-glass.

While he waited for the thief to make his appearance, he began to wonder what that dark shadow was which fell across the edge of the chest. He looked and looked—and did not want to believe his eyes. But the thing, which at first seemed shadowy, became more and more clear to him; and soon he saw that it was something real. It was no less a thing than an elf who sat there—astride the edge of the chest!

To be sure, the boy had heard stories about elves, but he had never dreamed that they were such tiny creatures. He was no taller than a hand's breadth—this one, who sat on the edge of the chest. He had an old, wrinkled and beardless face, and was dressed in a black frock coat, knee-breeches and a broad-brimmed black hat. He was very trim and smart. He had taken from the chest an embroidered piece, and sat and looked at the old-fashioned handiwork with such an air of veneration, that he did not observe the boy had awakened.

The boy was surprised to see the elf, but he was not particularly frightened. It was impossible to be afraid of one who was so little. And since the elf was so absorbed in his own thoughts that he neither saw nor heard, the boy thought that it would be great fun to play a trick on him; to push him over into the chest and shut the lid on him, or something of that kind.

He had hardly set eyes on that butterfly-snare, before he reached over and snatched it and jumped up and swung it alongside the edge of the chest. He hardly knew how he had managed it—but he had actually snared the elf. The poor little chap lay, head downward, in the bottom of the long snare, and could not free himself.

The first moment the boy was only particular to swing the snare backward and forward; to prevent the elf from getting a foothold and clambering up.

The elf began to begged, oh! so pitifully, for his freedom. He had brought them good luck—these many years—he said, and deserved better treatment. Now, if the boy would set him free, he would give him an old coin, a silver spoon, and a gold penny, as big as the case on his father's silver watch.

The boy didn't think that this was much of an offer; but it so happened—that after he had gotten the elf in his power, he was afraid of him. He felt that he had entered into an agreement with something weird and uncanny; something which did not belong to his world, and he

was only too glad to get rid of the horrid thing. For this reason he agreed at once to the bargain, and held the snare still, so the elf could crawl out of it. But when the elf was almost out of the snare, the boy happened to think that he ought to have bargained for large estates, and all sorts of good things. He should at least have made this stipulation: that the elf must conjure the sermon into his head. "What a fool I was to let him go!" thought he, and began to shake the snare violently, so the elf would tumble down again.

But the instant the boy did this, he received such a stinging box on the ear, that he thought his head would fly in pieces. He was dashed— first against one wall, then against the other; he sank to the floor, and lay there—senseless.

When he awoke, he was alone in the cottage. The chest-lid was down, and the butterfly-snare hung in its usual place by the window. If he had not felt how the right cheek burned, from that box on the ear, he would have been tempted to believe the whole thing had been a dream. "At any rate, father and mother will be sure to insist that it was nothing else," thought he. "They are not likely to make any allowances for that old sermon, on account of the elf. It's best for me to get at that reading again," thought he.

But as he walked toward the table, he noticed something remarkable. It couldn't be possible that the cottage had grown. But why was he obliged to take so many more steps than usual to get to the table? And what was the matter with the chair? It looked no bigger than it did a while ago; but now he had to step on the rung first, and then clamber up in order to reach the seat. It was the same thing with the table. He could not look over the top without climbing to the arm of the chair.

"What in all the world is this?" said the boy. "I believe the elf has bewitched both the armchair and the table—and the whole cottage."

The Commentary lay on the table and, to all appearances, it was not

changed; but there must have been something queer about that too, for he could not manage to read a single word of it, without actually standing right in the book itself.

He read a couple of lines, and then he chanced to look up. With that, his glance fell on the looking-glass; and then he cried aloud: "Look! There's another one!" For in the glass he saw plainly a little, little creature who was dressed in a hood and leather breeches.

"Why, that one is dressed exactly like me!" said the boy, and clasped his hands in astonishment. But then he saw that the thing in the mirror did the same thing. Then he began to pull his hair and pinch his arms and swing round; and instantly he did the same thing after him; he, who was seen in the mirror.

The boy ran around the glass several times, to see if there wasn't a little man hidden behind it, but he found no one there; and then he began to shake with terror. For now he understood that the elf had bewitched him, and that the creature whose image he saw in the glass— was he, himself.

THE WILD GEESE

The boy simply could not make himself believe that he had been transformed into an elf. "It can't be anything but a dream. If I wait a few moments, I'll surely be turned back into a human being again."

He placed himself before the glass and closed his eyes. He opened them again after a couple of minutes, and then expected to find that it had all passed over—but it hadn't. He was—and remained—just as little. In other respects, he was the same as before. The thin, straw-coloured hair; the freckles across his nose; the patches on his leather breeches and the darns on his stockings, were all like themselves, with this exception—that they had become diminished.

No, it would do no good for him to stand still and wait, of this he was certain. He must try something else. And he thought the wisest thing that he could do was to try and find the elf, and make his peace with him.

He cried and prayed and promised everything he could think of. Nevermore would he break his word to anyone; never again would he be naughty; and never, never would he fall asleep again over the sermon. If he might only be a human being once more, he would be such a good and helpful and obedient boy. But no matter how much he promised—it did not help him the least little bit.

Suddenly he remembered that he had heard his mother say, all the tiny folk made their home in the cowsheds; and, at once, he concluded to go there, and see if he couldn't find the elf. It was a lucky thing that the cottage-door stood partly open, for he never could have reached the bolt and opened it; but now he slipped through without any difficulty.

When he came out in the hallway, he looked around for his wooden shoes; for in the house, to be sure, he had gone about in his stocking-feet. He wondered how he should manage with these big, clumsy wooden shoes; but just then, he saw a pair of tiny shoes on the doorstep.

When he observed that the elf had been so thoughtful that he had also bewitched the wooden shoes, he was even more troubled. It was evidently his intention that this affliction should last a long time.

On the wooden board-walk in front of the cottage, hopped a gray sparrow. He had hardly set eyes on the boy before he called out: "Teetee! Teetee! Look at Nils goosey-boy! Look at Thumbietot! Look at Nils Holgersson Thumbietot!"

Instantly, both the geese and the chickens turned and stared at the boy; and then they set up a fearful cackling. "Good enough for him! Cock-el-i-coo, he has pulled my comb." crowed the rooster. "Serves him right!" cried the hens. The geese got together in a tight group, stuck their heads together and asked: "Who can have done this?"

But the strangest thing of all was, that the boy understood what they said. He was so astonished, that he stood there as if rooted to the doorstep, and listened. "It must be because I am changed into an elf," said he. "This is probably why I understand bird-talk."

He thought it was unbearable that the hens would not stop saying that it served him right. He threw a stone at them and shouted:

"Shut up, you pack!"

However, he was no longer the sort of boy the hens need fear. The whole henyard made a rush for him, and formed a ring around him; then they all cried at once: "Served you right! Ka, ka, kada, served you right!"

The boy tried to get away, but the chickens ran after him and screamed, until he thought he'd lose his hearing. It is more than likely that he never could have gotten away from them, if the house cat hadn't come along just then. As soon as the chickens saw the cat, they quieted down and pretended to be thinking of nothing else than just to scratch in the earth for worms.

Immediately the boy ran up to the cat. "You dear pussy!" said he, "you must know all the corners and hiding places about here? You'll be a

good little kitty and tell me where I can find the elf."

The cat did not reply at once. He seated himself, curled his tail into a graceful ring around his paws—and stared at the boy. It was a large black cat with one white spot on his chest. His fur lay sleek and soft, and shone in the sunlight. The claws were drawn in, and the eyes were a dull gray, with just a little narrow dark streak down the centre. The cat looked thoroughly good-natured and inoffensive.

"I know well enough where the elf lives," he said in a soft voice, "but I'm not going to tell you that."

"Dear pussy, you must tell me where the elf lives!" said the boy. "Can't you see how he has bewitched me?"

The cat opened his eyes a little, so that the green wickedness began to shine forth. He spun round and purred with satisfaction before he replied. "Shall I perhaps help you because you have so often grabbed me by the tail?" he said at last.

Then the boy was furious and forgot entirely how little and helpless he was now. "Oh! I can pull your tail again, I can," said he, and ran toward the cat.

The next instant the hair on the cat's body stood on end. The back was bent; the legs had become elongated; the claws scraped the ground; the tail had grown thick and short; the ears were laid back; the mouth was frothy; and the eyes were wide open and glistened like sparks of red fire.

The boy didn't want to let himself be scared by a cat, and he took a step forward. Then the cat made one spring and landed right on the boy; knocked him down and stood over him—his forepaws on his chest, and his jaws wide apart—over his throat.

The boy felt how the sharp claws sank through his vest and shirt and into his skin; and how the sharp eye-teeth tickled his throat. He shrieked for help, as loudly as he could, but no one came. He thought surely that his last hour had come. Then he felt that the cat drew in his claws and let go the hold on his throat.

"I'll let you go this time, for my mistress's sake. I only wanted you to know which one of us two has the power now." With that the cat walked away—looking as smooth and pious as he did when he first appeared on the scene. The boy was so crestfallen that he didn't say a word, but only hurried to the cowhouse to look for the elf.

There were not more than three cows, all told. But when the boy came in, there was such a bellowing and such a kick-up, that one might easily have believed that there were at least thirty.

"Moo, moo, moo," sang the three of them in unison. He couldn't hear what they said, for each one tried to out-bellow the others.

The boy wanted to ask after the elf, but he couldn't make himself heard because the cows were in full uproar. They carried on as they used to do when he let a strange dog in on them. They kicked with their hind

legs, shook their necks, stretched their heads, and measured the distance with their horns.

"Come here!" said Mayrose, "and you'll get a kick that you won't forget in a hurry!"

"Come here," said Gold Lily, "and you shall dance on my horns!"

"Come here, and you shall taste how it felt when you threw your wooden shoes at me, as you did last summer!" bawled Star.

Mayrose was the oldest and the wisest of them, and she was the very maddest. "Come here!" said she, "that I may pay you back for the many times that you have jerked the milk pail away from your mother; and for all the tears when she has stood here and wept over you!"

The boy wanted to tell them how he regretted that he had been unkind to them; and that never, never—from now on—should he be anything but good, if they would only tell him where the elf was. But the cows didn't listen to him. They made such a racket that he began to fear one of them would succeed in breaking loose; and he thought that the best thing for him to do was to go quietly away from the cowhouse.

When he came out, he was thoroughly disheartened. He could understand that no one on the place wanted to help him find the elf. He crawled up on the broad hedge which fenced in the farm, and which was overgrown with briers and lichen. There he sat down to think about how it would go with him, if he never became a human being again. When father and mother came home from church, there would be a surprise for them. The whole township would come to stare at him. Perhaps father and mother would take him with them, and show him at the market place in Kivik. Birds of passage came on their travels. They travelled over the East sea, by way of Smygahuk, and were now on their way North. The wild geese, who came flying in two long rows, which met at an angle.

When the wild geese saw the tame geese, who walked about the farm, they sank nearer the earth, and called: "Come along! Come along!

We're off to the hills!"

The tame geese could not resist the temptation to raise their heads and listen, but they answered very sensibly: "We're pretty well off where we are. We're pretty well off where we are."

It was an uncommonly fine day, so light and bracing. And with each new wild geese-flock that flew by, the tame geese became more and more unruly. A couple of times they flapped their wings, but then an old mother-goose would always say to them: "Now don't be silly. Those creatures will have to suffer both hunger and cold."

There was a young gander whom the wild geese had fired with a passion for adventure. "If another flock comes this way, I'll follow them," said he.

Then there came a new flock, who shrieked like the others, and the young gander answered: "Wait a minute! Wait a minute! I'm coming."

He spread his wings and raised himself into the air; but he was so unaccustomed to flying, that he fell to the ground again.

At any rate, the wild geese must have heard his call, for they turned and flew back slowly to see if he was coming.

"Wait, wait!" he cried, and made another attempt to fly. All this the boy heard, where he lay on the hedge. "It would be a great pity," thought he, "if the big goosey-gander should go away. It would be a big loss to father and mother if he was gone." When he thought of this, once again he entirely forgot that he was little and helpless. He took one leap right down into the goose-flock, and threw his arms around the neck of the goosey-gander. "Oh, no! You don't fly away this time, sir!" cried he.

But just about then, the gander was considering how he should go to work to raise himself from the ground. He couldn't

stop to shake the boy off, hence he had to go along with him—up in the air.

They bore on toward the heights so rapidly, that the boy fairly gasped. Before he had time to think that he ought to let go his hold around the gander's neck, he was so high up that he would have been killed instantly, if he had fallen to the ground.

The only thing that he could do to make himself a little more comfortable, was to try and get upon the gander's back. And there he wriggled himself forthwith; but not without considerable trouble. And it was not an easy matter, either, to hold himself secure on the slippery back. He had to dig deep into feathers and down with both hands, to keep from tumbling to the ground.

THE BIG CHECKED CLOTH

The boy had grown so giddy that it was a long while before he came to himself. The winds howled and beat against him, and the rustle of feathers and swaying of wings sounded like a whole storm. Thirteen geese flew around him, flapping their wings and honking.

After a bit, he regained just enough sense to understand that he ought to find out where the geese were taking him. But this was not so easy, for he didn't know how he should ever muster up courage enough to look down. He was sure he'd faint if he attempted it.

The wild geese were not flying very high because the new travelling companion could not breathe in the very thinnest air. For his sake they also flew a little slower than usual.

At last the boy just made himself cast one glance down to earth. Then he thought that a great big rug lay spread beneath him, which was made up of an incredible number of large and small checks. "Where in all the world am I now?" he wondered.

He saw nothing but check upon check. Some were broad and ran crosswise, and some were long and narrow—all over, there were angles and corners. Nothing was round, and nothing was crooked. "What kind of a big, checked cloth is this that I'm looking down on?" said the boy to himself without expecting anyone to answer him.

But instantly the wild geese who flew about him called out: "Fields and meadows. Fields and meadows."

Then he recognised that the bright green checks were rye fields. The yellowish-gray checks were stubble-fields—the remains of the oat-crop which had grown there the summer before. The brownish ones were old clover meadows: and the black ones, deserted grazing lands or ploughed-up fallow pastures.

The boy could not keep from laughing when he saw how checked everything looked. But when the wild geese heard him laugh, they called out—kind o' reprovingly: "Fertile and good land. Fertile and good land."

The boy had already become serious. "To think that you can laugh; you, who have met with the most terrible misfortune that can possibly happen to a human being!" thought he. And for a moment he was pretty serious; but it wasn't long before he was laughing again. Now that he had grown somewhat accustomed to the ride and the speed, so that he could think of something besides holding himself on the gander's back.

They came to one place where there were a number of big, clumsy-looking buildings with great, tall chimneys, and all around these were a lot of smaller houses. "This is Jordberga Sugar Refinery," cried the roosters. The boy shuddered as he sat there on the goose's back. He ought to have recognised this place, for it was not very far from his home.

Here he had worked the year before as a watch boy; but, to be sure, nothing was exactly like itself when one saw it like that—from up above.

And think! Just think! Osa the goose girl and little Mats, who were his comrades last year! Indeed the boy would have been glad to know if

they still were anywhere about here. Fancy what they would have said, had they suspected that he was flying over their heads!

Whenever the wild geese happened across any tame geese, they had the best fun! They flew forward very slowly and called down: "We're off to the hills. Are you coming along? Are you coming along?" But the tame geese answered: "It's still winter in this country. You're out too soon. Fly back! Fly back!"

The wild geese lowered themselves that they might be heard a little better, and called: "Come along! We'll teach you how to fly and swim." Then the tame geese got mad and wouldn't answer them with a single honk.

The wild geese sank themselves still lower—until they almost touched the ground—then, quick as lightning, they raised themselves, just as if they'd been terribly frightened. "Oh, oh, oh!" they exclaimed. "Those things were not geese. They were only sheep, they were only sheep." The ones on the ground were beside themselves with rage and shrieked.

When the boy heard all this teasing he laughed. Then he remembered how badly things had gone with him, and he cried. But the next second, he was laughing again.

02

AKKA FROM KEBNEKAISE

EVENING

The big tame goosey-gander that had followed them up in the air, felt very proud of being permitted to travel back and forth over the South country with the wild geese, and crack jokes with the tame birds. But in spite of his keen delight, he began to tire as the afternoon wore on. He tried to take deeper breaths and quicker wing-strokes, but even so he remained several goose-lengths behind the others.

When the wild geese who flew last, noticed that the tame one couldn't keep up with them, they began to call to the goose who rode in the centre of the angle and led the procession: "Akka from Kebnekaise! Akka from Kebnekaise!" "What do you want of me?" asked the leader. "The white one will be left behind; the white one will be left behind." "Tell him it's easier to fly fast than slow!" called the leader, and raced on as before.

The goosey-gander certainly tried to follow the advice, and increase his speed; but then he became so exhausted that he sank away down to the drooping willows that bordered the fields and meadows.

"Akka, Akka!" again cried those who flew last. "Can't you let me fly in peace?" asked the leader, and she sounded even madder than before.

"The white one is ready to collapse." "Tell him that he who has not the strength to fly with the flock, can go back home!" cried the leader.

"Oh! Is that the way the wind blows?" thought the goosey-gander.

He understood at once that the wild geese had never intended to take him along. They had only lured him away from home in sport.

He flew slowly behind the rest, while he deliberated whether he should turn back or continue. Finally, the little creature that he carried on his back said: "Dear Morten Goosey-gander, you know well enough that it is simply impossible for you, who have never flown, to go with the wild geese all the way up to Lapland. Won't you turn back before you kill yourself?"

But as soon as it dawned on him that this puny creature actually believed that he couldn't make the trip, he decided to stick it out. "If you say another word about this, I'll drop you into the first ditch we ride over!" said he, and at the same time his fury gave him so much strength that he began to fly almost as well as any of the others.

It isn't likely that he could have kept this pace up very long, neither was it necessary; for, just then, the sun sank quickly; and at sunset the geese flew down, and before the boy and the goosey-gander knew what had happened, they stood on the shores of Vomb Lake. "They probably intend that we shall spend the night here," thought the boy, and jumped down from the goose's back.

For now the sun was away and frost came from the lake, and darkness sank down from heaven, and terror stole forward on the twilight's trail, and in the forest it began to patter and rustle.

Now the good humour which the boy had felt when he was up in the air, was gone, and in his misery he looked around for his travelling companions. He had no one but them to cling to now. The goosey-gander was lying prostrate on the spot where he had alighted; and it looked as if he were ready to die. His neck lay flat against the ground, his eyes were closed, and his breathing sounded like a feeble hissing.

"Dear Morten Goosey-Gander," said the boy, "try to get a swallow of water! It isn't two steps to the lake."

But the goosey-gander didn't stir. The boy had certainly been cruel to all animals, and to the goosey-gander in times gone by; but now he felt that the goosey-gander was the only comfort he had left, and he was dreadfully afraid of losing him.

At once the boy began to push and drag him, to get him into the water, but the goosey-gander was big and heavy, and it was mighty hard work for the boy; but at last he succeeded.

The goosey-gander got in head first. For an instant he lay motionless in the slime, but soon he poked up his head, shook the water from his eyes and sniffed. Then he swam, proudly, between reeds and seaweed.

The white goosey-gander had the good fortune to spy a perch. He grabbed it quickly, swam ashore with it, and laid it down in front of the boy. "Here's a thank you for helping me into the water," said he.

It was the first time the boy had heard a friendly word that day. He was so happy that he wanted to throw his arms around the goosey-gander's neck, but he refrained; and he was also thankful for the gift.

He felt to see if he still had his sheath-knife with him; and, sure enough, there it hung—on the back button of his trousers, although it was so diminished that it was hardly as long as a match. Well, at any rate, it served to scale and cleanse fish with; and it wasn't long before the perch was eaten.

While the boy ate, the goosey-gander stood silently beside him. But when he had swallowed the last bite, he said in a low voice: "It's a fact that we have run across a stuck-up goose folk who despise all tame birds."

"Yes, I've observed that," said the boy.

"What a triumph it would be for me if I could follow them clear up to Lapland, and show them that even a tame goose can do things!"

"Yes," said the boy, and drawled it out because he didn't believe the goosey-gander could ever do it; yet he didn't wish to contradict him. "But I don't think I can get along all alone on such a journey," said the goosey-

gander. "I'd like to ask if you couldn't come along with me?" The boy, of course, hadn't expected anything but to return to his home as soon as possible, and he was so surprised that he hardly knew what he should reply.

"I suppose I really ought to go home to father and mother," said the boy. "Oh! I'll get you back to them some time in the fall," said the goosey-gander. "I shall not leave you until I put you down on your own doorstep."

The boy thought it might be just as well for him if he escaped showing himself before his parents for a while. He was not disinclined to favour the scheme, and was just on the point of saying that he agreed to it—when they heard a loud rumbling behind them. It was the wild geese who had come up from the lake—all at one time—and stood shaking the water from their backs. After that they arranged themselves in a long row—with the leader-goose in the centre—and came toward them.

The goosey-gander only had time to whisper to the boy: "Speak up quickly for yourself, but don't tell them who you are!"—before the geese were upon them.

When the wild geese had stopped in front of them, they curtsied with their necks many times, and the goosey-gander did likewise many more times. As soon as the ceremonies were over, the leader-goose said: "Now I presume we shall hear what kind of creatures you are."

"There isn't much to tell about me," said the goosey-gander. "I was born in Skanor last spring. In the fall I was sold to Holger Nilsson of West Vemminghög, and there I have lived ever since." "You don't seem to have any pedigree to boast of," said the leader-goose. "What is it, then, that makes you so high-minded that you wish to associate with wild geese?" "It may be because I want to show you wild geese that we tame ones may also be good for something," said the goosey-gander. "Yes, it would be well if you could show us that," said the leader-goose. "We have already observed how much you know about flying; but you are more skilled, perhaps, in other sports. Possibly you are strong in a

swimming match?" "No, I can't boast that I am," said the goosey-gander. It seemed to him that the leader-goose had already made up her mind to send him home, so he didn't much care how he answered. "I never swam any farther than across a marl-ditch," he continued. "Then I presume you're a crack sprinter," said the goose. "I have never seen a tame goose run, nor have I ever done it myself," said the goosey-gander; and he made things appear much worse than they really were.

The big white one was sure now that the leader-goose would say that under no circumstances could they take him along. He was very much astonished when she said: "You answer questions courageously; and he who has courage can become a good travelling companion, even if he is ignorant in the beginning. What do you say to stopping with us for a couple of days, until we can see what you are good for?" "That suits me!" said the goosey-gander—and he was thoroughly happy.

Thereupon the leader-goose pointed with her bill and said: "But who is that you have with you?." "That's my comrade," said the goosey-gander. "He's been a goose-tender all his life. He'll be useful all right to take with us on the trip." "Yes, he may be all right for a tame goose," answered the wild one. "What do you call him?" The goosey-gander—hesitantly, not knowing what he should hit upon in a hurry, for he didn't want to reveal the fact that the boy had a human name. "Oh! his name is Thumbietot," he said at last. "Does he belong to the elf family?" asked the leader-goose. "At what time do you wild geese usually retire?" said the goosey-gander quickly—trying to evade that last question. "My eyes close of their own accord about this time."

One could easily see that the goose who talked with the gander was very old. Her entire feather outfit was ice-gray, without any dark streaks. The head was larger, the legs coarser, and the feet were more worn than any of the others. The feathers were stiff; the shoulders knotty; the neck thin. All this was due to age. It was only upon the eyes that time had had

no effect. They shone brighter—as if they were younger—than any of the others!

She turned, very haughtily, toward the goosey-gander. "Understand, Mr. Tame-goose, that I am Akka from Kebnekaise! And that the goose who flies nearest me—to the right—is Iksi from Vassijaure, and the one to the left, is Kaksi from Nuolja! That the second right-hand goose is Kolmi from Sarjektjakko, and the second, left, is Neljä from Svappavaara; and behind them fly Viisi from Oviksfjällen and Kuusi from Sjangeli! And know that these, as well as the six goslings who fly last—three to the right, and three to the left—are all high mountain geese of the finest breed! You must not take us for land-lubbers who strike up a chance acquaintance with any and everyone! And you must not think that we permit anyone to share our quarters, that will not tell us who his ancestors were."

When Akka, the leader-goose, talked in this way, the boy stepped briskly forward. It had distressed him that the goosey-gander, who had spoken up so glibly for himself, should give such evasive answers when it concerned him. "I don't care to make a secret of who I am," said he. "My name is Nils Holgersson. I'm a farmer's son, and, until to-day, I have been a human being; but this morning—" He got no further. As soon as he had said that he was human the leader-goose staggered three steps backward, and the rest of them even farther back. They all extended their necks and hissed angrily at him.

"I have suspected this ever since I first saw you here on these shores," said Akka; "and now you can clear out of here at once. We tolerate no human beings among us."

"It isn't possible," said the goosey-gander, meditatively, "that you wild geese can be afraid of anyone who is so tiny! By to-morrow, of course, he'll turn back home. You can surely let him stay with us overnight. None of us can afford to let such a poor little creature wander off by himself in the night—among weasels and foxes!"

The wild goose came nearer. But it was evident that it was hard for her to master her fear. "I have been taught to fear everything in human shape—be it big or little," said she. "But if you will answer for this one, and swear that he will not harm us, he can stay with us to-night. But I don't believe our night quarters are suitable either for him or you, for we intend to roost on the broken ice out here."

She thought, of course, that the goosey-gander would be doubtful when he heard this, but he never let on. "She is pretty wise who knows how to choose such a safe bed," said he.

"You will be answerable for his return to his own to-morrow."

"Then I, too, will have to leave you," said the goosey-gander. "I have sworn that I would not forsake him."

"You are free to fly whither you will," said the leader-goose.

With this, she raised her wings and flew out over the ice and one after another the wild geese followed her.

The boy was very sad to think that his trip to Lapland would not come off, and, in the bargain, he was afraid of the chilly night quarters. "It will be worse and worse," said he. "In the first place, we'll freeze to death on the ice."

But the gander was in a good humour. "There's no danger," said he. "Only make haste, I beg of you, and gather together as much grass and litter as you can well carry."

When the boy had his arms full of dried grass, the goosey-gander grabbed him by the shirt-band, lifted him, and flew out on the ice, where the wild geese were already fast asleep, with their bills tucked under their wings.

"Now spread out the grass on the ice, so there'll be something to stand on, to keep me from freezing fast. You help me and I'll help you," said the goosey-gander.

This the boy did. And when he had finished, the goosey-gander

tucked him under his wing. "I think you'll lie snug and warm there," said the goosey-gander as he covered him with his wing.

The boy was so imbedded in down that he couldn't answer, and he was nice and comfy. Oh, but he was tired!—And in less than two winks he was fast asleep.

NIGHT

In the middle of the night the loosened ice-cake moved about, until one corner of it touched the shore. Now it happened that Mr. Smirre Fox, who lived at this time in Övid Cloister Park—on the east side of the lake—caught a glimpse of that one corner, while he was out on his night chase.

When Smirre was very near to the geese, his claws scraped the ice, and the geese awoke, flapped their wings, and prepared for flight. But Smirre was too quick for them. He darted forward as though he'd been shot; grabbed a goose by the wing, and ran toward land again.

The boy had awakened when the goosey-gander spread his wings. He had tumbled down on the ice and was sitting there, dazed. He hadn't grasped the whys and wherefores of all this confusion, until he saw a little long-legged dog who ran over the ice with a goose in his mouth.

In a minute the boy was after that dog, to try and take the goose away from him. He must have heard the goosey-gander call to him: "Have a care, Thumbietot! Have a care!" But the boy thought that such a little runt of a dog was nothing to be afraid of and he rushed ahead.

The wild goose that Smirre Fox tugged after him, heard the clatter as the boy's wooden shoes beat against the ice, and she could hardly believe her ears. "Does that infant think he can take me away from the fox?" she wondered. "The first thing he knows, he'll fall through a crack in the ice," thought she.

But dark as the night was, the boy saw distinctly all the cracks and holes there were, and took daring leaps over them. This was because he had the elf's good eyesight now, and could see in the dark.

And just as Smirre Fox was working his way up to the land-edge, the boy shouted: "Drop that goose, you sneak!"

Smirre didn't know who was calling to him, and wasted no time in looking around, but increased his pace. The fox made straight for the forest.

The boy shouted, again and again, to that dog, to make him drop his game. "What kind of a dog are you, who can steal a whole goose and not feel ashamed of yourself? Drop her, I say, or I'll tell your master how you behave!" The boy ran so fast that the thick beech-trees appeared to be running past him—backward, but he caught up with Smirre. Finally, he was so close to him that he got a hold on his tail. "Now I'll take the goose from you anyway," cried he, and held on as hard as ever he could, but he hadn't strength enough to stop Smirre. The fox dragged him along until the dry foliage whirled around him.

But now it began to dawn on Smirre how harmless the thing was that pursued him. He stopped short, put the goose on the ground, and stood on her with his forepaws, so she couldn't fly away. He was just about to bite off her neck—but then he couldn't resist the desire to tease the boy a little. "Hurry off and complain to the master, for now I'm going to bite the goose to death!" said he.

Certainly the one who was surprised when he saw what a pointed nose, and heard what a hoarse and angry voice that dog which he was pursuing had,—was the boy! But now he was so enraged because the fox had made fun of him, that he never thought of being frightened. He took a firmer hold on the tail, braced himself against a beech trunk; and just as the fox opened his jaws over the goose's throat, he pulled as hard as he could. Smirre was so astonished that he let himself be pulled

backward a couple of steps—and the wild goose got away. She fluttered upward feebly and heavily. One wing was so badly wounded that she could barely use it. In addition to this, she could not see in the night darkness of the forest but was as helpless as the blind. Therefore she could in no way help the boy; so she groped her way through the branches and flew down to the lake again.

Then Smirre made a dash for the boy. "If I don't get the one, I shall certainly have the other," said he. The boy was so gay after his success that in the beginning, he laughed and made fun of the fox. But Smirre was persevering—as old hunters generally are—and the boy began to fear that he should be captured in the end. Then he caught sight of a little, young beech-tree that had shot up as slender as a rod, that it might soon reach the free air above the canopy of branches which the old beeches spread above it. Quick as a flash, he let go of the fox-tail and climbed the beech tree. Smirre Fox was so excited that he continued to dance around after his tail.

"Don't bother with the dance any longer!" said the boy.

But Smirre couldn't endure the humiliation of his failure to get the better of such a little tot, so he lay down under the tree, that he might keep a close watch on him.

The boy didn't have any too good a time of it where he sat, astride a frail branch. The young beech did not , so the boy couldn't get over to another tree, and he didn't dare to come down again. He was so cold and numb that he almost lost his hold around the branch; and he was dreadfully sleepy; but he didn't dare fall asleep for fear of tumbling down.

Finally, more and more sunbeams came bursting through space, and soon the night's terrors were driven away, and such a marvellous lot of living things came forward.

Then the boy understood that the sun had said to all these tiny creatures: "Wake up now, and come out of your nests! I'm here! Now

you need be afraid of nothing."

The wild-goose call was heard from the lake, as they were preparing for flight; and soon all fourteen geese came flying through the forest. The boy tried to call to them, but they flew so high that his voice couldn't reach them. They probably believed the fox had eaten him up; and they didn't trouble themselves to look for him.

The boy came near crying with regret; but the sun stood up there— orange-coloured and happy—and put courage into the whole world. "It isn't worth while, Nils Holgersson, for you to be troubled about anything, as long as I'm here," said the sun.

GOOSE-PLAY *Monday, March twenty-first.*

Just as the morning was verging on forenoon, a goose came flying, all by herself, under the thick tree-canopy. She groped her way hesitatingly, between the stems and branches, and flew very slowly. As soon as Smirre Fox saw her, he left his place under the beech tree, and sneaked up toward her. The wild goose didn't avoid the fox, but flew very close to him. Smirre made a high jump for her but he missed her; and the goose went on her way down to the lake.

It was not long before another goose came flying. She took the same route as the first one; and flew still lower and slower. She, too, flew close to Smirre Fox, and he made such a high spring for her, that his ears brushed her feet. But she, too, got away from him unhurt, and went her way toward the lake, silent as a shadow.

A little while passed and then there came another wild goose. She flew still slower and lower; and it seemed even more difficult for her to find her way between the beech-branches. Smirre made a powerful spring! He was within a hair's breadth of catching her; but that goose also managed to save herself.

Just after she had disappeared, came a fourth. She flew so slowly, and so badly, that Smirre Fox thought he could catch her without much effort, but he was afraid of failure now, and concluded to let her fly past—unmolested. She took the same direction the others had taken; and just as she was come right above Smirre, she sank down so far that he was tempted to jump for her. He jumped so high that he touched her with his tail. But she flung herself quickly to one side and saved her life.

Before Smirre got through panting, three more geese came flying in a row. They flew just like the rest, and Smirre made high springs for them all, but he did not succeed in catching any one of them.

After that came five geese; but these flew better than the others. And although it seemed as if they wanted to lure Smirre to jump, he withstood the temptation. After quite a long time came one single goose. It was the thirteenth. This one was so old that she was gray all over, without a dark speck anywhere on her body. She didn't appear to use one wing very well, but flew so wretchedly and crookedly, that she almost touched the ground. Smirre not only made a high leap for her, but he pursued her, running and jumping all the way down to the lake. But not even this time did he get anything for his trouble.

When the fourteenth goose came along, it looked very pretty because it was white. And as its great wings swayed, it glistened like a light, in the dark forest. When Smirre Fox saw this one, he mustered all his resources and jumped half-way up to the tree-canopy. But the white one flew by unhurt like the rest.

Suddenly Smirre remembered his prisoner and raised his eyes toward the young beech-tree. And just as he might have expected—the boy had disappeared.

But Smirre didn't have much time to think about him; for now the first goose came back again from the lake and flew slowly under the canopy. In spite of all his ill luck, Smirre was glad that she came back, and

darted after her with a high leap. But he had been in too much of a hurry, and hadn't taken the time to calculate the distance, and he landed at one side of the goose. Then there came still another goose; then a third; a fourth; and so on, until the angle closed in with the old ice-gray one, and the big white one. They all flew low and slow. Just as they swayed in the vicinity of Smirre Fox, they sank down—kind of inviting-like—for him to take them. Smirre ran after them and made leaps a couple of fathoms high—but he couldn't manage to get hold of a single one of them.

It was the most awful day that Smirre Fox had ever experienced.

Smirre was no young fox. He had had the dogs after him many a time, and had heard the bullets whizz around his ears. He had lain in hiding, down in the lair, while the dachshunds crept into the crevices and all but found him. But all the anguish that Smirre Fox had been forced to suffer under this hot chase, was not to be compared with what he suffered every time that he missed one of the wild geese.

In the afternoon Smirre was so exhausted that he grew delirious. He saw nothing before his eyes but flying geese. He made leaps for sun-spots which he saw on the ground; and for a poor little butterfly that had come out of his chrysalis too soon.

When Smirre Fox sank down on a pile of dry leaves, weak and powerless and almost ready to give up the ghost, they stopped teasing him.

"Now you know, Mr. Fox, what happens to the one who dares to come near Akka of Kebnekaise!" they shouted in his ear; and with that they left him in peace.

03
THE WONDERFUL JOURNEY OF
NILS

ON THE FARM *Thursday, March twenty-fourth.*

A lady squirrel had been captured in the hazelbrush that grew on the shores of Vomb Lake, and was carried to a farmhouse close by. All the folks on the farm—both young and old—were delighted with the pretty creature with the bushy tail, the wise, inquisitive eyes, and the natty little feet. They intended to amuse themselves all summer by watching its nimble movements; its ingenious way of shelling nuts; and its droll play. They immediately put in order an old squirrel cage with a little green house and a wire-cylinder wheel. The little house, which had both doors and windows, the lady squirrel was to use as a dining room and bedroom. For this reason they placed therein a bed of leaves, a bowl of milk and some nuts. The cylinder wheel, on the other hand, she was to use as a play-house, where she could run and climb and swing round.

The people believed that they had arranged things very comfortably for the lady squirrel, and they were astonished because she didn't seem to be contented; but, instead, she sat there, downcast and moody, in a corner of her room. Every now and again, she would let out a shrill, agonised cry. She did not touch the food; and not once did she swing round on the wheel. "It's probably because she's frightened," said the farmer folk.

Naturally there was a great deal of excitement and bustle in the kitchen, and probably no one there took time to think about the squirrel, or to wonder how she was getting on. But there was an old grandma in the house who was too aged to take a hand in the baking; this she herself understood, but just the same she did not relish the idea of being left out of the game. She felt rather downhearted; and for this reason she did not go to bed but seated herself by the sitting-room window and looked out.

They had opened the kitchen door on account of the heat; and through it a clear ray of light streamed out on the yard; and it became so well lighted out there that the old woman could see all the cracks and holes in the plastering on the wall opposite. She also saw the squirrel cage which hung just where the light fell clearest. And she noticed how the squirrel ran from her room to the wheel, and from the wheel to her room, all night long, without stopping an instant. She thought it was a strange sort of unrest that had come over the animal; but she believed, of course, that the strong light kept her awake.

Between the cow-house and the stable there was a broad, handsome carriage-gate; this too came within the light-radius. As the night wore on, the old grandma saw a tiny creature, no bigger than a hand's breadth, cautiously steal his way through the gate. He was dressed in leather breeches and wooden shoes like any other working man. The old grandma knew at once that it was the elf, and she was not the least bit frightened. She had always heard that the elf kept himself somewhere about the place, although she had never seen him before; and an elf, to be sure, brought good luck wherever he appeared.

As soon as the elf came into the stone-paved yard, he ran right up to the squirrel cage. And since it hung so high that he could not reach it, he went over to the store-house after a rod; placed it against the cage, and swung himself up—in the same way that a sailor climbs a rope. When he had reached the cage, he shook the door of the little green house as if he

wanted to open it; but the old grandma didn't move; for she knew that the children had put a padlock on the door, as they feared that the boys on the neighbouring farms would try to steal the squirrel. When the boy could not get the door open, the lady squirrel came out to the wire wheel. There they held a long conference together. And when the boy had listened to all that the imprisoned animal had to say to him, he slid down the rod to the ground, and ran out through the carriage-gate.

The old woman didn't expect to see anything more of the elf that night, nevertheless, she remained at the window. After a few moments had gone by, he returned. He rushed right up to the squirrel cage. The old woman saw that he carried something in his hands; but what it was she couldn't imagine. The thing he carried in his left hand he laid down on the pavement; but that which he held in his right hand he took with him to the cage. He kicked so hard with his wooden shoes on the little window that the glass was broken. He poked in the thing which he held in his hand to the lady squirrel. Then he slid down again, and took up that which he had laid upon the ground, and climbed up to the cage with that also. The next instant he ran off again with such haste.

But now it was the old grandma who could no longer sit still in the cottage; but who, very slowly, went out to the back yard and stationed herself in the shadow of the pump to await the elf's return. And there was one other who had also seen him and had become curious. This was the house cat. He crept along slyly and stopped close to the wall, just two steps away from the stream of light. They both stood and waited, long and patiently, on that chilly March night, and the old woman was just beginning to think about going in again, when she heard a clatter on the pavement, and saw that the little mite of an elf came trotting along once more, carrying a burden in each hand, as he had done before. That which he bore squealed and squirmed. And now a light dawned on the old grandma. She understood that the elf had hurried down to the hazel-

grove and brought back the lady squirrel's babies; and that he was carrying them to her so they shouldn't starve to death.

The old grandma stood very still, so as not to disturb them; and it did not look as if the elf had noticed her. He was just going to lay one of the babies on the ground so that he could swing himself up to the cage with the other one—when he saw the house cat's green eyes glisten close beside him. He stood there, bewildered, with a young one in each hand.

He turned around and looked in all directions; then he became aware of the old grandma's presence. Then he did not hesitate long; but walked forward, stretched his arms as high as he could reach, for her to take one of the baby squirrels.

The old grandma did not wish to prove herself unworthy of the confidence, so she bent down and took the baby squirrel, and stood there and held it until the boy had swung himself up to the cage with the other one. Then he came back for the one he had entrusted to her care.

The next morning, when the farm folk had gathered together for breakfast, it was impossible for the old woman to refrain from telling them of what she had seen the night before. They all laughed at her, of course, and said that she had been only dreaming. There were no baby squirrels this early in the year.

But she was sure of her ground, and begged them to take a look into the squirrel cage and this they did. And there lay on the bed of leaves, four tiny half-naked, half blind baby squirrels, who were at least a couple of days old.

When the farmer himself saw the young ones, he said: "Be it as it may with this; but one thing is certain, we, on this farm, have behaved in such a manner that we are shamed before both animals and human beings." And, thereupon, he took the mother squirrel and all her young ones from the cage, and laid them in the old grandma's lap. "Go thou

out to the hazel-grove with them," said he, "and let them have their freedom back again!'"

VITTSKÖVLE *Saturday, March twenty-sixth.*

Two days later, another strange thing happened. A flock of wild geese came flying one morning, and lit on a meadow down in Eastern Skåne not very far from Vittskövle manor.

When the wild geese had been feeding a while, several children came along. The goose who was on guard at once raised herself into the air with noisy wing-strokes, so the whole flock should hear that there was danger on foot. All the wild geese flew upward; but the white one trotted along on the ground unconcerned. When he saw the others fly he raised his head and called after them: "You needn't fly away from these! They are only a couple of children!"

The little creature who picked a pine-cone in pieces, that he might get at the seeds. The children were so close to him that he did not dare to run across the meadow to the white one. He concealed himself under a big, dry thistle-leaf, and at the same time gave a warning-cry. But the white one had evidently made up his mind not to let himself be scared. He walked along on the ground all the while; and not once did he look to see in what direction they were going. When he finally did look up, they were right upon him. He was so dumfounded, and became so confused, he forgot that he could fly, and tried to get out of their reach by running. But the children followed, chasing him into a ditch, and there they caught him. The larger of the two stuck him under his arm and carried him off.

When the boy, who lay under the thistle-leaf saw this, he sprang up as if he wanted to take the goosey-gander away from them; then he must have remembered how little and powerless he was, for he threw himself on the knoll and beat upon the ground with his clenched fists.

The goosey-gander cried with all his might for help: "Thumbietot, come and help me! Oh, Thumbietot, come and help me!" The boy began to laugh in the midst of his distress. "Oh, yes! I'm just the right one to help anybody, I am!" said he. Anyway he got up and followed the goosey-gander. "I can't help him," said he, "but I shall at least find out where they are taking him."

He could see their footprints on a narrow path which led to the woods, and these he continued to follow.

Soon he came to a cross-road. Here the children must have separated, for there were footprints in two directions. The boy looked now as if all hope had fled. Then he saw a little white down on a heather-knoll, and he understood that the goosey-gander had dropped this by the wayside to let him know in which direction he had been carried; and therefore he continued his search. He followed the children through the entire wood. The goosey-gander he did not see; but wherever he was likely to miss his way, lay a little white down to put him right.

The boy continued faithfully to follow the bits of down. They led him out of the wood, across a couple of meadows, up on a road, and finally through the entrance of a broad allée. When the boy saw that this was some great manor, he thought he knew what had become of the goosey-gander. "No doubt the children have carried the goosey-gander to the manor and sold him there. By this time he's probably butchered." he said to himself. But he did not seem to be satisfied with anything less than proof positive.

On the east wing, there was a high arch leading into the courtyard. When he heard footsteps behind him; he stole behind a water-barrel which stood near the arch, and hid himself in haste.

Those who came up were some twenty young men from a folk-high-school, out on a walking tour.

One of them went over to the water-barrel and stooped down to

drink. He had a tin box such as botanists use hanging about his neck. He evidently thought that this was in his way, for he threw it down on the ground. With this, the lid flew open, and one could see that there were a few spring flowers in it.

The botanist's box dropped just in front of the boy; and he must have thought that here was his opportunity to get into the castle and find out what had become of the goosey-gander. He smuggled himself quickly into the box and concealed himself as well as he could under the anemones and colt's -foot.

He was hardly hidden before the young man picked the box up, hung it around his neck, and slammed down the cover.

Finally the company went into the castle. But if the boy had hoped for a chance to crawl out of that box, he was deceived; for the student carried it upon him all the while, and the boy was obliged to accompany him through all the rooms. It was a tedious tramp. The teacher stopped every other minute to explain and instruct.

If that boy had ever in his life been cross and impatient, he was given a good lesson in patience that day. It must have been a whole hour now that he had lain perfectly still.

At last the teacher went out into the courtyard again. And there he discoursed upon the tireless labour of mankind to procure for themselves tools and weapons, clothes and houses and ornaments.

But this dissertation the boy escaped hearing; for the student who carried him was thirsty again, and stole into the kitchen to ask for a drink of water. When the boy was carried into the kitchen, he should have tried to look around for the goosey-gander. He had begun to move; and as he did this, he happened to press too hard against the lid—and it flew open. As botanists' box-lids are always flying open, the student thought no more about the matter but pressed it down again. Then the cook asked him if he had a snake in the box.

"No, I have only a few plants," the student replied. "It was certainly something that moved there," insisted the cook. The student threw back the lid to show her that she was mistaken. "See for yourself—if—"

But he got no further, for now the boy dared not stay in the box any longer, but with one bound he stood on the floor, and out he rushed. The maids hardly had time to see what it was that ran, but they hurried after it, nevertheless.

The teacher still stood and talked when he was interrupted by shrill cries. "Catch him, catch him!" shrieked those who had come from the kitchen; and all the young men raced after the boy, who glided away faster than a rat. They tried to intercept him at the gate, but it was not so easy to get a hold on such a little creature, so, luckily, he got out in the open.

The boy did not dare to run down toward the open allée, but turned in another direction. He rushed through the garden into the back yard. All the while the people raced after him, shrieking and laughing. The poor little thing ran as hard as ever he could to get out of their way; but still it looked as though the people would catch up with him.

As he rushed past a labourer's cottage, he heard a goose cackle, and saw a white down lying on the doorstep. There, at last, was the goosey-gander! He had been on the wrong track before. He climbed up the steps—and into the hallway. Farther he couldn't come, for the door was locked. He heard how the goosey-gander cried and moaned inside, but he couldn't get the door open. The hunters that were pursuing him came nearer and nearer, and, in the room, the goosey-gander cried more and more pitifully. In this direst of needs the boy finally plucked up courage and pounded on the door with all his might.

A child opened it, and the boy looked into the room. In the middle of the floor sat a woman who held the goosey-gander tight to clip his quill-feathers. She didn't want to do him any harm. It was her intention

to let him in among her own geese, had she only succeeded in clipping his wings so he couldn't fly away. But a worse fate could hardly have happened to the goosey-gander, and he shrieked and moaned with all his might.

And a lucky thing it was that the woman hadn't started the clipping sooner. Now only two quills had fallen under the shears' when the door was opened—and the boy stood on the door-sill. But a creature like that the woman had never seen before. She couldn't believe anything else but that it was Goa-Nisse himself; and in her terror she dropped the shears, clasped her hands—and forgot to hold on to the goosey-gander.

As soon as he felt himself freed, he ran toward the door. He grabbed the boy by the neck-band and carried him along with him. On the stoop he spread his wings and flew up in the air; at the same time he made a graceful sweep with his neck and seated the boy on his smooth, downy back. And off they flew—while all Vittskövle stood and stared after them.

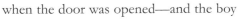

IN ÖVID CLOISTER PARK

All that day, when the wild geese played with the fox, the boy lay and slept in a deserted squirrel nest. When he awoke, along toward evening, he felt very uneasy. "Well, now I shall soon be sent home again! Then I'll have to exhibit myself before father and mother," thought he. But when he looked up and saw the wild geese, who lay and bathed in

Vomb Lake—not one of them said a word about his going. "They probably think the white one is too tired to travel home with me to-night," thought the boy.

The next morning the geese were awake at daybreak, long before sunrise. Now the boy felt sure that he'd have to go home; but, curiously enough, both he and the white goosey-gander were permitted to follow the wild ones on their morning tour. The boy couldn't comprehend the reason for the delay, but he figured it out in this way, that the wild geese did not care to send the goosey-gander on such a long journey until they had both eaten their fill.

The wild geese travelled over Övid's Cloister estate which was situated in a beautiful park east of the lake, and looked very imposing with its great castle; its well planned court surrounded by low walls and pavilions; its fine old-time garden with covered arbours, streams and fountains; its wonderful trees, trimmed bushes, and its evenly mown lawns with their beds of beautiful spring flowers.

When the wild geese rode over the estate there was no human being about. When they had carefully assured themselves of this, they lowered themselves toward the dog kennel, and shouted: "What kind of a little hut is this? What kind of a little hut is this?"

Instantly the dog came out of his kennel—furiously angry—and barked at the air.

"Do you call this a hut, you tramps! Can't you see that this is a great stone castle? Do you call this a hut? Have you seen huts with so many outhouses around them that they look like a whole village? You must know of a lot of huts that have their own church and their own parsonage; and that rule over the district and the peasant homes, wow, wow, wow? Do you call this a hut? You can't see a bit of land, from where you hang in the clouds, that does not obey commands from this hut, wow, wow, wow!"

All this the dog managed to cry out in one breath; and the wild geese flew back and forth over the estate, and listened to him until he was winded. But then they cried: "What are you so mad about? We didn't ask about the castle; we only wanted to know about your kennel, stupid!"

When the boy heard this joke, he laughed. "Think how many of these amusing things you would hear, if you could go with the wild geese through the whole country, all the way up to Lapland!" said he to himself. "And just now, when you are in such a bad fix, a trip like that would be the best thing you could hit upon."

The wild geese travelled to one of the wide fields, east of the estate, to eat grass-roots, and they kept this up for hours. In the meantime, the boy wandered in the great park which bordered the field. He hunted up a beech-nut grove and began to look up at the bushes, to see if a nut from last fall still hung there. But again and again the thought of the trip came over him, as he walked in the park. He pictured to himself what a fine time he would have if he went with the wild geese. To freeze and starve: that he believed he should have to do often enough; but as a recompense, he would escape both work and study. But he wondered what mother would say, if she knew that he had lived on raw fish and old winter-dried blossoms.

When the wild geese had finally eaten themselves full, they bore off toward the lake again, where they amused themselves with games until almost dinner time.

The wild geese challenged the white goosey-gander to take part in all kinds of sports. They had swimming races, running races, and flying races with him. The big tame one did his level best to hold his own, but the clever wild geese beat him every time. All the while, the boy sat on the goosey-gander's back and encouraged him, and had as much fun as the rest.

"This is just the life that suits me," thought the boy when he crept in

under the gander's wing. "But tomorrow, I suppose I'll be sent home."

He wasn't afraid of anything—except being sent home; but not even on Wednesday did the geese say anything to him about going. That day passed in the same way as Tuesday; and the boy grew more and more contented with the outdoor life.

On Wednesday he believed that the wild geese thought of keeping him with them; but he lost hope again.

Thursday began just like the other days; the geese fed on the broad meadows, and the boy hunted for food in the park. After a while Akka came to him, and asked if he had found anything to eat. No, he had not; and then she looked up a dry caraway herb, that had kept all its tiny seeds intact.

When the boy had eaten, Akka said that she thought he ran around in the park altogether too recklessly. She wondered if he knew how many enemies he had to guard against—he, who was so little. No, he didn't know anything at all about that. Then Akka began to enumerate them for him.

Whenever he walked in the park, she said, that he must look out for the fox and the marten; when he came to the shores of the lake, he must think of the otters; as he sat on the stone wall, he must not forget the weasels, who could creep through the smallest holes; and if he wished to lie down and sleep on a pile of leaves, he must first find out if the adders were not sleeping their winter sleep in the same pile. As soon as he came out in the open fields, he should keep an eye out for hawks and buzzards; for eagles and falcons that soared in the air. In the bramble-bush he could be captured by the sparrow-hawks; magpies and crows were found everywhere and in these he mustn't place any too much confidence. As soon as it was dusk, he must keep his ears open and listen for the big owls, who could come right up to him before he was aware of their presence.

The boy was not particularly afraid to die, but he didn't like the idea of being eaten up, so he asked Akka what he should do to protect himself from the carnivorous animals.

Akka answered at once that the boy should try to get on good terms with all the small animals in the woods and fields: with the squirrel-folk, and the hare-family; with bullfinches and the titmice and woodpeckers and larks. If he made friends with them, they could warn him against dangers, find hiding places for him, and protect him.

But later in the day, when the boy tried to profit by this counsel, and turned to Sirle Squirrel to ask for his protection, it was evident that he did not care to help him. "You surely can't expect anything from me, or the rest of the small animals!" said Sirle. "Don't you think we know that you are Nils the goose boy, who tore down the swallow's nest last year, crushed the starling's eggs, threw baby crows in the marl-ditch, caught thrushes in snares, and put squirrels in cages? You just help yourself as well as you can; and you may be thankful that we do not form a league against you, and drive you back to your own kind!"

This was just the sort of answer the boy would not have let go unpunished, in the days when he was Nils the goose boy. But now he was only fearful lest the wild geese, too, had found out how wicked he could be. It was true that he didn't have the power to do much harm now, but, little as he was, he could have destroyed many birds' nests, if he'd been in a mind to. Now he had been good. All day Thursday he thought it was surely on account of his wickedness that the wild geese did not care to take him along up to Lapland. And in the evening, when he heard that Sirle Squirrel's wife had been stolen, and her children were starving to death, he made up his mind to help them.

When the boy came into the park on Friday, he heard the bulfinches sing in every bush, of how Sirle Squirrel's wife had been carried away from her children by cruel robbers, and how Nils, the goose boy, had

risked his life among human beings, and taken the little squirrel children to her.

The boy was absolutely certain that both Akka and the wild geese had heard all this. But still Friday passed and not one word did they say about his remaining with them.

Until Saturday the wild geese fed in the fields around Övid, undisturbed by Smirre Fox.

But on Saturday morning, when they came out in the meadows, he lay in wait for them, and chased them from one field to another, and they were not allowed to eat in peace. Akka came to a decision quickly, raised herself into the air and flew with her flock several miles away, over plains and hills. They did not stop before they had arrived in the district of Vittskövle. But at Vittskövle the goosey-gander was stolen. If the boy had not used all his powers to help him he would never again have been found.

On Saturday evening, as the boy came back to Vomb Lake with the goosey-gander, he thought that he had done a good day's work; and he speculated a good deal on what Akka and the wild geese would say to him. The wild geese were not at all sparing in their praises, but they did not say the word he was longing to hear.

Then Sunday came again. A whole week had gone by since the boy had been bewitched, and he was still just as little.

But he didn't appear to be giving himself any extra worry on account of this thing. On Sunday afternoon he sat huddled together in a big, fluffy osier-bush, down by the lake, and blew on a reed-pipe. """"""

He had seen Akka, and all the wild geese, coming toward him in a long row. They walked so uncommonly slow and dignified-like, that the boy immediately understood that now he should learn what they intended to do with him.

When they stopped at last, Akka said: "You may well have reason to wonder at me, Thumbietot, who have not said thanks to you for saving

me from Smirre Fox. But I am one of those who would rather give thanks by deeds than words. I have sent word to the elf that bewitched you. At first he didn't want to hear anything about curing you; but I have sent message upon message to him, and told him how well you have conducted yourself among us. He greets you, and says, that as soon as you turn back home, you shall be human again."

But think of it! Just as happy as the boy had been when the wild geese began to speak, just that miserable was he when they had finished. He didn't say a word, but turned away and wept.

The boy was thinking of the care-free days and the banter; and of adventure and freedom and travel, high above the earth, that he should miss, and he actually bawled with grief. "I don't want to be human," said he. "I want to go with you to Lapland." "I'll tell you something," said Akka. "That elf is very touchy, and I'm afraid that if you do not accept his offer now, it will be difficult for you to coax him another time."

He had not cared for his father or mother; not for the school teacher; nor for his school-mates. All that they had wished to have him do—whether it had been work or play—he had only thought tiresome. Therefore there was no one whom he missed or longed for.

"I want to go with you to Lapland. That's why I've been good for a whole week!" "I don't want to forbid you to come along with us as far as you like," said Akka, "but think first if you wouldn't rather go home again. A day may come when you will regret this." "No," said the boy, "that's nothing to regret. I have never been as well off as here with you."

"Well then, let it be as you wish," said Akka.

"Thanks!" said the boy, and he felt so happy that he had to cry for very joy.

04

GLIMMINGE CASTLE

BLACK RATS AND GRAY RATS

In south-eastern Skåne—not far from the sea there is an old castle called Glimminge. It is a big and substantial stone house; and can be seen over the plain for miles around. It is not more than four stories high; but it is so ponderous that an ordinary farmhouse, which stands on the same estate, looks like a little children's playhouse in comparison.

At the time when Nils Holgersson wandered around with the wild geese, there were no human beings in Glimminge castle; but for all that, it was not without inhabitants. Every summer there lived a stork couple in a large nest on the roof. In a nest in the attic lived a pair of gray owls; in the secret passages hung bats; in the kitchen oven lived an old cat; and down in the cellar there were hundreds of old black rats.

Rats are not held in very high esteem by other animals; but the black rats at Glimminge castle were an exception. They were always mentioned with respect, because they had shown great valour in battle with their enemies; and much endurance under the great misfortunes which had befallen their kind. They nominally belong to a rat-folk who, at one time, had been very numerous and powerful, but who were now dying out. During a long period of time, the black rats owned Skåne and the whole country. They were found in every cellar; in every attic; in larders and cowhouses and barns; in breweries and flour-mills; in churches and castles; in every man-constructed building. But now they were banished from all

this—and were almost exterminated. Only in one and another old and secluded place could one run across a few of them; and nowhere were they to be found in such large numbers as in Glimminge castle. The people had certainly struggled with the black rats, but they couldn't do them any harm worth mentioning. Those who had conquered them were gray rats.

At first, these gray rats never dare to venture into the city, which was owned by the black rats. They marched forward in small and large companies to conquer the whole country.

It is almost impossible to comprehend why the black rats did not muster themselves into a great, united war-expedition to exterminate the gray rats, while these were still few in numbers. But the black rats were so certain of their power that they could not believe it possible for them to lose it. They sat still on their estates, and in the meantime the gray rats took from them farm after farm, city after city. They were starved out, forced out, rooted out. In Skåne they had not been able to maintain themselves in a single place except Glimminge castle.

The old castle had such secure walls and such few rat passages led through these, that the black rats had managed to protect themselves, and to prevent the gray rats from crowding in. Night after night, year after year, the struggle had continued between the aggressors and the defenders; but the black rats had kept faithful watch, and had fought with the utmost contempt for death, and, thanks to the fine old house, they had always conquered.

The gray rats that lived in the courtyard at Glimminge and in the vicinity, kept up a continuous warfare and tried to watch out for every possible chance to capture the castle. The gray rats must have known that it was because the human kind used Glimminge castle as a grain storehouse that the gray ones could not rest before they had taken possession of the place.

THE STORK *Monday, March twenty-eighth.*

Early one morning the wild geese who stood and slept on the ice in Vomb Lake were awakened by long calls from the air. "Trirop, Trirop!" it sounded, "Trianut, the crane, sends greetings to Akka, the wild goose, and her flock. To-morrow will be the day of the great crane dance on Kullaberg."

Akka raised her head and answered at once: "Greetings and thanks! Greetings and thanks!"

With that, the cranes flew farther; and the wild geese heard them for a long while—where they travelled and called out over every field, and every wooded hill: "Trianut sends greetings. To-morrow will be the day of the great crane dance on Kullaberg."

The wild geese were very happy over this invitation. "You're in luck," they said to the white goosey-gander, "to be permitted to attend the great crane dance on Kullaberg!" "Is it then so remarkable to see cranes dance?" asked the goosey-gander. "It is something that you have never even dreamed about!" replied the wild geese.

"Now we must think out what we shall do with Thumbietot to-morrow—so that no harm can come to him, while we run over to Kullaberg," said Akka. "Thumbietot shall not be left alone!" said the goosey-gander. "If the cranes won't let him see their dance, then I'll stay with him."

"No human being has ever been permitted to attend the Animal's Congress, at Kullaberg," said Akka, "and I shouldn't dare to take Thumbietot along. But we'll discuss this more at length later in the day. Now we must first and foremost think about getting something to eat."

With that Akka gave the signal to adjourn. On this day she also sought her feeding-place a good distance away, on Smirre Fox's account, and she didn't alight until she came to the swampy meadows a little south

of Glimminge castle.

On one side of the swampy meadow, there was a broad stone hedge. Toward evening when the boy finally raised his head, to speak to Akka, his glance happened to rest on this hedge. He uttered a little cry of surprise, and all the wild geese instantly looked up, and stared in the same direction. At first, both the geese and the boy thought that all the round, gray stones in the hedge had acquired legs, and were starting on a run; but soon they saw that it was a company of rats who ran over it. They moved very rapidly, and ran forward, tightly packed, line upon line, and were so numerous that, for some time, they covered the entire stone hedge.

The boy had been afraid of rats, even when he was a big, strong human being. Then what must his feelings be now, when he was so tiny that two or three of them could overpower him? One shudder after another travelled down his spinal column as he stood and stared at them.

But strangely enough, the wild geese seemed to feel the same aversion toward the rats that he did. When they were gone, they shook themselves as if their feathers had been mud-spattered.

"Such a lot of gray rats abroad!" said Iksi. "That's not a good omen."

For all of a sudden a big bird came down in the midst of the geese. He had procured for himself large black wings, long red legs, and a thick bill, which was too large for the little head, and weighed it down until it gave him a sad and worried look.

Akka at once straightened out the folds of her wings, and curtsied many times as she approached the stork. She wasn't specially surprised to see him in Skåne so early in the spring, because she knew that the male storks are in the habit of coming in good season to take a look at the nest, and see that it hasn't been damaged during the winter, before the female storks go to the trouble of flying over the East sea. But she wondered very much what it might signify that he sought her out, since storks prefer to associate with members of their own family.

"I can hardly believe that there is anything wrong with your house, Herr Ermenrich," said Akka.

A stork can seldom open his bill without complaining. But it was difficult for him to speak out. He stood for a long time and only clattered with his bill; afterward he spoke in a hoarse and feeble voice. He complained about everything: the nest—which was situated at the very top of the roof-tree at Glimminge castle—had been totally destroyed by winter storms; and no food could he get any more in Skåne. The people of Skåne were appropriating all his possessions. They dug out his marshes and laid waste his swamps. He intended to move away, and never return to it again.

Then the stork suddenly asked the geese if they had seen the gray rats who were marching toward Glimminge castle. When Akka replied that she had seen the horrid creatures, he began to tell her about the brave black rats who, for years, had defended the castle. "But this night Glimminge castle will fall into the gray rats' power," sighed the stork.

"And why just this night, Herr Ermenrich?" asked Akka.

"Well, because nearly all the black rats went over to Kullaberg last night," said the stork, "since they had counted on all the rest of the animals also hurrying there. But you see that the gray rats have stayed at home; and now they are mustering to storm the castle to-night, when it will be defended by only a few old creatures who are too feeble to go over to Kullaberg. They'll probably accomplish their purpose. But I have lived here in harmony with the black rats for so many years, that it does not please me to live in a place inhabited by their enemies."

Akka understood now that the stork had become so enraged over the gray rats' mode of action, that he had sought her out as an excuse to complain about them. "Have you sent word to the black rats, Herr Ermenrich?" she asked. "No," replied the stork, "that wouldn't be of any use. Before they can get back, the castle will be taken." "You mustn't be so sure of that, Herr Ermenrich," said Akka. "I know an old wild goose,

I do, who will gladly prevent outrages of this kind."

The stork raised his head and stared at Akka. She had neither claws nor bill that were fit for fighting; and, in the bargain, she was a day bird, and as soon as it grew dark she fell helplessly asleep, while the rats did their fighting at night.

But Akka had evidently made up her mind to help the black rats. She called Iksi from Vassijaure, and ordered him to take the wild geese over to Vonib Lake; and when the geese made excuses, she said authoritatively: "I believe it will be best for us all that you obey me. I must fly over to the big stone house, and if you follow me, the people on the place will be sure to see us, and shoot us down. The only one that I want to take with me on this trip is Thumbietot. He can be of great service to me because he has good eyes, and can keep awake at night."

The boy was in his most contrary mood that day. And when he heard what Akka said, he raised himself to his full height and stepped forward, his hands behind him and his nose in the air, and he intended to say that he, most assuredly, did not wish to take a hand in the fight with gray rats. She might look around for assistance elsewhere.

But the instant the boy was seen, the stork began to move. He had stood before, as storks generally stand, with head bent downward and the bill pressed against the neck. But now a gurgle was heard deep down in his windpipe; as though he would have laughed. Quick as a flash, he lowered the bill, grabbed the boy, and tossed him a couple of metres in the air. This feat he performed seven times, while the boy shrieked and the geese shouted: "What are you trying to do, Herr Ermenrich? That's not a frog. That's a human being, Herr Ermenrich."

Finally the stork put the boy down entirely unhurt. Thereupon he said to Akka, "I'll fly back to Glimminge castle now, mother Akka. All who live there were very much worried when I left. You may be sure they'll be very glad when I tell them that Akka, the wild goose, and

Thumbietot, the human elf, are on their way to rescue them." With that the stork craned his neck, raised his wings, and darted off like an arrow when it leaves a well-drawn bow. Akka understood that he was making fun of her, but she didn't let it bother her. She waited until the boy had found his wooden shoes, which the stork had shaken off; then she put him on her back and followed the stork. The boy had become so furious with the stork, that he actually sat and puffed. That long, red-legged thing believed he was of no account just because he was little; but he would show him what kind of a man Nils Holgersson from West Vemminghög was.

A couple of moments later Akka stood in the storks' nest. It had a wheel for foundation, and over this lay several grass-mats, and some twigs. The nest was so old that many shrubs and plants had taken root up there; and when the mother stork sat on her eggs in the round hole in the middle of the nest, she not only had the beautiful outlook over a goodly portion of Skåne to enjoy, but she had also the wild brier-blossoms and house-leeks to look upon.

On the edge of the stork-nest sat two gray owls, an old, gray-streaked cat, and a dozen old, decrepit rats with protruding teeth and watery eyes. They were not exactly the sort of animals one usually finds living peaceably together.

All the black rats were silent. One could see that they were in deep despair, and probably knew that they could neither defend their own lives nor the castle. The two owls sat and rolled their big eyes, and twisted their great, encircling eyebrows, and talked in hollow, ghost-like voices, about the awful cruelty of the gray rats, and that they would have to move away from their nest, because they had heard it said of them that they spared neither eggs nor baby birds. The old gray-streaked cat was positive that the gray rats would bite him to death, since they were coming into the castle in such great numbers, and he scolded the black

rats incessantly. "How could you be so idiotic as to let your best fighters go away?" said he. "How could you trust the gray rats? It is absolutely unpardonable!"

The twelve black rats did not say a word. But the stork, despite his misery, could not refrain from teasing the cat. "Don't worry so, Monsie house-cat!" said he. "Can't you see that mother Akka and Thumbietot have come to save the castle? You can be certain that they'll succeed. Now I must stand up to sleep—and I do so with the utmost calm. Tomorrow, when I awaken, there won't be a single gray rat in Glimminge castle."

The boy winked at Akka, and made a sign—as the stork stood upon the very edge of the nest, with one leg drawn up, to sleep—that he wanted to push him down to the ground; but Akka restrained him. She did not seem to be the least bit angry. Instead, she said in a confident tone of voice: "It would be pretty poor business if one who is as old as I am could not manage to get out of worse difficulties than this. If only Mr. and Mrs. Owl, who can stay awake all night, will fly off with a couple of messages for me, I think that all will go well."

Both owls were willing. Then Akka bade the gentleman owl that he should go and seek the black rats who had gone off, and counsel them to hurry home immediately. The lady owl she sent to Flammea, the steeple-owl, who lived in Lund cathedral, with a commission which was so secret that Akka only dared to confide it to her in a whisper.

THE RAT CHARMER

It was getting on toward midnight when the gray rats after a diligent search succeeded in finding an open air-hole in the cellar. This was pretty high upon the wall; but the rats got up on one another's shoulders, and it wasn't long before the most daring among them sat in the air-hole,

ready to force its way into Glimminge castle, outside whose walls so many of its forebears had fallen.

One after another of the gray rats followed the leader. They all kept very quiet; and all expected to be ambushed by the black rats. Not until so many of them had crowded into the cellar that the floor couldn't hold any more, did they venture farther.

Immediately upon their entrance the gray rats caught the scent of the grain, which was stored in great bins on the floor. But it was not as yet time for them to begin to enjoy their conquest. Not one of the narrow peep-holes did they leave uninspected, but they found no black rats.

The gray ones groped their way into the lord of the castle's great banquet hall—which stood there cold and empty, like all the other rooms in the old house. They even groped their way to the upper story, which had but one big, barren room. The only place they did not think of exploring was the big stork-nest on the roof—where, just at this time, the lady owl awakened Akka, and informed her that Flammea, the steeple owl, had granted her request, and had sent her the thing she wished for.

Since the gray rats had so conscientiously inspected the entire castle, they felt at ease. They took it for granted that the black rats had flown, and didn't intend to offer any resistance; and, with light hearts, they ran up into the grain bins.

But the gray rats had hardly swallowed the first wheat-grains, before the sound of a little shrill pipe was heard from the yard. The gray rats raised their heads, listened anxiously, ran a few steps as if they intended to leave the bin, then they turned back and began to eat once more.

Again the pipe sounded a sharp and piercing note—and now something wonderful happened. One rat, two rats—yes, a whole lot of rats left the grain, jumped from the bins and hurried down cellar by the shortest cut, to get out of the house. Still there were many gray rats left. These thought of all the toil and trouble it had cost them to win

Glimminge castle, and they did not want to leave it. But again they caught the tones from the pipe, and had to follow them. With wild excitement they rushed up from the bins, slid down through the narrow holes in the walls, and tumbled over each other in their eagerness to get out.

In the middle of the courtyard stood a tiny creature, who blew upon a pipe. All round him he had a whole circle of rats who listened to him, astonished and fascinated; and every moment brought more. Once he took the pipe from his lips—only for a second—put his thumb to his nose and wiggled his fingers at the gray rats; and then it looked as if they wanted to throw themselves on him and bite him to death; but as soon as he blew on his pipe they were in his power.

When the tiny creature had played all the gray rats out of Glimminge castle, he began to wander slowly from the courtyard out on the highway; and all the gray rats followed him, because the tones from that pipe sounded so sweet to their ears that they could not resist them.

The tiny creature walked before them and charmed them along with him, on the road to Vallby. He led them into all sorts of crooks and turns and bends, and wherever he went they had to follow. He blew continuously on his pipe, which appeared to be made from an animal's horn. No one knew, either, who had made it. Flammea, the steeple-owl, had found it in a niche, in Lund cathedral. She had shown it to Bataki, the raven; and they had both figured out that this was the kind of horn that was used in former times by those who wished to gain power over rats and mice. But the raven was Akka's friend; and it was from him she had learned that treasure like this. And it was true that the rats could not resist the pipe. The boy walked before them and played as long as the starlight lasted—and all the while they followed him. He played at daybreak; he played at sunrise; and the whole time the entire procession of gray rats followed him, and were enticed farther and farther away from the big grain loft at Glimminge castle.

05

THE GREAT CRANE DANCE ON KULLABERG

Tuesday, March twenty-ninth.

Although there are many magnificent buildings in Skåne, it must be acknowledged that there's not one among them that has such pretty walls as old Kullaberg. These remarkable mountain walls, with the blue sea beneath them, and the clear penetrating air above them, is what makes Kullaberg so dear to the people that great crowds of them haunt the place every day as long as the summer lasts. Every year the animals gather there for a big play-meeting. This is a custom that has been observed since time immemorial.

It is always beautiful weather on this day. The cranes are good weather prophets, and would not call the animals together if they expected rain. The air is clear, and nothing obstructs the vision.

But what the animals, on the other hand, observe, is one and another little dark cloud that comes slowly forward over the plain. And look! one of these clouds comes gradually along the coast of Öresund, and up toward Kullaberg. When the cloud has come just over the playground it stops, and, simultaneously, the entire cloud begins to ring and chirp, as if it was made of nothing but tone. It rises and sinks, rises and sinks, but all the while it rings and chirps. At last the whole cloud falls down over a knoll—all at once—and the next instant the knoll is entirely covered with gray larks, pretty red-white-gray bulfinches, speckled starlings and greenish-yellow titmice.

To the great reunion held the year that Nils Holgersson travelled around with the wild geese, came Akka and her flock—later than all the others. And that was not to be wondered at, for Akka had to fly over the whole of Skåne to get to Kullaberg. Beside, as soon as she awoke, she had been obliged to go out and hunt for Thumbietot, who, for many hours, had gone and played to the gray rats, and lured them far away from Glimminge castle. But it was not Akka who discovered the boy where he walked with his long following, and quickly sank down over him and caught him with the bill and swung into the air with him, but it was Herr Ermenrich, the stork! For Herr Ermenrich had also gone out to look for him; and after he had borne him up to the stork-nest, he begged his forgiveness for having treated him with disrespect the evening before. This pleased the boy immensely, and the stork and he became good friends. Akka, too, showed him that she felt very kindly toward him; she stroked her old head several times against his arms, and commended him because he had helped those who were in trouble.

But this one must say to the boy's credit: that he did not want to accept praise which he had not earned. "No, mother Akka," he said, "you mustn't think that I lured the gray rats away to help the black ones. I only wanted to show Herr Ermenrich that I was of some consequence."

He had hardly said this before Akka turned to the stork and asked if he thought it was advisable to take Thumbietot along to Kullaberg. "I mean, that we can rely on him as upon ourselves," said she. The stork at once advised, most enthusiastically, that Thumbietot be permitted to come along. "Certainly you shall take Thumbietot along to Kullaberg, mother Akka," said he. "It is fortunate for us that we can repay him for all that he has endured this night for our sakes. And since it still grieves me to think that I did not conduct myself in a becoming manner toward him the other evening, it is I who will carry him on my back—all the way to the meeting place."

Just as it has ever been the custom on Kullaberg, it was the crows who began the day's games and frolics with their flying-dance. They did not have to wait in vain, either; for as soon as the crows had finished, the hares came running. They dashed forward in a long row, without any apparent order. In some of the figures, one single hare came; in others, they ran three and four abreast. They had all raised themselves on two legs, and they rushed forward with such rapidity that their long ears swayed in all directions. As they ran, they spun round, made high leaps and beat their forepaws against their hind-paws so that they rattled. Some performed a long succession of somersaults, others doubled themselves up and rolled over like wheels; one stood on one leg and swung round; one walked upon his forepaws. There was no regulation whatever, but there was much that was droll in the hares' play; and the many animals who stood and watched them began to breathe faster.

Hundreds of wood-grouse in shining dark-brown array, and with bright red eyebrows, flung themselves up into a great oak that stood in the centre of the playground. The one who sat upon the topmost branch fluffed up his feathers, lowered his wings, and lifted his tail so that the white covert-feathers were seen. Thereupon he stretched his neck and sent forth a couple of deep notes from his thick throat. "Tjack, tjack, tjack," it sounded. More than this he could not utter. It only gurgled a few times way down in the throat. Then he closed his eyes and whispered: "Sis, sis, sis. Hear how pretty! Sis, sis, sis." While the first wood grouse was sissing, the three nearest began to sing; and before they had finished their song, the ten who sat lower down joined in; and thus it continued from branch to branch, until the entire hundred grouse sang and gurgled and sissed. They all fell into the same ecstasy during their song, and this affected the other animals like a contagious transport. Lately the blood had flowed lightly and agreeably; now it began to grow heavy and hot. "Yes, this is surely spring," thought all the animal folk.

"Winter chill has vanished. The fires of spring burn over the earth."

When the black grouse saw that the brown grouse were having such success, they could no longer keep quiet. As there was no tree for them to light on, they rushed down on the playground, where the heather stood so high that only their beautifully turned tail-feathers and their thick bills were visible—and they began to sing: "Orr, orr, orr."

Just as the black grouse began to compete with the brown grouse, something unprecedented happened. While all the animals thought of nothing but the grouse-game, a fox stole slowly over to the wild geese's knoll. He glided very cautiously, and came way up on the knoll before anyone noticed him. Suddenly a goose caught sight of him; and as she could not believe that a fox had sneaked in among the geese for any good purpose, she began to cry: "Have a care, wild geese! Have a care!" The fox struck her across the throat, but the wild geese had already heard the cry and they all raised themselves in the air. And when they had flown up, the animals saw Smirre Fox standing on the wild geese's knoll, with a dead goose in his mouth.

But because he had in this way broken the play-day's peace, such a punishment was meted out to Smirre Fox. Not a fox wished to lighten the sentence, since they all knew that the instant they attempted anything of the sort, they would be driven from the playground, and would nevermore be permitted to enter it. Smirre was banished from hunting grounds, home, resting places and retreats, which he had hitherto owned; and he must tempt fortune in foreign lands. So that all foxes in Skåne should know that Smirre was outlawed in the district, the oldest of the foxes bit off his right earlap. As soon as this was done, all the young foxes threw themselves on Smirre. For him there was no alternative except to take flight; and with all the young foxes in hot pursuit, he rushed away.

All this happened while black grouse and brown grouse were going

on with their games. But these birds lose themselves so completely in their song, that they neither hear nor see. Nor had they permitted themselves to be disturbed.

The forest birds' contest was barely over, before the stags came forward to show their wrestling game. There were several pairs of stags who fought at the same time. They rushed at each other with tremendous force, struck their antlers dashingly together, so that their points were entangled; and tried to force each other backward. The heather-heaths were torn up beneath their hoofs; the breath came like smoke from their nostrils; out of their throats strained hideous bellowings, and the froth oozed down on their shoulders.

On the knolls round about there was breathless silence while the skilled stag-wrestlers clinched. In all the animals new emotions were awakened. Each and all felt courageous and, strong; enlivened by returning powers; born again with the spring; sprightly, and ready for all kinds of adventures. They felt no enmity toward each other, although, everywhere, wings were lifted, neck-feathers raised and claws sharpened. If the stags had continued another instant, a wild struggle would have arisen on the knolls, for all had been gripped with a burning desire to show that they too were full of life because the winter's impotence was over and strength surged through their bodies.

A whisper went from knoll to knoll: "The cranes are coming!"

And then came the gray, dusk-clad birds with plumes in their wings. The big birds came gliding down the knoll with an abandon that was full of mystery. As they glided forward they swung round—half flying, half dancing. With wings gracefully lifted, they moved with an inconceivable rapidity. There was something marvellous and strange about their dance. It was as though gray shadows had played a game which the eye could scarcely follow. There was witchcraft in it. All those who had never before been on Kullaberg understood why the whole meeting took its

name from the crane's dance. There was wildness in it; but yet the feeling which it awakened was a delicious longing. No one thought any more about struggling. Instead, both the winged and those who had no wings, all wanted to raise themselves eternally, lift themselves above the clouds, seek that which was hidden beyond them, leave the oppressive body that dragged them down to earth and soar away toward the infinite.

Such longing after the unattainable, after the hidden mysteries back of this life, the animals felt only once a year; and this was on the day when they beheld the great crane dance.

06

IN RAINY WEATHER

Wednesday, March thirtieth.

It was the first rainy day of the trip. As long as the wild geese had remained in the vicinity of Vomb Lake, they had had beautiful weather; but on the day when they set out to travel farther north, it began to rain, and for several hours the boy had to sit on the goose-back, soaking wet, and shivering with the cold.

In the morning when they started, it had been clear and mild. The wild geese had flown high up in the air—evenly, and without haste—with Akka at the head maintaining strict discipline, and the rest in two oblique lines back of her. They had not taken the time to shout any witty sarcasms to the animals on the ground; but, as it was simply impossible for them to keep perfectly silent, they sang out continually—in rhythm with the wing-strokes—their usual coaxing call: "Where are you? Here am I. Where are you? Here am I."

Just as the first spring-showers pattered against the ground, there arose such shouts of joy from all the small birds in groves and pastures, that the whole air rang with them and the boy leaped high where he sat. "Now we'll have rain. Rain gives us spring; spring gives us flowers and green leaves; green leaves and flowers give us worms and insects; worms and insects give us food; and plentiful and good food is the best thing there is," sang the birds.

The wild geese, too, were glad of the rain which came to awaken the growing things from their long sleep, and to drive holes in the ice-roofs on the lakes. They were not able to keep up that seriousness any

longer, but began to send merry calls over the neighbourhood.

Thus it had sounded while the first showers fell, and when all were still glad of the rain. But when it continued to fall the whole afternoon, the wild geese grew impatient, and cried to the thirsty forests around Ivös lake: "Haven't you got enough yet? Haven't you got enough yet?"

In the afternoon, when they had lighted under a little stunted pine, in the middle of a large morass, where all was wet, and all was cold; where some knolls were covered with snow, and others stood up naked in a puddle of half-melted ice-water. The boy lay tucked in under the goosey-gander's wing, but could not sleep because he was cold and wet. He heard such a lot of rustling and rattling and stealthy steps and menacing voices, that he was terror-stricken and didn't know where he should go. He must go somewhere, where there was light and heat, if he wasn't going to be entirely scared to death.

"If I should venture where there are human beings, just for this night?" thought the boy. "Only so I could sit by a fire for a moment, and get a little food. I could go back to the wild geese before sunrise."

He crept from under the wing and slid down to the ground. He didn't awaken either the goosey-gander or any of the other geese, but stole, silently and unobserved, through the morass. He didn't know exactly where on earth he was: if he was in Skåne, in Småland, or in Blekinge. But just before he had gotten down in the morass, he had caught a glimpse of a large village, and thither he directed his steps. It wasn't long, either, before he discovered a road; and soon he was on the village street, which was long, and had planted trees on both sides, and was bordered with garden after garden.

The houses were of wood, and very prettily constructed. Most of them had gables and fronts, edged with carved mouldings, and glass doors, with here and there a coloured pane, opening on verandas. While the boy walked about and viewed the houses, he could hear, all the way

out to the road, how the people who sat in the warm cottages chattered and laughed. The words he could not distinguish, but he thought it was just lovely to hear human voices. "I wonder what they would say if I knocked and begged to be let in," thought he.

This was, of course, what he had intended to do all along, but now he felt again that shyness which always came over him now when he was near human beings. "I'll take a look around the town for a while longer," thought he, "before I ask anyone to take me in."

On one house there was a balcony. And just as the boy walked by, the doors were thrown open, and a yellow light streamed through the fine, sheer curtains. Then a pretty young fru came out on the balcony and leaned over the railing. "It's raining; now we shall soon have spring," said she. When the boy saw her he felt a strange anxiety. It was as though he wanted to weep. For the first time he was a bit uneasy because he had shut himself out from the human kind.

Shortly after that he walked by a shop. Outside the shop stood a red corn-drill. He stopped and looked at it; and finally crawled up to the driver's place, and seated himself. When he had got there, he smacked with his lips and pretended that he sat and drove. He thought what fun it would be to be permitted to drive such a pretty machine over a grainfield. For a moment he forgot what he was like now; then he remembered it, and jumped down quickly from the machine. Then a greater unrest came over him. After all, human beings were very wonderful and clever.

He walked by the post-office, and then he thought of all the newspapers which came every day, with news from all the four corners of the earth. He saw the apothecary's shop and the doctor's home, and he thought about the power of human beings, which was so great that they were able to battle with sickness and death. He came to the church. Then he thought how human beings had built it, that they might hear about another world than the one in which they lived, of God and the

resurrection and eternal life. And the longer he walked there, the better he liked human beings.

It is so with children that they never think any farther ahead than the length of their noses. That which lies nearest them, they want promptly, without caring what it may cost them. Nils Holgersson had not understood what he was losing when he chose to remain an elf; but now he began to be dreadfully afraid that, perhaps, he should never again get back to his right form. How in all the world should he go to work in order to become human?.

He crawled up on a doorstep, and seated himself in the pouring rain and meditated. "This thing is certainly much too difficult for one who has learned as little as I have," he thought at last. "It will probably wind up by my having to go back among human beings after all. I must ask the minister and the doctor and the schoolmaster and others who are learned, and may know a cure for such things."

This he concluded that he would do at once.Just about then he saw that a big owl came flying along, and alighted on one of the trees that bordered the village street. The next instant a lady owl, who sat under the cornice of the house, began to call out: "Kivitt, Kivitt! Are you at home again, Mr. Gray Owl? What kind of a time did you have abroad?"

"Thank you, Lady Brown Owl. I had a very comfortable time," said the gray owl. "Has anything out of the ordinary happened here at home during my absence?"

"Not here in Blekinge, Mr. Gray Owl; but in Skåne a marvellous thing has happened! A boy has been transformed by an elf into a goblin no bigger than a squirrel; and since then he has gone to Lapland with a tame goose."

"That's a remarkable bit of news, a remarkable bit of news. Can he never be human again, Lady Brown Owl? Can he never be human again?"

"That's a secret, Mr. Gray Owl; but you shall hear it just the same.

The elf has said that if the boy watches over the goosey-gander, so that he comes home safe and sound, and—"

"What more, Lady Brown Owl? What more? What more?"

"Fly with me up to the church tower, Mr. Gray Owl, and you shall hear the whole story! I fear there may be someone listening down here in the street." With that, the owls flew their way; but the boy flung his cap in the air, and shouted: "If I only watch over the goosey-gander, so that he gets back safe and sound, then I shall become a human being again. Hurrah! Hurrah! Then I shall become a human being again!"

He shouted "hurrah" until it was strange that they did not hear him in the houses—but they didn't, and he hurried back to the wild geese, out in the wet morass, as fast as his legs could carry him.

07

BY RONNEBY RIVER

Friday, April first.

Neither the wild geese nor Smirre Fox had believed that they should ever run across each other after they had left Skåne. Smirre Fox so far he had kept himself in the northern parts of the province; and since he had not as yet seen any manor parks, or hunting grounds filled with game and dainty young deer, he was more disgruntled than he could say.

One afternoon, when Smirre tramped around in the desolate forest district of Mellanbygden, not far from Ronneby River, he saw a flock of wild geese fly through the air. Instantly he observed that one of the geese was white and then he knew, of course, with whom he had to deal.

Smirre began immediately to hunt the geese—just as much for the pleasure of getting a good square meal, as for the desire to be avenged. He saw that they flew eastward until they came to Ronneby River. Then they changed their course, and followed the river toward the south. He understood that they intended to seek a sleeping-place along the river-banks, and he thought that he should be able to get hold of a pair of them without much trouble. But when Smirre finally discovered the place where the wild geese had taken refuge, he observed they had chosen such a well-protected spot, that he couldn't get near.

It was cold and blustery spring-winter; all the trees were nude. The wild geese thanked their good fortune that they had found a sand-strip large enough for them to stand upon, on a steep mountain wall. In front of them rushed the river, which was strong and violent in the snow-melting time; behind them they had an impassable mountain rock wall,

and overhanging branches screened them. They couldn't have it better.

The geese were asleep instantly; but the boy couldn't get a wink of sleep. He could see nothing, and only hear a little; and he thought if any harm came to the goosey-gander, he couldn't save him.

Smirre stood on the mountain's summit and looked down upon the wild geese. "You can't climb such a steep mountain; you can't swim in such a wild torrent; and there isn't the tiniest strip of land below the mountain which leads to the sleeping-place." But as Smirre lay lay there, that he wished the wild geese were dead, even if he, himself, should not have the satisfaction of eating them.

When Smirre's resentment had reached this height, he heard rasping in a large pine that grew close to him, and saw a squirrel come down from the tree, hotly pursued by a marten. Neither of them noticed Smirre; and he sat quietly and watched the chase, which went from tree to tree. He looked at the squirrel, who moved among the branches as lightly as though he'd been able to fly. He looked at the marten, who was not as skilled at climbing as the squirrel, but who still ran up and along the branches just as securely as if they had been even paths in the forest.

As soon as the squirrel had been captured, and the chase was ended, Smirre walked over to the marten. He greeted the marten in a very friendly manner, and wished him good luck with his catch. The marten, with his long and slender body, his fine head, his soft skin, and his light brown neck-piece, looked like a little marvel of beauty—but in reality was nothing but a crude forest dweller—hardly answered him. "It surprises me," said Smirre, "that such a fine hunter as you are should be satisfied with chasing squirrels when there is much better game within reach." Here he paused; but when the marten only grinned impudently at him, he continued: "Can it be possible that you haven't seen the wild geese that stand under the mountain wall? or are you not a good enough climber to get down to them?"

This time he had no need to wait for an answer. The marten rushed up to him with back bent, and every separate hair on end. "Have you seen wild geese?" he hissed. "Where are they? Tell me instantly, or I'll bite your neck off!" "No! you must remember that I'm twice your size—so be a little polite. I ask nothing better than to show you the wild geese."

The next instant the marten was on his way down the steep; and while Smirre sat and watched how he swung his snake-like body from branch to branch, he thought: "That pretty tree-hunter has the wickedest heart in all the forest. I believe that the wild geese will have me to thank for a bloody awakening."

But just as Smirre was waiting to hear the geese's death-rattle, he saw the marten tumble from branch to branch—and plump into the river so the water splashed high. Soon thereafter, wings beat loudly and strongly and all the geese went up in a hurried flight.

Smirre intended to hurry after the geese, but he was so curious to know how they had been saved, that he sat there until the marten came clambering up. That poor thing was soaked in mud, and stopped every now and then to rub his head with his forepaws. "Now wasn't that just what I thought—that you were a booby, and would go and tumble into the river?" said Smirre, contemptuously.

"I haven't acted boobyishly. You don't need to scold me," said the marten. "I sat—all ready—on one of the lowest branches and thought how I should manage to tear a whole lot of geese to pieces, when a little creature, no bigger than a squirrel, jumped up and threw a stone at my head with such force, that I fell into the water; and before I had time to pick myself up—"

The marten didn't have to say any more. Smirre was already a long way off in pursuit of the wild geese. In the meantime Akka had flown southward. She followed the river as long as she saw it winding through the moon-lit landscape like a black, shining snake. In this way she came way

down to Djupafors—where the river first hides itself in an underground channel—and then clear and transparent, as though it were made of glass, rushes down in a narrow cleft, and breaks into bits against its bottom in glittering drops and flying foam. Below the white falls lay a few stones, between which the water rushed away in a wild torrent cataract. Here mother Akka alighted. This was another good sleeping-place—especially this late in the evening, when no human beings moved about.

The geese fell asleep instantly, while the boy could find no rest in sleep, but sat beside them that he might watch over the goosey-gander.

After a while, Smirre came running along the river-shore. He spied the geese immediately where they stood out in the foaming whirlpools, and understood that he couldn't get at them here, either. Still he couldn't make up his mind to abandon them, but seated himself on the shore and looked at them. He felt very much humbled, and thought that his entire reputation as a hunter was at stake.

All of a sudden, he saw an otter come creeping up from the falls with a fish in his mouth. Smirre approached him. "You're a remarkable one, who can content yourself with catching a fish, while the stones are covered with geese!" said Smirre. The otter didn't turn his head once in the direction of the river. He was a vagabond—like all otters—and had fished many times by Vomb Lake, and probably knew Smirre Fox. "I know very well how you act when you want to coax away a salmon-trout, Smirre," said he.

"Oh! is it you, Gripe?" said Smirre, and was delighted; for he knew that this particular otter was a quick and accomplished swimmer. "I don't wonder that you do not care to look at the wild geese, since you can't manage to get out to them." But the otter, who had swimming-webs between his toes, and a stiff tail—which was as good as an oar—and a skin that was water-proof, didn't wish to have it said of him that there was a waterfall that he wasn't able to manage. He turned toward the

stream; and as soon as he caught sight of the wild geese, he threw the fish away, and rushed down the steep shore and into the river.

If the nightingales in Djupafors had been at home, they would have sung for many a day of Gripe's struggle with the rapid. For the otter was thrust back by the waves many times, and carried down river; but he fought his way steadily up again. He swam forward in still water; he crawled over stones, and gradually came nearer the wild geese. It was a perilous trip, which might well have earned the right to be sung by the nightingales.

Smirre followed the otter's course with his eyes as well as he could. At last he saw that the otter was in the act of climbing up to the wild geese. But just then it shrieked shrill and wild. The otter tumbled backward into the water, and dashed away as if he had been a blind kitten. An instant later, there was a great crackling of geese's wings. They raised themselves and flew away to find another sleeping-place.

The otter soon came on land. He said nothing, but commenced to lick one of his forepaws. When Smirre sneered at him because he hadn't succeeded, he broke out: "It was not the fault of my swimming-art, Smirre. I had raced all the way over to the geese, and was about to climb up to them, when a tiny creature came running, and jabbed me in the foot with some sharp iron. It hurt so, I lost my footing, and then the current took me."

He didn't have to say any more. Smirre was already far away on his way to the wild geese.

Once again Akka and her flock had to take a night fly. Fortunately, the moon had not gone down; and with the aid of its light, she succeeded in finding another of those sleeping-places which she knew in that neighbourhood. A little south of the city and not far from the sea, lies Ronneby health-spring, with its bath house and spring house; with its big hotel and summer cottages for the spring's guests. All these stand

empty and desolate in winter—which the birds know perfectly well; and many are the bird-companies who seek shelter on the deserted buildings' balustrades and balconies during hard storm-times.

Here the wild geese lit on a balcony, and, as usual, they fell asleep at once. The balcony faced south, so the boy had an outlook over the sea. And since he could not sleep, he sat there and saw how pretty it looked when sea and land meet.

The boy observed how mild and friendly nature was; and he began to feel calmer than he had been before, that night. Then, suddenly, he heard a sharp and ugly yowl from the bath-house park; and when he stood up he saw, in the white moonlight, a fox standing on the pavement under the balcony. For Smirre had followed the wild geese once more. But when he had found the place where they were quartered, he had understood that it was impossible to get at them in any way; then he had not been able to keep from yowling with chagrin.

When the fox yowled in this manner, old Akka, the leader-goose, was awakened. Although she could see nothing, she thought she recognised the voice. "Is it you who are out to-night, Smirre?" said she. "Yes," said Smirre, "it is I; and I want to ask what you geese think of the night?"

"Do you mean to say that it is you who have sent the marten and otter against us?" asked Akka. "A good turn shouldn't be denied," said Smirre. "You once played the goose-game with me, now I have begun to play the fox-game with you; and I'm not inclined to let up on it so long as a single one of you still lives even if I have to follow you the world over!"

"You, Smirre, ought at least to think whether it is right for you, who are weaponed with both teeth and claws, to hound us in this way; we, who are without defence," said Akka.

Smirre thought that Akka sounded scared, and he said quickly: "If you, Akka, will take that Thumbietot—who has so often opposed me—and throw him down to me, I'll promise to make peace with you. Then

I'll never more pursue you or any of yours." "I'm not going to give you Thumbietot," said Akka. "From the youngest of us to the oldest, we would willingly give our lives for his sake!" "Since you're so fond of him," said Smirre, "I'll promise you that he shall be the first among you that I will wreak vengeance upon."

Akka said no more, and after Smirre had sent up a few more yowls, all was still. The boy lay all the while awake. Now it was Akka's words to the fox that prevented him from sleeping. Never had he dreamed that he should hear anything so great as that anyone was willing to risk life for his sake. From that moment, it could no longer be said of Nils Holgersson that he did not care for anyone.

08

KARLSKRONA

Saturday, April second.

It was a moonlight evening in Karlskrona—calm and beautiful. But earlier in the day, there had been rain and wind; and the people must have thought that the bad weather still continued, for hardly one of them had ventured out on the streets.

While the city lay there so desolate, Akka, the wild goose, and her flock, came flying toward it over Vemmön and Pantarholmen. They couldn't remain inland because they were disturbed by Smirre Fox wherever they lighted.

When the boy rode along high up in the air, and looked at the sea and the islands which spread themselves before him, he thought that everything appeared so strange and spook-like. He thought that just for this one night he wanted to be brave, and not afraid—when he saw something that really frightened him. It was a high cliff island, which was covered with big, angular blocks; and between the blocks shone specks of bright, shining gold.

After the geese descended, the boy was astonished that he could have seen things so awry. In the first place, the big stone blocks were nothing but houses. The whole island was a city; and the shining gold specks were street lamps and lighted window-panes. There were boats and ships of every description, that lay anchored all around the island. On the side which lay toward the land were mostly row-boats and sailboats and small coast steamers; but on the side that faced the sea lay armour-clad battleships.

Now what city might this be? That, the boy could figure out because he saw all the battleships. All his life he had loved ships, although he had had nothing to do with any, except the galleys which he had sailed in the road ditches. He knew very well that this city—where so many battleships lay—couldn't be any place but Karlskrona.

This was a pretty safe place for those who wanted to get away from a fox, and the boy began to wonder if he couldn't venture to crawl in under the goosey-gander's wing for this one night. It would do him good to get a little sleep. He should try to see a little more of the dock and the ships after it had grown light.

The boy himself thought it was strange that he could keep still and wait until the next morning to see the ships. He certainly had not slept five minutes before he slipped out from under the wing and slid down the lightning-rod and the waterspout all the way down to the ground.

Soon he stood on a big square which spread itself in front of the church. It was a lucky thing that the square was entirely deserted. There wasn't a human being about—unless he counted a statue that stood on a high pedestal. The boy gazed long at the statue, which represented a big, brawny man in a three-cornered hat, long waistcoat, knee-breeches and coarse shoes, and wondered what kind of a one he was. He held a long stick in his hand, and he looked as if he would know how to make use of it, too—for he had an awfully severe countenance, with a big, hooked nose and an ugly mouth.

"What is that long-lipped thing doing here?" said the boy at last. He had never felt so small and insignificant as he did that night. He tried to jolly himself up a bit by saying something audacious. Then he thought no more about the statue, but betook himself to a wide street which led down to the sea.

But the boy hadn't gone far before he heard that someone was following him. Someone was walking behind him, who stamped on the

stone pavement with heavy footsteps, and pounded on the ground with a hard stick. It sounded as if the bronze man up in the square had gone out for a promenade.

The boy listened after the steps, while he ran down the street, and he became more and more convinced that it was the bronze man. The ground trembled, and the houses shook. The boy grew panic-stricken when he thought of what he had just said to him.

"Perhaps he is only out walking for recreation," thought the boy. "Surely he can't be offended with me for the words I spoke. They were not at all badly meant."

The boy turned into a side street which led east. First and foremost, he wanted to get away from the one who tramped after him. But he heard that the bronze man had switched off to the same street; and then the boy was so scared that he didn't know what he would do with himself. Then he saw on his right an old frame church, which lay a short distance away from the street in the centre of a large grove. Not an instant did he pause to consider, but rushed on toward the church. "If I can only get there, then I'll surely be shielded from all harm," thought he.

As he ran forward, he suddenly caught sight of a man who stood on a gravel path and beckoned to him. "There is certainly someone who will help me!" thought the boy; he became intensely happy, and hurried off in that direction. But when he came up to the man who stood on the edge of the gravel path, upon a low pedestal, he was absolutely thunderstruck; for he saw that the entire man was made of wood.

He stood there and stared at him. He was a thick-set man on short legs, with a broad, ruddy countenance, shiny, black hair and full black beard. On his head he wore a wooden hat; on his body, a brown wooden coat; around his waist, a black wooden belt; on his legs he had wide wooden knee-breeches and wooden stockings; and on his feet black wooden shoes. He was newly painted and newly varnished, so that he glistened and shone in the moonlight. This undoubtedly had a good deal to do with giving him such a good-natured appearance, that the boy at once placed confidence in him.

In his left hand he held a wooden slate, and there the boy read:

Most humbly I beg you, Though voice I may lack: Come drop a penny, do; But lift my hat!

Oh ho! the man was only a poor-box. The boy felt that he had been done. And now he remembered that grandpa had also spoken of the wooden man, and said that all the children in Karlskrona were so fond of him. He had something so old-timy about him, that one could well take him to be many hundred years old; and at the same time, he looked so strong and bold, and animated—just as one might imagine that folks looked in olden times. But now the boy heard him. He turned from the street and came into the churchyard. He followed him here too! Where should the boy go?

Just then he saw the wooden man bend down to him and stretch forth his big, broad hand. It was impossible to believe anything but good of him; and with one jump, the boy stood in his hand. The wooden man lifted him to his hat—and stuck him under it.

The boy was just hidden, and the wooden man had just gotten his arm in its right place again, when the bronze man stopped in front of him and banged the stick on the ground, so that the wooden man shook on his pedestal. Thereupon the bronze man said in a strong and resonant voice: "Who might this one be?"

The wooden man's arm went up, so that it creaked in the old woodwork, and he touched his hat brim as he replied: "Rosenbom, by Your Majesty's leave. Once upon a time boatswain on the man-of-war, Dristigheten; after completed service, sexton at the Admiral's church—and, lately, carved in wood and exhibited in the churchyard as a poor-box."

The boy gave a start when he heard that the wooden man said

"Your Majesty." For now, when he thought about it, he knew that the statue on the square represented the one who had founded the city. It was probably no less an one than Charles the Eleventh himself, whom he had encountered.

"Can he also tell me if he has seen a little brat who runs around in the city to-night? He's an impudent rascal, if I get hold of him, I'll teach him manners!" With that, he again pounded on the ground with his stick, and looked fearfully angry.

"By Your Majesty's leave, I have seen him," said the wooden man; and the boy was so scared that he commenced to shake where he sat under the hat and looked at the bronze man through a crack in the wood. But he calmed down when the wooden man continued: "Your Majesty is on the wrong track. That youngster certainly intended to run into the shipyard, and conceal himself there."

"Does he say so, Rosenbom? Well then, don't stand still on the pedestal any longer but come with me and help me find him. Four eyes are better than two, Rosenbom."

But the wooden man answered in a doleful voice: "I would most humbly beg to be permitted to stay where I am. I look well and sleek because of the paint, but I'm old and mouldy, and cannot stand moving about."

The bronze man was not one of those who liked to be contradicted. "What sort of notions are these? Come along, Rosenbom!" Then he raised his stick and gave the other one a resounding whack on the shoulder. "Does Rosenbom not see that he holds together?"

With that they broke off and walked forward on the streets of Karlskrona—large and mighty—until they came to a high gate, which led to the shipyard. Just outside and on guard walked one of the navy's jack-tars, but the bronze man strutted past him and kicked the gate open without the jack-tar's pretending to notice it.

As soon as they had gotten into the shipyard, they saw before them a wide, expansive harbor separated by pile-bridges. "Where does Rosenbom think it most advisable for us to begin the search?" said the bronze man.

"Such an one as he could most easily conceal himself in the hall of models," replied the wooden man.

On a narrow land-strip which stretched to the right from the gate, all along the harbour, lay ancient structures. The bronze man walked over to a building with low walls, small windows, and a conspicuous roof. He pounded on the door with his stick until it burst open; and tramped up a pair of worn-out steps. Soon they came into a large hall, which was filled with tackled and full-rigged little ships. The boy understood without being told, that these were models for the ships which had been built for the Swedish navy.

When the boy was carried around among all this, he was awed. "Fancy that such big, splendid ships have been built here in Sweden!" he thought to himself.

He had plenty of time to see all that was to be seen in there; for when the bronze man saw the models, he forgot everything else. He examined them all, from the first to the last, and asked about them. And Rosenbom, the boatswain on the Dristigheten, told as much as he knew of the ships' builders, and of those who had manned them; and of the fates they had met.

Both he and the bronze man had the most to say about the fine old wooden ships. The new battleships they didn't exactly appear to understand. "I can hear that Rosenbom doesn't know anything about these new-fangled things," said the bronze man. "Therefore, let us go and look at something else; for this amuses me, Rosenbom."

By this time he had entirely given up his search for the boy, who felt calm and secure where he sat in the wooden hat.

Thereupon both men wandered through the big establishment. And the very last, they went into an open court, where the galley models of old men-of-war were grouped; and a more remarkable sight the boy had never beheld; for these models had inconceivably powerful and terror-striking faces. They were big, fearless and savage: filled with the same proud spirit that had fitted out the great ships. They were from another time than his. He thought that he shrivelled up before them.

But when they came in here, the bronze man said to the wooden man: "Take off thy hat, Rosenbom, for those that stand here! They have all fought for the fatherland."

And Rosenbom—like the bronze man—had forgotten why they had begun this tramp. Without thinking, he lifted the wooden hat from his head and shouted:

"I take off my hat to the one who chose the harbour and founded the shipyard and recreated the navy; to the monarch who has awakened all this into life!"

"Thanks, Rosenbom! That was well spoken. Rosenbom is a fine man. But what is this, Rosenbom?"

For there stood Nils Holgersson, right on the top of Rosenbom's bald pate. He wasn't afraid any longer; but raised his white toboggan hood, and shouted: "Hurrah for you, Longlip!"

The bronze man struck the ground hard with his stick, for now the sun ran up, and, at the same time, both the bronze man and the wooden man vanished—as if they had been made of mists. The wild geese flew up from the church tower, and swayed back and forth over the city. Instantly they caught sight of Nils Holgersson; and then the big white one darted down from the sky and fetched him.

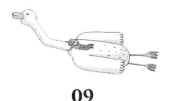

09

ÖLAND's SOUTHERN POINT

Sunday, April third.

The wild geese went out on a wooded island to feed. There they happened to run across a few gray geese, who were surprised to see them—since they knew very well that their kinsmen, the wild geese, usually travel over the interior of the country.

A gray goose, who appeared to be as old and as wise as Akka herself, said: "Smirre Fox will be sure to follow you all the way up to Lapland. If I were in your place, I shouldn't travel north over Småland, but would take the outside route over Öland instead, so that he'll be thrown off the track entirely. You must remain for a couple of days on Öland's southern point. There you'll find lots of food and lots of company. I don't believe you'll regret it, if you go over there."

It was certainly very sensible advice. As soon as the wild geese had eaten all they could hold, they started on the trip to Öland.

April third to sixth.

On the most southerly part of Öland lies a royal demesne, which is called Ottenby. It is a rather large estate which extends from shore to shore, straight across the island; and it is remarkable because it has always been a haunt for large bird-companies.

It was a low sand-shore with stones and pools, and a lot of cast-up sea-weed. If the boy had been permitted to choose, it isn't likely that he would have thought of alighting there; but the birds probably looked upon this as a veritable paradise. Ducks and geese walked about and fed

on the meadow; nearer the water, ran snipe, and other coast-birds. The loons lay in the sea and fished, but the life and movement was upon the long sea-weed banks along the coast. There the birds stood side by side close together and picked grub-worms—which must have been found there in limitless quantities for it was very evident that there was never any complaint over a lack of food.

The great majority were going to travel farther, and had only alighted to take a short rest; and as soon as the leader of a flock thought that his comrades had recovered themselves sufficiently he said, "If you are ready now, we may as well move on."

"No, wait, wait! We haven't had anything like enough," said the followers.

"You surely don't believe that I intend to let you eat so much that you will not be able to move?" said the leader, and flapped his wings and started off.

Along the outermost sea-weed banks lay a flock of swans. They didn't bother about going on land, but rested themselves by lying and rocking on the water. Now and then they dived down with their necks and brought up food from the sea-bottom. When they had gotten hold of anything very good, they indulged in loud shouts that sounded like trumpet calls.

When the boy heard that there were swans on the shoals, he hurried out to the sea-weed banks. He had never before seen wild swans at close range. He had luck on his side, so that he got close up to them.

The boy was not the only one who had heard the swans. Both the wild geese and the gray geese and the loons swam out between the banks, laid themselves in a ring around the swans and stared at them. The swans ruffled their feathers, raised their wings like sails, and lifted their necks high in the air. Occasionally one and another of them swam up to a goose, or a great loon, or a diving-duck, and said a few words. And then

it appeared as though the one addressed hardly dared raise his bill to reply.

But then there was a little loon—a tiny mischievous baggage—who couldn't stand all this ceremony. He dived suddenly, and disappeared under the water's edge. Soon after that, one of the swans let out a scream, and swam off so quickly that the water foamed. Then he stopped and began to look majestic once more. But soon, another one shrieked in the same way as the first one, and then a third.

The little loon wasn't able to stay under water any longer, but appeared on the water's edge, little and black and venomous. The swans rushed toward him; but when they saw what a poor little thing it was, they turned abruptly—as if they considered themselves too good to quarrel with him. Then the little loon dived again, and pinched their feet. It certainly must have hurt; and the worst of it was, that they could not maintain their dignity. At once they took a decided stand. They began to beat the air with their wings so that it thundered; came forward a bit—as though they were running on the water—got wind under their wings, and raised themselves.

When the swans were gone they were greatly missed; and those who had lately been amused by the little loon's antics scolded him for his thoughtlessness.

The next morning it was just as cloudy. The wild geese walked about on the meadow and fed; but the boy had gone to the seashore to gather mussels. There were plenty of them; and when he thought that the next day, perhaps, they would be in some place where they couldn't get any food at all, he concluded that he would try to make himself a little bag, which he could fill with mussels. He found an old sedge on the meadow, which was strong and tough; and out of this he began to braid a knapsack. He worked at this for several hours, but he was well satisfied with it when it was finished.

At dinner time all the wild geese came running and asked him if he had seen anything of the white goosey-gander. "No, he has not been with me," said the boy. "We had him with us all along until just lately," said Akka, "but now we no longer know where he's to be found."

The boy jumped up, and was terribly frightened. He asked if any fox or eagle had put in an appearance, or if any human being had been seen in the neighbourhood. But no one had noticed that. The goosey-gander had probably lost his way in the mist.

The boy started off immediately to hunt for him. The mist shielded him, so that he could run wherever he wished without being seen, but it also prevented him from seeing. He ran southward along the shore—all the way down to the lighthouse and the mist cannon on the island's extreme point. It was the same bird confusion everywhere, but no goosey-gander. He ventured over to Ottenby estate, and he searched every one of the old, hollow oaks in Ottenby grove, but he saw no trace of the goosey-gander.

He searched until it began to grow dark. Then he had to turn back again to the eastern shore. He walked with heavy steps, and was fearfully blue. He didn't know what would become of him if he couldn't find the goosey-gander. There was no one whom he could spare less.

But when he wandered over the sheep meadow, what was that big, white thing that came toward him in the mist if it wasn't the goosey-gander? He was all right, and very glad that, at last, he had been able to find his way back to the others. The mist had made him so dizzy, he said, that he had wandered around on the big meadow all day long. The boy threw his arms around his neck, for very joy, and begged him to take care of himself, and not wander away from the others. And he promised, positively, that he never would do this again. No, never again.

But the next morning, when the boy went down to the beach and hunted for mussels, the geese came running and asked if he had seen the

goosey-gander. No, of course he hadn't. "Well, then the goosey-gander was lost again. He had gone astray in the mist, just as he had done the day before."

The boy ran off in great terror and began to search. He found one place where the Ottenby wall was so tumble-down that he could climb over it. Later, he went about, first on the shore which gradually widened and became so large that there was room for fields and meadows and farms—then up on the flat highland, which lay in the middle of the island, and where there were no buildings except windmills, and where the turf was so thin that the white cement shone under it.

Meanwhile, he could not find the goosey-gander; and as it drew on toward evening, and the boy must return to the beach, he couldn't believe anything but that his travelling companion was lost. He was so depressed, he did not know what to do with himself.

He had just climbed over the wall again when he heard a stone crash down close beside him. As he turned to see what it was, he thought that he could distinguish something that moved on a stone pile which lay close to the wall. He stole nearer, and saw the goosey-gander come trudging wearily over the stone pile, with several long fibres in his mouth. The goosey-gander didn't see the boy, and the boy did not call to him, but thought it advisable to find out first why the goosey-gander time and again disappeared in this manner.

And he soon learned the reason for it. Up in the stone pile lay a young gray goose, who cried with joy when the goosey-gander came. The boy crept near, so that he heard what they said; then he found out that the gray goose had been wounded in one wing, so that she could not fly, and that her flock had travelled away from her, and left her alone. She had been near death's door with hunger, when the white goosey-gander had heard her call, the other day, and had sought her out. Ever since, he had been carrying food to her. They had both hoped that she would be

well before they left the island, but, as yet, she could neither fly nor walk. She was very much worried over this, but he comforted her with the thought that he shouldn't travel for a long time. At last he bade her good-night, and promised to come the next day.

The boy let the goosey-gander go; and as soon as he was gone, he stole, in turn, up to the stone heap. He was angry because he had been deceived, and now he wanted to say to that gray goose that the goosey-gander was his property. He was going to take the boy up to Lapland, and there would be no talk of his staying here on her account. But now, when he saw the young gray goose close to, he understood. She had the prettiest little head; her feather-dress was like soft satin, and the eyes were mild and pleading.

When she saw the boy, she wanted to run away; but the left wing was out of joint and dragged on the ground, so that it interfered with her movements. "You mustn't be afraid of me," said the boy, and didn't look nearly so angry as he had intended to appear. "I'm Thumbietot, Morten Goosey-gander's comrade," he continued. Then he stood there, and didn't know what he wanted to say.

As soon as Thumbietot said who he was, she lowered her neck and head very charmingly before him, and said in a voice that was so pretty that he couldn't believe it was a goose who spoke: "I am very glad that you have come here to help me. The white goosey-gander has told me that no one is as wise and as good as you." She said this with such dignity, that the boy grew really embarrassed. "This surely can't be any bird," thought he. "It is certainly some bewitched princess."

He was filled with a desire to help her, and ran his hand under the feathers, and felt along the wing-bone. The bone was not broken, but there was something wrong with the joint. He got his finger down into the empty cavity. "Be careful, now!" he said; and got a firm grip on the bone-pipe and fitted it into the place where it ought to be. He did it very

quickly and well, considering it was the first time that he had attempted anything of the sort. But it must have hurt very much, for the poor young goose uttered a single shrill cry, and then sank down among the stones without showing a sign of life. The boy was terribly frightened. He had only wished to help her, and now she was dead. He made a big jump from the stone pile, and ran away. He thought it was as though he had murdered a human being.

The next morning it was clear and free from mist, and Akka said that now they should continue their travels. The boy jumped up on the goosey-gander's back, and the white one followed the flock—albeit slowly and unwillingly. The boy was mighty glad that they could fly away from the island. He was conscience-stricken on account of the gray goose, and had not cared to tell the goosey-gander how it had turned out when he had tried to cure her. But suddenly the goosey-gander turned. He couldn't go with the others when he knew that she lay alone and ill. But when he was over the stone pile, there lay no young gray goose between the stones. "Dunfin! Dunfin! Where art thou?" called the goosey-gander.

"The fox has probably been here and taken her," thought the boy. But at that moment he heard a pretty voice answer the goosey-gander. "Here am I, goosey-gander; here am I! I have only been taking a morning bath." And up from the water came the little gray goose—fresh and in good trim—and told how Thumbietot had pulled her wing into place, and that she was entirely well, and ready to follow them on the journey.

The drops of water lay like pearl-dew on her shimmery satin-like feathers, and Thumbietot thought once again that she was a real little princess.

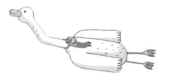

10

LITTLE KARL's ISLAND

THE STORM *Friday, April eighth.*

The wild geese had spent the night on Öland's northern point, and were now on their way to the continent. A strong south wind blew over Kalmar Sound, and they had been thrown northward. Still they worked their way toward land with good speed. But when they were nearing the first islands a powerful rumbling was heard, as if a lot of strong-winged birds had come flying; and the water under them, all at once, became perfectly black. Akka drew in her wings so suddenly that she almost stood still in the air. Thereupon, she lowered herself to light on the edge of the sea. But before the geese had reached the water, the west storm caught up with them. Already, it drove before it fogs, salt scum and small birds; it also snatched with it the wild geese, threw them on end, and cast them toward the sea.

It was a rough storm. The wild geese tried to turn back, time and again, but they couldn't do it and were driven out toward the East sea. The storm had already blown them past Öland, and the sea lay before them—empty and desolate. There was nothing for them to do but to keep out of the water.

When Akka observed that they were unable to turn back she thought that it was needless to let the storm drive them over the entire East sea. Therefore she sank down to the water. Now the sea was raging, and increased in violence with every second. The sea-green billows rolled

forward, with seething foam on their crests. Each one surged higher than the other. But the wild geese were not afraid of the swells. On the contrary, this seemed to afford them much pleasure. They did not strain themselves with swimming, but lay and let themselves be washed up with the wave-crests, and down in the water-dales, and had just as much fun as children in a swing. Their only anxiety was that the flock should be separated. The few land-birds who drove by, up in the storm, cried with envy: "There is no danger for you who can swim."

But the wild geese were certainly not out of all danger. In the first place, the rocking made them helplessly sleepy. Akka called out all the while: "Don't go to sleep, wild geese! He that falls asleep will get away from the flock. He that gets away from the flock is lost."

Despite all attempts at resistance one after another fell asleep; and Akka herself came pretty near dozing off, when she suddenly saw something round and dark rise on the top of a wave. "Seals! Seals! Seals!" cried Akka in a high, shrill voice, and raised herself up in the air with resounding wing-strokes. It was just at the crucial moment. Before the last wild goose had time to come up from the water, the seals were so close to her that they made a grab for her feet.

They lit on the water again, as soon as they dared venture. But when they had rocked upon the waves for a while, they became sleepy again. And when they fell asleep, the seals came swimming. If old Akka had not been so wakeful, not one of them would have escaped.

The storm continued all day, and, at last, Akka began to wonder if she and her flock would perish. They were now dead tired, and nowhere did they see any place where they might rest. Toward evening she no longer dared to lie down on the sea, because now it filled up all of a sudden with large ice-cakes, which struck against each other, and she feared they should be crushed between these. A couple of times the wild geese tried to stand on the ice-crust; but one time the wild storm swept

them into the water; another time, the merciless seals came creeping up on the ice.

At sundown the wild geese were once more up in the air. The heavens were cloud-bedecked, the moon hid itself, and the darkness came quickly. At the same time all nature was filled with a horror which caused the most courageous hearts to quail. Down on the sea, the ice-drifts crashed against each other with a loud rumbling noise. The seals tuned up their wild hunting songs. It was as though heaven and earth were, about to clash.

THE SHEEP

The boy sat for a moment and looked down into the sea. Suddenly he thought that it began to roar louder than ever. He looked up. Right in front of him—only a couple of metres away—stood a rugged and bare mountain-wall. At its base the waves dashed into a foaming spray. The wild geese flew straight toward the cliff, and the boy did not see how they could avoid being dashed to pieces against it. Hardly had he wondered that Akka hadn't seen the danger in time, when they were over by the mountain. Then he also noticed that in front of them was the half-round entrance to a grotto. Into this the geese steered; and the next moment they were safe.

The first thing the wild geese thought of—before they gave themselves time to rejoice over their safety—was to see if all their comrades were also harboured. Kaksi from Nuolja, the first left-hand goose, was missing—and no one knew anything about her fate.

When the wild geese discovered that no one but Kaksi had been separated from the flock, they took the matter lightly. Kaksi was old and wise. She knew all their byways and their habits, and she, of course, would know how to find her way back to them.

Then the wild geese began to look around in the cave. Enough daylight came in through the opening, so that they could see the grotto was both deep and wide. They were delighted to think they had found such a fine night harbour, when one of them caught sight of some shining, green dots, which glittered in a dark corner. "These are eyes!" cried Akka. "There are big animals in here." They rushed toward the opening, but Thumbietot called to them: "There is nothing to run away from! It's only a few sheep who are lying alongside the grotto wall."

When the wild geese had accustomed themselves to the dim daylight in the grotto, they saw the sheep very distinctly. The grown-up ones might be about as many as there were geese; but beside these there were a few little lambs. An old ram with long, twisted horns appeared to be the most lordly one of the flock. The wild geese went up to him with much bowing and scraping. "Well met in the wilderness!" they greeted, but the big ram lay still, and did not speak a word of welcome.

Then the wild geese thought that the sheep were displeased because they had taken shelter in their grotto. "It is perhaps not permissible that we have come in here?" said Akka. "But we cannot help it, for we are wind-driven. We have wandered about in the storm all day, and it would be very good to be allowed to stop here to-night." After that a long time passed before any of the sheep answered with words; but, on the other hand, it could be heard distinctly that a pair of them heaved deep sighs. . Finally an old ewe, who had a long and pathetic face and a doleful voice, said: "There isn't one among us that refuses to let you stay; but this is a house of mourning, and we cannot receive guests as we did in former days." "You needn't worry about anything of that sort," said Akka. "If you knew what we have endured this day, you would surely understand that we are satisfied if we only get a safe spot to sleep on."

When Akka said this, the old ewe raised herself. "I believe that it would be better for you to fly about in the worst storm than to stop here.

But, at least, you shall not go from here before we have had the privilege of offering you the best hospitality which the house affords."

She conducted them to a hollow in the ground, which was filled with water. Beside it lay a pile of bait and husks and chaff; and she bade them make the most of these. "We have had a severe snow-winter this year, on the island," she said. "The peasants who own us came out to us with hay and oaten straw, so we shouldn't starve to death. And this trash is all there is left of the good cheer."

The geese rushed to the food instantly. They thought that they had fared well, and were in their best humour. They must have observed, of course, that the sheep were anxious; but they knew how easily scared sheep generally are, and didn't believe there was any actual danger on foot. As soon as they had eaten, they intended to stand up to sleep as usual. But then the big ram got up, and walked over to them.

"I cannot assume the responsibility of letting you geese remain, without telling you that it is unsafe here," said he. "We cannot receive night guests just now." At last Akka began to comprehend that this was serious. "We shall go away, since you really wish it," said she. "But won't you tell us first, what it is that troubles you? We know nothing about it. We do not even know where we are." "This is Little Karl's Island!" said the ram. "It lies outside of Gottland, and only sheep and seabirds live here." "Perhaps you are wild sheep?" said Akka. "We're not far removed from it," replied the ram. "We have nothing to do with human beings. It's an old agreement between us and some peasants on a farm in Gottland, that they shall supply us with fodder in case we have snow-winter; and as a recompense they are permitted to take away those of us who become superfluous. The island is small, so it cannot feed very many of us. But otherwise we take care of ourselves all the year round, and we do not live in houses with doors and locks, but we reside in grottoes like these."

"Do you stay out here in the winter as well?" asked Akka, surprised. "We do," answered the ram. "We have good fodder up here on the mountain, all the year around." "I think it sounds as if you might have it better than other sheep," said Akka. "But what is the misfortune that has befallen you?" "It was bitter cold last winter. The sea froze, and then three foxes came over here on the ice, and here they have been ever since. Otherwise, there are no dangerous animals here on the island." "Oh, oh! do foxes dare to attack such as you?" "Oh, no! not during the day; then I can protect myself and mine," said the ram, shaking his horns. "But they sneak upon us at night when we sleep in the grottoes. We try to keep awake, but one must sleep some of the time; and then they come upon us. They have already killed every sheep in the other grottoes, and there were herds that were just as large as mine."

"It isn't pleasant to tell that we are so helpless," said the old ewe. "We cannot help ourselves any better than if we were tame sheep." "Do you think that they will come here to-night?" asked Akka. "There is nothing else in store for us," answered the old ewe. "They were here last night, and stole a lamb from us. They'll be sure to come again, as long as there are any of us alive. This is what they have done in the other places." "But if they are allowed to keep this up, you'll become entirely exterminated," said Akka. "Oh! it won't be long before it is all over with the sheep on Little Karl's Island," said the ewe.

Akka stood there hesitatingly. It was not pleasant, by any means, to venture out in the storm again, and it wasn't good to remain in a house where such guests were expected. When she had pondered a while, she turned to Thumbietot. "I wonder if you will help us, as you have done so many times before," said she. Yes, that he would like to do, he replied. "It is a pity for you not to get any sleep!" said the wild goose, "but I wonder if you are able to keep awake until the foxes come, and then to awaken us, so we may fly away." The boy was so very glad of this—for anything

was better than to go out in the storm again—so he promised to keep awake. He went down to the grotto opening, crawled in behind a stone, that he might be shielded from the storm, and sat down to watch.

When the boy had been sitting there a while, the storm seemed to abate. The sky grew clear, and the moonlight began to play on the waves. The boy stepped to the opening to look out. The grotto was rather high up on the mountain. A narrow path led to it. It was probably here that he must await the foxes.

The boy heard a claw scrape against a stone. He saw three foxes coming up the steep; and as soon as he knew that he had something real to deal with, he was calm again, and not the least bit scared. It struck him that it was a pity to awaken only the geese, and to leave the sheep to their fate. He thought he would like to arrange things some other way.

He ran quickly to the other end of the grotto, shook the big ram's horns until he awoke, and, at the same time, swung himself upon his back. "Get up, sheep, and we'll try to frighten the foxes a bit!" said the boy.

He had tried to be as quiet as possible, but the foxes must have heard some noise; for when they came up to the mouth of the grotto they stopped and deliberated. "It was certainly someone in there that moved," said one. "I wonder if they are awake." "Oh, go ahead, you!" said another. "At all events, they can't do anything to us."

When they came farther in, in the grotto, they stopped and sniffed. "Who shall we take to-night?" whispered the one who went first. "To-night we will take the big ram," said the last. "After that, we'll have easy work with the rest."

The boy sat on the old ram's back and saw how they sneaked along. "Now butt straight forward!" whispered the boy. The ram butted, and the first fox was thrust—top over tail—back to the opening. "Now butt to the left!" said the boy, and turned the big ram's head in that direction. The ram measured a terrific assault that caught the second fox in the

side. He rolled around several times before he got to his feet again and made his escape. The boy had wished that the third one, too, might have gotten a bump, but this one had already gone.

"Now I think that they've had enough for to-night," said the boy. "I think so too," said the big ram. "Now lie down on my back, and creep into the wool! You deserve to have it warm and comfortable, after all the wind and storm that you have been out in."

HELL's HOLE

The next day the big ram went around with the boy on his back, and showed him the island. It consisted of a single massive mountain. It was like a large house with perpendicular walls and a flat roof. First the ram walked up on the mountain-roof and showed the boy the good grazing lands there, and he had to admit that the island seemed to be especially created for sheep. There wasn't much else than sheep-sorrel and such little spicy growths as sheep are fond of that grew on the mountain.

But indeed there was something beside sheep fodder to look at, for one who had gotten well up on the steep. To begin with, the largest part of the sea—which now lay blue and sunlit, and rolled forward in glittering swells—was visible. Only upon one and another point, did the foam spray up. To the east lay Gottland, with even and long-stretched coast; and to the southwest lay Great Karl's Island, which was built on the same plan as the little island. When the ram walked to the very edge of the mountain roof, so the boy could look down the mountain walls, he noticed that they were simply filled with birds' nests; and in the blue sea beneath him, lay surf-scoters and eider-ducks and kittiwakes and guillemots and razor-bills—so pretty and peaceful—busying themselves with fishing for small herring.

"This is really a favoured land," said the boy. "You live in a pretty place, you sheep." "Oh, yes! it's pretty enough here," said the big ram. It was as if he wished to add something; but he did not, only sighed. "If you go about here alone you must look out for the crevices which run all around the mountain," he continued after a little. And this was a good warning, for there were deep and broad crevices in several places. The largest of them was called Hell's Hole. That crevice was many fathoms deep and nearly one fathom wide. "If anyone fell down there, it would certainly be the last of him," said the big ram. The boy thought it sounded as if he had a special meaning in what he said.

Then he conducted the boy down to the narrow strip of shore. Now he could see those giants which had frightened him the night before, at close range. They were nothing but tall rock-pillars. The big ram called them "cliffs." The boy couldn't see enough of them. He thought that if there had ever been any trolls who had turned into stone they ought to look just like that.

Although it was pretty down on the shore, the boy liked it still better on the mountain height. It was ghastly down here; for everywhere they came across dead sheep. It was here that the foxes had held their orgies. He saw skeletons whose flesh had been eaten, and bodies that were half-eaten, and others which they had scarcely tasted, but had allowed to lie untouched. It was heart-rending to see how the wild beasts had thrown themselves upon the sheep just for sport—just to hunt them and tear them to death.

The big ram did not pause in front of the dead, but walked by them in silence. But the boy, meanwhile, could not help seeing all the horror.

Then the big ram went up on the mountain height again; but when he was there he stopped and said: "If someone who is capable and wise could see all the misery which prevails here, he surely would not be able to rest until these foxes had been punished." "The foxes must live, too,"

said the boy. "Yes," said the big ram, "those who do not tear in pieces more animals than they need for their sustenance, they may as well live. But these are felons." "The peasants who own the island ought to come here and help you," insisted the boy. "They have rowed over a number of times," replied the ram, "but the foxes always hid themselves in the grottoes and crevices, so they could not get near them, to shoot them." "You surely cannot mean, father, that a poor little creature like me should be able to get at them, when neither you nor the peasants have succeeded in getting the better of them." "He that is little and spry can put many things to rights," said the big ram.

They talked no more about this, and the boy went over and seated himself among the wild geese who fed on the highland. Although he had not cared to show his feelings before the ram, he was very sad on the sheep's account, and he would have been glad to help them. "I can at least talk with Akka and Morten goosey-gander about the matter," thought he. "Perhaps they can help me with a good suggestion."

A little later the white goosey-gander took the boy on his back and went over the mountain plain, and in the direction of Hell's Hole at that.

He wandered, care-free, on the open mountain roof—apparently unconscious of how large and white he was. He didn't seek protection behind tufts, or any other protuberances, but went straight ahead. It was strange that he was not more careful, for it was apparent that he had fared badly in yesterday's storm. He limped on his right leg, and the left wing hung and dragged as if it might be broken.

He acted as if there were no danger, pecked at a grass-blade here and another there, and did not look about him in any direction. The boy lay stretched out full length on the goose-back, and looked up toward the blue sky. He was so accustomed to riding now, that he could both stand and lie down on the goose-back.

When the goosey-gander and the boy were so care-free, they did not

observe, of course, that the three foxes had come up on the mountain plain.

And the foxes, who knew that it was well-nigh impossible to take the life of a goose on an open plain, thought at first that they wouldn't chase after the goosey-gander. But they finally sneaked down on one of the long passes, and tried to steal up to him.

They were not far off when the goosey-gander made an attempt to raise himself into the air. He spread his wings, but he did not succeed in lifting himself. When the foxes seemed to grasp the fact that he couldn't fly, they hurried forward with greater eagerness than before. They no longer concealed themselves in the cleft, but came up on the highland. They hurried as fast as they could, behind tufts and hollows, and came nearer and nearer the goosey-gander—without his seeming to notice that he was being hunted. At last the foxes were so near that they could make the final leap. Simultaneously, all three threw themselves with one long jump at the goosey-gander.

But still at the last moment he must have noticed something, for he ran out of the way, so the foxes missed him. This, at any rate, didn't mean very much, for the goosey-gander only had a couple of metres headway, and, in the bargain, he limped. Anyway, the poor thing ran ahead as fast as he could.

The boy sat upon the goose-back—backward—and shrieked and called to the foxes. "You have eaten yourselves too fat on mutton, foxes. You can't catch up with a goose even." He teased them so that they became crazed with rage and thought only of rushing forward.

The white one ran right straight to the big cleft. When he was there, he made one stroke with his wings, and got over. Just then the foxes were almost upon him.

The goosey-gander hurried on with the same haste before the boy patted him on the neck, and said: "Now you can stop, goosey-gander."

At that instant they heard a number of wild howls behind them, and a scraping of claws, and heavy falls. But of the foxes they saw nothing more.

The next morning the lighthouse keeper on Great Karl's Island found a bit of bark poked under the entrance-door, and on it had been cut, in slanting, angular letters: "The foxes on the little island have fallen down into Hell's Hole. Take care of them!"

And this the lighthouse keeper did, too.

11

THE LEGEND OF SMÅLAND

Tuesday, April twelfth.

The wild geese had made a good trip over the sea, and had lighted in Tjust Township, in northern Småland. That township didn't seem able to make up its mind whether it wanted to be land or sea. Fiords ran in everywhere, and cut the land up into islands and peninsulas and points and capes. The sea was so forceful that the only things which could hold themselves above it were hills and mountains. All the lowlands were hidden away under the water exterior.

The wild geese alighted upon a limestone island a good way in on Goose-fiord. With the first glance at the shore they observed that spring had made rapid strides while they had been away on the islands. The big, fine trees were not as yet leaf-clad, but the ground under them was brocaded with white anemones, gagea, and blue anemones.

When the wild geese saw the flower-carpet they feared that they had lingered too long in the southern part of the country. Akka said instantly that there was no time in which to hunt up any of the stopping places in Småland. By the next morning they must travel northward, over Östergötland.

The boy should then see nothing of Småland, and this grieved him. He had heard more about Småland than he had about any other province, and he had longed to see it with his own eyes.

The summer before, when he had served as goose-boy with a farmer in the neighbourhood of Jordberga, he had met a pair of Småland children, almost every day, who also tended geese. These

children had irritated him terribly with their Småland.

Osa, the goose-girl, was much too wise for that. But the one who could be aggravating with a vengeance was her brother, little Mats.

"Have you heard, Nils Goose-boy, how it went when Småland and Skåne were created?" he would ask, and if Nils Holgersson said no, he began immediately to relate the old joke-legend.

"Well, it was at that time when our Lord was creating the world. While he was doing his best work, Saint Peter came walking by. He stopped and looked on, and then he asked if it was hard to do. 'Well, it isn't exactly easy,' said our Lord. Saint Peter stood there a little longer, and when he noticed how easy it was to lay out one landscape after another, he too wanted to try his hand at it. 'Perhaps you need to rest yourself a little,' said Saint Peter, 'I could attend to the work in the meantime for you.' But this our Lord did not wish. 'I do not know if you are so much at home in this art that I can trust you to take hold where I leave off,' he answered. Then Saint Peter was angry, and said that he believed he could create just as fine countries as our Lord himself.

"It happened that our Lord was just then creating Småland. It wasn't even half-ready but it looked as though it would be an indescribably pretty and fertile land. It was difficult for our Lord to say no to Saint Peter, and aside from this, he thought very likely that a thing so well begun no one could spoil. Therefore he said: If you like, we will prove which one of us two understands this sort of work the better. You, who are only a novice, shall go on with this which I have begun,

and I will create a new land.' To this Saint Peter agreed at once; and so they went to work—each one in his place.

"Our Lord moved southward a bit, and there he undertook to create Skåne. It wasn't long before he was through with it, and soon he asked if Saint Peter had finished, and would come and look at his work. 'I had mine ready long ago,' said Saint Peter; and from the sound of his voice it could be heard how pleased he was with what he had accomplished.

"When Saint Peter saw Skåne, he had to acknowledge that there was nothing but good to be said of that land. It was a fertile land and easy to cultivate, with wide plains wherever one looked, and hardly a sign of hills. It was evident that our Lord had really contemplated making it such that people should feel at home there. 'Yes, this is a good country,' said Saint Peter, 'but I think that mine is better.' 'Then we'll take a look at it,' said our Lord.

"The land was already finished in the north and east when Saint Peter began the work, but the southern and western parts; and the whole interior, he had created all by himself. Now when our Lord came up there, where Saint Peter had been at work, he was so horrified that he stopped short and exclaimed: 'What on earth have you been doing with this land, Saint Peter?'

"Saint Peter, too, stood and looked around—perfectly astonished. He had had the idea that nothing could be so good for a land as a great deal of warmth. Therefore he had gathered together an enormous mass of stones and mountains, and erected a highland, and this he had done so that it should be near the sun, and receive much help from the sun's heat. Over the stone-heaps he had spread a thin layer of soil, and then he had thought that everything was well arranged.

"But while he was down in Skåne, a couple of heavy showers had come up, and more was not needed to show what his work amounted to. When our Lord came to inspect the land, all the soil had been washed away, and the naked mountain foundation shone forth all over. Where it

was about the best, lay clay and heavy gravel over the rocks, but it looked so poor that it was easy to understand that hardly anything except spruce and juniper and moss and heather could grow there. But what there was plenty of was water. It had filled up all the clefts in the mountain; and lakes and rivers and brooks; these one saw everywhere, to say nothing of swamps and morasses, which spread over large tracts. And the most exasperating thing of all was, that while some tracts had too much water, it was so scarce in others, that whole fields lay like dry moors, where sand and earth whirled up in clouds with the least little breeze.

"'What can have been your meaning in creating such a land as this?' said our Lord. Saint Peter made excuses, and declared he had wished to build up a land so high that it should have plenty of warmth from the sun. 'But then you will also get much of the night chill,' said our Lord, 'for that too comes from heaven. I am very much afraid the little that can grow here will freeze.'

"This, to be sure, Saint Peter hadn't thought about.

"'Yes, here it will be a poor and frost-bound land,' said our Lord, 'it can't be helped.'"

When little Mats had gotten this far in his story, Osa, the goose-girl, protested: "I cannot bear, little Mats, to hear you say that it is so miserable in Småland," said she. "You forget entirely how much good soil there is there. Only think of Möre district, by Kalmar Sound! I wonder where you'll find a richer grain region. There are fields upon fields, just like here in Skåne. The soil is so good that I cannot imagine anything that couldn't grow there."

"I can't help that," said little Mats. "I'm only relating what others have said before."

"And I have heard many say that there is not a more beautiful coast land than Tjust. Think of the bays and islets, and the manors, and the groves!" said Osa. "And don't you remember," continued Osa, "the school teacher

said that such a lively and picturesque district as that bit of Småland which lies south of Lake Vettern is not to be found in all Sweden? Think of the beautiful sea and the yellow coast-mountains,with its match factory, and all the big establishments there!" "Yes, that's true enough," little Mats admitted.

All of a sudden he had looked up. "Now we are pretty stupid," said he. "All this, of course, lies in our Lord's Småland, in that part of the land which was already finished when Saint Peter undertook the job. It's only natural that it should be pretty and fine there. But in Saint Peter's Småland it looks as it says in the legend. And it wasn't surprising that our Lord was distressed when he saw it," continued little Mats, as he took up the thread of his story again. "Saint Peter didn't lose his courage, at all events, but tried to comfort our Lord. 'Don't be so grieved over this!' said he. 'Only wait until I have created people who can till the swamps and break up fields from the stone hills.'

"That was the end of our Lord's patience—and he said: 'No! you can go down to Skåne and make the Skåninge, but the Smålander I will create myself.' And so our Lord created the Smålander, and made him quick-witted and contented and happy and thrifty and enterprising and capable, that he might be able to get his livelihood in his poor country."

Then little Mats was silent; and if Nils Holgersson had also kept still, all would have gone well; but he couldn't possibly refrain from asking how Saint Peter had succeeded in creating the Skåninge.

"Well, what do you think yourself?" said little Mats, and looked so scornful that Nils Holgersson threw himself upon him, to thrash him. But Mats was only a little tot, and Osa, the goose-girl, who was a year older than he, ran forward instantly to help him. Good-natured though she was, she sprang like a lion as soon as anyone touched her brother. And Nils Holgersson did not care to fight a girl, but turned his back, and didn't look at those Småland children for the rest of the day.

12

THE CROWS

THE EARTHEN CROCK

In the southwest corner of Småland lies a township called Sonnerbo. It is a rather smooth and even country. In the beginning of April when the snow finally melts away in Sonnerbo, it is apparent that that which lies hidden under it is only dry, sandy heaths, bare rocks, and big, marshy swamps.

At the time when Nils Holgersson travelled around with the wild geese, a little cabin stood there, with a bit of cleared ground around it. But the people who had lived there at one time, had, for some reason or other, moved away. The little cabin was empty, and the ground lay unused.

When the tenants left the cabin they closed the damper, fastened the window-hooks, and locked the door. But no one had thought of the broken window-pane which was only stuffed with a rag. After the showers of a couple of summers, the rag had moulded and shrunk, and, finally, a crow had succeeded in poking it out.

The ridge on the heather-heath was really not as desolate as one might think, for it was inhabited by a large crow-folk. Naturally, the crows did not live there all the year round. They moved to foreign lands in the winter; in the autumn they travelled from one grain-field to another all over Götaland, and picked grain; during the summer, they spread themselves over the farms in Sonnerbo township, and lived upon

eggs and berries and birdlings; but every spring, when nesting time came, they came back to the heather-heath.

The one who had poked the rag from the window was a crow-cock named Garm Whitefeather; but he was never called anything but Fumle or Drumle, or out and out Fumle-Drumle, because he always acted awkwardly and stupidly, and wasn't good for anything except to make fun of. Fumle-Drumle was bigger and stronger than any of the other crows, but that didn't help him in the least; he was—and remained—a butt for ridicule. And it didn't profit him, either, that he came from very good stock. If everything had gone smoothly, he should have been leader for the whole flock, because this honour had, from time immemorial, belonged to the oldest Whitefeather. But long before Fumle-Drumle was born, the power had gone from his family, and was now wielded by a cruel wild crow, named Wind-Rush.

This transference of power was due to the fact that the crows on crow-ridge desired to change their manner of living. Possibly there are many who think that everything in the shape of crow lives in the same way; but this is not so. There are entire crow-folk who lead honourable lives—that is to say, they only eat grain, worms, caterpillars, and dead animals; and there are others who lead a regular bandit's life, who throw themselves upon baby-hares and small birds, and plunder every single bird's nest they set eyes on.

The ancient Whitefeathers had been strict and temperate; and as long as they had led the flock, the crows had been compelled to conduct themselves in such a way that other birds could speak no ill of them. But the crows were numerous, and poverty was great among them. They didn't care to go the whole length of living a strictly moral life, so they rebelled against the Whitefeathers, and gave the power to Wind-Rush, who was the worst nest-plunderer and robber that could be imagined— if his wife, Wind-Air, wasn't worse still. Under their government the crows had begun to lead such a life that now they were more feared than pigeon-hawks and leech-owls.

Naturally, Fumle-Drumle had nothing to say in the flock. The crows were all of the opinion that he did not in the least take after his forefathers, and that he wouldn't suit as a leader. No one would have mentioned him, if he hadn't constantly committed fresh blunders. A few, who were quite sensible, sometimes said perhaps it was lucky for Fumle-Drumle that he was such a bungling idiot, otherwise Wind-Rush and Wind-Air would hardly have allowed him—who was of the old chieftain stock—to remain with the flock.

None of the crows knew that it was Fumle-Drumle who had pecked the rag out of the window; and had they known of this, they would have been very much astonished. Such a thing as daring to approach a human being's dwelling, they had never believed of him. He kept the thing to himself very carefully; and he had his own good reasons for it. Wind-Rush always treated him well in the daytime, and when the others were around; but one very dark night, when the comrades sat on the night branch, he was attacked by a couple of crows and nearly murdered. After that he moved every night, after dark, from his usual sleeping quarters into the empty cabin.

Now one afternoon, when the crows had put their nests in order on crow-ridge, they happened upon a remarkable find. Wind-Rush, Fumle-Drumle, and a couple of others had flown down into a big hollow in one corner of the heath. The hollow was nothing but a gravel-pit, but the crows could not be satisfied with such a simple explanation; they flew down in it continually, and turned every single sand-grain to get at the reason why human beings had digged it. While the crows were pottering around down there, a mass of gravel fell from one side. They rushed up to it, and had the good fortune to find amongst the fallen stones and stubble—a large earthen crock, which was locked with a wooden clasp!

Naturally they wanted to know if there was anything in it, and they tried both to peck holes in the crock, and to bend up the clasp, but they had no success.

They stood perfectly helpless and examined the crock, when they heard someone say: "Shall I come down and assist you crows?" They glanced up quickly. On the edge of the hollow sat a fox and blinked down at them. He was one of the prettiest foxes—both in colour and form—that they had ever seen. The only fault with him was that he had lost an ear.

"If you desire to do us a service," said Wind-Rush, "we shall not say nay." At the same time, both he and the others flew up from the hollow. Then the fox jumped down in their place, bit at the jar, and pulled at the lock—but he couldn't open it either.

"Can you make out what there is in it?" said Wind-Rush. The fox rolled the jar back and forth, and listened attentively. "It must be silver money," said he.

This was more than the crows had expected. "Do you think it can be silver?" said they, and their eyes were ready to pop out of their heads with greed; for remarkable as it may sound, there is nothing in the world which crows love as much as silver money.

"Hear how it rattles!" said the fox and rolled the crock around once more. "Only I can't understand how we shall get at it." "That will surely be impossible," said the crows. The fox stood and rubbed his head against his left leg, and pondered. Now perhaps he might succeed, with the help of the crows, in becoming master of that little imp who always eluded him. "Oh! I know someone who could open the crock for you," said the fox. "Then tell us! Tell us!" cried the crows; and they were so excited that they tumbled down into the pit. "That I will do, if you'll first promise me that you will agree to my terms," said he.

Then the fox told the crows about Thumbietot, and said that if they could bring him to the heath he would open the crock for them. But in payment for this counsel, he demanded that they should deliver Thumbietot to him, as soon as he had gotten the silver money for them. The crows had no reason to spare Thumbietot, so agreed to the compact at once.

KIDNAPPED BY CROWS *Wednesday, April thirteenth.*

The wild geese were up at daybreak, starting out on the journey toward Östergötland. The island in Goosefiord, where they had slept, was small and barren, but in the water all around it were growths which they could eat their fill upon. It was worse for the boy, however. He couldn't manage to find anything eatable.

As he stood there hungry and drowsy, and looked around in all directions, his glance fell upon a pair of squirrels, who played upon the wooded point, directly opposite the rock island. He wondered if the squirrels still had any of their winter supplies left, and asked the white goosey-gander to take him over to the point, that he might beg them for a couple of hazelnuts.

Instantly the white one swam across the sound with him; but as luck would have it the squirrels had so much fun chasing each other from tree to tree, that they didn't bother about listening to the boy. They drew farther into the grove. He hurried after them, and was soon out of the goosey-gander's sight—who stayed behind and waited on the shore.

The boy waded forward between some white anemone-stems— which were so high they reached to his chin—when he felt that someone caught hold of him from behind, and tried to lift him up. He turned round and saw that a crow had grabbed him by the shirt-band. He tried to break loose, but before this was possible, another crow ran up, gripped him by the stocking, and knocked him over.

If Nils Holgersson had immediately cried for help, the white goosey-gander certainly would have been able to save him; but the boy probably thought that he could protect himself, unaided, against a couple of crows. He kicked and struck out, but the crows didn't let go their hold, and they soon succeeded in raising themselves into the air with him. To make matters worse, they flew so recklessly that his head struck against a branch. He received a hard knock over the head, it grew black before his eyes, and he lost consciousness.

When he opened his eyes once more, he found himself high above the ground. He regained his senses slowly. When he glanced down, he saw that under him was spread a tremendously big woolly carpet, which was woven in greens and reds, and in large irregular patterns. When the crows descended, he saw at once that the big carpet under him was the earth, which was dressed in green and brown cone-trees and naked leaf-trees, and that the holes and tears were shining fiords and little lakes.

He began to ask himself a lot of questions. Why wasn't he sitting on the goosey-gander's back? Why did a great swarm of crows fly around him? And why was he being pulled and knocked hither and thither so that he was about to break to pieces?

Then, all at once, the whole thing dawned on him. He had been kidnapped by a couple of crows. The white goosey-gander was still on the shore, waiting, and to-day the wild geese were going to travel to Östergötland. He was being carried southwest; this he understood because the sun's disc was behind him. The big forest-carpet which lay beneath him was surely Småland.

After a bit, one of them flapped his wings in a manner which meant: "Look out! Danger!" Soon thereafter they came down in a spruce forest, pushed their way between prickly branches to the ground, and put the boy down under a thick spruce, where he was so well concealed that not even a falcon could have sighted him.

Fifty crows surrounded him, with bills pointed toward him to guard him. "Now perhaps I may hear, crows, what your purpose is in carrying me off", said he. But he was hardly permitted to finish the sentence before a big crow hissed at him: "Keep still! or I'll bore your eyes out."

It was evident that the crow meant what she said; and there was nothing for the boy to do but obey. So he sat there and stared at the crows, and the crows stared at him.

The longer he looked at them, the less he liked them. It was dreadful how dusty and unkempt their feather dresses were—as though they knew neither baths nor oiling. Their toes and claws were grimy with dried-in mud, and the corners of their mouths were covered with food drippings. These were very different birds from the wild geese—that he observed.

"It is certainly a real robber-band that I've fallen in with," thought he.

Just then he heard the wild geese's call above him. "Where are you? Here am I. Where are you? Here am I."

He understood that Akka and the others had gone out to search for him; but before he could answer them the big crow who appeared to be the leader of the band hissed in his ear: "Think of your eyes!" And there was nothing else for him to do but to keep still.

A moment later the crows gave the signal to break up; and since it was still their intention, apparently, to carry him along in such a way that one held on to his shirt-band, and one to a stocking, the boy said: "Is there not one among you so strong that he can carry me on his back? You have already travelled so badly with me that I feel as if I were in pieces. Only let me ride! I'll not jump from the crow's back, that I promise you."

"Oh! you needn't think that we care how you have it," said the leader. But now the largest of the crows—a dishevelled and uncouth

one, who had a white feather in his wing—came forward and said: "It would certainly be best for all of us, Wind-Rush, if Thumbietot got there whole, rather than half, and therefore, I shall carry him on my back." "I have no objection," said Wind-Rush. "But don't lose him!"

With this, much was already gained, and the boy actually felt pleased again. "There is nothing to be gained by losing my grit because I have been kidnapped by the crows," thought he. "I'll surely be able to manage those poor little things."

The crows continued to fly southwest, over Småland. It was a glorious morning—sunny and calm; and the birds down on the earth were singing their best love songs. In a high, dark forest sat the thrush himself with drooping wings and swelling throat, and struck up tune after tune. "How pretty you are! How pretty you are! How pretty you are!" sang he. "No one is so pretty. No one is so pretty. No one is so pretty." As soon as he had finished this song, he began it all over again.

But just then the boy rode over the forest; and when he had heard the song a couple of times, and marked that the thrush knew no other, he put both hands up to his mouth as a speaking trumpet, and called down: "We've heard all this before. We've heard all this before." "Who is it? Who is it? Who is it? Who makes fun of me?" asked the thrush, and tried to catch a glimpse of the one who called. "It is Kidnapped-by-Crows who makes fun of your song," answered the boy. At that, the crow-chief turned his head and said: "Be careful of your eyes, Thumbietot!" But the boy thought, "Oh! I don't care about that. I want to show you that I'm not afraid of you!"

Farther and farther inland they travelled; and there were woods and lakes everywhere. In a birch-grove sat the wood-dove on a naked branch, and before him stood the lady-dove. He blew up his feathers, cocked his head, raised and lowered his body, until the breast-feathers rattled against the branch. All the while he cooed: "Thou, thou, thou art the loveliest in all the forest. No one in the forest is so lovely as thou, thou, thou!"

But up in the air the boy rode past, and when he heard Mr. Dove he couldn't keep still. "Don't you believe him! Don't you believe him!" cried he.

"Who, who, who is it that lies about me?" cooed Mr. Dove, and tried to get a sight of the one who shrieked at him. "It is Caught-by-Crows that lies about you," replied the boy. Again Wind-Rush turned his head toward the boy and commanded him to shut up, but Fumle-Drumle, who was carrying him, said: "Let him chatter, then all the little birds will think that we crows have become quick-witted and funny birds." "Oh! they're not such fools, either," said Wind-Rush; but he liked the idea just the same, for after that he let the boy call out as much as he liked.

In one place they saw a pretty old manor. It lay with the forest back of it, and the sea in front of it; had red walls and a turreted roof; great sycamores about the grounds, and big, thick gooseberry-bushes in the orchard. On the top of the weathercock sat the starling, and sang so loud that every note was heard by the wife, who sat on an egg in the heart of a pear tree. "We have four pretty little round eggs. We have the whole nest filled with fine eggs." sang the starling.

When the starling sang the song for the thousandth time, the boy rode over the place. He put his hands up to his mouth, as a pipe, and called: "The magpie will get them. The magpie will get them."

"Who is it that wants to frighten me?" asked the starling, and flapped his wings uneasily. "It is Captured-by-Crows that frightens you," said the boy. This time the crow-chief didn't attempt to hush him up. Instead, both he and his flock were having so much fun that they cawed with satisfaction.

The farther inland they came, the larger were the lakes, and the more plentiful were the islands and points. And on a lake-shore stood a

drake and kowtowed before the duck. "I'll be true to you all the days of my life. I'll be true to you all the days of my life," said the drake. "It won't last until the summer's end," shrieked the boy. "Who are you?" called the drake. "My name's Stolen-by-Crows," shrieked the boy.

At dinner time the crows lighted in a food-grove. They walked about and procured food for themselves, but none of them thought about giving the boy anything. Then Fumle-Drumle came riding up to the chief with a dog-rose branch, with a few dried buds on it. "Here's something for you, Wind-Rush," said he. "This is pretty food, and suitable for you." Wind-Rush sniffed contemptuously. "And I who thought that you would be pleased with them!" said Fumle-Drumle; and threw away the dog-rose branch as if in despair. But it fell right in front of the boy, and he wasn't slow about grabbing it and eating until he was satisfied.

When the crows had eaten, they began to chatter. They became so excited that they all talked at once. "What kind of an accomplishment is that—to steal little kittens?" said one. "I once chased a young hare who was almost full-grown. That meant to follow him from covert to covert." He got no further before another took the words from him. "It may be fun, perhaps, to annoy hens and cats, but I find it still more remarkable that a crow can worry a human being. I once stole a silver spoon—"

But now the boy thought he was too good to sit and listen to such gabble. "Now listen to me, you crows!" said he. "I think you ought to be ashamed of yourselves to talk about all your wickedness. I have lived amongst wild geese for three weeks, and of them I have never heard or seen anything but good. You must have a bad chief, since he permits you to rob and murder in this way. You ought to begin to lead new lives, for I can tell you that human beings have grown so tired of your wickedness they are trying with all their might to root you out. And then there will soon be an end of you."

When Wind-Rush and the crows heard this, they were so furious that they intended to throw themselves upon him and tear him in pieces. But Fumle-Drumle laughed and cawed, and stood in front of him. "Oh, no, no!" said he, and seemed absolutely terrified. "What think you that Wind-Air will say if you tear Thumbietot in pieces before he has gotten that silver money for us?" "It has to be you, Fumle-Drumle, that's afraid of women-folk," said Rush. But, at any rate, both he and the others left Thumbietot in peace.

The sun had gone down, but it was still perfect daylight when the crows reached the large heather-heath. Wind-Rush sent a crow on ahead, to say that he had met with success; and when it was known, Wind-Air, with several hundred crows from Crow-Ridge, flew to meet the arrivals. In the midst of the deafening cawing which the crows emitted, Fumle-Drumle said to the boy: "You have been so comical and so jolly during the trip that I am really fond of you. Therefore I want to give you some good advice. As soon as we light, you'll be requested to do a bit of work which may seem very easy to you; but beware of doing it!"

Soon thereafter Fumle-Drumle put Nils Holgersson down in the bottom of a sandpit. The boy flung himself down, rolled over, and lay there as though he was simply done up with fatigue. Such a lot of crows fluttered about him that the air rustled like a wind-storm, but he didn't look up.

"Thumbietot," said Wind-Rush, "get up now! You shall help us with a matter which will be very easy for you."

The boy didn't move, but pretended to be asleep. Then Wind-Rush took him by the arm, and dragged him over the sand to an earthen crock of old-time make, that was standing in the pit. "Get up, Thumbietot," said he, "and open this crock!" "Why can't you let me sleep?" said the boy. "I'm too tired to do anything to-night. Wait until to-morrow!"

"Open the crock!" said Wind-Rush, shaking him. "How shall a poor

little child be able to open such a crock? Why, it's quite as large as I am myself." "Open it!" commanded Wind-Rush once more, "or it will be a sorry thing for you." The boy got up, tottered over to the crock, fumbled the clasp, and let his arms fall. "I'm not usually so weak," said he. "If you will only let me sleep until morning, I think that I'll be able to manage with that clasp."

But Wind-Rush was impatient, and he rushed forward and pinched the boy in the leg. That sort of treatment the boy didn't care to suffer from a crow. He jerked himself loose quickly, ran a couple of paces backward, drew his knife from the sheath, and held it extended in front of him. "You'd better be careful!" he cried to Wind-Rush.

This one too was so enraged that he didn't dodge the danger. He rushed at the boy, just as though he'd been blind, and ran so straight against the knife, that it entered through his eye into the head. The boy drew the knife back quickly, but Wind-Rush only struck out with his wings, then he fell down—dead.

"Wind-Rush is dead! The stranger has killed our chieftain, Wind-Rush!" cried the nearest crows, and then there was a terrible uproar. Some wailed, others cried for vengeance. They all ran or fluttered up to the boy, with Fumle-Drumle in the lead. But he acted badly as usual. He only fluttered and spread his wings over the boy, and prevented the others from coming forward and running their bills into him.

The boy thought that things looked very bad for him now. He couldn't run away from the crows, and there was no place where he could hide. Then he happened to think of the earthen crock. He took a firm hold on the clasp, and pulled it off. Then he hopped into the crock to hide in it. But the crock was a poor hiding place, for it was nearly filled to the brim with little, thin silver coins. The boy couldn't get far enough down, so he stooped and began to throw out the coins.

Until now the crows had fluttered around him in a thick swarm and pecked at him, but when he threw out the coins they immediately forgot their thirst for vengeance, and hurried to gather the money. The boy threw out handfuls of it, and all the crows—yes, even Wind-Air herself—picked them up. And everyone who succeeded in picking up a coin ran off to the nest with the utmost speed to conceal it.

When the boy had thrown out all the silver pennies from the crock he glanced up. Not more than a single crow was left in the sandpit. That was Fumle-Drumle, with the white feather in his wing; he who had carried Thumbietot. "You have rendered me a greater service than you understand," said the crow—with a very different voice, and a different intonation than the one he had used heretofore—"and I want to save your life. Sit down on my back, and I'll take you to a hiding place where you can be secure for to-night. To-morrow, I'll arrange it so that you will get back to the wild geese."

THE CABIN *Thursday, April fourteenth.*

The following morning when the boy awoke, he lay in a bed. When he saw that he was in a house with four walls around him, and a roof over him, he thought that he was at home.

He looked around the cabin once more, to try and discover if there was anything else which he might find useful to take along. "I may as well take what I need, since no one else cares about it," thought he. But most of the things were too big and heavy. The only things that he could carry might be a few matches perhaps.

He clambered up on the table, and swung with the help of the curtains up to the window-shelf. While he stood there and stuffed the matches into his bag, the crow with the white feather came in through the window. "Well here I am at last," said Fumle-Drumle as he lit on the table. "I couldn't get here any sooner because we crows have elected a

new chieftain in Wind-Rush's place." "Whom have you chosen?" said the boy. "Well, we have chosen one who will not permit robbery and injustice. We have elected Garm Whitefeather, lately called Fumle-Drumle," answered he, drawing himself up until he looked absolutely regal. "That was a good choice," said the boy and congratulated him. "You may well wish me luck," said Garm; then he told the boy about the time they had had with Wind-Rush and Wind-Air.

During this recital the boy heard a voice outside the window which he thought sounded familiar. "Is he here?"—inquired the fox. "Yes, he's hidden in there," answered a crow-voice. "Be careful, Thumbietot!" cried Garm. "Wind-Air stands without with that fox who wants to eat you." More he didn't have time to say, for Smirre dashed against the window. The old, rotten window-frame gave way, and the next second Smirre stood upon the window-table. Garm Whitefeather, who didn't have time to fly away, he killed instantly. Thereupon he jumped down to the floor, and looked around for the boy. He tried to hide behind a big oakum-spiral, but Smirre had already spied him, and was crouched for the final spring. The cabin was so small, and so low, the boy understood that the fox could reach him without the least difficulty. But just at that moment the boy was not without weapons of defence. He struck a match quickly, touched the curtains, and when they were in flames, he threw them down upon Smirre Fox. When the fire enveloped the fox, he was seized with a mad terror. He thought no more about the boy, but rushed wildly out of the cabin.

But it looked as if the boy had escaped one danger to throw himself into a greater one. From the tuft of oakum which he had flung at Smirre the fire had spread to the bed-hangings. He jumped down and tried to smother it, but it blazed too quickly now. The cabin was soon filled with smoke, and Smirre Fox, who had remained just outside the window, began to grasp the state of affairs within. "Well, Thumbietot," he called out, "which do you choose now: to be broiled alive in there, or to come out here to me? Of course, I should prefer to have the pleasure of eating you; but in whichever way death meets you it will be dear to me."

The whole bed was now in a blaze, and smoke rose from the floor; and along the painted wall-strips the fire crept from rider to rider. The boy jumped up in the fireplace, and tried to open the oven door, when he heard a key which turned around slowly in the lock. It must be human beings coming. And in the dire extremity in which he found himself, he was not afraid, but only glad. He was already on the threshold when the door opened. He saw a couple of children facing him; but how they looked when they saw the cabin in flames, he took no time to find out; but rushed past them into the open.

He didn't dare run far. He knew, of course, that Smirre Fox lay in wait for him, and he understood that he must remain near the children. He turned round to see what sort of folk they were, but he hadn't looked at them a second before he ran up to them and cried: "Oh, good-day, Osa goose-girl! Oh, good-day, little Mats!"

For when the boy saw those children he forgot entirely where he was. Crows and burning cabin and talking animals had vanished from his memory. He was walking on a stubble-field, in West Vemminghög, tending a goose-flock; and beside him, on the field, walked those same Småland children, with their geese. As soon as he saw them, he ran up on the stone-hedge and shouted: "Oh, good-day, Osa goose-girl! Oh, good-day, little Mats!"

But when the children saw such a little creature coming up to them with outstretched hands, they grabbed hold of each other, took a couple of steps backward, and looked scared to death.

When the boy noticed their terror he woke up and remembered who he was. And then it seemed to him that nothing worse could happen to him than that those children should see how he had been bewitched.

Shame and grief because he was no longer a human being overpowered him. He turned and fled. He knew not whither.

But a glad meeting awaited the boy when he came down to the heath. For there, in the heather, he spied something white, and toward him came the white goosey-gander, accompanied by Dunfin. When the white one saw the boy running with such speed, he thought that dreadful fiends were pursuing him. He flung him in all haste upon his back and flew off with him.

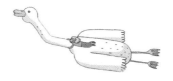

13

THE OLD PEASANT WOMAN

Thursday, April fourteenth.

Three tired wanderers were out in the late evening in search of a night harbour. When it was so dark that there was scarcely a glimmer of light left under the skies and the two who needed sleep journeyed on in a kind of half-sleep, they happened into a farmyard which was a long way off from all neighbours. And not only did it lie there desolate, but it appeared to be uninhabited as well. No smoke rose from the chimney; no light shone through the windows; no human being moved on the place. When the one among the three who could keep awake, saw the place, he thought: "Now come what may, we must try to get in here. Anything better we are not likely to find."

Soon after that, all three stood in the house-yard. Two of them fell asleep the instant they stood still, but the third looked about him eagerly, to find where they could get under cover. It was not a small farm. Beside the dwelling house and stable and smoke-house, there were long ranges with granaries and storehouses and cattlesheds. But it all looked awfully poor and dilapidated. The houses had gray, moss-grown, leaning walls, which seemed ready to topple over. In the roofs were yawning holes, and the doors hung aslant on broken hinges. It was apparent that no one had taken the trouble to drive a nail into a wall on this place for a long time.

Meanwhile, he who was awake had figured out which house was the cowshed. He roused his travelling companions from their sleep, and conducted them to the cowshed door. Luckily, this was not fastened with anything but a hook, which he could easily push up with a rod. He

heaved a sigh of relief at the thought that they should soon be in safety. But when the cowshed door swung open with a sharp creaking, he heard a cow begin to bellow. "Are you coming at last, mistress?" said she. "I thought that you didn't propose to give me any supper to-night."

The one who was awake stopped in the doorway, absolutely terrified when he discovered that the cowshed was not empty. But he soon saw that there was not more than one cow, and three or four chickens; and then he took courage again. "We are three poor travellers who want to come in somewhere, where no fox can assail us, and no human being capture us," said he. "We wonder if this can be a good place for us." "I cannot believe but what it is," answered the cow. "To be sure the walls are poor, but the fox does not walk through them as yet; and no one lives here except an old peasant woman, who isn't at all likely to make a captive of anyone. But who are you?" she continued, as she twisted in her stall to get a sight of the newcomers. "I am Nils Holgersson from Vemminghög, who has been transformed into an elf," replied the first of the incomers, "and I have with me a tame goose, whom I generally ride, and a gray goose." "Such rare guests have never before been within my four walls," said the cow, "and you shall be welcome, although I would have preferred that it had been my mistress, come to give me my supper."

The boy led the geese into the cowshed, which was rather large, and placed them in an empty manger, where they fell asleep instantly. For himself, he made a little bed of straw and expected that he, too, should go to sleep at once.

But this was impossible, for the poor cow, who hadn't had her supper, wasn't still an instant. She shook her flanks, moved around in the stall, and complained of how hungry she was. The boy couldn't get a wink of sleep, but lay there and lived over all the things that had happened to him during these last days.

He thought of Osa, the goose-girl, and little Mats, whom he had encountered so unexpectedly; and he fancied that the little cabin which he had set on fire must have been their old home in Småland. Now he recalled that he had heard them speak of just such a cabin, and of the big heather-heath which lay below it. Now Osa and Mats had wandered back there to see their old home again, and then, when they had reached it, it was in flames.

It was indeed a great sorrow which he had brought upon them, and it hurt him very much. If he ever again became a human being, he would try to compensate them for the damage and miscalculation.

Then his thoughts wandered to the crows. And when he thought of Fumle-Drumle who had saved his life, and had met his own death so soon after he had been elected chieftain, he was so distressed that tears filled his eyes. He had had a pretty rough time of it these last few days. But, anyway, it was a rare stroke of luck that the goosey-gander and Dunfin had found him. The goosey-gander had said that as soon as the geese discovered that Thumbietot had disappeared, they had asked all the small animals in the forest about him. They soon learned that a flock of Småland crows had carried him off. But the crows were already out of sight, and whither they had directed their course no one had been able to say. That they might find the boy as soon as possible, Akka had commanded the wild geese to start out—two and two—in different directions, to search for him. But after a two days' hunt, whether or not they had found him, they were to meet in northwestern Småland on a high mountain-top, which resembled an abrupt, chopped-off tower, and was called Taberg. After Akka had given them the best directions, and described carefully how they should find Taberg, they had separated.

The white goosey-gander had chosen Dunfin as travelling companion, and they had flown about hither and thither with the greatest anxiety for Thumbietot. During this ramble they had heard a

thrush, who sat in a tree-top, cry and wail that someone, who called himself Kidnapped-by-Crows, had made fun of him. They had talked with the thrush, and he had shown them in which direction that Kidnapped-by-Crows had travelled. Afterward, they had met a dove-cock, a starling and a drake; they had all wailed about a little culprit who had disturbed their song, and who was named Caught-by-Crows, Captured-by-Crows, and Stolen-by-Crows. In this way, they were enabled to trace Thumbietot all the way to the heather-heath in Sonnerbo township.

As soon as the goosey-gander and Dunfin had found Thumbietot, they had started toward the north, in order to reach Taberg. But it had been a long road to travel, and the darkness was upon them before they had sighted the mountain top. "If we only get there by to-morrow, surely all our troubles will be over," thought the boy, and dug down into the straw to have it warmer.

All the while the cow fussed and fumed in the stall. Then, all of a sudden, she began to talk to the boy. "Everything is wrong with me," said the cow. "I am neither milked nor tended. I have no night fodder in my manger, and no bed has been made under me. My mistress came here at dusk, to put things in order for me, but she felt so ill, that she had to go in soon again, and she has not returned."

"It's distressing that I should be little and powerless," said the boy. "I don't believe that I am able to help you." "You can't make me believe that you are powerless because you are little," said the cow. "All the elves that I've ever heard of, were so strong that they could pull a whole load of hay and strike a cow dead with one fist." The boy couldn't help laughing at the cow. "They were a very different kind of elf from me," said he. "But I'll loosen your halter and open the door for you, so that you can go out and drink in one of the pools on the place, and then I'll try to climb up to the hayloft and throw down some hay in your

manger."

The boy did as he had said; and when the cow stood with a full manger in front of her, he thought that at last he should get some sleep. But he had hardly crept down in the bed before she began, anew, to talk to him.

"You'll be clean put out with me if I ask you for one thing more," said the cow. "Oh, no I won't, if it's only something that I'm able to do," said the boy. "Then I will ask you to go into the cabin, directly opposite, and find out how my mistress is getting along. I fear some misfortune has come to her." "No! I can't do that," said the boy. "I dare not show myself before human beings." "'s urely you're not afraid of an old and sick woman," said the cow. "But you do not need to go into the cabin. Just stand outside the door and peep in through the crack!" "Oh! if that is all you ask of me, I'll do it of course," said the boy.

With that he opened the cowshed door and went out in the yard. Neither moon nor stars shone; the wind blew a gale, and the rain came down in torrents. "He was blown down twice before he got to the house: once the wind swept him into a pool, which was so deep that he came near drowning. But he got there nevertheless.

He clambered up a pair of steps, scrambled over a threshold, and came into the hallway. The cabin door was closed, but down in one corner a large piece had been cut away, that the cat might go in and out. It was no difficulty whatever for the boy to see how things were in the cabin.

He had hardly cast a glance in there before he staggered back and turned his head away. An old, gray-haired woman lay stretched out on the floor within. She neither moved nor moaned; and her face shone strangely white.

The boy remembered that when his grandfather had died, his face had also become so strangely white-like. Death had probably come to her

so suddenly that she didn't even have time to lie down on her bed.

When he told the cow what he had seen in the cabin, she stopped eating. "So my mistress is dead," said she. "Then it will soon be over for me as well." "There will always be someone to look out for you," said the boy comfortingly. "Ah! you don't know," said the cow, "that I am already twice as old as a cow usually is before she is laid upon the slaughter-bench. But then I do not care to live any longer, since she, in there, can come no more to care for me."

She said nothing more for a while, but the boy observed, no doubt, that she neither slept nor ate. It was not long before she began to speak again. "Is she lying on the bare floor?" she asked. "She is," said the boy. "She had a habit of coming out to the cowshed," she continued, "and talking about everything that troubled her. I understood what she said, although I could not answer her. These last few days she talked of how afraid she was lest there would be no one with her when she died. She was anxious for fear no one should close her eyes and fold her hands across her breast, after she was dead. Perhaps you'll go in and do this?" The boy hesitated. He remembered that when his grandfather had died, mother had been very careful about putting everything to rights. He knew this was something which had to be done. But, on the other hand, he felt that he didn't care go to the dead, in the ghastly night. When the boy said nothing, she did not repeat her request. Instead, she began to talk with him of her mistress.

There was much to tell, first and foremost, about all the children which she had brought up. They had been in the cowshed every day, and in the summer they had taken the cattle to pasture on the swamp and in the groves, so the old cow knew all about them. They had been splendid, all of them, and happy and industrious. A cow knew well enough what her caretakers were good for.

There was also much to be said about the farm. It had not always

been as poor as it was now. It was very large—although the greater part of it consisted of swamps and stony groves. There was not much room for fields, but there was plenty of good fodder everywhere. At one time there had been a cow for every stall in the cowshed; and the oxshed, which was now empty, had at one time been filled with oxen. And then there was life and gayety, both in cabin and cowhouse. When the mistress opened the cowshed door she would hum and sing, and all the cows lowed with gladness when they heard her coming.

But the good man had died when the children were so small that they could not be of any assistance, and the mistress had to take charge of the farm, and all the work and responsibility. She had been as strong as a man, and had both ploughed and reaped. In the evenings, when she came into the cowshed to milk, sometimes she was so tired that she wept. Then she dashed away her tears, and was cheerful again. "It doesn't matter. Good times are coming again for me too, if only my children grow up. Yes, if they only grow up."

But as soon as the children were grown, a strange longing came over them. They didn't want to stay at home, but went away to a strange country. Their mother never got any help from them. A couple of her children were married before they went away, and they had left their children behind, in the old home. And now these children followed the mistress in the cowshed, just as her own had done. They tended the cows, and were fine, good folk. And, in the evenings, when the mistress was so tired out that she could fall asleep in the middle of the milking, she would rouse herself again to renewed courage by thinking of them. "Good times are coming for me, too," said she—and shook off sleep—"when once they are grown."

But when these children grew up, they went away to their parents in the strange land. No one came back—no one stayed at home—the old mistress was left alone on the farm.

Probably she had never asked them to remain with her. "Think you, Rödlinna, that I would ask them to stay here with me, when they can go out in the world and have things comfortable?" she would say as she stood in the stall with the old cow. "Here in Småland they have only poverty to look forward to."

But when the last grandchild was gone, it was all up with the mistress. All at once she became bent and gray, and tottered as she walked; as if she no longer had the strength to move about. She stopped working. She did not care to look after the farm, but let everything go to rack and ruin. She didn't repair the houses; and she sold both the cows and the oxen. The only one that she kept was the old cow who now talked with Thumbietot. Her she let live because all the children had tended her.

She could have taken maids and farm-hands into her service, who would have helped her with the work, but she couldn't bear to see strangers around her, since her own had deserted her. Perhaps she was better satisfied to let the farm go to ruin, since none of her children were coming back to take it after she was gone. She did not mind that she herself became poor, because she didn't value that which was only hers. But she was troubled lest the children should find out how hard she had it. "If only the children do not hear of this! If only the children do not hear of this!" she sighed as she tottered through the cowhouse.

The children wrote constantly, and begged her to come out to them; but this she did not wish. She didn't want to see the land that had taken them from her. She was angry with it. "It's foolish of me, perhaps, that I do not like that land which has been so good for them," said she. "But I don't want to see it."

She never thought of anything but the children, and of this—that they must needs have gone. When summer came, she led the cow out to graze in the big swamp. All day she would sit on the edge of the swamp,

her hands in her lap; and on the way home she would say: "You see, Rödlinna, if there had been large, rich fields here, in place of these barren swamps, then there would have been no need for them to leave."

This last evening she had been more trembly and feeble than ever before. She could not even do the milking. She had leaned against the manger and talked about two strangers who had been to see her, and had asked if they might buy the swamp. They wanted to drain it, and sow and raise grain on it. This had made her both anxious and glad. "Do you hear, Rödlinna," she had said, "do you hear they said that grain can grow on the swamp? Now I shall write to the children to come home. Now they'll not have to stay away any longer; for now they can get their bread here at home." It was this that she had gone into the cabin to do—

The boy heard no more of what the old cow said. He had opened the cowhouse door and gone across the yard, and in to the dead whom he had but lately been so afraid of.

It was not so poor in the cabin as he had expected. It was well supplied with the sort of things one generally finds among those who have relatives in America. In a corner there was an American rocking chair; on the table before the window lay a brocaded plush cover; there was a pretty spread on the bed; on the walls, in carved-wood frames, hung the photographs of the children and grandchildren who had gone away; on the bureau stood high vases and a couple of candlesticks, with thick, spiral candles in them.

The boy searched for a matchbox and lighted these candles, not because he needed more light than he already had; but because he thought that this was one way to honour the dead.

Then he went up to her, closed her eyes, folded her hands across her breast, and stroked back the thin gray hair from her face.

He thought no more about being afraid of her. He was so deeply grieved because she had been forced to live out her old age in loneliness

and longing. He, at least, would watch over her dead body this night.

He hunted up the psalm book, and seated himself to read a couple of psalms in an undertone. But in the middle of the reading he paused—because he had begun to think about his mother and father.

Think, that parents can long so for their children! This he had never known. Think, that life can be as though it was over for them when the children are away! Think, if those at home longed for him in the same way that this old peasant woman had longed!

This thought made him happy, but he dared not believe in it. He had not been such a one that anybody could long for him.

But what he had not been, perhaps he could become.

Round about him he saw the portraits of those who were away. They were big, strong men and women with earnest faces. There were brides in long veils, and gentlemen in fine clothes; and there were children with waved hair and pretty white dresses. And he thought that they all stared blindly into vacancy—and did not want to see.

"Poor you!" said the boy to the portraits. "Your mother is dead. You cannot make reparation now, because you went away from her. But my mother is living!"

Here he paused, and nodded and smiled to himself. "My mother is living," said he. "Both father and mother are living."

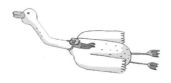

14

FROM TABERG TO THE BIG BIRD LAKE

Friday, April fifteenth.

The boy sat awake nearly all night, but toward morning he fell asleep and then he dreamed of his father and mother. They had both grown gray, and had old and wrinkled faces. They said that they had aged so because they had longed for him.

When the boy awoke the morning was come, with fine, clear weather. He gave morning feed to both geese and cow, and opened the cowhouse door so that the cow could go over to the nearest farm. When the cow came along all by herself the neighbours would no doubt understand that something was wrong with her mistress. They would hurry over to the desolate farm to see how the old woman was getting along, and then they would find her dead body and bury it.

The boy and the geese had barely raised themselves into the air, when they caught a glimpse of a high mountain, with almost perpendicular walls, and an abrupt, broken-off top; and they understood that this must be Taberg. On the summit stood Akka and all six goslings waited for them. There was a rejoicing, and a cackling, and a fluttering, and a calling which no one can describe, when they saw that the goosey-gander and Dunfin had succeeded in finding Thumbietot.

Later in the day, when the geese continued their journey, they flew up toward the blue valley. They were in holiday humour; shrieked and made such a racket that no one who had ears could help hearing them.

JARRO, THE WILD DUCK

Takern is certainly the largest and choicest bird lake in the whole country; and the birds may count themselves lucky as long as they own such a retreat. But it is uncertain just how long they will be in control of reeds and mud-banks, for human beings cannot forget that the lake extends over a considerable portion of good and fertile soil; and every now and then the proposition to drain it comes up among them. And if these propositions were carried out, the many thousands of water-birds would be forced to move from this quarter.

At the time when Nils Holgersson travelled around with the wild geese, there lived at Takern a wild duck named Jarro. He was a young bird, who had only lived one summer, one fall, and a winter; now, it was his first spring. He had just returned from South Africa, and had reached Takern in such good season that the ice was still on the lake.

One evening, when he and the other young wild ducks played at racing backward and forward over the lake, a hunter fired a couple of shots at them, and Jarro was wounded in the breast. In order that the one who had shot him shouldn't get him into his power, he continued to fly as long as he possibly could. He had flown a bit inland, and now he sank down before the entrance to one of the big farms which lie along the shores of Takern.

A moment later a young farm-hand happened along. He saw Jarro, and came and lifted him up. The farm-hand noticed that the bird was alive. He carried him very gently into the cottage, and showed him to the mistress of the house. She took Jarro from the farm-hand, stroked him on the back and wiped away the blood which trickled down through the neck-feathers. She looked him over very carefully; and she saw how pretty he was, with his dark-green, shining head, his white neck-band, his brownish-red back, and his blue wing-mirror. She promptly put a basket

in order, and tucked the bird into it. The mistress carried the basket across the floor to place it in the corner by the fireplace; but before she put it down Jarro was already fast asleep.

In a little while Jarro was awakened by someone who nudged him gently. When he opened his eyes he experienced such an awful shock that he almost lost his senses. Now he was lost; for there stood the one who was more dangerous than either human beings or birds of prey. It was Caesar—the long-haired dog—who nosed around him inquisitively.

How pitifully scared had he not been last summer, when he was still a little yellow-down duckling, every time it had sounded over the reed-stems: "Caesar is coming!" He had always hoped that he would never have to live through that moment when he should meet the brown and white spotted dog face to face.

But, to his sorrow, he must have fallen down in the very yard where Caesar lived, for there he stood right over him. "Who are you?" he growled. "How did you get into the house? Don't you belong down among the reed banks?"

It was with great difficulty that he gained the courage to answer. "Don't be angry with me, Caesar!" said he. "It isn't my fault. I have been wounded by a gunshot. It was the people themselves who laid me in this basket."

"Oho! so it's the folks themselves that have placed you here," said Caesar. "Then it is surely their intention to cure you; although, for my part, I think it would be wiser for them to eat you up. But, at any rate, you are tabooed in the house. You needn't look so scared. "

The next time Jarro awoke, he saw that a dish with grain and water stood before him. He was still quite ill, but he felt hungry nevertheless, and began to eat. When the mistress saw that he ate, she came up and petted him, and looked pleased. After that, Jarro fell asleep again. For several days he did nothing but eat and sleep.

One morning Jarro felt so well that he stepped from the basket and

wandered along the floor. But he hadn't gone very far before he keeled over, and lay there. Then came Caesar, opened his big jaws and grabbed him. Jarro believed that the dog was going to bite him to death; but Caesar carried him back to the basket without harming him. Thereafter Caesar and he became good friends, and every day, for several hours, Jarro lay and slept between Caesar's paws.

But an even greater affection than he felt for Caesar, did Jarro feel toward his mistress. Of her he had not the least fear; but rubbed his head against her hand when she came and fed him. Whenever she went out of the cottage he sighed with regret; and when she came back he cried welcome to her in his own language.

THE DECOY-DUCK *Sunday, April seventeenth.*

Jarro was so well that he could fly all about the house. Then he was petted a good deal by the mistress, and the little boy ran out in the yard and plucked the first grass-blades for him which had sprung up. Jarro thought that, although he was now so strong that he could fly down to Takern at any time, he shouldn't care to be separated from the human beings. He had no objection to remaining with them all his life.

But early one morning the mistress placed a halter, or noose, over Jarro, which prevented him from using his wings, and then she turned him over to the farm-hand who had found him in the yard. The farm-hand poked him under his arm, and went down to Takern with him.

The farm-hand got into a scow, laid Jarro in the bottom of the boat, and began to pole himself out on the lake. Jarro, who had now accustomed himself to expect only good of human beings, said to Caesar, who was also in the party, that he was very grateful toward the farm-hand for taking him out on the lake. But there was no need to keep him so closely guarded, for he did not intend to fly away. To this Caesar

made no reply. He was very close-mouthed that morning.

The only thing which struck Jarro as being a bit peculiar was that the farm-hand had taken his gun along. He couldn't believe that any of the good folk in the cottage would want to shoot birds. And, beside, Caesar had told him that the people didn't hunt at this time of the year.

The farm-hand went over to one of the little reed-enclosed mud-islets. There he stepped from the boat, gathered some old reeds into a pile, and lay down behind it. Jarro was permitted to wander around on the ground, with the halter over his wings, and tethered to the boat, with a long string.

Suddenly Jarro caught sight of some young ducks and drakes, in whose company he had formerly raced backward and forward over the lake. They were a long way off, but Jarro called them to him with a couple of loud shouts. They responded, and a large and beautiful flock approached. Before they got there, Jarro began to tell them about his marvellous rescue, and of the kindness of human beings. Just then, two shots sounded behind him. Three ducks sank down in the reeds— lifeless—and Caesar bounced out and captured them.

Then Jarro understood. The human beings had only saved him that they might use him as a decoy-duck. And they had also succeeded. Three ducks had died on his account. He thought he should die of shame. He thought that even his friend Caesar looked contemptuously at him; and when they came home to the cottage, he didn't dare lie down and sleep beside the dog.

The next morning Jarro was again taken out on the shallows. This time, too, he saw some ducks. But when he observed that they flew toward him, he called to them: "Away! Away! Be careful! Fly in another direction! There's a hunter hidden behind the reed-pile. I'm only a decoy-bird!" And he actually succeeded in preventing them from coming within shooting distance.

Jarro had scarcely had time to taste of a grass-blade, so busy was he in keeping watch. He called out his warning as soon as a bird drew nigh. But he did not wish that any bird should meet with misfortune on his account. And, thanks to Jarro's vigilance, the farm-hand had to go home without firing off a single shot.

Caesar looked less displeased than on the previous day; and when evening came he took Jarro in his mouth, carried him over to the fireplace, and let him sleep between his forepaws. Nevertheless, Jarro was no longer contented in the cottage, but was grievously unhappy. His heart suffered at the thought that humans never had loved him. When the mistress, or the little boy, came forward to caress him, he stuck his bill under his wing and pretended that he slept.

For several days Jarro continued his distressful watch-service; and already he was known all over Takern. Then it happened one morning, while he called as usual: "Have a care, birds! Don't come near me! I'm only a decoy-duck," that a grebe-nest came floating toward the shallows where he was tied. This was nothing especially remarkable. It was a nest from the year before; and since grebe-nests are built in such a way that they can move on water like boats, it often happens that they drift out toward the lake. Still Jarro stood there and stared at the nest, because it came so straight toward the islet that it looked as though someone had steered its course over the water.

As the nest came nearer, Jarro saw that a little human being sat in the nest and rowed it forward with a pair of sticks. And this little human called to him: "Go as near the water as you can, Jarro, and be ready to fly. You shall soon be freed."

A few seconds later the grebe-nest lay near land, but the little oarsman did not leave it, but sat huddled up between branches and straw. Jarro too held himself almost immovable. He was actually paralysed with fear lest the rescuer should be discovered.

The next thing which occurred was that a flock of wild geese came along. Then Jarro woke up to business, and warned them with loud shrieks; but in spite of this they flew backward and forward over the shallows several times. They held themselves so high that they were beyond shooting distance; still the farm-hand let himself be tempted to fire a couple of shots at them. These shots were hardly fired before the little creature ran up on land, drew a tiny knife from its sheath, and, with a couple of quick strokes, cut loose Jarro's halter. "Now fly away, Jarro, before the man has time to load again!" cried he, while he himself ran down to the grebe-nest and poled away from the shore.

The hunter had had his gaze fixed upon the geese, and hadn't observed that Jarro had been freed; but Caesar had followed more carefully that which happened; and just as Jarro raised his wings, he dashed forward and grabbed him by the neck.

Jarro cried pitifully; and the boy who had freed him said quietly to Caesar: "If you are just as honourable as you look, surely you cannot wish to force a good bird to sit here and entice others into trouble."

Caesar heard these words. "Fly, Jarro!" said he. "You are certainly too good to be a decoy-duck. It wasn't for this that I wanted to keep you here; but because it will be lonely in the cottage without you."

THE LOWERING OF THE LAKE *Wednesday, April twentieth.*

It was indeed very lonely in the cottage without Jarro. The housewife missed the glad quacking which he had indulged in every time she entered the house. But the one who longed most for Jarro, was the little boy, Per Ola. He was but three years old, and the only child; and in all his life he had never had a playmate like Jarro. When he heard that Jarro had gone back to Takern and the wild ducks, he couldn't be satisfied with this, but thought constantly of how he should get him back again.

Per Ola had talked a good deal with Jarro while he lay still in his basket, and he was certain that the duck understood him. He begged his mother to take him down to the lake that he might find Jarro, and persuade him to come back to them. Mother wouldn't listen to this; but the little one didn't give up his plan on that account.

The day after Jarro had disappeared, Per Ola was running about in the yard. He played by himself as usual, but Caesar lay on the stoop; and when mother let the boy out, she said: "Take care of Per Ola, Caesar!"

Now if all had been as usual, Caesar would also have obeyed the command, and the boy would have been so well guarded that he couldn't have run the least risk. But Caesar was not like himself these days. He knew that the farmers who lived along Takern had held frequent conferences about the lowering of the lake; and that they had almost settled the matter. The ducks must leave, and Caesar should nevermore behold a glorious chase. He was so preoccupied with thoughts of this misfortune, that he did not remember to watch over Per Ola.

And the little one had scarcely been alone in the yard a minute, before he realised that now the right moment was come to go down to Takern and talk with Jarro. He opened a gate, and wandered down

toward the lake on the narrow path which ran along the banks. When Per Ola came down to the lake-shore, he called Jarro several times. Thereupon he stood for a long time and waited, but no Jarro appeared. When Jarro didn't come to him, the little boy thought that it would be easier to find him if he went out on the lake.

There were several good craft lying along the shore, but they were tied. The only one that lay loose, and at liberty, was an old leaky scow which was so unfit that no one thought of using it. But Per Ola scrambled up in it without caring that the whole bottom was filled with water. He had not strength enough to use the oars, but instead, he seated himself to swing and rock in the scow. Per Ola was soon riding around on Takern, and calling for Jarro.

When the old scow was rocked like this—out to sea—its Cracks opened wider and wider, and the water actually streamed into it. Per Ola didn't pay the slightest attention to this. At last Jarro caught sight of Per Ola. Jarro was unspeakably happy to find that one of the humans really loved him. He shot down toward Per Ola, like an arrow, seated himself beside him, and let him caress him. But suddenly Jarro noticed the condition of the scow. It was half-filled with water, and was almost ready to sink. Jarro tried to tell Per Ola that he, who could neither fly nor swim, must try to get upon land; but Per Ola didn't understand him. Then Jarro did not wait an instant, but hurried away to get help.

Jarro came back in a little while, and carried on his back a tiny thing, who was much smaller than Per Ola himself. Instantly, the little one ordered Per Ola to pick up a long, slender pole that lay in the bottom of the scow, and try to pole it toward one of the reed-islands. Per Ola obeyed him, and he and the tiny creature, together, steered the scow. With a couple of strokes they were on a little reed-encircled island, and now Per Ola was told that he must step on land. And just the very moment that Per Ola set foot on land, the scow was filled with water,

and sank to the bottom.

Meanwhile the folks on the farm had discovered that the boy had disappeared, and had started to search for him. But no matter how much they sought they did not find him.

Caesar, the dog, understood very well that the farmer-folk were looking for Per Ola, but he did nothing to lead them on the right track; instead, he lay still as though the matter didn't concern him.

Later in the day, Per Ola's footprints were discovered down by the boat-landing. And then came the thought that the old, leaky scow was no longer on the strand. Then one began to understand how the whole affair had come about.

The farmer and his helpers immediately took out the boats and went in search of the boy. They rowed around on Takern until way late in the evening, without seeing the least shadow of him.

In the evening, Per Ola's mother hunted around on the strand. Everyone else was convinced that the boy was drowned, but she could not bring herself to believe this. She searched all the while. She searched between reeds and bulrushes; tramped and tramped on the muddy shore, never thinking of how deep her foot sank, and how wet she had become. She was unspeakably desperate. Her heart ached in her breast. She did not weep, but wrung her hands and called for her child in loud piercing tones.

Round about her she heard swans' and ducks' and curlews' shrieks. It was strange that they did not quiet down after sunset. But she heard all these uncountable bird-throngs, which lived along Takern, send forth cry upon cry. Several of them followed her wherever she went; others came rustling past on light wings. All the air was filled with moans and lamentations.

She understood much better than ever before, how birds fared. They had their constant worries for home and children; they, as she.

There was surely not such a great difference between them and her as she had heretofore believed. Then she happened to think that it was as good as settled that these thousands of swans and ducks and loons would lose their homes here by Takern. She mused on this. It appeared to be an excellent and agreeable accomplishment to change a lake into fields and meadows, but let it be some other lake than Takern; some other lake, which was not the home of so many thousand creatures.

She wondered if this was why her son had been lost—just today. Was it God's meaning that sorrow should come and open her heart—just to-day—before it was too late to avert the cruel act?

She walked rapidly up to the house, and began to talk with her husband about this. She spoke of the lake, and of the birds, and said that she believed it was God's judgment on them both. And she soon found that he was of the same opinion.

He stood and pondered if God's hand was back of the fact that Takern had taken his son from him on the day before he was to draw up the contract to lay it waste. The wife didn't have to say many words to him, before he answered: "It may be that God does not want us to interfere with His order. I'll talk with the others about this to-morrow, and I think we'll conclude that all may remain as it is."

While the farmer-folk were talking this over, Caesar lay before the fire. He raised his head and listened very attentively. When he thought that he was sure of the outcome, he walked up to the mistress, took her by the skirt, and led her to the door. "But Caesar!" said she, and wanted to break loose. "Do you know where Per Ola is?" she exclaimed. Caesar barked joyfully, and threw himself against the door. She opened it, and Caesar dashed down toward Takern. The mistress was so positive he knew where Per Ola was, that she rushed after him. And no sooner had they reached the shore than they heard a child's cry out on the lake.

Per Ola had had the best day of his life, in company with

Thumbietot and the birds; but now he had begun to cry because he was hungry and afraid of the darkness. And he was glad when father and mother and Caesar came for him.

15

THE HOMESPUN CLOTH AND THE BREAKING UP OF THE ICE

Saturday, April twenty-third.

Östergötland was made up of a large plain, which lay wedged in between two mountainous forest-tracts—one to the north, the other to the south. The two forest-heights lay there, a lovely blue, and shimmered in the morning light, as if they were decked with golden veils; and the plain, which simply spread out one winter-naked field after another, was, in and of itself, prettier to look upon than gray homespun.

But the people must have been contented on the plain, because it was generous and kind, and they had tried to decorate it in the best way possible. High up—where the boy rode by—he thought that cities and farms, churches and factories, castles and railway stations were scattered over it, like large and small trinkets. It shone on the roofs, and the window-panes glittered like jewels. Yellow country roads, shining railway-tracks and blue canals ran along between the districts like embroidered loops. Linköping lay around its cathedral like a pearl-setting around a precious stone; and the gardens in the country were like little brooches and buttons. There was not much regulation in the pattern, but it was a display of grandeur which one could never tire of looking at.

For a time they had followed an old, hilly country road, which wound around cliffs, and ran forward under wild mountain-walls—when the boy suddenly let out a shriek. He had been sitting and swinging his foot back and forth, and one of his wooden shoes had slipped off.

"Goosey-gander, goosey-gander, I have dropped my shoe!" cried the boy. The goosey-gander turned about and sank toward the ground; then the boy saw that two children, who were walking along the road, had picked up his shoe. "Goosey-gander, goosey-gander," screamed the boy excitedly, "fly upward again! It is too late. I cannot get my shoe back again."

Down on the road stood Osa, the goose-girl, and her brother, little Mats, looking at a tiny wooden shoe that had fallen from the skies.

Osa stood silent a long while, and pondered over the find. At last she said, slowly and thoughtfully: "Do you remember, little Mats, that when we ourselves came home to our cabin, we saw a goblin who was dressed in the same way, and who also straddled the back of a goose— and flew away. Maybe it was the same one who rode along on his goose up here in the air and dropped his wooden shoe."

"Yes, it must have been," said little Mats.

They turned the wooden shoe about and examined it carefully.

"Wait, little Mats!" said Osa, the goose-girl. "There is something written on one side of it."

"Why, so there is! but they are such tiny letters."

"Let me see! It says—it says: 'Nils Holgersson from W. Vemminghög.' That's the most wonderful thing I've ever heard!" said little Mats.

Thursday, April twenty-eighth.

The morning sun darted its clear rays upon the ice, which did not look dark and forbidding, like most spring ice, but sparkled temptingly. As far as they could see, the ice was firm and dry. The rain had run down into cracks and hollows, or been absorbed by the ice itself. The children saw only the sound ice.

Osa, the goose girl, and little Mats were on their way North, and they could not help thinking of all the steps they would be saved if they could cut straight across the lake instead of going around it. They knew, to be sure, that spring ice is treacherous, but this looked perfectly secure. They could see that it was several inches thick near the shore. They saw a path which they might follow, and the opposite shore appeared to be so near that they ought to be able to get there in an hour.

"Come, let's try!" said little Mats. "If we only look before us, so that we don't go down into some hole, we can do it."

So they went out on the lake. The ice was not very slippery, but rather easy to walk upon. There was more water on it than they expected to see, and here and there were cracks, where the water purled up. One had to watch out for such places; but that was easy to do in broad daylight, with the sun shining.

The children advanced rapidly, and talked only of how sensible they were to have gone out on the ice instead of tramping the slushy road.

When they had been walking a while they came to Vin Island, where an old woman had sighted them from her window. She rushed from her cabin, waved them back, and shouted something which they could not hear. They understood perfectly well that she was warning them not to come any farther; but they thought there was no immediate danger. It would be stupid for them to leave the ice when all was going so well!

They went on past Vin Island and had a stretch of seven miles of ice ahead of them. Out there was so much water that the children were obliged to take roundabout ways; but that was sport to them. They vied with each other as to which could find the soundest ice. They were neither tired nor hungry. The whole day was before them, and they laughed at each obstacle they met.

Now and then they cast a glance ahead at the farther shore. It still appeared far away, although they had been walking a good hour. They were rather surprised that the lake was so broad.

"The shore seems to be moving farther away from us," little Mats

observed.

Out there the children were not protected against the wind, which was becoming stronger and stronger every minute, and was pressing their clothing so close to their bodies that they could hardly go on. The cold wind was the first disagreeable thing they had met with on the journey.

But the amazing part of it was that the wind came sweeping along with a loud roar. They had walked to the west of the big island, Valen; now they thought they were nearing the north shore. Suddenly the wind began to blow more and more, while the loud roaring increased so rapidly that they began to feel uneasy.

All at once it occurred to them that the roar was caused by the foaming and rushing of the waves breaking against a shore. Even this seemed improbable, since the lake was still covered with ice.

At all events, they paused and looked about. They noticed far in the west a white bank which stretched clear across the lake. At first they thought it was a snowbank alongside a road. Later they realized it was the foam-capped waves dashing against the ice! They took hold of hands and ran without saying a word. Open sea lay beyond in the west, and suddenly the streak of foam appeared to be moving eastward. They wondered if the ice was going to break all over. They felt now that they were in great danger.

"Osa," said little Mats, "this must be the breaking up of the ice!"

"Why, so it is, little Mats, but as yet we can get to land. Run for your life!" said Osa.

As a matter of fact, the wind and waves had a good deal of work to do yet to clear the ice from the lake. The hardest part was done when the ice-cake burst into pieces, but all these pieces must be broken and hurled against each other, to be crushed, worn down, and dissolved. There was still a great deal of hard and sound ice left, which formed large, unbroken surfaces.

The greatest danger for the children lay in the fact that they had no general view of the ice. They did not see the places where the gaps were so wide that they could not possibly jump over them, nor did they know where to find any floes that would hold them, so they wandered aimlessly back and forth, going farther out on the lake instead of nearer land. At last, confused and terrified, they stood still and wept.

Then a flock of wild geese in rapid flight came rushing by. They shrieked loudly and sharply; but the strange thing was that above the geese-cackle the little children heard these words:

"You must go to the right, the right!" They began at once to follow the advice; but before long they were again standing irresolute, facing another broad gap.

Again they heard the geese shrieking above them, and again, amid the geese-cackle, they distinguished a few words:

"Stand where you are! Stand where you are!"

The children did not say a word to each other, but obeyed and stood still. Soon after that the ice-floes floated together, so that they could cross the gap. Then they took hold of hands again and ran. They were afraid not only of the peril, but of the mysterious help that had come to them.

Soon they had to stop again, and immediately the sound of the voice reached them.

"Straight ahead, straight ahead!" it said.

This leading continued for about half an hour; by that time they had reached Ljunger Point, where they left the ice and waded to shore. They were still terribly frightened, even though they were on firm land. They did not stop to look back at the lake—where the waves were pitching the ice-floes faster and faster—but ran on. When they had gone a short distance along the point, Osa paused suddenly.

"Wait here, little Mats," she said; "I have forgotten something."

Osa went down to the strand again, where she stopped to rummage in her bag. Finally she fished out a little wooden shoe, which she placed on a stone where it could be plainly seen. Then she ran to little Mats without once looking back.

But the instant her back was turned, a big white goose shot down from the sky, like a streak of lightning, snatched the wooden shoe, and flew away with it.

16

THE FLOOD

THE NEW WATCH-DOG *May first to fourth.*

There was a terrible storm raging in the district north of Lake Mälar, which lasted several days. The sky was a dull gray, the wind whistled, and the rain beat. Both people and animals knew the spring could not be ushered in with anything short of this; nevertheless they thought it unbearable.

The safest refuge for water-fowl in the whole Mälar district is Hjälsta Bay. It has low shores, shallow water and is also covered with reeds. It is the home of a great many swans, and the owner of the old castle nearby has prohibited all shooting on the bay, so that they might be unmolested.

The geese stood on a clump of reeds with perfect composure, and slept. Nils Holgersson was too hungry to sleep.

"It is necessary for me to get something to eat," he said.

He did not stop to deliberate, but hopped down on a stump that had drifted in amongst the reeds. Then he picked up a little stick and began to pole toward shore.

Just as he was landing, he heard a splash in the water. He stopped short. First he saw a lady swan asleep in her big nest quite close to him, then he noticed that a fox had taken a few steps into the water and was sneaking up to the swan's nest.

"Hi, hi, hi! Get up, get up!" cried the boy, beating the water with his

stick.

The lady swan rose, but not so quickly but that the fox could have pounced upon her had he cared to. However, he refrained and instead hurried straight toward the boy.

Thumbietot saw the fox coming and ran for his life. The boy was a good runner, but it stands to reason that he could not race with a fox!

Not far from the bay there were a number of little cabins. Naturally the boy ran in that direction, but he realized that long before he could reach the nearest cabin the fox would catch up to him.

Once the fox was so close that it looked as if the boy would surely be his prey, but Nils quickly sprang aside and turned back toward the bay. By that move the fox lost time, and before he could reach the boy the latter had run up to two men who were on their way home from work.

The men were tired and sleepy; they had noticed neither boy nor fox, although both had been running right in front of them. Nor did the boy ask help of the men; he was content to walk close beside them.

"Surely the fox won't venture to come up to the men," he thought.

But presently the fox came pattering along. He probably counted on the men taking him for a dog, for he went straight up to them.

"Whose dog can that be sneaking around here?" queried one.

The other paused and glanced back.

"Go along with you!" he said, and gave the fox a kick that sent it to the opposite side of the road. "What are you doing here?"

After that the fox kept at a safe distance, but followed all the while.

Presently the men reached a cabin and entered it. The boy intended to go in with them; but when he got to the stoop he saw a big, shaggy watch-dog rush out from his kennel to greet his master. Suddenly the boy changed his mind and remained out in the open.

"Listen, watch-dog!" whispered the boy as soon as the men had shut the door. "I wonder if you would like to help me catch a fox to-night?"

The dog had poor eyesight and had become irritable and cranky from being chained.

"What, I catch a fox?" he barked angrily. "Who are you that makes fun of me? You just come within my reach and I'll teach you not to fool with me!"

"You needn't think that I'm afraid to come near you!" said the boy, running up to the dog.

When the dog saw him he was so astonished that he could not speak.

"I'm the one they call Thumbietot, who travels with the wild geese," said the boy, introducing himself. "Haven't you heard of me?"

"I believe the sparrows have twittered a little about you," the dog returned. "They say that you have done wonderful things for one of your size."

"I've been rather lucky up to the present," admitted the boy. "But now it's all up with me unless you help me! There's a fox at my heels. He's lying in wait for me around the corner."

"Don't you suppose I can smell him?" retorted the dog. "But we'll soon be rid of him!" With that the dog sprang as far as the chain would allow, barking and growling for ever so long. "Now I don't think he will show his face again to-night!" said the dog.

"It will take something besides a fine bark to scare that fox!" the boy remarked. "He'll soon be here again, and that is precisely what I wish, for I have set my heart on your catching him."

"Are you poking fun at me now?" asked the dog.

"Only come with me into your kennel, and I'll tell you what to do."

The boy and the watch-dog crept into the kennel and crouched there, whispering.

By and by the fox stuck his nose out from his hiding place. He scented the boy all the way to the kennel, but halted at a safe distance and sat down to think of some way to coax him out.

Suddenly the watch-dog poked his head out and growled at him: "Go away, or I'll catch you!"

"I'll sit here as long as I please for all of you!" defied the fox.

"Go away!" repeated the dog threateningly, "or there will be no more hunting for you after to-night."

But the fox only grinned and did not move an inch.

"I know how far your chain can reach," he said.

"I have warned you twice," said the dog, coming out from his kennel. "Now blame yourself!"

With that the dog sprang at the fox and caught him without the least effort, for he was loose. The boy had unbuckled his collar.

There was a hot struggle, but it was soon over. The dog was the victor. The fox lay on the ground and dared not move.

"Don't stir or I'll kill you!" snarled the dog. Then he took the fox by the scruff of the neck and dragged him to the kennel. There the boy was ready with the chain. He placed the dog collar around the neck of the fox, tightening it so that he was securely chained. During all this the fox had to lie still, for he was afraid to move.

"Now, Smirre Fox, I hope you'll make a good watch-dog," laughed the boy when he had finished.

17

OSA, THE GOOSE GIRL, AND LITTLE MATS

The year that Nils Holgersson travelled with the wild geese everybody was talking about two little children, a boy and a girl, who tramped through the country. They were from Sunnerbo township, in Småland, and had once lived with their parents and four brothers and sisters in a little cabin on the heath.

While the two children, Osa and Mats, were still small, a poor, homeless woman came to their cabin one night and begged for shelter. Although the place could hardly hold the family, she was taken in and the mother spread a bed for her on the floor. In the night she coughed so hard that the children fancied the house shook. By morning she was too ill to continue her wanderings. The children's father and mother were as kind to her as could be. They gave up their bed to her and slept on the floor, while the father went to the doctor and brought her medicine.

The first few days the sick woman behaved like a savage; she demanded constant attention and never uttered a word of thanks. Later she became more subdued and finally begged to be carried out to the heath and left there to die.

When her hosts would not hear of this, she told them that the last few years she had roamed about with a band of gipsies. She herself was not of gipsy blood, but was the daughter of a well-to-do farmer. She had run away from home and gone with the nomads. She believed that a gipsy woman who was angry at her had brought this sickness upon her.

Nor was that all: The gipsy woman had also cursed her, saying that all who took her under their roof or were kind to her should suffer a like fate. She believed this, and therefore begged them to cast her out of the house and never to see her again. She did not want to bring misfortune down upon such good people. But the peasants refused to do her bidding. It was quite possible that they were alarmed, but they were not the kind of folk who could turn out a poor, sick person.

Soon after that she died, and then along came the misfortunes. Before, there had never been anything but happiness in that cabin. Its inmates were poor, yet not so very poor. The father was a maker of weavers' combs, and mother and children helped him with the work. Father made the frames, mother and the older children did the binding, while the smaller ones planed the teeth and cut them out. They worked from morning until night, but the time passed pleasantly, especially when father talked of the days when he travelled about in foreign lands and sold weavers' combs. Father was so jolly that sometimes mother and the children would laugh until their sides ached at his funny quips and jokes.

The weeks following the death of the poor vagabond woman lingered in the minds of the children like a horrible nightmare. They knew not if the time had been long or short, but they remembered that they were always having funerals at home. One after another they lost their brothers and sisters. At last it was very still and sad in the cabin.

The mother kept up some measure of courage, but the father was not a bit like himself. He could no longer work nor jest, but sat from morning till night, his head buried in his hands, and only brooded.

Once—that was after the third burial—the father had broken out into wild talk, which frightened the children. He said that he could not understand why such misfortunes should come upon them. They had done a kindly thing in helping the sick woman. Could it be true, then, that the evil in this world was more powerful than the good? The mother

tried to reason with him, but she was unable to soothe him.

A few days later the eldest was stricken. She had always been the father's favourite, so when he realized that she, too, must go, he fled from all the misery. The mother never said anything, but she thought it was best for him to be away, as she feared that he might lose his reason. He had brooded too long over this one idea: that God had allowed a wicked person to bring about so much evil.

After the father went away they became very poor. For awhile he sent them money, but afterward things must have gone badly with him, for no more came.

The day of the eldest daughter's burial the mother closed the cabin and left home with the two remaining children, Osa and Mats. She went down to Skåne to work in the beet fields, and found a place at the Jordberga sugar refinery. She was a good worker and had a cheerful and generous nature. Everybody liked her. Many were astonished because she could be so calm after all that she had passed through, but the mother was very strong and patient. When any one spoke to her of her two sturdy children, she only said: "I shall soon lose them also," without a quaver in her voice or a tear in her eye. She had accustomed herself to expect nothing else.

But it did not turn out as she feared. Instead, the sickness came upon herself. She had gone to Skane in the beginning of summer; before autumn she was gone, and the children were left alone.

While their mother was ill she had often said to the children they must remember that she never regretted having let the sick woman stop with them. It was not hard to die when one had done right, she said, for then one could go with a clear conscience.

Before the mother passed away, she tried to make some provision for her children. She asked the people with whom she lived to let them remain in the room which she had occupied. If the children only had a

shelter they would not become a burden to any one. She knew that they could take care of themselves.

Osa and Mats were allowed to keep the room on condition that they would tend the geese, as it was always hard to find children willing to do that work. It turned out as the mother expected: they did maintain themselves. The girl made candy, and the boy carved wooden toys, which they sold at the farm houses. They had a talent for trading and soon began buying eggs and butter from the farmers, which they sold to the workers at the sugar refinery. Osa was the older, and, by the time she was thirteen, she was as responsible as a grown woman. She was quiet and serious, while Mats was lively and talkative. His sister used to say to him that he could outcackle the geese.

When the children had been at Jordberga for two years, there was a lecture given one evening at the schoolhouse. Evidently it was meant for grown-ups, but the two Småland children were in the audience. The lecturer talked about the dread disease called the White Plague, which every year carried off so many people in Sweden.

After the lecture they waited outside the schoolhouse. When the lecturer came out they took hold of hands and walked gravely up to him, asking if they might speak to him.

The stranger must have wondered at the two rosy, baby-faced children standing there talking with an earnestness more in keeping with people thrice their age; but he listened graciously to them. They related what had happened in their home, and asked the lecturer if he thought their mother and their sisters and brothers had died of the sickness he had described.

"Very likely," he answered. "It could hardly have been any other disease."

If only the mother and father had known what the children learned that evening, they might have protected themselves. If they had burned the clothing of the vagabond woman; if they had scoured and aired the cabin and had not used the old bedding, all whom the children mourned might have been living yet. The lecturer said he could not say positively, but he believed that none of their dear ones would have been sick had they understood how to guard against the infection.

Osa and Mats waited awhile before putting the next question, for that was the most important of all. It was not true then that the gipsy woman had sent the sickness because they had befriended the one with whom she was angry. It was not something special that had stricken only them. The lecturer assured them that no person had the power to bring sickness upon another in that way.

Thereupon the children thanked him and went to their room. They talked until late that night.

The next day they gave notice that they could not tend geese another year, but must go elsewhere. Where were they going? Why, to try to find their father. They must tell him that their mother and the other children had died of a common ailment and not something special brought upon them by an angry person. They were very glad that they had found out about this. Now it was their duty to tell their father of it, for probably he was still trying to solve the mystery.

Osa and Mats set out for their old home on the heath. When they arrived they were shocked to find the little cabin in flames. They went to the parsonage and there they learned that a railroad workman had seen their father at Malmberget, far up in Lapland. He had been working in a mine and possibly was still there. When the clergyman heard that the children wanted to go in search of their father he brought forth a map and showed them how far it was to Malmberget and tried to dissuade them from making the journey, but the children insisted that they must find their father. He had left home believing something that was not true. They must find him and tell him that it was all a mistake.

They did not want to spend their little savings buying railway tickets, therefore they decided to go all the way on foot, which they never regretted, as it proved to be a remarkably beautiful journey.

Before they were out of Småland, they stopped at a farm house to buy food. The housewife was a kind, motherly soul who took an interest in the children. She asked them who they were and where they came from, and they told her their story. "Dear, dear! Dear, dear!" she interpolated time and again when they were speaking. Later she petted the children and stuffed them with all kinds of goodies, for which she would not accept a penny. When they rose to thank her and go, the woman asked them to stop at her brother's farm in the next township. Of course the children were delighted.

"Give him my greetings and tell him what has happened to you," said the peasant woman.

This the children did and were well treated. From every farm after that it was always: "If you happen to go in such and such a direction, stop there or there and tell them what has happened to you."

In every farm house to which they were sent there was always a consumptive. So Osa and Mats went through the country unconsciously teaching the people how to combat that dreadful disease.

One day, while still in Lapland, Akka took the boy to Malmberget, where they discovered little Mats lying unconscious at the mouth of the pit. He and Osa had arrived there a short time before. That morning he had been roaming about, hoping to come across his father. He had ventured too near the shaft and been hurt by flying rocks after the setting off of a blast.

Thumbietot ran to the edge of the shaft and called down to the miners that a little boy was injured.

Immediately a number of labourers came rushing up to little Mats. Two of them carried him to the hut where he and Osa were staying.

They did all they could to save him, but it was too late.

Thumbietot felt so sorry for poor Osa. He wanted to help and comfort her; but he knew that if he were to go to her now, he would only frighten her—such as he was!

The night after the burial of little Mats, Osa straightway shut herself in her hut. She sat alone recalling, one after another, things her brother had said and done. There was so much to think about that she did not go straight to bed, but sat up most of the night. The more she thought of her brother the more she realized how hard it would be to live without him. At last she dropped her head on the table and wept.

"What shall I do now that little Mats is gone?" she sobbed.

It was far along toward morning and Osa, spent by the strain of her hard day, finally fell asleep.

She dreamed that little Mats softly opened the door and stepped into the room.

"Osa, you must go and find father," he said.

"How can I when I don't even know where he is?" she replied in her dream.

"Don't worry about that," returned little Mats in his usual, cheery way. "I'll send some one to help you."

Just as Osa, the goose girl, dreamed that little Mats had said this, there was a knock at the door. It was a real knock—not something she heard in the dream, but she was so held by the dream that she could not tell the real from the unreal. As she went on to open the door, she thought:

"This must be the person little Mats promised to send me."

She was right, for it was Thumbietot come to talk to her about her father.

When he saw that she was not afraid of him, he told her in a few words where her father was and how to reach him.

While he was speaking, Osa, the goose girl, gradually regained consciousness; when he had finished she was wide awake.

Then she was so terrified at the thought of talking with an elf that she could not say thank you or anything else, but quickly shut the door.

As she did that she thought she saw an expression of pain flash across the elf's face, but she could not help what she did, for she was beside herself with fright. She crept into bed as quickly as she could and drew the covers over her head.

Although she was afraid of the elf, she had a feeling that he meant well by her. So the next day she made haste to do as he had told her.

18

WITH THE LAPLANDERS

One afternoon in July it rained frightfully up around Lake Luossajaure. The Laplanders, who lived mostly in the open during the summer, had crawled under the tent and were squatting round the fire drinking coffee. While the Laplanders were chatting over their coffee cups, a row boat coming from the Kiruna side pulled ashore at the Lapps' quarters. A workman and a young girl, between thirteen and fourteen, stepped from the boat. The girl was Osa. The Lapp dogs bounded down to them, barking loudly, and a native poked his head out of the tent opening to see what was going on.

"You're just in time, Söderberg!" he said. "The coffee pot is on the fire. No one can do any work in this rain, so come in and tell us the news."

The workman went in, and, with much ado and amid a great deal of laughter and joking, places were made for Söderberg and Osa, though the tent was already crowded to the limit with natives. Osa understood none of the conversation. She sat dumb and looked around. All this was new to her.

Suddenly she lowered her glance, conscious that every one in the tent was looking at her. Söderberg must have said something about her, for now both Lapp men and Lapp women took the short pipes from their mouths and stared at her in open-eyed wonder and awe. The Laplander at her side patted her shoulder and nodded, saying in Swedish, "bra, bra!" (good, good!) A Lapp woman filled a cup to the brim with coffee and passed it under difficulties, while a Lapp boy, who was about

her own age, wriggled and crawled between the squatters over to her.

Osa felt that Söderberg was telling the Laplanders that she had just buried her little brother, Mats. She wished he would find out about her father instead.

The elf had said that he lived with the Lapps, who camped west of Lake Luossajaure, and she had begged leave to ride up on a sand truck to seek him, as no regular passenger trains came so far. Both labourers and foremen had assisted her as best they could. An engineer had sent Söderberg across the lake with her, as he spoke Lappish. She had hoped to meet her father as soon as she arrived. Her glance wandered anxiously from face to face, but she saw only natives. Her father was not there.

She noticed that the Lapps and the Swede, Söderberg, grew more and more earnest as they talked among themselves. The Lapps shook their heads and tapped their foreheads, as if they were speaking of some one that was not quite right in his mind.

She became so uneasy that she could no longer endure the suspense and asked Söderberg what the Laplanders knew of her father.

"They say he has gone fishing," said the workman. "They're not sure that he can get back to the camp to-night; but as soon as the weather clears, one of them will go in search of him."

Thereupon he turned to the Lapps and went on talking to them. He did not wish to give Osa an opportunity to question him further about Jon Esserson.

THE NEXT MORNING

Ola Serka himself, who was the most distinguished man among the Lapps, had said that he would find Osa's father, but he appeared to be in no haste and sat huddled outside the tent, thinking of Jon Esserson and wondering how best to tell him of his daughter's arrival. It would

require diplomacy in order that Jon Esserson might not become alarmed
and flee. He was an odd sort of man who was afraid of children. He
used to say that the sight of them made him so melancholy that he could
not endure.

While Ola Serka deliberated, Osa, the goose girl, and Aslak, the
young Lapp boy who had stared so hard at her the night before, sat on
the ground in front of the tent and chatted.

Aslak had been to school and could speak Swedish. He was telling
Osa about the life of the "Saméfolk," assuring her that they fared better
than other people.

Osa thought that they lived wretchedly, and told him so.

"You don't know what you are talking about!" said Aslak curtly.
"Only stop with us a week and you shall see that we are the happiest
people on earth."

Old Ola understood more Swedish than he was willing to have any
one know, and he had overheard his son's remarks. While he was
listening, it had suddenly flashed on him how he should handle this
delicate matter of telling Jon Esserson that his daughter had come in
search of him.

Ola Serka went down to Lake Luossajaure and had walked a short
distance along the strand, when he happened upon a man who sat on a
rock fishing.

The fisherman was gray-haired and bent. His eyes blinked wearily
and there was something slack and helpless about him. He looked like a
man who had tried to carry a burden too heavy for him, or to solve a
problem too difficult for him, who had become broken and despondent
over his failure.

"You must have had luck with your fishing, Jon, since you've been
at it all night?" said the mountaineer in Lappish, as he approached.

The fisherman gave a start, then glanced up. The bait on his hook

was gone and not a fish lay on the strand beside him. He hastened to rebait the hook and throw out the line. "There's a matter that I wanted to talk over with you," said Ola. "You know that I had a little daughter who died last winter, and we have always missed her in the tent."

"Yes, I know," said the fisherman abruptly, a cloud passing over his face—as though he disliked being reminded of a dead child.

"It's not worth while to spend one's life grieving," said the Laplander.

"I suppose it isn't."

"Now I'm thinking of adopting another child. Don't you think it would be a good idea?"

"That depends on the child, Ola."

"I will tell you what I know of the girl," said Ola. Then he told the fisherman that around midsummer-time, two strange children—a boy and a girl—had come to the mines to look for their father, but as their father was away, they had stayed to await his return. While there, the boy had been killed by a blast of rock.

Thereupon Ola gave a beautiful description of how brave the little girl had been, and of how she had won the admiration and sympathy of everyone.

"Is that the girl you want to take into your tent?" asked the fisherman.

"Yes," returned the Lapp. "When we heard her story we were all deeply touched and said among ourselves that so good a sister would also make a good daughter, and we hoped that she would come to us."

The fisherman sat quietly thinking a moment. It was plain that he continued the conversation only to please his friend, the Lapp.

"I presume the girl is one of your race?"

"No," said Ola, "she doesn't belong to the Saméfolk."

"Perhaps she's the daughter of some new settler and is accustomed

to the life here?"

"No, she's from the far south," replied Ola, as if this was of small importance.

The fisherman grew more interested.

"Then I don't believe that you can take her," he said. "It's doubtful if she could stand living in a tent in winter, since she was not brought up that way."

"She will find kind parents and kind brothers and sisters in the tent," insisted Ola Serka. "It's worse to be alone than to freeze."

The fisherman became more and more zealous to prevent the adoption. It seemed as if he could not bear the thought of a child of Swedish parents being taken in by Laplanders.

"You said just now that she had a father in the mine."

"He's dead," said the Lapp abruptly.

"I suppose you have thoroughly investigated this matter, Ola?"

"What's the use of going to all that trouble?" disdained the Lapp. "I ought to know! Would the girl and her brother have been obliged to roam about the country if they had a father living? Would two children have been forced to care for themselves if they had a father? The girl herself thinks he's alive, but I say that he must be dead."

The man with the tired eyes turned to Ola.

"What is the girl's name, Ola?" he asked.

The mountaineer thought awhile, then said:

"I can't remember it. I must ask her."

"Ask her! Is she already here?"

"She's down at the camp."

"What, Ola! Have you taken her in before knowing her father's wishes?"

"What do I care for her father! If he isn't dead, he's probably the kind of man who cares nothing for his child. He may be glad to have

another take her in hand."

The fisherman threw down his rod and rose with an alertness in his movements that bespoke new life.

"I don't think her father can be like other folk," continued the mountaineer. "I dare say he is a man who is haunted by gloomy forebodings and therefore can not work steadily. What kind of a father would that be for the girl?"

While Ola was talking the fisherman started up the strand.

"Where are you going?" queried the Lapp.

"I'm going to have a look at your foster-daughter, Ola."

"Good!" said the Lapp. "Come along and meet her. I think you'll say that she will be a good daughter to me."

The Swede rushed on so rapidly that the Laplander could hardly keep pace with him.

After a moment Ola said to his companion:

"Now I recall that her name is Osa—this girl I'm adopting."

The other man only kept hurrying along and old Ola Serka was so well pleased that he wanted to laugh aloud.

When they came in sight of the tents, Ola said a few words more.

"She came here to us Saméfolk to find her father and not to become my foster-child. But if she doesn't find him, I shall be glad to keep her in my tent."

The fisherman hastened all the faster.

"I might have known that he would be alarmed when I threatened to take his daughter into the Lapps' quarters," laughed Ola to himself.

When the man from Kiruna, who had brought Osa to the tent, turned back later in the day, he had two people with him in the boat, who sat close together, holding hands—as if they never again wanted to part.

They were Jon Esserson and his daughter. Both were unlike what they had been a few hours earlier.

The father looked less bent and weary and his eyes were clear and good, as if at last he had found the answer to that which had troubled him so long.

Osa, the goose girl, did not glance longingly about, for she had found some one to care for her, and now she could be a child again.

19

HOMEWARD BOUND!

THE FIRST TRAVELLING DAY *Saturday, October first.*

The boy sat on the goosey-gander's back and rode up amongst the clouds. Some thirty geese, in regular order, flew rapidly southward. There was a rustling of feathers and the many wings beat the air so noisily that one could scarcely hear one's own voice. Akka from Kebnekaise flew in the lead; after her came Yksi and Kaksi, Kolme and Neljä, Viisi and Kuusi, Morten Goosey-Gander and Dunfin. The six goslings which had accompanied the flock the autumn before had now left to look after themselves. Instead, the old geese were taking with them twenty-two goslings that had grown up in the glen that summer. Eleven flew to the right, eleven to the left; and they did their best to fly at even distances, like the big birds.

The poor youngsters had never before been on a long trip and at first they had difficulty in keeping up with the rapid flight.

"Akka from Kebnekaise! Akka from Kebnekaise!" they cried in plaintive tones.

"What's the matter?" said the leader-goose sharply.

"Our wings are tired of moving, our wings are tired of moving!" wailed the young ones.

"The longer you keep it up, the better it will go," answered the leader-goose, without slackening her speed. And she was quite right, for when the goslings had flown two hours longer, they complained no more

of being tired.

But in the mountain glen they had been in the habit of eating all day long, and very soon they began to feel hungry.

"Akka, Akka, Akka from Kebnekaise!" wailed the goslings pitifully.

"What's the trouble now?" asked the leader-goose.

"We're so hungry, we can't fly any more!" whimpered the goslings. "We're so hungry, we can't fly any more!"

"Wild geese must learn to eat air and drink wind," said the leader-goose, and kept right on flying.

It actually seemed as if the young ones were learning to live on wind and air, for when they had flown a little longer, they said nothing more about being hungry.

The goose flock was still in the mountain regions, and the old geese called out the names of all the peaks as they flew past, so that the youngsters might learn them. When they had been calling out a while:

"This is Porsotjokko, this is Särjaktjokko, this is Sulitelma," and so on, the goslings became impatient again.

"Akka, Akka, Akka!" they shrieked in heart-rending tones.

"What's wrong?" said the leader-goose.

"We haven't room in our heads for any more of those awful names!" shrieked the goslings.

"The more you put into your heads the more you can get into them," retorted the leader-goose, and continued to call out the queer names.

Now, at last, the goslings' wings had grown, so that the geese could start for the south. The boy was so happy that he laughed and sang as he rode on the goose's back. It was not only on account of the darkness and cold that he longed to get away from Lapland; there were other reasons too.

The first weeks of his sojourn there the boy had not been the least

bit homesick. He thought he had never before seen such a glorious country. The only worry he had had was to keep the mosquitoes from eating him up.

The boy had seen very little of the goosey-gander, because the big, white gander thought only of his Dunfin and was unwilling to leave her for a moment. On the other hand, Thumbietot had stuck to Akka , and they had passed many happy hours together.

Akka had taken him with them on long trips. He had stood on snow-capped Mount Kebnekaise, had looked down at the glaciers and visited many high cliffs. Akka had shown him deep-hidden mountain dales and had let him peep into caves where mother wolves brought up their young.

Ever since he had seen Osa, he longed for the day when he might go home with Morten Goosey-Gander and be a normal human being once more. He wanted to be himself again, so that Osa would not be afraid to talk to him and would not shut the door in his face.

Yes, indeed, he was glad that at last they were speeding southward.

20

LEGENDS FROM HÄRJEDALEN

Tuesday, October fourth.

The boy had had three days' travel in the rain and mist and longed for some sheltered nook, where he might rest awhile.

At last the geese alighted to feed and ease their wings a bit. To his great relief the boy saw an observation tower on a hill close by, and dragged himself to it.

When he had climbed to the top of the tower he found a party of tourists there, so he quickly crawled into a dark corner and was soon sound asleep.

At last, when the tourists were gone, and the boy could crawl from his hiding place, he saw no wild geese, and no Morten Goosey-Gander came to fetch him. He called, "Here am I, where are you?" as loud as he could, but his travelling companions did not appear. Not for a second did he think they had deserted him; but he feared that they had met with some mishap and was wondering what he should do to find them, when Bataki, the raven, lit beside him.

The boy never dreamed that he should greet Bataki with such a glad welcome as he now gave him.

"Dear Bataki," he burst forth. "How fortunate that you are here! Maybe you know what has become of Morten Goosey-Gander and the wild geese?"

"I've just come with a greeting from them," replied the raven. "Akka saw a hunter prowling about on the mountain and therefore dared not stay to wait for you, but has gone on ahead. Get up on my back and you

shall soon be with your friends."

The boy quickly seated himself on the raven's back and Bataki would soon have caught up with the geese had he not been hindered by a fog. Bataki flew along above the fog in clear air and sparkling sunshine, but the wild geese must have circled down among the damp clouds, for it was impossible to sight them. The boy and the raven called and shrieked, but got no response.

"Well, this is a stroke of ill luck!" said Bataki finally. "But we know that they are travelling toward the south, and of course I'll find them as soon as the mist clears."

The boy was distressed at the thought of being parted from Morten Goosey-Gander just now, when the geese were on the wing, and the big white one might meet with all sorts of mishaps. After Thumbietot had been sitting worrying for two hours or more, he remarked to himself that, thus far, there had been no mishap, and it was not worth while to lose heart.

Just then he heard a rooster crowing down on the ground, and instantly he bent forward on the raven's back and called out:

"What's the name of the country I'm travelling over?"

"It's called Härjedalen, Härjedalen, Härjedalen," crowed the rooster.

"How does it look down there where you are?" the boy asked.

"Cliffs in the west, woods in the east, broad valleys across the whole country," replied the rooster.

"Thank you," cried the boy. "You give a clear account of it."

When they had travelled a little farther, he heard a crow cawing down in the mist.

"What kind of people live in this country?" shouted the boy.

"Good, thrifty peasants," answered the crow. "Good, thrifty peasants."

"What do they do?" asked the boy. "What do they do?"

"They raise cattle and fell forests," cawed the crow.

"Thanks," replied the boy. "You answer well."

A bit farther on he heard a human voice yodeling and singing down in the mist.

It was not long before the mist went away as suddenly as it had come. Then the boy saw a beautiful landscape, with high cliffs as in Jämtland, but there were no large, flourishing settlements on the mountain slopes. The villages lay far apart, and the farms were small. Bataki followed the stream southward till they came within sight of a village. There he alighted in a stubble field and let the boy dismount.

"In the summer grain grew on this ground," said Bataki. "Look around and see if you can't find something eatable."

The boy acted upon the suggestion and before long he found a blade of wheat. As he picked out the grains and ate them, Bataki talked to him.

"Do you see that mountain towering directly south of us?" he asked.

"Yes, of course, I see it," said the boy.

"It is called Sonfjället," continued the raven; "you can imagine that wolves were plentiful there once upon a time."

"Perhaps you remember a good wolf story you could tell me?" said the boy.

"I've been told that a long, long time ago the wolves from Sonfjället are supposed to have waylaid a man who had gone out to peddle his wares," began Bataki. It was winter time and the wolves made for him as he was driving over the ice on Lake Ljusna. There were about nine or ten, and the man from Hede had a poor old horse, so there was very little hope of his escaping.

"When the man heard the wolves howl and saw how many there were after him, he lost his head, and it did not occur to him that he

ought to dump his casks and jugs out of the sledge, to lighten the load. He only whipped up the horse and made the best speed he could, but he soon observed that the wolves were gaining on him. The shores were desolate and he was fourteen miles from the nearest farm. He thought that his final hour had come, and was paralyzed with fear.

"While he sat there, terrified, he saw something move in the brush, which had been set in the ice to mark out the road; and when he discovered who it was that walked there, his fear grew more and more intense.

"Wild beasts were not coming toward him, but a poor old woman, named Finn-Malin, who was in the habit of roaming about on highways and byways. She was a hunchback, and slightly lame, so he recognized her at a distance.

"The old woman was walking straight toward the wolves. The sledge had hidden them from her view, and the man comprehended at once that, if he were to drive on without warning her, she would walk right into the jaws of the wild beasts, and while they were rending her, he would have time enough to get away.

"The old woman walked slowly, bent over a cane. It was plain that she was doomed if he did not help her, but even if he were to stop and take her into the sledge, it was by no means certain that she would be safe. More than likely the wolves would catch up with them, and he and she and the horse would all be killed. He wondered if it were not better to sacrifice one life in order that two might be spared—this flashed upon him the minute he saw the old woman. He had also time to think how it would be with him afterward—if perchance he might not regret that he had not succoured her; or if people should some day learn of the meeting and that he had not tried to help her. It was a terrible temptation.

"'I would rather not have seen her,' he said to himself.

"Just then the wolves howled savagely. The horse reared, plunged forward, and dashed past the old beggar woman. She, too, had heard the howling of the wolves, and, as the man from Hede drove by, he saw that the old woman knew what awaited her. She stood motionless, her mouth open for a cry, her arms stretched out for help. But she neither cried nor tried to throw herself into the sledge. Something seemed to have turned her to stone. 'It was I,' thought the man. 'I must have looked like a demon as I passed.'

"He tried to feel satisfied, now that he was certain of escape; but at that very moment his heart reproached him. Never before had he done a dastardly thing, and he felt now that his whole life was blasted.

"'Let come what may,' he said, and reined in the horse, 'I cannot leave her alone with the wolves!'

"It was with great difficulty that he got the horse to turn, but in the end he managed it and promptly drove back to her.

"'Be quick and get into the sledge,' he said gruffly; for he was mad with himself for not leaving the old woman to her fate.

"'You might stay at home once in awhile, you old hag!' he growled. 'Now both my horse and I will come to grief on your account.'

"The old woman did not say a word, but the man from Hede was in no mood to spare her.

"'the horse has already tramped thirty-five miles to-day, and the load hasn't lightened any since you got up on it!' he grumbled, 'so that you must understand he'll soon be exhausted.'

"The sledge runners crunched on the ice, but for all that he heard how the wolves panted, and knew that the beasts were almost upon him.

"'It's all up with us!' he said. 'Much good it was, either to you or to me, this attempt to save you, Finn-Malin!'

"Up to this point the old woman had been silent—like one who is accustomed to take abuse—but now she said a few words.

"'I can't understand why you don't throw out your wares and lighten the load. You can come back again to-morrow and gather them up.'

"The man realized that this was sound advice and was surprised that he had not thought of it before. He tossed the reins to the old woman, loosed the ropes that bound the casks, and pitched them out. The wolves were right upon them, but now they stopped to examine that which was thrown on the ice, and the travellers again had the start of them.

"'If this does not help you,' said the old woman, 'you understand, of course, that I will give myself up to the wolves voluntarily, that you may escape.'

"While she was speaking the man was trying to push a heavy brewer's vat from the long sledge. As he tugged at this he paused, as if he could not quite make up his mind to throw it out; but, in reality, his mind was taken up with something altogether different.

"''s urely a man and a horse who have no infirmities need not let a feeble old woman be devoured by wolves for their sakes!' he thought. 'There must be some other way of salvation. Why, of course, there is! It's only my stupidity that hinders me from finding the way.'

"Again he started to push the vat, then paused once more and burst out laughing.

"The old woman was alarmed and wondered if he had gone mad, but the man from Hede was laughing at himself because he had been so stupid all the while. It was the simplest thing in the world to save all three of them. He could not imagine why he had not thought of it before.

"'Listen to what I say to you, Malin!' he said. 'It was splendid of you to be willing to throw yourself to the wolves. But you won't have to do that because I know how we can all three be helped without endangering the life of any. Remember, whatever I may do, you are to sit still and drive down to Linsäll. There you must waken the townspeople and tell them that I'm alone out here on the ice, surrounded by wolves, and ask

them to come and help me.'

"The man waited until the wolves were almost upon the sledge. Then he rolled out the big brewer's vat, jumped down, and crawled in under it.

"It was a huge vat, large enough to hold a whole Christmas brew. The wolves pounced upon it and bit at the hoops, but the vat was too heavy for them to move. They could not get at the man inside.

"He knew that he was safe and laughed at the wolves. After a bit he was serious again.

"'For the future, when I get into a tight place, I shall remember this vat, and I shall bear in mind that I need never wrong either myself or others, for there is always a third way out of a difficulty if only one can hit upon it.'"

With this Bataki closed his narrative.

The boy noticed that the raven never spoke unless there was some special meaning back of his words, and the longer he listened to him, the more thoughtful he became.

"I wonder why you told me that story?" remarked the boy.

"I just happened to think of it as I stood here, gazing up at Sonfjället," replied the raven.

Now they had travelled farther down Lake Ljusna and in an hour or so they came to Kolsätt, close to the border of Hälsingland. Here the raven alighted near a little hut that had no windows—only a shutter. From the chimney rose sparks and smoke, and from within the sound of heavy hammering was heard.

"Whenever I see this smithy," observed the raven, "I'm reminded that, in former times, there were such skilled blacksmiths here in Härjedalen, more especially in this village—that they couldn't be matched in the whole country."

"I remember one about a smith from Härjedalen who once invited

two other master blacksmiths—one from Dalecarlia and one from Vermland—to compete with him at nail-making. The challenge was accepted and the three blacksmiths met here at Kolsätt. The Dalecarlian began. He forged a dozen nails, so even and smooth and sharp that they couldn't be improved upon. After him came the Vermlander. He, too, forged a dozen nails, which were quite perfect and, moreover, he finished them in half the time that it took the Dalecarlian. When the judges saw this they said to the Härjedal smith that it wouldn't be worth while for him to try, since he could not forge better than the Dalecarlian or faster than the Vermlander.

"'I sha'n't give up! There must be still another way of excelling,' insisted the Härjedal smith.

"He placed the iron on the anvil without heating it at the forge; he simply hammered it hot and forged nail after nail, without the use of either anvil or bellows. None of the judges had ever seen a blacksmith wield a hammer more masterfully, and the Härjedal smith was proclaimed the best in the land."

With these remarks Bataki subsided, and the boy grew even more thoughtful.

"I wonder what your purpose was in telling me that?" he queried.

"The story dropped into my mind when I saw the old smithy again," said Bataki in an offhand manner.

The two travellers rose again into the air and the raven carried the boy southward till they came to Lillhärdal Parish, where he alighted on a leafy mound at the top of a ridge.

"I wonder if you know upon what mound you are standing?" said Bataki.

The boy had to confess that he did not know.

"This is a grave," said Bataki. "Beneath this mound lies the first settler in Härjedalen."

"Perhaps you have a story to tell of him too?" said the boy.

"I haven't heard much about him, but I think he was a Norwegian. He had served with a Norwegian king, got into his bad graces, and had to flee the country.

"Later he went over to the Swedish king, who lived at Upsala, and took service with him. But, after a time, he asked for the hand of the king's sister in marriage, and when the king wouldn't give him such a high-born bride, he eloped with her. By that time he had managed to get himself into such disfavour that it wasn't safe for him to live either in Norway or Sweden, and he did not wish to move to a foreign country. 'But there must still be a course open to me,' he thought. With his servants and treasures, he journeyed through Dalecarlia until he arrived in the desolate forests beyond the outskirts of the province. There he settled, built houses and broke up land. Thus, you see, he was the first man to settle in this part of the country."

As the boy listened to the last story, he looked very serious.

"I wonder what your object is in telling me all this?" he repeated.

Bataki twisted and turned and screwed up his eyes, and it was some time before he answered the boy.

"Since we are here alone," he said finally, "I shall take this opportunity to question you regarding a certain matter.

"Have you ever tried to ascertain upon what terms the elf who transformed you was to restore you to a normal human being?"

"The only stipulation I've heard anything about was that I should take the white goosey-gander up to Lapland and bring him back to Skåne, safe and sound."

"I thought as much," said Bataki; "for when last we met, you talked confidently of there being nothing more contemptible than deceiving a friend who trusts one. You'd better ask Akka about the terms. You know, I dare say, that she was at your home and talked with the elf."

"Akka hasn't told me of this," said the boy wonderingly.

"She must have thought that it was best for you not to know just what the elf did say. Naturally she would rather help you than Morten Goosey-Gander.»

"It is singular, Bataki, that you always have a way of making me feel unhappy and anxious," said the boy.

"I dare say it might seem so," continued the raven, "but this time I believe that you will be grateful to me for telling you that the elf's words were to this effect: You were to become a normal human being again if you would bring back Morten Goosey-Gander that your mother might lay him on the block and chop his head off."

The boy leaped up.

"That's only one of your base fabrications," he cried indignantly.

"You can ask Akka yourself," said Bataki. "I see her coming up there with her whole flock. And don't forget what I have told you today. There is usually a way out of all difficulties, if only one can find it. I shall be interested to see what success you have."

21

THE TREASURE ON THE ISLAND

Wednesday, October fifth.

To-day the boy took advantage of the rest hour, when Akka was feeding apart from the other wild geese, to ask her if that which Bataki had related was true, and Akka could not deny it. The boy made the leader-goose promise that she would not divulge the secret to Morten Goosey-Gander. The big white gander was so brave and generous that he might do something rash were he to learn of the elf's stipulations.

Later the boy sat on the goose-back, glum and silent, and hung his head. He heard the wild geese call out to the goslings that now they were in Dalarne, they could see Städjan in the north, and that now they were flying over Österdal River to Horrmund Lake and were coming to Vesterdal River. But the boy did not care even to glance at all this.

"I shall probably travel around with wild geese the rest of my life," he remarked to himself, "and I am likely to see more of this land than I wish."

He was quite as indifferent when the wild geese called out to him that now they had arrived in Vermland and that the stream they were following southward was Klarälven.

"I've seen so many rivers already," thought the boy, "why bother to look at one more?"

Even had he been more eager for sight-seeing, there was not very much to be seen, for northern Vermland is nothing but vast,

monotonous forest tracts, through which Klarälven winds—narrow and rich in rapids. Here and there one can see a charcoal kiln, a forest clearing, or a few low, chimneyless huts, occupied by Finns. But the forest as a whole is so extensive one might fancy it was far up in Lapland.

ON THEIR WAY TO THE SEA *Friday, October seventh.*

The wild geese had flown straight south; but when they left Fryksdalen they veered in another direction, travelling over western Vermland and Dalsland, toward Bohuslän.

That was a jolly trip! The goslings were now so used to flying that they complained no more of fatigue, and the boy was fast recovering his good humour.

"Do you know, Morten Goosey-Gander, that it will be rather monotonous for us to stay at home all winter after having been on a trip like this," he said, as they were flying far up in the air. "I'm sitting here thinking that we ought to go abroad with the geese."

"Surely you are not in earnest!" said the goosey-gander. Since he had proved to the wild geese his ability to travel with them all the way to Lapland, he was perfectly satisfied to get back to the goose pen in Holger Nilsson's cow shed.

The boy sat silently a while and gazed down on Vermland, where the birch woods, leafy groves, and gardens were clad in red and yellow autumn colours.

"I don't think I've ever seen the earth beneath us as lovely as it is to-day!" he finally remarked. "The lakes are like blue satin bands. Don't you think it would be a pity to settle down in West Vemminghög and never see any more of the world?"

"I thought you wanted to go home to your mother and father and show them what a splendid boy you had become?" said the goosey-

gander.

All summer he had been dreaming of what a proud moment it would be for him when he should alight in the house yard before Holger Nilsson's cabin and show Dunfin and the six goslings to the geese and chickens, the cows and the cat, and to Mother Holger Nilsson herself, so that he was not very happy over the boy's proposal.

"Now, Morten Goosey-Gander, don't you think yourself that it would be hard never to see anything more that is beautiful!" said the boy.

"I would rather see the fat grain fields of Söderslätt than these lean hills," answered the goosey-gander. "But you must know very well that if you really wish to continue the trip, I can't be parted from you."

"That is just the answer I had expected from you," said the boy, and his voice betrayed that he was relieved of a great anxiety.

"I might possibly miss not being in danger of my life at least once every day or two," he thought. "Anyhow it's best to be content with things as they are."

He did not speak of this idea to the big white gander, because the geese were now flying over Bohuslän with all the speed they could muster, and the goosey-gander was puffing so hard that he would not have had the strength to reply.

The sun was far down on the horizon, and disappeared every now and then behind a hill; still the geese kept forging ahead.

As the boy gazed at the broad, endless sea and the red evening sun, which had such a kindly glow that he dared to look straight at it, he felt a sense of peace and calm penetrate his soul.

THE GIFT OF THE WILD GEESE

The geese stood sleeping on a little rock islet just beyond Fjällbacka. When it drew on toward midnight, and the moon hung high in the

335

heavens, old Akka shook the sleepiness out of her eyes. After that she walked around and awakened Yksi and Kaksi, Kolme and Neljä, Viisi and Kuusi, and, last of all, she gave Thumbietot a nudge with her bill that startled him.

"What is it, Mother Akka?" he asked, springing up in alarm.

"Nothing serious," assured the leader-goose. "It's just this: we seven who have been long together want to fly a short distance out to sea to-night, and we wondered if you would care to come with us."

The boy knew that Akka would not have proposed this move had there not been something important on foot, so he promptly seated himself on her back. The flight was straight west. The wild geese first flew over a belt of large and small islands near the coast, then over a broad expanse of open sea, till they reached the large cluster known as the Väder Islands. All of them were low and rocky, and in the moonlight one could see that they were rather large.

Akka looked at one of the smallest islands and alighted there. It consisted of a round, gray stone hill, with a wide cleft across it, into which the sea had cast fine, white sea sand and a few shells.

As the boy slid from the goose's back. He stood gazing admiringly at two beautiful shells, but when Akka spoke his name, he glanced up.

"You must have wondered, Thumbietot, why we turned out of our course to fly here to the West Sea," said Akka.

"To be frank, I did think it strange," answered the boy. "But I knew, of course, that you always have some good reason for whatever you do."

"You have a good opinion of me," returned Akka, "but I almost fear you will lose it now, for it's very probable that we have made this journey in vain.

"Many years ago it happened that two of the other old geese and myself encountered frightful storms during a spring flight and were wind-driven to this island. When we discovered that there was only open

sea before us, we feared we should be swept so far out that we should never find our way back to land, so we lay down on the waves between these bare cliffs, where the storm compelled us to remain for several days.

"We suffered terribly from hunger; once we ventured up to the cleft on this island in search of food. We couldn't find a green blade, but we saw a number of securely tied bags half buried in the sand. We hoped to find grain in the bags and pulled and tugged at them till we tore the cloth. However, no grain poured out, but shining gold pieces. For such things we wild geese had no use, so we left them where they were. We haven't thought of the find in all these years; but this autumn something has come up to make us wish for gold.

"We do not know that the treasure is still here, but we have travelled all this way to ask you to look into the matter."

With a shell in either hand the boy jumped down into the cleft and began to scoop up the sand. He found no bags, but when he had made a deep hole he heard the clink of metal and saw that he had come upon a gold piece. Then he dug with his fingers and felt many coins in the sand. So he hurried back to Akka.

"The bags have rotted and fallen apart," he exclaimed, "and the money lies scattered all through the sand."

"That's well!" said Akka. "Now fill in the hole and smooth it over so no one will notice the sand has been disturbed."

The boy did as he was told, but when he came up from the

cleft he was astonished to see that the wild geese were lined up, with Akka in the lead, and were marching toward him with great solemnity.

The geese paused in front of him, and all bowed their heads many times, looking so grave that he had to doff his cap and make an obeisance to them.

"The fact is," said Akka, "we old geese have been thinking that if Thumbietot had been in the service of human beings and had done as much for them as he has for us they would not let him go without rewarding him well."

"I haven't helped you; it is you who have taken good care of me," returned the boy.

"We think also," continued Akka, "that when a human being has attended us on a whole journey he shouldn't be allowed to leave us as poor as when he came."

"I know that what I have learned this year with you is worth more to me than gold or lands," said the boy.

"Since these gold coins have been lying unclaimed in the cleft all these years, I think that you ought to have them," declared the wild goose.

"I thought you said something about needing this money yourselves," reminded the boy.

"We do need it, so as to be able to give you such recompense as will make your mother and father think you have been working as a goose boy with worthy people."

The boy turned half round and cast a glance toward the sea, then faced about and looked straight into Akka's bright eyes.

"I think it strange, Mother Akka, that you turn me away from your service like this and pay me off before I have given you notice," he said.

"As long as we wild geese remain in Sweden, I trust that you will stay with us," said Akka. "I only wanted to show you where the treasure

was while we could get to it without going too far out of our course."

"All the same it looks as if you wished to be rid of me before I want to go," argued Thumbietot. "After all the good times we have had together, I think you ought to let me go abroad with you."

When the boy said this, Akka and the other wild geese stretched their long necks straight up and stood a moment, with bills half open, drinking in air.

"That is something I haven't thought about," said Akka, when she recovered herself. "Before you decide to come with us, you had better hear that the elf couldn't give you easier terms, and said 'You can tell Nils Holgersson from me that he would do well to return soon with his goose, for matters on the farm are in a bad shape. His father has had to forfeit a bond for his brother, whom he trusted. He has bought a horse with borrowed money, and the beast went lame the first time he drove it. Since then it has been of no earthly use to him. Tell Nils Holgersson that his parents have had to sell two of the cows and that they must give up the croft unless they receive help from somewhere.'"

When the boy heard this he frowned and clenched his fists so hard that the nails dug into his flesh.

"It is cruel of the elf to make the conditions so hard for me that I can not go home and relieve my parents, but he sha'n't turn me into a traitor to a friend! My father and mother are square and upright folk. I know they would rather forfeit my help than have me come back to them with a guilty conscience."

22

THE JOURNEY TO VEMMINGHÖG

Thursday, November third.

One day in the beginning of November the wild geese flew over Halland Ridge and into Skåne. For several weeks they had been resting on the wide plains around Falköping.

Nils Holgersson had tried to keep a stout heart; but it was hard for him to reconcile himself to his fate. "If I were only well out of Skåne and in some foreign land," he had thought, "I should know for certain that I had nothing to hope for, and would feel easier in my mind."

Finally, one morning, the geese started out and flew toward Halland.

When the wild geese continued the journey farther south, along the narrow coast-lands, the boy leaned over the goose's neck and did not take his glance from the ground.

He saw the hills gradually disappear and the plain spread under him, open sea came clear up to firm land. Here there were no more forests: here the plain was supreme. It spread all the way to the horizon. A land that lay so exposed, with field upon field, reminded the boy of Skåne. He felt both happy and sad as he looked at it.

"I can't be very far from home," he thought.

Many times during the trip the goslings had asked the old geese: "How does it look in foreign lands?"

"Wait, wait! You shall soon see," the old geese had answered.

When the wild geese had passed Halland Ridge and gone a distance

into Skåne, Akka called out:

"Now look down! Look all around! It is like this in foreign lands."

Just then they flew over Söder Ridge. The whole long range of hills was clad in beech woods, and beautiful, turreted castles peeped out here and there.

"Does it look like this in foreign lands?" asked the goslings.

"It looks exactly like this wherever there are forest-clad ridges," replied Akka, "only one doesn't see many of them. Wait! You shall see how it looks in general."

Akka led the geese farther south to the great Skåne plain. Little beech-encircled meadow lakes, each of them adorned by its own stately manor, shimmered here and there.

"Now look down! Look carefully!" called the leader-goose. "Thus it is in foreign lands, from the Baltic coast all the way down to the high Alps. Farther than that I have never travelled."

When the goslings had seen the plain, the leader-goose flew down the Öresund coast. Swampy meadows sloped gradually toward the sea. In some places were high, steep banks, in others drift-sand fields, where the sand lay heaped in banks and hills.

"Now look down! Look well! This is how it looks along the coasts in foreign lands."

After Akka had been flying about in this manner a long time she alighted suddenly on a marsh in Vemminghög township and the boy could not help thinking that she had travelled over Skåne just to let him see that his was a country which could compare favourably with any in the world.

From the moment that he had seen the first willow grove his heart ached with homesickness.

23

HOME AT LAST

Tuesday, November eighth.

The atmosphere was dull and hazy. The wild geese had been feeding on the big meadow around Skerup church and were having their noonday rest when Akka came up to the boy.

"It looks as if we should have calm weather for awhile," she remarked, "and I think we'll cross the Baltic to-morrow."

"Indeed!" said the boy abruptly, for his throat contracted so that he could hardly speak. All along he had cherished the hope that he would be released from the enchantment while he was still in Skåne.

"We are quite near West Vemminghög now," said Akka, "and I thought that perhaps you might like to go home for awhile. It may be some time before you have another opportunity to see your people."

"Perhaps I had better not," said the boy hesitatingly, but something in his voice betrayed that he was glad of Akka's proposal.

"If the goosey-gander remains with us, no harm can come to him," Akka assured. "I think you had better find out how your parents are getting along. You might be of some help to them, even if you're not a normal boy."

"You are right, Mother Akka. I should have thought of that long ago," said the boy impulsively. The next second he and the leader-goose were on their way to his home. It was not long before Akka alighted behind the stone hedge encircling the little farm.

"It seems to me only yesterday that I first saw you come flying through the air."

"I wonder if your father has a gun," said Akka suddenly.

"You may be sure he has," returned the boy. "It was just the gun that kept me at home that Sunday morning when I should have been at church."

"Then I don't dare to stand here and wait for you," said Akka. "You had better meet us at Smygahök early to-morrow morning, so that you may stay at home over night."

"Oh, don't go yet, Mother Akka!" begged the boy, jumping from the hedge.

He could not tell just why it was, but he felt as if something would happen, either to the wild goose or to himself, to prevent their future meeting.

"No doubt you see that I'm distressed because I cannot get back my right form; but I want to say to you that I don't regret having gone with you last spring," he added. "I would rather forfeit the chance of ever being human again than to have missed that trip."

Akka breathed quickly before she answered.

"There's a little matter I should have mentioned to you before this, but since you are not going back to your home for good, I thought there was no hurry about it. Still it may as well be said now."

"You know very well that I am always glad to do your bidding," said the boy.

"If you have learned anything at all from us, Thumbietot, you no longer think that the humans should have the whole earth to themselves," said the wild goose, solemnly. "Remember you have a large country and you can easily afford to leave a few bare rocks, a few shallow lakes and swamps, a few desolate cliffs and remote forests to us poor, dumb creatures, where we can be allowed to live in peace. All my days I have been hounded and hunted. It would be a comfort to know that there is a refuge somewhere for one like me."

"Indeed, I should be glad to help if I could," said the boy, "but it's not likely that I shall ever again have any influence among human beings."

"Well, we're standing here talking as if we were never to meet again," said Akka, "but we shall see each other to-morrow, of course. Now I'll return to my flock."

She spread her wings and started to fly, but came back and stroked Thumbietot up and down with her bill before she flew away.

It was broad daylight, but no human being moved on the farm and the boy could go where he pleased. He hastened to the cow shed, because he knew that he could get the best information from the cows.

It looked rather barren in their shed. In the spring there had been three fine cows there, but now there was only one—Mayrose. It was quite apparent that she yearned for her comrades. Her head drooped sadly, and she had hardly touched the feed in her crib.

"Good day, Mayrose!" said the boy, running fearlessly into her stall. "How are mother and father? How are the cat and the chickens? What has become of Star and Gold-Lily?"

When Mayrose heard the boy's voice she started, and appeared as if she were going to gore him. But she was not so quick-tempered now as formerly, and took time to look well at Nils Holgersson.

He was just as little now as when he went away, and wore the same clothes; yet he was completely changed. The Nils Holgersson that went away in the spring had a heavy, slow gait, a drawling speech, and sleepy eyes. The one that had come back was lithe and alert, ready of speech, and had eyes that sparkled and danced. He had a confident bearing that commanded respect, little as he was. Although he himself did not look happy, he inspired happiness in others.

"Moo!" bellowed Mayrose. "They told me that he was changed, but I couldn't believe it. Welcome home, Nils Holgersson! Welcome home! This is the first glad moment I have known for ever so long!"

"Thank you, Mayrose!" said the boy, who was very happy to be so well received.

"Now tell me all about father and mother."

"They have had nothing but hardship ever since you went away," said Mayrose. "The horse has been a costly care all summer, for he has stood in the stable the whole time and not earned his feed. Your father is too soft-hearted to shoot him and he can't sell him. It was on account of the horse that both Star and Gold-Lily had to be sold."

There was something else the boy wanted badly to know, but he was diffident about asking the question point blank. Therefore he said:

"Mother must have felt very sorry when she discovered that Morten Goosey-Gander had flown?"

"She wouldn't have worried much about Morten Goosey-Gander had she known the way he came to leave. She grieves most at the thought of her son having run away from home with a goosey-gander."

"Does she really think that I stole the goosey-gander?" said the boy.

"What else could she think?"

"Father and mother must fancy that I've been roaming about the country, like a common tramp?"

"They think that you've gone to the dogs," said Mayrose. "They have mourned you as one mourns the loss of the dearest thing on earth."

As soon as the boy heard this, he rushed from the cow shed and down to the stable.

It was small, but clean and tidy. Everything showed that his father had tried to make the place comfortable for the new horse. In the stall stood a strong, fine animal that looked well fed and well cared for.

"Good day to you!" said the boy. "I have heard that there's a sick horse in here. Surely it can't be you, who look so healthy and strong."

The horse turned his head and stared fixedly at the boy.

"Are you the son?" he queried. "I have heard many bad reports of

him. But you have such a good face, I couldn't believe that you were he, did I not know that he was transformed into an elf."

"I know that I left a bad name behind me when I went away from the farm," admitted Nils Holgersson. "My own mother thinks I am a thief. But what matters it—I sha'n't tarry here long. Meanwhile, I want to know what ails you."

"Pity you're not going to stay," said the horse, "for I have the feeling that you and I might become good friends. I've got something in my foot—the point of a knife, or something sharp—that's all that ails me. It has gone so far in that the doctor can't find it, but it cuts so that I can't walk. If you would only tell your father what's wrong with me, I'm sure that he could help me."

"It's well that you have no real illness," remarked Nils Holgersson. "I must attend to this at once, so that you will be all right again. You don't mind if I do scratching on your hoof with my knife, do you?"

Nils Holgersson had just finished, when he heard the sound of voices. He opened the stable door a little and peeped out.

His father and mother were coming down the lane. It was easy to see that they were broken by many sorrows. His mother had many lines on her face and his father's hair had turned gray. She was talking with him about getting a loan from her brother-in-law.

"No, I don't want to borrow any more money," his father said, as they were passing the stable. "There's nothing quite so hard as being in debt. It would be better to sell the cabin."

"If it were not for the boy, I shouldn't mind selling it," his mother demurred. "But what will become of him, if he returns some day, wretched and poor—as he's likely to be—and we not here?"

"You're right about that," the father agreed. "But we shall have to ask the folks who take the place to receive him kindly and to let him know that he's welcome back to us. We sha'n't say a harsh word to him, no matter what he may be, shall we mother?"

"No, indeed! If I only had him again, so that I could be certain he is not starving and freezing on the highways, I'd ask nothing more!"

Then his father and mother went in, and the boy heard no more of their conversation.

He was happy and deeply moved when he knew that they loved him so dearly, although they believed he had gone astray. He longed to rush into their arms. "But perhaps it would be an even greater sorrow were they to see me as I now am."

While he stood there, hesitating, a cart drove up to the gate. The boy smothered a cry of surprise, for who should step from the cart and go into the house yard but Osa, the goose girl, and her father!

They walked hand in hand toward the cabin. When they were about half way there, Osa stopped her father and said:

"Now remember, father, you are not to mention the wooden shoe or the geese or the little brownie who was so like Nils Holgersson that if it was not himself it must have had some connection with him."

"Certainly not!" said Jon Esserson. "I shall only say that their son has been of great help to you on several occasions—when you were trying to find me—and that therefore we have come to ask if we can't do them a service in return, since I'm a rich man now and have more than I need, thanks to the mine I discovered up in Lapland."

They went into the cabin, and the boy would have liked to hear what they talked about in there; but he dared not venture near the house. It was not long before they came out again, and his father and mother accompanied them as far as the gate.

His parents were strangely happy. They appeared to have gained a new hold on life.

When the visitors were gone, father and mother lingered at the gate gazing after them.

"I don't feel unhappy any longer, since I've heard so much that is good of our Nils," said his mother.

"Perhaps he got more praise than he really deserved," put in his father thoughtfully.

"Wasn't it enough for you that they came here specially to say they wanted to help us because our Nils had served them in many ways? I think, father, that you should have accepted their offer."

"No, mother, I don't wish to accept money from any one, either as a gift or a loan. In the first place I want to free myself from all debt, then we will work our way up again. We're not so very old, are we, mother?" The father laughed heartily as he said this.

"I believe you think it will be fun to sell this place, upon which we have expended such a lot of time and hard work," protested the mother.

"Oh, you know why I'm laughing," the father retorted. "It was the thought of the boy's having gone to the bad that weighed me down until I had no strength or courage left in me. Now that I know he still lives and has turned out well, you'll see that Holger Nilsson has some grit left."

The mother went in alone, and the boy made haste to hide in a corner, for his father walked into the stable. He went over to the horse and examined its hoof, to try to discover what was wrong with it.

"What's this!" he cried, discovering some letters scratched on the hoof. "Remove the sharp piece of iron from the foot," he read and glanced around inquiringly. However, he ran his fingers along the under side of the hoof and looked at it carefully.

"I verily believe there is something sharp here!" he said.

The boy sat huddled in a corner, it happened that other callers came to the farm.

The fact was that when Morten Goosey-Gander found himself so near his old home he simply could not resist the temptation of showing his wife and children to his old companions on the farm. So he took

Dunfin and the goslings along, and made for home.

There was not a soul in the barn yard when the goosey-gander came along. He alighted, confidently walked all around the place, and showed Dunfin how luxuriously he had lived when he was a tame goose.

When they had viewed the entire farm, he noticed that the door of the cow shed was open.

"Look in here a moment," he said, "then you will see how I lived in former days. It was very different from camping in swamps and morasses, as we do now."

The goosey-gander stood in the doorway and looked into the cow shed. "There's not a soul in here," he said. "Come along, Dunfin, and you shall see the goose pen. Don't be afraid; there's no danger."

Forthwith the goosey-gander, Dunfin, and all six goslings waddled into the goose pen, to have a look at the elegance and comfort in which the big white gander had lived before he joined the wild geese.

"Wait! there's some fodder in it now." With that he rushed to the trough and began to gobble up the oats.

But Dunfin was nervous.

"Let's go out again!" she said.

"Only two more grains," insisted the goosey-gander. The next second he let out a shriek and ran for the door, but it was too late! The door slammed, the mistress stood without and bolted it. They were locked in!

The father had removed a sharp piece of iron from the horse's hoof and stood contentedly stroking the animal when the mother came running into the stable.

"Come, father, and see the capture I've made!"

"No, wait a minute!" said the father. "Look here, first. I have discovered what ailed the horse."

"I believe our luck has turned," said the mother. "Only fancy! the big white goosey-gander that disappeared last spring must have gone off

with the wild geese. He has come back to us with seven wild geese. They walked straight into the goose pen, and I've shut them all in."

"That's extraordinary," remarked the father. "But best of all is that we don't have to think any more that our boy stole the goosey-gander when he went away."

"You're quite right, father," she said. "But I'm afraid we'll have to kill them to-night. In two days is Morten Gooseday and we must make haste if we expect to get them to market in time."

"I think it would be outrageous to butcher the goosey-gander, now he has returned to us with such a large family," protested Holger Nilsson.

"If times were easier we'd let him live; but since we're going to move from here, we can't keep geese. Come along now and help me carry them into the kitchen," urged the mother.

They went out together and in a few moments the boy saw his father coming along with Morten Goosey-Gander and Dunfin—one under each arm. He and his wife went into the cabin.

The goosey-gander cried: "Thumbietot, come and help me!"—as he always did when in peril—although he was not aware that the boy was at hand.

Nils Holgersson heard him, yet he lingered at the door of the cow shed. He did not hesitate because he knew that it would be well for him if the goosey-gander were beheaded—at that moment he did not even remember this—but because he shrank from being seen by his parents.

"They have a hard enough time of it already," he thought. "Must I bring them a new sorrow?" But when the door closed on the goosey-gander, the boy was aroused. He dashed across the house yard, sprang up on the board-walk leading to the entrance door and ran into the hallway, where he kicked off his wooden shoes in the old accustomed way, and walked toward the door.

All the while it went so much against the grain to appear before his father and mother that he could not raise his hand to knock.

"But this concerns the life of the goosey-gander," he said to himself—"he who has been my best friend ever since I last stood here."

In a twinkling the boy remembered all that he and the goosey-gander had suffered on ice-bound lakes and stormy seas and among wild beasts of prey. His heart swelled with gratitude; he conquered himself and knocked on the door.

"Is there some one who wishes to come in?" asked his father.

"Mother, you sha'n't touch the goosey-gander!" cried the boy.

Instantly both the goosey-gander and Dunfin, who lay on a bench with their feet tied, gave a cry of joy, so that he was sure they were alive.

Some one else gave a cry of joy—his mother!

"My, but you have grown tall and handsome!" she exclaimed.

The boy had not entered the cabin, but was standing on the doorstep, like one who is not quite certain how he will be received.

"The Lord be praised that I have you back again!" said his mother, laughing and crying. "Come in, my boy! Come in!"

"Welcome!" added his father, and not another word could he utter.

But the boy still lingered at the threshold. He could not comprehend why they were so glad to see him—such as he was. Then his mother came and put her arms around him and drew him into the room, and he knew that he was all right.

"Mother and father!" he cried. "I'm a big boy. I am a human being again!"

24

THE PARTING WITH THE WILD GEESE

Wednesday, November ninth.

The boy arose before dawn and wandered down to the coast. He was standing alone on the strand east of Smyge fishing hamlet before sunrise. He had already been in the pen with Morten Goosey-Gander to try to rouse him, but the big white gander had no desire to leave home. He did not say a word, but only stuck his bill under his wing and went to sleep again.

To all appearances the weather promised to be almost as perfect as it had been that spring day when the wild geese came to Skåne. There was hardly a ripple on the water; the air was still and the boy thought of the good passage the geese would have. He himself was as yet in a kind of daze—sometimes thinking he was an elf, sometimes a human being. When he saw a stone hedge alongside the road, he was afraid to go farther until he had made sure that no wild animal or vulture lurked behind it. Very soon he laughed to himself and rejoiced because he was big and strong and did not have to be afraid of anything.

When he reached the coast he stationed himself, big as he was, at the very edge of the strand, so that the wild geese could see him.

It was a busy day for the birds of passage. Bird calls sounded on the air continuously. The boy smiled as he thought that no one but himself understood what the birds were saying to one another. Presently wild geese came flying; one big flock following another.

"Just so it's not my geese that are going away without bidding me farewell," he thought. He wanted so much to tell them how everything had turned out, and to show them that he was no longer an elf but a human being.

There came a flock that flew faster and cackled louder than the others, and something told him that this must be the flock, but now he was not quite so sure about it as he would have been the day before.

The flock slackened its flight and circled up and down along the coast.

The boy knew it was the right one, but he could not understand why the geese did not come straight down to him. They could not avoid seeing him where he stood. He tried to give a call that would bring them down to him, but only think! his tongue would not obey him. He could not make the right sound! He heard Akka's calls, but did not understand what she said.

"What can this mean? Have the wild geese changed their language?" he wondered.

He waved his cap to them and ran along the shore calling.

"Here am I, where are you?"

But this seemed only to frighten the geese. They rose and flew farther out to sea. At last he understood. They did not know that he was human, had not recognized him. He could not call them to him because human beings can not speak the language of birds. He could not speak their language, nor could he understand it.

Although the boy was very glad to be released from the enchantment, still he thought it hard that because of this he should be parted from his old comrades.

He sat down on the sands and buried his face in his hands. What was the use of his gazing after them any more?

Presently he heard the rustle of wings. Old mother Akka had found

it hard to fly away from Thumbietot, and turned back, and now that the boy sat quite still she ventured to fly nearer to him. Suddenly something must have told her who he was, for she lit close beside him.

Nils gave a cry of joy and took old Akka in his arms. The other wild geese crowded round him and stroked him with their bills. They cackled and chattered and wished him all kinds of good luck, and he, too, talked to them and thanked them for the wonderful journey which he had been privileged to make in their company.

All at once the wild geese became strangely quiet and withdrew from him, as if to say:

"Alas! he is a man. He does not understand us: we do not understand him!"

Then the boy rose and went over to Akka; he stroked her and patted her. He did the same to Yksi and Kaksi, Kolme and Neljä, Viisi and Kuusi—the old birds who had been his companions from the very start.

After that he walked farther up the strand. He knew perfectly well that the sorrows of the birds do not last long, and he wanted to part with them while they were still sad at losing him.

As he crossed the shore meadows he turned and watched the many flocks of birds that were flying over the sea. All were shrieking their coaxing calls—only one goose flock flew silently on as long as he could follow it with his eyes. The wedge was perfect, the speed good, and the wing strokes strong and certain.

The boy felt such a yearning for his departing comrades that he almost wished he were Thumbietot again and could travel over land and sea with a flock of wild geese.

國家圖書館出版品預行編目資料

騎鵝歷險記（中英雙語典藏版）／賽爾瑪·拉格洛芙
（Selma Lagerlöf）作；鐘文君、Bertil Lybeck繪；李
毓昭譯. -- 初版. -- 臺中市：晨星，2022.06
　　面；　公分. --（愛藏本；109）
中英雙語典藏版
譯自：The Wonderful Adventures of Nils
ISBN 978-626-320-139-2（精裝）

881.3596　　　　　　　　　　　　　111006867

愛藏本：109

騎鵝歷險記（中英雙語典藏版）
The Wonderful Adventures of Nils

作者｜賽爾瑪·拉格洛芙（Selma Lagerlof）
繪者｜鐘文君；Bertil Lybeck 繪
譯者｜李毓昭

責任編輯｜謝宜真、呂曉婕
封面設計｜鐘文君
美術編輯｜黃偵瑜
文字校潤｜謝宜真、呂曉婕

填寫線上回函，立刻享有
晨星網路書店50元購書金

負責人｜陳銘民
發行所｜晨星出版有限公司
　　　　行政院新聞局局版台業字第 2500 號
總經銷｜知己圖書股份有限公司
地址｜台北市 106 辛亥路一段 30 號 9 樓
　　　TEL：02-23672044 / 23672047　FAX：02-23635741
　　　台中市 407 工業 30 路 1 號
　　　TEL：04-23595819　FAX：04-23595493
E-mail｜service@morningstar.com.tw
晨星網路書店｜www.morningstar.com.tw
法律顧問｜陳思成律師
郵政劃撥｜15060393　知己圖書股份有限公司
讀者服務專線｜04-2359-5819#230

印刷｜上好印刷股份有限公司

出版日期｜2022 年 6 月 15 日
定價｜新台幣 320 元
ISBN 978-626-320-139-2